Yours, Unexpectedly

ALSO BY SUSAN FOX

Love, Unexpectedly

His, Unexpectedly

WRITING AS SUSAN LYONS

Sex Drive

She's on Top

Touch Me

Hot in Here

Champagne Rules

ANTHOLOGIES

The Naughty List

Some Like It Rough

Men on Fire

Unwrap Me

The Firefighter

Yours, Unexpectedly

SUSAN FOX

BRAVA

KENSINGTON PUBLISHING CORP.
www.kensingtonbooks.com

BRAVA BOOKS are published by

Kensington Publishing Corp.
119 West 40th Street
New York, NY 10018

All Kensington titles, imprints, and distributed lines are available at special quantity discounts for bulk purchases for sales promotion, premiums, fund-raising, educational, or institutional use.

Special book excerpts or customized printings can also be created to fit specific needs. For details, write or phone the office of the Kensington Special Sales Manager: Kensington Publishing Corp., 119 West 40th Street, New York, NY 10018. Attn. Special Sales Department. Phone: 1-800-221-2647.

Brava and the B logo are Reg. U.S. Pat. & TM Off.

ISBN-13: 978-0-7582-5931-8
ISBN-10: 0-7582-5931-X

First Kensington Trade Paperback Printing: December 2011

10 9 8 7 6 5 4 3 2 1

Printed in the United States of America

Chapter 1

Absorbed in the slide show of images of me and my fiancé, Matt, in the digital photo frame on my desk, I took a moment to register the growl of a throaty car engine outside my open bedroom window. One glance and—"Oh my God!" I leaped to my feet. The yellow MGB convertible cruising to a stop was my sister Jenna's. Which meant that the hottie with windblown brown hair in the driver's seat was her man, come to make things right with her.

I flew out of my room and almost crashed into Jenna in the hall. My sister, now twenty-nine, had always been the gorgeous one in the family—in a totally natural way she took for granted. Nothing, not even the male-driven angst she'd been through in the past couple of days, could change that. Her blue sundress was perfect with her tanned skin, her hair tumbled in sunny curls over her shoulders, and even the shadows around her eyes brought out their dramatic greenish-blue.

"Jenna! That's your car!" And in it, fingers crossed, the cure for those mauve shadows. I'd always loved her—even despite her gorgeousness, her flakiness, and my issues with my sisters in general—but in the past days we'd grown closer and I really, really wanted things to work out for her.

"What?" She shook her head, frowning in puzzlement. "No, my car's in California. What are you talking about, Merilee?"

When her old MGB had broken down last week just as she'd started her journey home from Santa Cruz to Vancouver, she'd left it at a repair shop and hitched a ride with the man who'd turned her life upside down. And yes, the car outside was definitely hers, which meant this had to be *the guy*—the stranger she'd fallen for, broken up with, and been angsting over. "Look!" I grabbed her hand and dragged her over to the window.

Her ocean-colored eyes went wide, wider, and wider still as she stared out. "What?" She sounded utterly stunned.

"It's Mark, it's Mark! It is, isn't it?" He hadn't flown to Indonesia to start his marine biology project; he'd gone down to California to pick up her car. He'd come for her—a windblown knight in a butter-yellow MGB—and he was going to make everything all right. It was like the happy, tear-jerker ending of every romantic movie.

Finally, emotion flooded her face: hope, and a joy so powerful that . . . that I felt the sour tang of jealousy in my mouth. *I* was the one getting married in two days. *I* was the one who was supposed to feel on top of the world.

Ack! What was *wrong* with me these days?

Jenna dashed out my bedroom door and I ran after her, shoving aside my stupid, petty, irrational doubts and recapturing my excitement for her. In the hall, I yelled, "Theresa, Kat!"

Theresa opened her bedroom door. My oldest sister looked all fresh and pretty in shorts and an avocado-colored top that made green flecks dance in her hazel eyes. Frowning, she held up her cell phone. "What is it? I'm talking to Damien."

At least she'd only been *talking* to her boyfriend, who was on a book tour in the States, and not having phone sex, which from what she said occupied an awful lot of their time. I still couldn't get over the change in my uptight professor sister since she'd hooked up with Damien. She'd always intimidated the hell out of me, but now she'd softened and was easier to relate to. Love had worked magic. Love and phone sex.

"Jenna's Mark is here," I answered, loud enough for Kat to hear, too, in her bedroom where she'd holed up with her hottie from Montreal. Ms. Sociability, the girl who had a million friends but the worst luck when it came to love, had finally found herself a winner.

Theresa's face lit up. "Seriously?" Into the phone she said, "Have to go, talk to you later, love you." She tossed the phone onto her bed, then faced me again, brow pinching. "That man better not hurt Jenna again."

Kat's bedroom door opened a crack and she stuck her head out, reddish-brown curls in disarray. "Mark's here? Really?"

"Outside, in Jenna's MGB." I turned to Theresa. "He won't hurt her." I crossed my fingers, hoping it was true. Yeah, maybe I was a teeny bit envious, but my sister—all my sisters—deserved happiness. "He's come to apologize. I'm sure of it."

Theresa's frown slid into a smile. "It is our summer for happy endings, isn't it? All of us Fallon girls."

Her, with her new love, Damien, the thriller writer she'd met on the plane from Sydney. Kat, with the sexy photographer who'd won her heart on the train ride from Montreal. And me of course, marrying the boy I'd loved forever. Which was exciting. Of course, it was. Along with kind of scary. And confusing. Which it shouldn't have been. . . .

This wasn't the time to worry about it. Mark had come for Jenna, and I didn't want to miss a moment.

Kat said, "Gotta pull some clothes on."

So that's why she'd only opened the door a crack. "Ew!

TMI." It was squirmy enough to hear her gush and rave about Kama Sutra sex with the fabulous Naveen, much less know exactly when and where—like right now, across the hall—it was going on.

"Don't let anything happen without me," she called as she slammed the door.

Theresa and I darted down the hall and pounded down the staircase, then raced out the open front door of the family home. Halfway between the MGB and the steps, Jenna stood with her guy. His arms were around her shoulders and hers around his waist.

As Theresa and I went over, Kat and Nav hurried up behind us. Mom's Mercedes pulled up and she climbed out and walked briskly toward us in her business suit. For once, my lawyer mom who had to control the world didn't jump in with questions. She was so smart she'd have sized up the situation in a nanosecond.

As we all moved closer to Jenna, I figured Mark had to know we were serving notice that if he messed with her, he'd have us to answer to. Within the family, we might snipe and nag and bitch, but when it came to outsiders, we protected our own.

I sized the guy up: a rangy, well-muscled bod shown off by cargo shorts and a black tank, angular features, a tan that made his sky-blue eyes even more dramatic. Even rumpled and windblown, he was a total hottie. Was I disloyal to Matt, to think that? Of course, my fiancé was handsome, but he didn't have Mark's intense, utterly masculine vibe.

Mark's piercing blue eyes took in our presence. Then he gazed down at Jenna and, oh yeah, I was watching a romantic movie. He shut us out as if we didn't exist, and focused entirely on her with a passionate intensity that gave me shivers. What would it be like to have a man look at me that way? My guy was loving and considerate, but . . .

I brushed the thought away and listened.

Mark told Jenna he'd postponed his trip to Indonesia where he was scheduled to head a coral reef restoration project and had instead taken a red-eye down to California so he could bring her much-loved car back to her—because to her, that car symbolized freedom.

I nodded. Yeah, Jenna'd always been all about freedom.

Then he said, "I was wrong. I shouldn't have asked you to change. I fell in love with you just the way you are. You're a wonderful person."

A silent "Aw" rose in my throat. He was romancing her so absolutely perfectly. Again, I wondered what that would be like. My Matt and I had been together since we were seven. He'd never had to romance me, never had to do something grand and dramatic to win me, because love had always been there.

I'd always thought words like *radiant* and *glowing* belonged in ads, not real life. My sister's face proved me wrong.

Vaguely, I was aware of Dad driving up and coming over to join us, but I was utterly caught up in what Jenna was telling her lover. When she said she'd just asked a travel agent to book her a flight to Bali for right after my wedding, I barely suppressed a gasp. She said she had been afraid of commitment, but now she was ready to build a future with Mark.

It was her own grand, romantic gesture. Did he have any idea how huge this was for her?

Maybe so. The way he touched her cheek was so tender it brought tears to my eyes. "You mean you'd give up all the variety for one man, one cause?" he asked huskily.

"We'll create our own variety. Side by side, as partners. That'll be all the excitement I can handle."

"And it'll be more excitement and more joy than I'd ever hoped for."

"You and me both."

Excitement. Joy. Yes, I saw those emotions on their faces, along with tenderness and passion. I'd seen the same feelings shared by Theresa and her Damien, and Kat and Nav. Intense, sexy, and romantic.

When was the last time Matt and I had looked at each other that way? Or had we ever? Tenderness, yes, but passion? Excitement? Pure, blazing joy? All week, seeing my sisters come home one by one from all over the world, bursting with the excitement of new, passionate love affairs, I'd felt . . . what?

Kind of flat. Maybe even unhappy, a little depressed. Off. In the week before my own wedding, the wedding I'd dreamed of since I was a little girl, when I should have been brimming with excitement, I'd felt empty. Left out. Like everyone else was having all the fun.

That was childish. In this family, I should know I'd never be the center of attention, and just stop wanting it.

Except . . . was that really all it was? Or did it go deeper? Was it about Matt and me? Though I was eleven years younger than Theresa, eight years younger than Jenna, I felt—okay, I felt *settled.* Settled into a comfortable relationship that never ignited the kind of sparks I now saw flying between Jenna and Mark as they kissed like they were merging their souls.

Well, shit. Comfortable, rather than exciting. Settled, at the ripe old age of twenty-one. This was bad. Definitely bad. For fourteen years I'd told myself I was the Fallon sister who'd found her soul mate, the perfect love, and now . . .

Pre-wedding jitters. Everyone has them.

Then why was my heart racing and why, even as I joined my family in clapping and cheering for Jenna and Mark, did I feel left out and envious? I was the one getting *married*, and rather than looking forward to my beautiful white wedding, I was wanting what my sisters had.

My heart lodged in my throat, beating so hard it threatened to choke me. I tried to swallow as Jenna and her guy eased an inch or two apart. "We belong together," he said with absolute conviction.

"We do. I've been falling for you since . . . oh, probably since the moment you ordered strawberry pie."

"I've been falling for you since I first looked into your eyes."

It was one of those *aw, isn't that sweet?* moments, but instead of enjoying it, my brain was spinning. That was how it had been for Matt and me, recognizing from the beginning that we were soul mates: M&M. Except we'd been seven. Children, not adults. We'd grown up together. He'd been at our house so often, Mom and Dad said it was almost like having a son. I'd never dated anyone but him. We'd fumbled through learning about sex together. And the sex was great. Tender and affectionate and really . . . comfortable.

I put a hand to my chest, over my racing heart, and pressed down, trying to calm it. What a bitch I was, being disloyal to Matt, my best friend, the one person in the world who'd always been there for me. Always put me first.

But . . . why did he never look at me with passionate intensity? Why did I never feel sparks flying, like he couldn't wait to be alone with me and strip my clothes off? Did he really, really love me or was it just *comfortable* being with me?

Oh, shit, I couldn't seem to draw air into my lungs. Was I going to pass out?

As per usual, no one was paying me the slightest notice. Things with my family had improved in the past week, but I would never be the center of attention in a family where everyone else was, in their own way, larger than life.

I could have fainted dead away and no one would have noticed. They were all, "You'll stay for dinner"; "I've been on the road for the last two days without a shower or change of clothes"; "I'm sure Jenna will help you find the shower." Blah, blah, and they'd be having sex in that shower, too, and everyone knew it.

Hot sex. Steamy hot sex. Not *comfortable* sex. Matt and I had been lovers for five years now, and never once had we made out in the shower. What did that mean?

Yesterday, I'd visited Gran. I'd always loved her so much, and it broke my heart that now she had Alzheimer's and mostly was pretty out of it. Still, somehow that had freed me to pour out all the stupid, toxic shit I'd been feeling since my sisters arrived home: the crazy jealousy, the uncertainty, the fear that my future wasn't going to be the blissful one I'd always dreamed of.

She had stared out the window the whole time I talked, not saying a word. When I kissed her and said I had to go, she caught my hand and said, "Every woman deserves passion. Have you found yours?"

Did she even know it was me? Was this one of her lucid moments, or was she just rambling?

I'd told myself that Matt, marriage to Matt, was my passion. But now . . . why was I almost hyperventilating? What did this all *mean*? Ack! I was supposed to be getting *married*!

I managed to take a shallow breath and said, with certainty, "I have to see Matt." I didn't have a clue to what I was going to say, but I could tell him anything, couldn't I? We'd figure this out together, like we sorted out every other problem in our lives. Surely, he'd know why I had this strange ache in my chest.

Jenna, who was leading Mark inside, showed no sign of having heard. Mom and Dad had their heads together discussing Mark, and so did Kat and Nav. Theresa glanced at her watch, probably wondering if she could catch Damien again. Nope, I might as well not have been there.

I went to grab my keys, not bothering to change out of my old shorts and tee.

Not a soul was in sight when I started up the hand-me-down Toyota Dad had passed on to me when I was sixteen. The car almost steered itself toward Matt's house, a route I'd used to bike when I was younger. "The beaten path," his mom called it. And that reminded me, Adele would be there. A nurse, she worked some pretty weird shifts, but she and Matt had agreed to spend one mom-son night at home in the busy week before the wedding. She was great, a loving, hardworking single mom, but right now I couldn't face her.

I pulled over to dial Matt on my cell. The phone rang, then rang again. "Damn it, Matt, where are you? I need you." It rang again, then once more, and finally he answered.

"You're there." I exhaled in relief. "Are you with your mom?"

"Hey, M. No, she just got home from work. She's having a shower, then we'll get dinner going."

"I'm on my way over. Need to talk to you. Meet me at your place?" When Matt and I were eighteen, we'd helped his mom convert their two-car garage into a tiny apartment for him.

"Sure. What's up?"

"Uh . . . Jenna's guy, the one she met hitchhiking from California, showed up."

"Hey, that's cool. And so . . ."

"I need to talk to you."

"Are you okay? You've been acting kind of strange the past few days."

He'd noticed. I shouldn't be surprised; it went with that soul mate thing. "Just meet me, okay?"

Ten minutes later, when I drove down the back alley, I saw a car in the Townsend driveway—a sporty black convertible that definitely didn't belong to Matt or Adele. The top was up, drops of water glistened on the black paint, and a guy in shorts, flip-flops, and nothing else was leaning over it, rubbing the car's body with a cloth.

A hot guy. Momentarily distracted from my worries, I appreciated the view: great butt, muscles flexing under the lightly tanned skin of a buff back, water drops glistening on strong arms and legs. Wow. If this was a car commercial, women would sure be buying.

Curious to find out who he was, I pulled up behind the Miata.

The guy turned, smiled, grabbed a gray T-shirt, and pulled it over his head, and I realized it was Matt.

My Matt. The center of my life for the last fourteen years.

I blinked. That image of the hot car-commercial guy had been weird, almost like a hallucination. This was the old familiar Matt coming toward me as I stepped out of my car—casual in baggy cargo shorts and a loose, faded University of British Columbia tee, his dirty-blond hair showing a few summer-gold streaks. My girlfriends said he was hot, that he looked like a younger, lighter-haired Bradley Cooper. Sure, he was good looking, but to me he wasn't movie star handsome; he was just good old Matt, the boy I'd grown up with.

"Merilee?" He tilted his head quizzically. His blue eyes, the shade of well-washed denim—yeah, they were kind of the color of Bradley Cooper's—were warm with concern as he tugged me into a hug. "Are you all right?"

His arms had always given me shelter. When my family ignored me, or I was pissed off at my sisters, or when I was suffering the pain that had finally been diagnosed as endometriosis, he'd been the one to comfort and support me.

Yet, now, maybe for the first time ever, I didn't feel at home in his arms. Or perhaps I was tired of feeling at home and wanted something more. I pushed away from him, not knowing how to say what I needed to. I sensed that once I started, things between us would change forever.

Stalling, I said, "What are you doing with the car?"

"It was supposed to be a surprise. It's Leon's brother's and he loaned it to me. I'm washing and polishing it. Then some of our friends are going to do the whole 'Just Married' thing with it, so we can drive it from the wedding."

Just Married. Not long ago, it had sounded like the best thing in the whole world, but now . . . "M, what are we doing?" The words burst out of my mouth. "Is this the right thing?"

"Doing?" He frowned, processing, then said, "You don't mean . . . getting married?"

I nodded.

His eyes widened. "You're kidding, right? I mean, I know you've been having some, uh, pre-wedding nerves, but that's normal, isn't it?"

"I guess." Everyone said so, but what I felt seemed stronger. Maybe I was wrong, though. This was why we needed to talk. "I don't know. Are you feeling any, you know, nerves? Doubts?"

He shrugged. "Not really. I mean, we're young like everyone keeps telling us, but I want to marry you. We've always wanted that. Moving up the date from next year—"

"Should we have?" I broke in. Maybe the timing was wrong. "We always said we'd get married after we got our B.A.'s." And right before starting the year-long program to get our education degrees. Then I was going to teach middle-grade kids, and he'd teach high school.

That was something else we'd been planning for years. We really were *settled*.

"But then you were diagnosed," he said.

Matt had nagged me into asking a doctor about what my sisters and mom had for years blown off as being normal menstrual cramps. I'd had surgery for endometriosis a couple of months ago. The diagnosis had made Matt and I rethink things. We'd always wanted kids and never once imagined I might face infertility at the age of twenty-one.

"Yeah." I nodded, mentally retracing the steps that had led us to move up the wedding. "Then you saw that last-minute deal on the cruise." A Mexican Riviera cruise—a perfect honeymoon and pure R&R. After the surgery, recuperation, and being crazy busy catching up on missed course work and exams, I was desperate to lie back and do nothing.

"It all came together," he said, "as if it was meant to be."

That was how it had felt. Yes, I remembered. But now . . . I squeezed my lips together, then parted them and heard myself say, "But maybe it wasn't meant to be."

He frowned. "What are you saying?"

Words poured out, giving voice to all the doubts and fears I'd been trying to ignore all week. "Maybe we shouldn't do it. Get married. Not now." Oh, God, was I totally crazy? I'd loved Matt since grade two.

"Jeez, Merilee, you're talking crazy. We've loved each other since we were seven."

It was spooky how he so often read my mind, or our minds were on the same track. I didn't even have the privacy of my own thoughts. "I know that!" I snapped. "Do you think I don't know that? I still love you, M, but . . ."

His hands gripped my shoulders, hard. "Calm down, you're not making any sense."

"I can't calm down. I don't want to calm down. This is important." He had to see that. Maybe once I explained, he'd make everything right. He'd say something, sweep me off my feet, show me he really, really, totally and utterly loved me, and that we could be just as exciting and passionate as my sisters and their guys. He'd do that *thing*—that grand romantic thing like Jenna's man had just done—that would show me I was crazy to have second thoughts.

Fingers biting into me, pinning me down, he stared into my eyes. "How can you have cold feet about getting married Saturday, when we've been talking about getting married all our lives?"

"I don't know!" I wriggled my shoulders until he dropped his hands, then I took a step back, away from him. "Maybe *because* we've been talking about it all our lives." He was *still* talking, not *doing* anything. "Maybe because I've known you all my life." And because of that, I should know better than to hope for a dramatic, romantic gesture.

He shook his head, looking frustrated and pissed off. "I don't get it. You always said we're soul mates. We're M&M. A couple."

"I'm not sure this is the right time." The more he tried to persuade me, the more *sense* he made, the less right the whole thing felt. Instincts counted just as much as logic, and what my instincts craved was *not* a bunch of rational discussion.

"Everything's booked." He snapped out the words. "Theresa made that project plan and you and your sisters have put everything together in under two weeks. Location, minister, reception, food, music. We've had the damned stag and stagette."

He was right, and at first I'd been thrilled to bits about the wedding, but now I felt trapped. "Stop being so logical." Even that silly stagette had given me doubts, as I'd been showered with sexy, kinky gifts I couldn't imagine us ever using.

He strode a couple of paces away from me. I heard him take a deep breath, then he turned around and faced me, his expression one of strained patience. "What do you want, Merilee?"

I blinked. What did I want? What had I been hoping for when I came here? Did I want him to fight for me? To sweep me up in his arms and . . . do what? To find that perfect romantic thing, the way Damien had when he asked Theresa to stay over in Honolulu with him. The way Nav had, playing stranger on the train with Kat. The way Mark had, flying down to California to bring Jenna's car to her.

I didn't want *settled*. I didn't want *comfortable*. I wanted what my sisters had: a grand, romantic, larger than life love. Was there any hope Matt could give it to me?

Stunned, Matt Townsend stared at the girl he knew better than anyone else in the world, and felt as if he didn't know her at all. Had she lost her freaking mind?

He struggled to hold on to his patience. After all the initial excitement about announcing the wedding, she'd grown increasingly moody. He'd figured it was the sister effect as her older sisters—the three-pack, as the family called them—had returned to Vancouver one by one. The Fallon girls pushed each other's buttons, and it was especially bad for Merilee, the unplanned baby who'd come along eight years after Jenna. Rebecca and James Fallon and the three-pack hadn't rearranged their lives to make room for the newcomer.

That had always annoyed Matt. Merilee was such a sweet person, but her family was so self-absorbed they barely noticed her. He did, though. He noticed, he valued, he loved her. He looked after her.

And now he was pissed off with her. She was talking crazy, and couldn't even say what she wanted. "Merilee?" he prompted, struggling to keep his voice even. "You don't want to call off the wedding, right?" When he put it that bluntly, she'd come to her senses. She wasn't going to dump him flat on his ass two days before their wedding.

"I think"—she sniffled and swiped a hand across eyes the blue of a spring morning—"that maybe I do." Tears began to roll.

Her tears usually made him want to cradle her in his arms and make everything better. This time he just gaped at her. She hadn't really said that, had she? "Are you nuts?"

"Oh, Matt," she wailed, "try to understand."

"Understand?" Anger and hurt rose in him, and his voice along with them. "Shit, Merilee, what the hell's going on?" Trying to regain control—he was *not*, would never be, a guy like his dad who lost his temper—he paced jerkily across the alley, then turned to stare at her. He'd done everything for this girl, focused his life on her for fourteen years. She was *not* betraying and abandoning him. "Two weeks ago, you said getting married was your dream come true."

"It was." She stared back at him, eyes huge and drenched with tears. Her shoulders were rounded inside one of his old T-shirts and she looked small and forlorn. Her dark honey-blond hair lay in gleaming curls on her shoulders, incongruously bouncy, as if it hadn't gotten the message that she was miserable.

He had, and he was feeling pretty damned crappy. Except he still couldn't really believe it. "It was," he said harshly, "and now it isn't. What's changed?"

"My sisters came home," she said, so softly he could barely hear.

"Your family's trying to talk you out of getting married?" Shit. He'd always thought the Fallons liked him. He'd been at family dinners for the past week, and everyone had been friendly. They'd even been getting along better with each other, too. And now they'd stabbed him in the back.

"No." She shook her head. "No, it's not that. Oh, M, I don't know how to say this."

Insulted, he said, "You can tell me anything. You know that."

She took a deep breath, then words flew out on the exhale. "I feel middle-aged."

Relief sent him rushing over to grip her shoulders comfortingly. Now it all made sense. "Sweetheart, you're worn out." When her surgery was scheduled, they'd discussed her skipping a semester at university, but she'd wanted to catch up on her courses and exams so they'd graduate together next year. Besides, once they were on their honeymoon, she'd have a week of total rest.

She closed her eyes for a long moment, then opened them and gazed up at him. "I am tired, but that's not what I meant. We're so, you know, settled and comfortable as a couple."

"Settled and comfortable?" Those didn't sound like bad things, except for the tone of her voice.

"I mean, we're all stable and b-boring"—she ducked her head, again not meeting his eyes—"and there's no spark or excitement or p-passion."

His hands jerked off her shoulders as if she'd scalded him. She thought he was boring? That their love life sucked? Well, just *shit!* His hands clenched, unclenched, clenched again. Yeah, he wasn't the most exciting guy in the world. How could he be when his mom had told him, at the age of six, that he had to be the man of the house—then at age seven he'd begun protecting Merilee as well?

Through an effort of will, he straightened his clenched fingers. A good man didn't give in to anger. He didn't beat up on women; he protected them. Matt was *not* a temperamental, irresponsible, violent man like his father, the man who had finally—thank God—abandoned him and his mom when he was six.

Matt had thought his maturity and consideration were qualities Merilee loved. Jesus, she'd said so. He'd never had a clue she was unhappy. He wanted to yell at her, to shake her, but he fought to keep his temper in check.

She gazed up, cheeks flushing. "I didn't tell you all the things I got at the stagette."

"What?" Startled out of his anger, he stared at her. She'd gone from dropping that bomb to talking about the stagette? Who was this girl?

"I was so totally embarrassed. Like, there were Ben Wa balls."

Balls? To play some kind of game? He scrubbed his hands roughly over his face, hoping this was all some horrible dream. "What are you talking about?"

"V-vaginal balls."

Vaginal balls? He gaped at her, his anger and frustration momentarily forgotten. "Seriously?"

"I mean, can you just imagine? That's not, I mean, we wouldn't . . ." She buried her face against his chest and automatically he put his arms around her.

Oh, yeah, he could imagine. Sometimes he'd wanted to try something a little kinky in bed, but he never said anything, afraid she'd think he was a perv. Afraid, too, of where it might take him. Of turning into a man like his dad.

Like that one time, after a night at the pub with their friends, she'd been giggling about being a naughty girl for drinking so much. He was horny and he'd had too much to drink, too, and, joking around, he'd said naughty girls should be punished. She'd teased, "I dare you." Then he'd pulled the long scarf off her neck, tied her hands above her head, forced her on her stomach, and spanked her. He'd hit Merilee. Yeah, he'd only been fooling around, but he'd actually hit her.

Only when she'd cried out in pain had he come to his senses and stopped. Horrified, he'd sobered up immediately and untied her. The shock in her eyes was more than he could bear. He'd apologized profusely and she'd forgiven him, even promised to forget it ever happened, and after that he'd taken care to always be gentle with her.

Merilee was sweet and wholesome, not kinky or skanky. Some of his guy friends boasted about their girlfriends, and sometimes—yeah, he was a red-blooded male—he was envious. But often he just thought the behavior was slutty. Like, sexting a crotch shot, or giving a bunch of dudes blow jobs at a party? No, thanks. Merilee had morals and he respected that.

He wasn't surprised those vaginal balls had embarrassed her. Yet she said she wanted more spark, excitement, passion. Things she didn't find with him. Yeah, that cut deep. There were different kinds of passion. Their love was like a steady golden candle, not sparks and fireworks.

They'd grown up together. Never even dated anyone else. Best friends who, yeah, were comfortable together. What the hell was wrong with that?

As for sparks, how could he and M have ignited sparks? From the bits of girl talk he'd overheard with their friends, it seemed like sparks happened when you first met someone and fell for them.

And what was Merilee's idea of excitement anyhow? Going out dancing? A picnic on the beach? They did those things occasionally and he liked them, too, but money and time were in short supply.

They'd always been so practical. *She* had, too; it wasn't just him. If she'd wanted something different, why the hell hadn't she said so? She had no trouble deciding what movie to see, what kind of pizza to order, what kind of careers they should both have. Mostly, he went along because it all sounded fine to him.

But *this*, this business about calling off the wedding—no, it didn't sound fucking *fine* at all.

"Matt, are you furious? Hurt?" Warm breath brushed his neck. "Say something. Tell me how you feel."

"I feel . . ." Betrayed. Mad. Frustrated. Shocked. "Shitty."

She wound her arms around his waist and held him tightly. "I'm sorry, so sorry. I do love you, but over the past few days, it's just been feeling wrong."

It felt wrong to marry the guy she loved?

Her arms felt like a vise, so he shoved free of them. Those

blue eyes welling with tears didn't match up with what she was saying. "Then if it feels *wrong*," he said bitterly, "we'll call it off. We'll call the whole damned thing off." The words flew out of his mouth, surprising him.

Surprising her, too, from her expression. "The whole thing?"

"Us," he spat the word out. And now, with all those crappy feelings taking over, he was on a roll. "We're *settled*, we don't have passion, we're *wrong*. Call it quits."

"I didn't. . . . You aren't saying you want to break up?"

Break up. Break up with Merilee? Those words brought him back to reality. The idea was unthinkable. But so was her calling off the wedding. He shook his head, not knowing anything anymore. "I . . . I don't know." He hadn't felt so shitty in his entire life. "What are you saying?"

"Just that we shouldn't be getting married Saturday."

"But . . ." He tried to think it through. "Then what? We're the same two people. Settled, comfortable, all those things you don't like. We're not suddenly going to get *exciting*, whatever the hell you mean by that word."

Expression stunned, she said, "I didn't think that far ahead."

When he tried to, he felt only a bleak chill in his heart. Pissed and hurt though he might be, he told her the truth. "I can't imagine life without you."

"Me either."

They stared at each other for a long moment. He felt like screaming, crying, punching his fist through a wall. The same shit his dad had done, except sometimes that fist hit his mom instead. When Matt was a boy, every time he'd acted out, his mom had said he was behaving like his dad, he was breaking her heart.

Yeah, he could hold it together. "We're in no shape to decide the big stuff right now. We're both in shock. Let's take it one step at a time. First step's cancelling the wedding."

She blinked back tears and nodded. "Okay, yes, I can think about that. Though my family will be furious. The money they've laid out, all the planning. Oh, Matt, I got Theresa and Kat and Jenna to come all the way here for nothing."

Nothing. Their beautiful wedding, the happiest day of their lives, had turned into *nothing*. In fact, maybe their whole fourteen-year relationship was turning into nothing. Tears burned behind his eyes and he clenched his fists, hot tension vibrating up his arms and tightening his shoulders.

"I'll tell Mom," he said, his voice raw. For years, his mother had thought of Merilee as her daughter. "And I'll call the cruise lines."

"Theresa will draw up one of her project plans," she said bleakly. "To cancel everything else." She stepped away from him. "I need to go, so I can tell everyone and get things started."

"You shouldn't drive." Nor should he, and the last thing he wanted was to be confined in a car with her, but he'd always looked after her. "I'll give you a ride home."

She held up her hands. "No. Please. I'll go slow, but I need a few minutes alone."

Torn, he said, "Promise you'll be careful?"

"Promise." Her blue eyes were huge, wet, and swollen.

They stared at each other for long seconds, then she said in a plaintive voice, "Love you, M."

It was what they always said when they said good-bye. The only time he'd ever heard her say it so sadly was when the doctor had diagnosed her endometriosis and they'd realized they might never have the children they both wanted so badly. Yeah, they could adopt, but they'd had that soul mate thing going on and wanted to create their own babies. Maybe it had been a sign. A sign that they weren't soul mates after all.

But now, as he'd always done, he gave her what she

wanted. "Love you, M." And it was true. She'd betrayed him, angered him, shattered him, but love didn't die in the space of minutes. Would it, though? For fourteen years, his future had been certain. Now . . . He couldn't think about it.

In the past, they'd always kissed good-bye. Today, he folded his arms across his chest.

Merilee turned and walked toward her car.

When she had driven away, Matt dragged his hands across his face. Then, because he couldn't help worrying, couldn't help caring, he pulled his cell from his pocket and called her house. He had ambivalent feelings about her family. They were good people, interesting ones, yet they rarely gave Merilee what she needed.

When her mother answered, he said, "Rebecca, Merilee's on her way home. If she doesn't make it, call me. And when she does, be there for her. All of you. She needs you."

"But, what . . . ?" Rarely was the high-powered litigator ever at a loss for words.

"It's her story to tell. Just, for once, would you put her first?"

"Put her first? But, we—"

He hung up, cutting her off. No, they didn't put Merilee first. He was the one who'd done that.

Everything in his life was based on being half of M&M, and now that was gone. He gave a choked sob, unable to hold back the tears any longer.

Chapter 2

Shivers wracked me as I drove home, creeping along well below the speed limit. It was a sunny late afternoon in June, yet I was freezing. I'd never felt so alone. Matt and I might be breaking up? No, I couldn't go there. One step at a time: tell my family the wedding was off.

As a toddler, I'd learned a sad truth. While my parents and sisters occasionally lavished attention on "the baby," as they called me then, more often they were too busy to even notice me. I tried to be a good girl, hoping that would get their attention and win their love, but I was just too blah in comparison to smart, successful Theresa; popular, active Kat; and gorgeous, kooky Jenna.

But right from when we first met, Matt had seen me. He'd always seen me, he'd thought I was special, he'd made me feel loved. He'd been my other half.

Now I was solo. Single. Alone. Matt might say he loved me, but it wasn't a real, true, strong love. He said he felt shitty, but he hadn't protested passionately and fought for me. He seemed ready to let our whole relationship go, just like that. It broke my heart. But it told me I'd made the right decision about the wedding.

And now there was my family. I hated to think how they'd react.

Maybe I could pull a Jenna. Aim my car in a different direction and see where the winds took me. Except I wasn't a free spirit like her, and even Jenna was learning about responsibility. The responsible thing was to tell my family I'd made a huge mistake. There were plans, so many plans, to cancel before Saturday.

God, I was tired. And cold. And lonely. And sad. So sad. My head ached from crying and from all the tears still waiting to be shed. I wanted to lock myself in my room and hide away from the world. Maybe for the rest of my life.

I parked outside the family home and got out slowly. Rubbing my hands over my chilled arms, I put one foot in front of the other and headed for the front steps.

It opened when I was halfway there, and Mom stepped out, frowning. "Merilee? Matt called."

"He told you?" What right did he have? And yet it took some of the pressure off me.

"He said you had something to tell us. He was worried about you." She peered intently. "Oh, Merilee, what's wrong? You've been crying." Quickly, she came down the steps and put her arms around me.

Hugs from my mom were rare, which made them special. I let myself sink into the comfort of her embrace, compassionate and loving and not judgmental. Not judgmental *yet*, because she didn't yet know how badly I'd messed up. That thought kept me from dissolving in tears.

If Matt had dumped me, I could have indulged in a crying jag and everyone would have sympathized. But I'd initiated this, and I had to pull myself together and explain.

She stroked up and down my back soothingly. "Come inside, dear. Tell us about it. Then we'll figure out what to do."

That was Mom, the lawyer. Like Theresa, rational analysis and action plans were her *thing*. Though I had to admit that, this week, they'd both loosened up a little, especially when it came to Jenna's broken heart. They'd actually realized they couldn't always fix things, that sometimes the best a person could give was understanding and love. I could sure use some of that right now.

Her arm around my waist, Mom guided me up the front steps as if I were a little girl. "Your dad and sisters are waiting for you in the family room. Naveen volunteered to make dinner and Mark's napping."

Though it'd likely be more of a family tribunal than a healing circle, it would be good to tell everyone in one fell swoop. Maybe they'd even understand and commiserate. Yeah, sure, what were the chances? Especially when I'd always lorded it over my sisters that I was lucky in love.

That had been my position in the family. Theresa was the brainiac, Kat was Ms. Sociability, and Jenna was the free spirit. When I'd been growing up, they'd all had that larger-than-life thing going on, but once I found Matt I hadn't minded so much.

Now I'd blown the one thing I was good at. It wasn't me who was lucky in love any longer; it was them.

My steps slowed as we approached the family room, but Mom's firm arm didn't let me stop. In the doorway, I stepped away from her and went in first, gazing at the group scattered around on couches and comfy chairs. Looks of puzzlement, concern, and minor annoyance greeted me.

Jenna flicked back long curls still damp from the shower. "Hey, M, what's going on?"

"We're calling off the w-wedding." A hiccupy sob broke the last word.

The group reacted with a chorus of gasps and exclamations. Mom snapped, "What's gotten into Matt?"

"It wasn't him. It was my idea."

That was met with dead silence. Shock. They all knew how much I'd always wanted to marry Matt.

Then Kat said, in a tone that mixed sympathy and impatience in a way that only a Fallon sister could achieve, "Merilee, every bride gets the jitters."

"Yes," Theresa said in her lecturing voice, "and you're tired and stressed out. Get a good night's sleep and things will look different in the morning."

"Not that I believe in marriage," Jenna put in, "but come on, sis, this is you and Matt."

Poor old Dad, a cancer researcher who was more comfortable dealing with DNA under a microscope than with his daughters, looked baffled. "Merilee, I thought this was what you always wanted."

Well, duh, Dad. So did I.

Mom stepped in front of me, took my hand and squeezed it, and looked me straight in the eye. "Is this jitters, dear, or something more? You have to think seriously. Your sisters have gone to a lot of work pulling this wedding together on very short notice. If we take it apart, it's not magically going to go back together again."

Like Humpty Dumpty. And my whole life. I choked back a sob. Nothing was magically going to go back together again. Were Matt and I breaking up?

Again, I shoved that thought away. Trying to keep my voice steady, I told Mom, "I have thought seriously." Then I glanced past her at Theresa. "And I've slept on it, for several nights." Biting my lip, I studied my baffled father. "Dad, I thought it was what I wanted, too. But now it doesn't feel right. And Matt agrees with me." He'd talked about breaking up.

My mother shook her head, eyes narrowed and brow furrowed. "How can it not feel right? All we've ever heard from you is how perfect Matt is, how he's your soul mate, how you're two halves of a whole."

"A woman shouldn't be," Jenna said, rising and coming to stand beside Mom. They made such a contrast, Mom still in her tailored charcoal lawyer suit and Jenna in a turquoise tank top and one of her floaty hippie skirts, with damp golden hair rippling down past her shoulders. "You have to be independent," my sister went on, "and so does he. Then your love is given freely, out of want rather than need."

I didn't get what she was saying—all I'd ever wanted in my life was to be half of M&M—and it was all too airy-fairy Jenna-talk for my aching head. "I can't explain it," I said, addressing Mom again. "It just doesn't feel right. There's something wrong, or missing, or . . ." How could I tell these five people that Matt and I were boring, not passionate? It was too private, too humiliating.

Usually, I backed down in the face of my family's logic, pressure, the sheer force of their personalities. This time, I couldn't. I tilted my chin up. "I'm sorry, but the wedding's not going to happen."

The message finally seemed to be sinking in because Jenna touched my arm. "I'm really sorry, sis."

"We're all very sorry, dear," Mom said, looking a little lost. Give her a corporate criminal or a negligent doctor to prosecute and she was in her element, but messy emotions weren't her forte. Tentatively, she said, "Are you two still engaged, or . . . ?"

"I d-don't know." Were we breaking up? Or just taking a break to think things through? There was no ring on my finger to leave on or give back. Though my romantic heart had longed for one, I'd told Matt we should be practical; we needed the money for our discount honeymoon, apartment rent, groceries, and tuition. He'd listened like he always did, and agreed. They were great qualities—except for the times when I'd longed to be surprised, longed for him to take a stand, longed for drama and passion. Clearly, he'd never cared enough about me to be passionate. I gave a hiccupy little sob. "We haven't got that far."

"Oh, Merilee, I don't know what to say." Again, my mother wrapped her arms around me.

Kat and Theresa came over, too, murmuring words of sympathy, and somehow we all got tangled up in an awkward group hug. We might not be very experienced at giving each other unconditional support, but I could feel their love flowing into me.

Tears overflowed. "I'm sorry I messed this up so badly."

I could just feel words trembling on lips—complaints, accusations, rebukes—but no one spoke them and I was so grateful.

"Merilee?" It was Dad's voice.

The female circle broke apart and I saw him standing there, looking as ill at ease as I'd ever seen him. He wasn't a huggy person—even less than Mom—but now he stepped forward and gathered me in his arms. "Baby, I wish I could fix this for you." Baby. It was what they'd all called me when I was little, before I met Matt, before we turned into M&M and I became M.

I rested my wet face against the shoulder of his cotton shirt. "Oh, Daddy, I wish you could, too." As I said it, I realized I hadn't called him Daddy for a very long time.

He patted my back, kind of like someone burping a baby, but it was the thought that counted. "What do you need now?" he asked.

"I want to sleep. I want to take one of those pills the doctor gave me after the surgery, and sleep for hours. For days. I want to sleep past Saturday." But that wouldn't be responsible. I'd created the mess and I had to help clean it up. So, reluctantly, I stepped out of the shelter of his arms. "But I won't. Theresa, maybe you could make a list of the things that have to be done, and I'll start making calls."

"No, we'll do it. The three-pack. Right, Kat? Jenna?"

As they murmured agreement, Mom said, "I'll help, too. You go and sleep, dear. I know you're exhausted and hurting."

"That would be so nice." Everything ached. My head, my heart. "I can't believe what I'm putting you through. I drag the three-pack here from all over the world and then—"

"Don't apologize for that," Theresa broke in. "If you hadn't, I wouldn't have met Damien."

"Nav and I might never have gotten together," Kat said.

"And I wouldn't have hitched a ride with Mark," Jenna put in.

Great. Because Matt and I set a wedding date, my three sisters found true love—and M and I had maybe lost it. I couldn't bring myself to say I was happy for them, because I felt too shitty to be happy about anything. "I'm going to bed," I said, sounding as pathetic as I felt.

"Can we bring anything?" Mom asked. "Do anything? Some dinner? Someone to keep you company?"

I shook my head. "Not hungry. And I just want to be alone." That was what my life was going to be like now, so I might as well get used to it.

As I trailed out of the room, almost too tired to lift my feet, I heard Theresa say quietly, "She'll sleep on it. There's not much we could do tonight anyway, so let's hold off until morning. I'll make a list so we're prepared if she doesn't change her mind."

Didn't anyone ever listen to me? I wasn't going to change my mind.

Thank God for drugs. I actually slept for ten straight hours. When I woke, a little groggy and headachy, I wanted to take another pill and go back to sleep, but I forced myself up. I checked my cell. No, I hadn't missed a call from Matt.

How was he doing? What was he thinking? I could call, but if he did want to split up, I wasn't ready to hear it.

Instead, I headed for the shower. As that stupid cliché said, this was the first day of the rest of my life. Escaping it with drugs was tempting, but I wouldn't be such a wuss.

I let the water pour over me for ages, feeling as if it were washing away the old Merilee. The only problem was, I had no idea who the new one would be. But, surprisingly, when I went into my bedroom in my light summer robe, threw open the window, and heard a robin trilling, I felt a ripple of hope.

My decision about the wedding, tough as it had been, felt right. For the past week, I'd felt like Pigpen in those old Peanuts cartoons—except where he was enveloped in a cloud of dirt, my cloud had been doubt. Now the doubt was gone. I was clean, shiny, new. Vulnerable and scared, yes— and not ready to think about Matt and I actually breaking up—but kind of . . . alive, too.

A soft knock sounded on my door.

Was this shiny and vulnerable me ready to face the family? I took a breath of fresh summer air. Mom always said that putting off the inevitable never helped, so I called, "I'm up. Come in."

It was Kat. Usually, she was the most put-together one of us, even more so than Mom. But this morning, in her own robe and bare feet, hair mussed, no makeup, she looked . . . oddly, she looked a bit shiny and vulnerable herself. Her face glowed but her body language screamed uncertainty as she crossed the room toward me. "Hey, Merilee, how are you doing?"

Was she afraid I was going to break down and cry all over her? "Not too bad."

"Have you, uh, had second thoughts?"

So that was it. They were all hoping they didn't have to

spend the day making cancellation calls. "Sorry, I haven't changed my mind. I know that'd make it easier for everyone, but honestly, I think this is the right thing. And Matt agrees," I added bitterly. It probably shouldn't have been a surprise that he found me boring, not worth fighting for or romancing, because—hello—I wasn't the smartest, prettiest, sexiest, most exciting girl in the world. But he'd always told me I was special and I'd always believed he meant it.

Kat perched on the windowsill. "Well, if you're sure. I mean, you two know best." She shoved off the sill, took a couple of steps away, then turned again and, unexpectedly, hugged me. "I can't imagine how hard this must be for you."

Matt, who'd made me feel special, was talking about breaking up. Yeah, that was *hard*. Tears clogged my throat. If I said anything, I'd cry, and that wasn't how I wanted to start this day.

She stepped back, shaking her head, reddish-brown curls flying every which way. "Yeah, of course. What was I thinking? Well, look, Theresa has a list so I guess we'll all get started."

"I'll get dressed and come down and help."

She'd almost reached the door when I registered what she'd said. "Kat, what did you mean? When you said, 'What was I thinking?' You weren't going to try to fix things up, were you?" She was a romantic, too, even though her own love life had sucked before Nav.

"No, nothing like that." She bit her lip, like there was something she wanted to say but was holding back.

Were they all going to treat me like a baby who needed to be handled with kid gloves? "Spit it out, sis."

She shook her head, then impatiently raked a wayward curl out of her eye. On her hand, her left hand, something flashed.

My eyes widened and I dashed toward her. "Kat?"

Quickly her hand disappeared into the pocket of her robe. I dragged it out and stared at an engagement ring with a big, sparkly diamond. "You got engaged?" Pure happiness rushed through me, momentarily displacing my worries. "Oh, Kat, you and Nav got engaged!" I threw my arms around her.

She hugged me back. "I'm sorry. I meant to hide the ring."

"No. Jeez, you don't have to do that." I pushed her away and picked up her hand again so I could stare at the fabulous ring. Lucky Kat. Not that I'd have cared about the size of the ring. If Matt had surprised me with even the tiniest diamond chip, I'd have been thrilled out of my mind.

Ack. This wasn't about me. "I'm so happy for you. He's a terrific guy. Did he pop the question last night?"

She studied me warily, as if she wasn't sure whether I could handle this. "On the train, the night before we got to Vancouver."

"But . . . you never told us."

"It was your special time," she said quietly. "You deserved the spotlight."

She'd actually done that for me? Ruefully, I said, "And look how well that turned out. Well, wow, this is amazing." No, I wasn't jealous, wasn't jealous, wasn't jealous. Just because Kat was passionately in love with a dynamic, exciting man who thought she was the sexiest, loveliest woman ever created, a man who was a brilliant photographer and had a totally drool-worthy accent, who'd wooed and won her and proposed on a *train*, who'd given her a honking big diamond. . . .

Like hell I wasn't jealous. But I could at least try to do the mature thing and hide it. "It's an incredible ring. And you're really, really sweet to keep the engagement a secret. Not that you have to any longer."

"He wasn't planning to propose." Her eyes shone and she spoke quickly, eagerly. "But he had this ring, his own ring.

He gave it to me when he asked me to marry him, and no way would I let him replace it with another one, so we got it made over into a woman's ring."

"That's so romantic." He'd taken his own ring off his finger and given it to her. "Have you set the date?"

She glanced away, eyes shifting down to study her bare feet. "No."

"You have, haven't you? It's okay, you can tell me. I promise I won't fall to pieces."

Her head lifted again and she shook it firmly, curls tossing. "No, we haven't."

Though we Fallon girls were all really different from each other, I'd known Kat for twenty-one years. Something was going on that she wasn't telling me. And then it hit me. "Not . . . Saturday? You weren't thinking . . ."

"No, of course not!" The denial was too quick, too vehement.

"Oh, my God."

"But we won't. I don't know why we even—"

I gaped at her, stunned. "You came here to ask me if it was okay."

"No." Another vigorous head shake. Then, "Well, to see how you were doing. But it's crazy. Nav and I were in my room last night, drinking Grand Marnier and talking. You know, about the wedding being off, all the things that needed to be cancelled. And he said, 'If everything's in place for a wedding, then someone should get married.' We'd all had a lot to drink at dinner as well, and at the time it seemed like a good idea. But it *wasn't*. It was stupid and thoughtless and I'm so sorry for even thinking it."

They wanted to take my wedding? Seriously? I couldn't get my head around it, much less my battered, envious heart.

Kat loved me. For her to even think of this meant . . . what? That she wanted to grab on to Nav before he could get away? I tilted my head and studied her. "You got engaged a couple of weeks ago and you'd marry him tomorrow? Are you that sure, or is it just, you know, you've dated so many guys and had such crappy luck?"

One side of her mouth kicked up. "No, Merilee, it's not that I'm desperate."

"Sorry, I didn't mean—"

"It's okay. I can see why you'd ask. But you notice something? With all that dating, I never once got engaged."

That was true. She'd had dazzling love affairs that either crashed and burned or fizzled pathetically, but not a single engagement.

"Not even when I went out with someone for months and months." Her mouth twisted ruefully. "And no, it wasn't always because they dumped me. Sometimes I just knew it wasn't right. With Nav, it's totally different. I know him so well, and he's wonderful. This time it *is* right. There's no reason to wait." The certainty glowed in her eyes.

Probably my eyes used to look like that. But maybe Kat had a better reason. She had dated a ton of different guys, so she knew what she was looking for. Besides, she and Nav really did seem perfect together. They'd known each other two years, were best friends, and had all that romance and passion going for them. All my sisters were perfect with their new guys. That was what had made me realize Matt and I were . . . flawed.

Sometimes life just sucked. I'd done everything right for fourteen whole years. Why couldn't I have the glow, the perfect romance?

I took a breath and reminded myself I wasn't a spoiled baby. I was the shiny, new Merilee. Kat, who'd wanted to get married just as long as I had, had kept her engagement a secret so I could hog the limelight. Now I could give my sister this gift. "Look," I said slowly, "if you're both really sure, in the light of day with no booze in you, then yeah, go ahead. Someone might as well get married on Saturday. If you don't mind secondhand stuff." *My* venue, *my* wedding cake, *my* music.

"You'll have to get a dress, though," I told her. No one was wearing the floaty white-lace gown I'd chosen with stars in my eyes, imagining Matt watching me walk down the grassy aisle. Wryly, I added, "And a photographer." Her fiancé had been going to take the wedding photos as his gift to M and me.

She took my hands and squeezed them. "It's too much to ask."

It was. But seeing the hope in her eyes, I said, "You're not asking. I'm offering." It was a grand romantic gesture, and I loved my sister so I was making it.

"Would Matt be okay with it? Saturday was, you know . . ."

"His wedding, too." Yeah, I knew. "Phone and ask." No, that was cowardly, rude, just plain wrong. I still loved him and we had to be able to talk. To figure out what we were going to do. Whether we really were going to . . . break up. I swallowed another choking lump of tears. "No, I should talk to him." By phone, not in person. If I saw him, if he said to my face that we were over, I'd be toast.

Her brow furrowed. "This is pretty bizarre."

"Tell me about it." Doing the right thing wasn't always easy. "Go tell Theresa not to cancel anything yet, just our friends who'd RSVP'ed. I'll phone Matt."

She squeezed my hands harder. "I love you, Merilee."

In my family, when we used those words, they were usually followed by, "but you should do this or that," with an undertone of, "because I know better than you." Her simple, unqualified words meant a lot. "I love you, too." Only for a sister would I do this.

A thought struck me. "Oh, God, Kat. What about Theresa and Jenna? Will they be pissed off? I mean, what if Theresa and Damien want to get married on Saturday? Or Jenna and Mark?" Jenna, my free-spirited sister who thought marriage was an archaic institution? "Okay, not Jenna, but maybe Theresa?"

Kat released my hands, humor gleaming in her eyes. "Never thought of that. I could claim first dibs. Or maybe we could flip a coin. Or have a double wedding." Then she sobered. "Or forget the whole thing. That's the better thing to do."

Better? It would be easier for me and for Matt. Not for anyone else. The hurt, envious child in me wanted to scream, *Yes, forget it! Just forget it!* Slowly, I said, "You want this. I can see how much it means to you. Let's take it one step at a time. I'll call Matt, then we'll all talk."

Maybe he'd say no. If he did, would I side with him or my sister? In the past, there'd never have been a question because Matt and I were two halves of a whole. We never disagreed. He was such an easygoing guy, he went along with what I wanted.

Which, actually, could be a little annoying. It got tiring, having to make all the decisions.

"You're the best," Kat said fervently.

Me? As she left the room, her words lingered. Had anyone in my family ever said those words to me? Matt had, but not my family. Would he ever tell me that again?

Before I could wuss out, I squared my shoulders and picked up the phone.

Chapter 3

Coffee was better than tossing in bed, so Matt rose early. Last night, he'd told his mom about the wedding and had to deal with female outpourings of shock, anger, and sympathy. She'd wanted to cook dinner for him, look after him, but he couldn't handle that so he'd thanked her and said he needed to be alone.

He'd thought about calling his guy friends, but no way would they relate. They didn't get why he wanted to be with just one girl, much less get married, at so young an age.

The one person he'd always been able to talk to was now off limits. So, feeling really, really alone, he'd gone out and walked for hours, tramping the residential streets as evening turned into night. He walked as kids went inside for family dinners, then people watched TV together or played games outside, then bedroom lights went off.

When finally his body was exhausted, he went home and fell into bed, but he couldn't shut his brain off. What did he think about all this? How did he feel? What were he and Merilee going to do?

For fourteen years, everything in their relationship had seemed inevitable, like a cruise ship steaming happily and securely on its appointed route. Now he'd been cast overboard in a rowboat, with no idea which direction to row, or where Merilee was heading.

He'd just poured a second cup of strong morning coffee when his phone rang. The call display showed her number. His heart leaped. Had she changed her mind? Decided this was just crazy pre-wedding nerves? But . . .

As he stared at that ringing phone, a shocking truth surfaced in his tired brain. Maybe he didn't want her to change her mind. Maybe he didn't want that cruise ship to toss down a ladder so he could climb up.

Now what the hell was that all about?

He picked up the phone. "Merilee?"

"How are you?"

Like she cared. "How do you think I am? Damn, Merilee, why didn't you tell me this stuff long ago? Why'd you save it up until two days before the wedding?" They'd said they could tell each other anything, but it hadn't been true.

Probably he should ask how she was doing, but if she was feeling happy, he didn't want to hear it. Maybe, despite her tears yesterday, she was excited about the idea of *not* being half of a couple. Excited about dating other guys. Was that what she wanted? Boring old Matt wasn't good enough for her anymore?

"I didn't know how I felt until my sisters came home," she said softly. "And no, not because they told me I was crazy or tried to talk me out of it. But just being around them, it was kind of like a light shining on me and on our relationship. They've gone through all this stuff lately, and so have their guys. Sorting out who they are and what they want. I've never really done that. I kind of took everything for granted."

"Took it for granted?" he snapped disbelievingly. "You were the one with the wedding magazines, you were the one who said we should both be teachers. Last summer, you were the one who said we shouldn't go on that camping trip in the Okanagan because we needed to save our money for the future."

"You're saying I bossed you around?" She sounded offended.

Had she? It hadn't felt like it at the time. "I'm saying you knew what you wanted and told me, and we made plans together. In my books, that's not taking things for granted."

"N-no, but I guess . . . I don't even know what I mean. I'm so confused."

He snorted. "Tell me about it. Suddenly, I don't know anything." Grudgingly, he added, "Guess it's better to figure that out now, though, rather than after we'd been married a few years." It was a possibility he'd never imagined before, that their marriage wouldn't be happy. Him, the kid of divorced parents whose marriage had been hell. He'd wanted a do-over—a second chance at a loving family—and for some reason he'd never doubted that he and Merilee would make that happen. He gave a ragged laugh that held no humor. "I finally get what people were saying, about how young we are."

"We thought we knew better, but I guess not. Matt, thanks for not being too furious with me."

Furious. Was he? Since his dad left, he'd tried his best to never even feel anger much less express it, for fear he would let it out the same way his dad had: in violence. No, he wasn't furious, and he didn't want to hit Merilee. Shake her, maybe, and that scared him.

"You aren't, are you?" she asked anxiously. "Tell me you're not furious."

He reminded himself that this was the girl he'd always loved. "I'm unsettled, okay? I don't know what happens next." Should they break up? Did she want that? Did he? Where had his weird thought come from earlier, about not being so sure he wanted to climb back aboard their relationship and take up where they'd left off?

Not having a clue what he wanted, he kept quiet.

Thank God he'd taken today—the day before the wedding—off work. That thought reminded him that the boss at his summer job was his uncle, and a couple of his coworkers were also invited to the wedding that now wasn't going to happen. "I guess Theresa has a list? Guests who need to be told, stuff that needs to be cancelled?"

"Actually . . . Matt, this may be a terrible idea, but . . . well . . ."

"What now?" His patience for surprises was wearing really, really thin.

"Kat and Nav are engaged."

That caught him off guard and made him, for a moment, think about something other than himself. "Seriously? Well, I guess we saw that coming." They were a good couple. Outgoing Kat could be a bit of a steamroller and Nav had softened her.

"Actually, they got engaged on the train from Montreal and kept it a secret. Which was really considerate. It must've almost killed her. Anyhow, they want to get married and, uh . . ."

His brain was working sluggishly despite the caffeine, so it took him a moment. Then adrenaline jolted through him. "They want our wedding? You have to be kidding." Gripping the cell tightly, he paced across his converted-garage apartment.

"She didn't ask, but they'd been talking about the possibility, and so I said maybe, if it was okay with you. What do you think?"

That everyone had gone fucking crazy and he was fucking pissed off. "She didn't ask, but you said maybe? What are you talking about?"

"She and Nav had talked about it, but she decided not to ask, but I just somehow knew. And I thought I should be mature and offer."

His free hand clenched into a fist. Mature? It was *mature* to just hand over her wedding to someone else? Like a sweater she didn't want any longer, so she'd give it to her sister?

"What do you think?" she asked again, nervously.

He forced himself to unclench his fingers, but his body was still taut with anger and bitterness. What could he say? He was the nice guy, the responsible one who never lost his temper, the one who liked making other people happy. "Oh, hell, why not?" he snapped. "Why let a perfectly good wedding go to waste."

Across the phone line, he heard Merilee draw in a breath, or maybe a sob.

He ran a hand over his unshaven jaw and automatically apologized. "Sorry. I'm kind of all over the place."

Quietly she said, "Me, too. This is hard."

"Whatever," he ground out. *She* was finding this hard, after she'd initiated it? His heart bled. Not!

"Yeah," he said. "If they want the wedding, they can have it." That reminded him of something else. "They might as well take the damned cruise, too."

"Nav has that photography exhibit in Montreal, remember? Unless he postpones it. But I doubt he could. Well, I'll ask. Right away, because otherwise we'll need to cancel the cruise."

"I phoned last night. If we cancel, there's no refund. Not even of the return flights to L.A., because I booked the whole package as a last-minute sale."

"Oh, no."

"Yeah, it sucks." And it was all her fault. "If we find someone else who wants to go, we can swap them in and have them pay us, but we can't get a refund."

"We could really use that money."

They could. Though not for their first apartment; not

now. That was another thing they'd have to cancel. "I asked my mom if she knew anyone who might be interested in the cruise, but it's such last-minute notice, leaving Sunday. No one with a job can take off that quickly."

"I'll ask, too." She sighed. "I was really, really looking forward to lazing around and being pampered, and to exploring those Mexican towns."

He knew that. When he'd mentioned the cruise, she'd been so excited.

It reminded him that, despite her calling off the wedding, this was the girl he loved. She'd been under a lot of stress this year, and maybe that's why she'd suddenly gone crazy. "Look," he said slowly, feeling way more noble than she deserved, "why don't you go? Chances of finding someone else are slim, and rather than waste the money you should have a holiday."

"I couldn't."

Fine. Turn down his noble gesture. "Whatever," he snapped again. "Ask Kat, ask around. I'll do the same."

"Okay." She was quiet long enough that he knew there was something else on her mind.

"What?"

"If they do get married, do you want to go?"

He stifled a gasp, feeling like he'd been sucker-punched.

"You know Kat would invite you to her wedding, but . . ."

"No. No way." He did *not* want to see another woman walk down the aisle on Saturday. He scowled. "Are you going?"

"I don't want to. But this can't be about me, right? If my sister gets married, that's what I have to focus on. Her happiness."

She could do that? Clearly, she was nowhere as upset as he was. "Then you just have a *wonderful* time." He clicked off his cell.

* * *

A half hour later, Matt got an e-mail from Merilee saying that Kat and Nav were going ahead with the wedding. He didn't reply. Needing to do something, anything, he left his garage apartment without the slightest idea of where he was heading.

His mom must have been hanging out at the kitchen window. As soon as he stepped into the yard, she hurried out the back door of the house in her old yellow terrycloth bathrobe and slippers. She had booked the day off from her nursing job, planning to give herself a luxury day at a spa in preparation for the wedding rehearsal and dinner.

There hadn't been many luxuries in their lives since his abusive dad had walked out on them when Matt was six. His mom had moved them to Vancouver, partly to get away from bad memories, partly to be close to her parents and have their help with Matt. But life hadn't cut them a break. Only a couple months later, his grandparents died in their sleep of carbon monoxide poisoning when their furnace malfunctioned. Since then, it had been just him and his mom. She'd worked her butt off to support them and he'd pulled his weight, too, taking part-time jobs and helping out around the house.

Now she gave him a big hug. "Oh, honey, how are you doing? I didn't want to disturb you if you were sleeping, but . . ."

He returned the hug. "I'll survive."

She reached up to flick her hand over his hair, just a quick ruffle. "I hate to see you hurting. You're still my little boy."

He shrugged. When he was six, she'd told him he was the man of the house. He'd always tried to be grown-up and responsible, to look after her. And yet she insisted on calling him her little boy. Had to be a mom thing.

"No change in plans?" she asked. "Have you talked to Merilee this morning?"

"We talked. There's no change in *our* plans." He swallowed a hard, bitter lump in his throat. "Kat and her new guy—turns out he's actually her fiancé—are getting married instead."

"What? Kat and . . . What?" She plunked her hands on her hips and stared up at him, expression outraged. "They're stealing your wedding? That's terrible."

"Merilee called me to ask if it was okay."

"Hmph. What's the girl thinking?"

He sighed. The edge of his anger had dulled, probably because he was so tired and depressed. "What does it matter? Her sisters have gone to a lot of work organizing everything. Someone might as well take advantage of it."

"But that's just bizarre."

He shrugged. "It's the Fallons. They do things their own way."

"That they do." Though the Fallon family had been a part of both their lives since he met Merilee—providing him a place to go after school and a hot meal when his mom was working shifts—she'd never been too comfortable with Merilee's parents. Dr. James Fallon, a scientist researching the genetic links to cancer, was an easy man to respect but not an easy one to get close to. And Rebecca's idea of fun was reading law journals, while his mom would rather veg out in front of the TV.

It didn't help that his mother believed she owed Rebecca big-time. It was Merilee's mom who'd insisted Adele sue the furnace repair company, had represented her without charge, and had won her a hefty settlement. Every penny of which his mom had invested for his own education.

Now she said grimly, "They boxed you in. You didn't feel you could say no."

It was true. "*No* isn't my favorite word."

She rubbed his shoulder. "You're a gem. But it is okay to say no every now and then."

When he shrugged, she said, "I bet you haven't had breakfast. I'll make you something."

"No thanks, I'm not hungry."

"You need to eat."

He rolled his eyes, not the least bit surprised. So much for it being okay to say no.

"And I need to cook for you," she went on, "so humor me. Come in and I'll make you anything. Mexican omelet, French toast, chocolate chip pancakes."

When he'd been a little boy, chocolate chip pancakes—the chips arranged to make a smiley face—had been the panacea for all ills. "Pancakes."

"Good." She took him by the arm, maybe afraid he'd escape or just needing to touch him, and steered him up the back walk. "You're not going, are you?"

"To Kat's wedding? No way."

"Good. What about Merilee?"

"She says she will. That it's about Kat, not about her."

"Hmph. She's taking this awfully well."

"Tell me about it." He held the door for his mom and they went into the kitchen, a cozy room that hadn't been updated since they moved in fifteen years ago.

Matt took his old seat at the yellow Formica table. They'd always sat across from each other at one end, leaving the other end as a place to spread out magazines, bills, homework, junk mail. Now, a red geranium plant and a folded-open travel magazine sat there. His mom never traveled except in her imagination. She rarely dated, and he knew it was because of his dad, but still, she really needed to get past it. Not all men were abusers.

She was fifty, which wasn't all that old these days, and not bad looking in a comfy, "mom" kind of way: trim build, brown hair with only a few strands of gray, casual clothing that suited her.

She went through the familiar motions of getting out ingredients and mixing them together without measuring. "What will you do about the apartment?"

He and Merilee had planned to move into an apartment at the beginning of July, when they got back from the cruise. "Give notice, I guess. We'll be out a month's rent."

She turned from the counter. "Give it a few days. Just in case. I know how much you both like the place. You never know, things might look different in a week or two. I'll cover the first month's rent, until you're sure."

Money was tight, and she was pretty obsessive about paying off the mortgage, so the offer meant a lot. "Thanks, Mom. Maybe you're right. I have no idea what's going to happen."

"No need to make any big decisions right now. Oh, I phoned a few friends and no one's able to take that cruise. I'll keep trying."

"Sure hope we can find someone. If we don't, I told Merilee that she should go."

"What?" She swung around to look at him.

"It's been a tough year for her, and she's tired and stressed." Which could well be why she was acting so strange.

"Huh." His mom slapped batter into a heated frying pan a little too vigorously. "It's been a tough year for you, too. You almost had to drag her off to the doctor kicking and screaming, then you handheld her though all the pre- and post-surgery stuff, and you helped her make up her course work and study." As if on autopilot, she pulled orange juice out of the fridge, poured two glasses, and put them on the table. "Not to mention, there was the emotional stress when you found out she might not be able to get pregnant."

She sat down across from him, elbows on the table, chin resting on her hands, and gazed at him, her blue eyes serious. "Matt, you know I've always loved Merilee and I trust the two of you to figure out what's right for you. But if you . . . break up, have you realized what it means? One day you'll meet another girl, probably one with no fertility issues."

"I, uh . . ." That had never occurred to him. When Merilee's doctor had said that, as a result of her endometriosis, she'd likely have problems conceiving, they'd both grieved, but he'd never wavered a moment in still wanting to be with her. He'd figured that, some years down the road, they'd consider adoption. And if not, then the two of them would still be happy together.

"You know you want kids. How many times have you said two's too small a family?"

It was. His mother was wonderful but he'd longed for a big, noisy, happy family. Feeling disloyal to her, he said, "I'm sorry. I didn't mean to hurt you."

"You didn't," she said firmly. "I did the best I could, and I know you know it. I'm just saying, you could have that big family with another girl."

He'd never choose a woman based on whether she could have kids. But if she could, he had to admit it would be awesome. And now he was feeling disloyal to Merilee. Which was insane, because she clearly felt no loyalty to him. God, what a shitty, crappy, fucking mess his life had turned into.

His mom popped up to press the chocolate chips into the tops of the nearly-firm pancakes, then flipped them over. She poured two cups of coffee and got maple syrup from the fridge. Normally, she insisted he pull his weight in the kitchen. It was rare to be pampered this way.

She turned the pancakes out onto plates and brought them over. Two big chocolate smiles grinned up at him. Despite himself, his lips curved slightly—not out of happiness, but out of knowing how much he and his mom loved each other. He cut a bite off the edge of one pancake. He always ate around the edges first and saved the smiles for last.

"Maybe you should go on the cruise," she said.

"Maybe you should," he countered. No one worked harder than her.

"Even if I could afford it, I can't get off work on such short notice." She cocked her head and studied him. "Here's a radical idea. What if you and Merilee went?"

He looked up from the bite of pancake he was cutting. "Huh?"

"Like we just said, it's been a tough year for both of you. No wonder you're confused and stressed out. Why not take a holiday, just as friends. You've always been best friends. Spend time apart, spend time together. Talk, play tourist, fatten yourselves up. Slather on sunscreen and lie out on deck chairs all day, listening to the ocean and the breeze."

"Go on our honeymoon as friends? That's as bizarre as Kat taking over our wedding." How could he be friends with Merilee right now, after what she'd done and the things she'd said?

"Who says you always have to do the conventional thing?"

Her comment cut close to the bone. He hadn't told her about the "boring, stable, no passion" part of his and Merilee's conversation, only said his fiancée was having second thoughts and they both wanted time to think things through. Now even his mom thought he was predictable. "I don't always do the conventional thing," he snapped. Though he hadn't yet eaten all the pancake edges, he deliberately took a slice out of one of the grins.

Go on the cruise with Merilee? That was the craziest idea he'd ever heard.

Friday at noon—before Kat went off to try on wedding dresses and Theresa left for the airport to pick up Damien, who was flying in from his book tour to attend the wedding—we all got together on the patio with platters of sandwiches we'd tossed together. Dad was up at the university, but Mom was there, all us sisters, and Kat's and Jenna's guys.

Theresa, who'd been working at warp speed all morning, hung up her cell and triumphantly added another tick to the spreadsheet she'd printed out. "We have a photographer, thanks to Nav's connections. She's a student and hasn't officially set up her business yet, but the photos on her website are terrific. So, aside from the bride and groom's clothes, that's everything I can do. I'm taking the afternoon off."

Jenna grinned. "Nothing like having your lover coming to get you motivated, Tree." She was into nicknames, and this one dated from when, as a toddler, she hadn't been able to pronounce her older sister's name properly. "We all know where you'll be spending the afternoon."

Mark leaned over to whisper something in her ear, which made her giggle. I figured he'd suggested they do the same.

Kat had enlisted Mom to go dress shopping with her, while Nav was going tux hunting.

Theresa had turned down the offer of a double wedding, saying she and Damien had so far only spent a few days together and were in no rush. Jenna had laughed her head off at the idea of getting married, and Mark had hugged her and said, "That's not our style."

They'd all refused the offer of the Mexican Riviera cruise, as had my parents and my relatives and friends. But Matt had called, sounding distant—at first I'd been afraid it was a *we should break up* call—and told me his mom's idea.

Now I put down the tuna sandwich I'd been nibbling on halfheartedly. "Matt's mom had a weird suggestion about the cruise."

"Weird?" Jenna said. "Weird can be interesting."

"This idea is interesting, all right, but I'm pretty sure it's dumb. She says maybe he and I should go, just as friends."

"What?" My mother frowned. "Go on your honeymoon as friends? What's Adele thinking?"

"She says we're both stressed out and it would give us a chance to relax. We could each spend as much time alone as we want, but we could also get together and talk. Maybe things would make more sense if we had a rest, a change of scene."

"A change of scene's great," Jenna said promptly. "It gives you a new perspective and you learn stuff about yourself."

"She's right," Mark said.

"You don't need to travel to learn about yourself," my mother said.

"It can help, though," Kat said. "If Nav hadn't been on that train from Montreal, I might never have seen him for who he really is. Or seen myself, either."

"With me," Theresa said, "it wasn't so much travel as meeting Damien. But because we were on an airplane for hours, we really got to talk."

"Talk?" Kat teased.

All of us sisters knew Theresa had joined the mile high club. Yet another of the things it wouldn't even occur to Matt and me to do.

Theresa flushed and shot Kat a warning look. "And in Honolulu," she went on quickly, "it was so different for me. I wasn't being a professor, I was being a girlfriend. A woman. It was new, and fun. I definitely got a fresh perspective."

Like sex on Waikiki Beach. Yeah, that'd give you perspective, all right.

"You should consider it, Merilee."

I almost choked on a bite of sandwich. Oh, yeah, she meant fresh perspective. And yes, I did need that. I was this new, shiny, vulnerable Merilee—and yet, I had no clue who that person was, at least not in relation to Matt. "All the same, sharing a cabin . . ."

"Nothing wrong with friends with benefits," Jenna said with a twinkle in her eye.

Matt and I had been lovers since we'd turned sixteen. *Comfortable* lovers. A boring couple. I doubted we'd fall back into bed anytime soon, but if we did . . . I shook my head. "I'm not sure that'd be a good idea."

"No," Kat said, "it's not going to solve anything. You'll just fall back into the way you've always been with each other."

If we slept together, she was right. Nothing would have changed.

"You have to break the old pattern," she said. "Don't you, Nav?"

"In a big way," he agreed. "That's the only way I won you, my love."

Ack. Enough with the grand romance.

"What does Matt think?" Mom asked.

"That it's crazy. He said that, to be fair, he was telling me about Adele's idea, but he thought she was nuts."

"Didn't he also suggest, earlier, that you go alone?" Jenna asked. "I think you should."

"I've never traveled anywhere on my own."

"There you go," Kat said promptly. "Breaking the pattern in a big way. Traveling on your own is fun. You meet lots of interesting people." She winked at Nav.

"A woman needs to be able to move around in the world on her own," Mom put in. "We all do that—the three-pack and I—in our own ways. You need to learn how, dear."

I'd been so looking forward to getting away: to the ocean, sun, visiting the ship's spa, swimming in the pool, eating and drinking, and then going ashore to visit Mexican towns and eat Mexican food. To dressing up and dancing, to strolling the deck in the moonlight. But with Matt. Not alone. I never did anything alone.

Maybe I'd meet someone else. I shivered, my body rejecting the idea even before my heart and mind did. It wasn't like we'd actually broken up. And even if we did, dating was way down the road for me. If it was even on my road at all. After fourteen years of loving one person, I couldn't imagine ever falling for another guy.

I bit back a groan and glanced around the table. "So, I don't know if you're saying I should go alone or go with Matt." Much easier to just stay home, but no one had recommended that option. I imagined a week of total rest. Then I'd be all refreshed to start my summer job working at a kids' day camp. Or would I? Maybe I'd just spend the week angsting.

"I think . . ." and "You should definitely . . ." advice from four female voices made a noisy, tangled mess that hurt my head.

Across the table, Jenna's Mark shot me a sympathetic glance.

"Merilee?" Nav's voice cut in, not louder than the female ones but decisive enough that it silenced all of them. "I don't mean to interfere."

"Go ahead. Everyone else is."

His lips twitched, then straightened. "If you let someone else tell you what to do, you're letting life happen to you. It's not a real decision. You've heard a lot of opinions. Take some quiet time and think about what you really want. And then do it. Whatever it is. To get what you want, you have to go after it. If I hadn't got off my arse and gone after Kat, I'd still be mooning around in secret."

"Hmm." I realized something. I'd probably never made a decision on my own in my entire life. Either my parents or sisters had told me what to do, or Matt and I had decided things together. Yes, with him I'd usually taken the lead, but we'd always discussed things. He'd had great input, and I'd never felt like I was on my own. "Thanks, Nav. That's good advice." Kat had done well, choosing this man.

His thick-lashed, chocolate eyes sparkled with humor. "That's what big brothers are for."

He startled a small laugh out of me. Then I glanced around at everyone again. "If I make my own decision, will you all respect it? Whether it's to go on the cruise with Matt, to go alone, or to stay home, rest, and think about where I want to go from here?"

Glances were exchanged, and I could see lips contort to hold back words, then finally everyone nodded.

Okay. It was up to me. Now there was a scary thought.

Chapter 4

Saturday morning, I had a good cry-fest in the shower. The day that was supposed to be the happiest of my life was Kat's and, even if I was the one who'd made that happen, it didn't stop me from feeling awful. Then, determined to be adult and generous, I pasted a smile on my face and resolved to keep it there all day.

Mom and the three-pack gave me sympathy hugs, but they were busy getting ready for the wedding, and Dad had holed up in his study. I got out the sewing machine to take in the side seams of the bridesmaid's dress that had been Kat's. Normally, we wore the same size, but I'd lost weight in the past months.

When I was finished, I put the dress on and studied myself in the mirror. The sundress was a rich shade of peach that was great with Kat's coloring. In it, I looked washed out. No, I *was* washed out. I'd look sucky in anything today.

My honey-blond hair was shoulder length and usually I wore it either pulled back in a ponytail or loose and wavy. For my wedding, I'd booked a salon visit to get it twisted up into a flattering style with soft tendrils dancing on my neck. Kat had gone to my appointment instead, and come back looking beautiful and elegant, yet still unmistakably Kat.

She was now in her room with Mom, Theresa, and Jenna, getting dressed.

I didn't want to join in, but I felt so alone, aimlessly brushing my hair, waiting, trying not to think. It was almost a relief when it was time to drive to VanDusen Gardens for the wedding.

The group gathered there was small. None of my and Matt's friends, of course. Very few of Kat and Nav's, given the short notice. None of his family, who were all in either India or England. I'd have felt sorry for Kat, but for the glow on her cheeks.

Relatives and family friends were there, having received phone calls to tell them it wasn't me getting married, but my sister. They treated me with kid gloves, clearly uncomfortable. They probably didn't know whether to murmur words of sympathy or scold me for being a silly girl who couldn't make up my mind. Which, obviously, I couldn't. I'd changed my mind about getting married, couldn't decide whether to go on the cruise, and didn't have a clue to what the heck I was doing with my life.

When Kat had asked if I wanted to be a bridesmaid along with my other two sisters, I'd said yes because I couldn't imagine not being part of her wedding. Still, when we all gathered on the grass at my favorite place in all of Vancouver, it felt freaky to line up with my bridesmaid's bouquet and begin the walk down the flower-bordered aisle.

Pacing slowly behind Jenna was exactly what I'd anticipated, but not staring ahead to see handsome Naveen Bharani beside the minister, beaming as he awaited his bride. Not stepping off to the side and turning to watch as Kat, radiant and stunning in the elegant satin gown she'd picked out yesterday, came toward him, her arms linked on either side in Mom and Dad's.

The joy in her eyes pierced my heart, but I fought to hold

my smile in place. I'd always believed that one day I'd take that walk down the aisle, joy fizzing in my veins like champagne bubbles at the thought of joining my life with Matt's.

Had I thrown that away? Could things work out between us? Kat had talked about changing our pattern, but we were the same two people we'd always been. We might love each other, but how could we create excitement and passion out of *comfort*? Or was I being totally childish to even want them?

Were Matt and I breaking up? Neither of us had said anything when we spoke on the phone. What was he doing now, and how was he feeling? Was he glad to be rid of boring old me?

The minister asked who gave this woman away. Together, Mom and Dad said, "We do." Grasping each other's hands, they stepped back and took their seats. I glanced at my sisters standing beside me and saw Theresa's gaze meet Damien's, and Jenna's catch Mark's. The two men sat side by side on white garden chairs, Mark next to my gran, who was sitting beside Mom.

Gran had brought us to VanDusen on so many Sunday outings. This afternoon, sitting there in her favorite green dress, with her white hair freshly styled, did she understand what was going on? I'd so wanted her to be lucid when I got married. Now I wished the same for Kat.

"Every woman deserves passion," Gran had told me. Surely she would recognize the passion between Kat and Nav, as well as the deep, abiding love.

My eyes were damp, but I absolutely refused to cry. If I did, even out of happiness for Kat, I might never stop.

I didn't listen to the minister's words. Instead, I shut off my mind and thought about my conversation with Matt that morning. He'd called to ask if I'd decided about the cruise.

"I can't imagine the two of us going," I said. "Wouldn't we fall back into the same old pattern?"

"Rut," he said bitterly. "You mean rut. I thought you enjoyed that *rut*."

"I did, but . . ." No, maybe we wouldn't fall into our comfortable pattern; more likely, we'd fight. We'd bickered more in the last two days than over the whole course of our relationship. "Same old pattern, or arguing all the time? Neither sounds like much fun."

"Looking for fun, are you? Sorry, I'm not much in the mood for it."

"I didn't mean—" Fine, I obviously couldn't say anything right. "I should stay home and do some thinking. But you could go."

"Like I said, I'm not much in the mood for fun. Guess the cabin will be empty." He hadn't said good-bye.

Now, his last words rang in my head as Kat and Nav exchanged rings and the vows they'd written yesterday. Our honeymoon cabin aboard the *Diamond Star* would sit empty, as empty as my heart felt right now. All my life, all I'd ever wanted was true love, to be half of a glorious romantic dream. Was this the end of M&M? If we broke up, could we salvage a friendship? Or would that be too hard for both of us?

But we hadn't broken up. Neither of us had taken that step. After this weekend, life would start getting back to normal and maybe we'd . . . what? Fall back into our comfortable rut? No, that wasn't right either. There was no good answer here.

I drew in a shaky breath, trying to hold myself together. Jenna leaned close to me so her shoulder touched mine. On my other side, Theresa did the same. Their silent support gave me strength to keep that smile on my face, even if it trembled.

I couldn't wait for this day—the day I'd once believed would be the happiest in my life—to be over.

* * *

Early Sunday morning, Matt's mom insisted on giving him a ride to the airport. She told him he should spend his money enjoying his holiday rather than paying for cab fare. Right now, enjoyment was the last thing on his mind.

When his mom drove into the terminal, he said, "Don't park. Just drop me off." He didn't want her fussing and crying.

"You're sure you'll be all right?"

"God, Mom. I'm a big boy." Fine, so he wasn't an experienced traveler. In fact this would be the first time he'd traveled outside of British Columbia except for driving across the border into Washington. But his mom had no more experience than he.

"You're still my little boy."

He was twenty-one. If he'd gotten married, would she still say that? He was so on edge these days, it was hard to keep his voice even. "I'm perfectly capable of checking in at the airport." Or at least he hoped he was, given how little sleep he'd had and how muddled his brain was. He was glad that he'd packed and organized everything earlier in the week, using the detailed checklist Theresa had drawn up back when this was supposed to be a honeymoon trip.

Yeah, he was going on the cruise. After spending Saturday imagining the wedding and the dinner reception, he'd realized he was desperate to get away. If Merilee was staying home, he was going to Mexico to sort out his thoughts and feelings.

When his mom parked in the loading zone, he pulled his backpack from the trunk and gave her a quick hug. "Love you. See you in a week."

"Love you, too, Matt. You try and have a good time."

Oh, sure. Still, he nodded, then waved as she pulled away. Letting out a sigh of relief at being alone, he slung his bag over one shoulder and went inside the terminal. He took Theresa's check-in checklist from his pocket, annoyed that he was relying on a Fallon, yet knowing that left to his own devices he'd forget something.

Customs form; that was first. He walked over to one of the stands and filled in the information, referring to his e-ticket to Los Angeles for the flight details. Next on the list: find the check-in counter.

He glanced around, then his backpack slid off his shoulder with a thump. Merilee? She stood inside the terminal, staring upward as she scanned the airline signs. At first he thought she'd come to see him, then he noticed that not only did she have her big tote bag over one shoulder, but one hand gripped the handle of a wheeled bag.

Oh, shit. Had she decided to go on the cruise after all?

Questions raced through Matt's mind, a jumble of emotions flooded him, and for the moment he just stood and studied her. It was the first time he'd seen her since Thursday night when she'd called off the wedding. She looked the same as always, which for some reason surprised him. He was the same Matt, and Merilee was the same girl he'd known for fourteen years. Everything had changed, yet nothing had.

No, his emotions had. He guessed he still loved her, but that was buried down below the hurt and anger.

Her gaze lowered and lit on him and her jaw dropped. She stood gaping as he hoisted his pack again and strode toward her. She looked pretty, as always, in beige cotton capris and a long-sleeved blue shirt that matched her eyes. But as he came closer, he saw that the soft skin of her face was stretched taut over the bones and deep purple shadows rimmed her eyes.

He felt like a shit for being glad.

"What are you doing here?" he demanded, afraid he knew the answer.

"I decided to go. I thought—" She shook her head, still looking stunned. "I thought you weren't going."

"I am."

"You said you weren't." Her tone was accusing.

"I changed my mind." She'd changed her mind about getting married; he could change his mind about the cruise.

"And didn't tell me?"

"You didn't tell me. Besides, I just decided last night. You were at the wedding reception having fun."

Her eyes narrowed. "I wasn't. I was alone in my room listening to everyone partying downstairs and out in the garden. And I couldn't stand it anymore. I knew I had to get away."

"Shit." Rarely had he sworn around Merilee, but now he didn't give a fuck. "What now?" Nice guy Matt would have told her to go ahead, he'd just go home. Screw that. She'd had her chance.

"I guess one of us should stay home," she said hesitantly.

"Damn right." The emotions he felt right now told him that his mom's idea about going as friends, sharing a cabin, was crazy.

"Um . . ." She gazed up at him expectantly.

"I don't want to stay home." Now that he'd decided to go, the thought of hanging around at home was unbearable. How could he gain fresh perspective in the same old place?

Her chin firmed and her blue eyes stared into his with determination. "Me either."

Generally, he was glad to do what others wanted. He rarely had strong feelings one way or the other and he liked making people happy. This time he did have strong feelings—and why should he care about making Merilee happy? "I don't care what you do," he lied. He tightened his grip on his pack and turned away. "I'm going."

He strode over to the automated check-in machine and resisted looking over his shoulder. She'd leave. Surely she would. She had to see they couldn't share a cabin.

Was he being a jerk? Too bad.

He hadn't hit her, hadn't even touched her. Still, he could hear his mom's voice in his head, saying that the strong man wasn't the one who bullied or dominated a woman, but the one who looked after her and supported her. He'd always done that for Merilee.

She needed a holiday more than he did.

He paused a moment, torn, then gathered his passport and boarding pass and forged ahead. No luggage to tag, just his carry-on backpack, so he could go straight through to Customs. The line was short at this time on a Sunday morning, and moving quickly.

Merilee could have a holiday at home. Her sisters were all heading off today, her parents would be at work, she'd have the house to herself. To sleep, think, do whatever she needed. If he stayed home, he'd have his mom fussing over him. Adele meant well, but sometimes a guy needed to get away from his mother, and she had trouble understanding that.

Women. His mom, Merilee. He almost wished he wasn't going on a cruise ship, but out on a wilderness hike with other guys.

He cleared Customs, went through Security, then located his departure gate. Theresa's list suggested picking up a bottle of water and a snack, which made sense. He chose a fruit granola bar rather than the chocolate kind Merilee loved. And he didn't buy M&Ms, a treat the two of them had shared forever.

He already had a novel in his backpack, so didn't study the book racks, but his gaze slid over the glossy magazine covers. The wedding mags popped out at him, the kind Merilee had pored over for the past decade. When he'd had a little spare cash, he used to pick one up for her because she'd never tired of planning their perfect wedding.

Muttering a curse under his breath, he turned away.

Returning to the departure gate, which was now almost

full, another curse escaped him. This time out loud. She was there. She had the *balls* to be there.

Her eyes widened as he headed over, and when he stood in front of her, she said, quietly but firmly, "I need to get away."

"So do I. I'm not backing down."

She tossed her hair. "Me either."

"Jesus." He stalked away, to sit as far from her as he could. Should he back down? The whole point of the trip was to get away. From her, and all the anger and confusion she'd made him feel. But shit, trailing home like a loser didn't feel right.

Hoisting his pack again, he went over to her. "Come here."

"Why?" she asked warily.

"To talk."

She glanced around at the other passengers, a few of whom were watching with curious expressions, then flounced to her feet. "Fine." She began to walk away, leaving her tote bag under her chair.

He pointed. "Take that."

"Fine." She grabbed it and followed him as he walked over to stand by a wall a little away from other passengers.

"You won't go back?" he asked.

"No, and I won't ask you to, either. You have as much right to go as I do."

He folded his arms across his chest and glared at her. "More." She was the one who'd bailed.

She shook her head, looking bemused. "We've never fought like this before."

"You've never called off our wedding before."

She sighed. "Matt, I'm sorry about everything and I know this isn't how things are supposed to be, but I wish you'd try to understand and—"

"We need ground rules."

"Pardon me?"

"I don't *understand* anything, except that if we're both going on this cruise, we need to set ground rules."

"How do you mean?"

"We have to share a cabin. So what are we, roommates?"

"Friends?" she asked hesitantly.

He glared some more. "I don't feel very friendly right now." Hadn't she managed to pick up on that?

The wounded look in her eyes made him sigh and say, "Yeah, before you say it, I've loved you for fourteen years. I guess that hasn't gone away, but right now I really don't want to see you."

"You mean, we'd share a cabin but, uh, stay out of each other's way? Not do things together?"

"Do things together?" She actually thought they might? "That's the last thing I want." Since grade two, they'd almost been joined at the hip. The only time they weren't together was when he played sports with the guys and had a beer at the pub afterward. He had no idea what he'd do on his own, but it was better than suffering the pain and turmoil he felt when he was with Merilee.

Right now, seeing the shadows under her eyes and the fragile slump of her shoulders, a part of him wanted to enfold her in his arms and take care of her. What a mess this was.

"All right," she said slowly. "Yes, you're right. Otherwise we'll fall back into the old—"

"Rut." He ground out the word. "And I doubt that very much." Not with all the negative shit he was feeling.

Damn it, he'd liked that rut. He'd been happy. Not ecstatic all the time, but happy, comfortable.

And yet . . . Maybe, even if it had been possible, he didn't want to jump back into that rut. He remembered his thought about being cast overboard, yet being in no hurry to climb back aboard. Something inside him—maybe a boy who'd never put himself first or a young man who didn't want to settle for a lifetime of *comfortable*—told him things needed to change. *He* needed to change.

"So," he said slowly, "we both want to break out of the rut." Finally confronting the issue they'd both avoided, one he hadn't even dared think about, he said, "That means we need to break up. Doesn't it?" Even as he spoke the words, he felt a pang deep in his heart. All he had in his life was his mom and Merilee. And yet, as he'd learned from seeing his mom with his dad, it was unhealthy to try to hang on to something that was broken. It was unhealthy not to recognize the truth and move on.

A stricken expression crossed Merilee's face. So softly he could barely hear, she said, "I don't know."

"If we hang on to our relationship, it's like a security net." As a kid whose dad had been an asshole, and whose grandparents had both died one horrible night, he'd valued love and security above all. But, he reminded himself, he was twenty-one. Not a kid. A grown-up who had to make adult decisions. "It *is* the rut."

Her eyes were huge and sad. "You're right," she said slowly. "We've always been M&M and I don't even know who I am as a person. We need to be on our own. I guess we need to find out who Merilee and Matt are as individuals."

That made sense, as much as anything made sense these days, yet he felt a sense of disbelief and shock. They'd really broken up?

Glancing past her, he had another shock. The departure gate was almost empty. "We have to board. Are you still going?"

Looking lost, she raised her eyes to him as if he could give her the answer. When he didn't say anything, she squared her shoulders. "I'm going."

*   *   *

I woke, a little groggy, and tried to get my bearings. Oh, right, the cabin on the *Diamond Star*. I glanced around the small room. No Matt. The covers on his bed were pulled up messily; his backpack sat on a chair with some clothing tumbling out of it. My own wheelie bag rested unopened on a luggage rack, and sunshine filtered between partially closed blinds. The time on the clock beside the bed said two o'clock.

Two o'clock? Had I actually slept for almost an entire day?

Yesterday, I'd stumbled through the day, exhausted and in shock. We'd broken up; we were flying to L.A. together; we were sharing the cabin we'd booked for our honeymoon. It was all like a bizarre parallel reality. I'd wanted to cry, but didn't have the energy. Matt had looked stunned, too, and we barely spoke a word.

My stomach growled and I desperately needed to pee. When I slipped out of bed, I found I was wearing the clothes I'd traveled in, minus my sandals and capris. My gosh, I'd been so exhausted I climbed into bed without even taking off my bra.

In the bathroom, I took care of the basics, then studied my face: puffy, with a pillow-mark across one cheek, but not as strained as yesterday. Basically, though, the same old Merilee.

Whatever happened to shiny and new? How could I be shiny and new when I looked just the same? How could I be shiny and new when I was sharing a cabin with Matt? Matt, my *ex*.

It was so unbelievable. Yet what he'd said made sense, and it confirmed my own fears. We'd been in a hopelessly boring rut, and I would never get a grand romantic gesture from him because he just didn't feel that way about me. He loved me, but he didn't really *love* me. It broke my heart, but I had to accept it.

My sisters had found guys who felt that special kind of love. I deserved that, too, didn't I?

Of course, it had taken them until they were thirtyish. . . .

I groaned. Why had I come? I must've been totally sleep deprived yesterday, or totally desperate, to climb on that plane.

I stared at my reflection again. However it had happened, I was here now. On a cruise ship, heading to Mexico. I could burrow under the covers again and spend the whole week being miserable, just as I'd feared I'd do if I stayed home. Or I could start figuring out who the new Merilee was. And what better place to do it than on a luxury ship—with a spa, great food, and a swimming pool, not to mention three shore excursions in Mexico?

As for Matt, he was clearly off doing his own thing, and that was good. He had to figure out who the new Matt was. And then . . . would we get back together? Or be *just friends*?

I had to believe that, with all the history and love we shared, we'd at least work through to being friends again. Right now, I couldn't start to imagine what my new life would look like, but I had to believe Matt would be a part of it. Losing him would be like losing a member of my family. Unthinkable. He had to feel the same way.

I peeled off my clothes and stepped into the shower, then emerged refreshed and ready to go. First, though, I should check messages. Wrapped in a towel, I picked up my cell from the bedside table.

Yesterday, before I joined the line-up to board the ship, I'd phoned Mom to tell her I'd arrived safely. When I'd told her Matt was here, too, and we'd broken up, I'd actually silenced her. Finally, she said, "How do you feel about all this?"

I told her I had no idea, then she said, "I hope you find out what you need to, Merilee. Whatever it ends up being. Your dad and I just want you to be happy."

This was the new and improved version of my mom. Two

weeks ago, she'd have lectured and not listened, but my family had come a long way since my sisters arrived home.

Anyway, that was yesterday and I was sure she'd have passed along the news. Sure enough, my cell showed missed calls. Before retrieving them, I threw back the curtains. Deep blue ocean, light blue sky—oh, yes, we were definitely cruising. Maybe there was a land view on the other side of the ship, but not on this one. Still, it was wonderful to have a window cabin rather than an interior one. I watched the ocean as I listened to the messages.

From Theresa: "Hi, Merilee. Damien and I just arrived in Boston." She'd gone with him while he finished the book tour launching his Australian thrillers in the U.S. "Mom filled me in on what's going on. Wow, that's sure not what you'd planned. Hope you're okay. And, Merilee, you've taken charge of your life, so stick with it and figure out the best course for *you*. Matt's a good guy, but let him look after himself and you look after yourself."

Shouldn't be a problem, since Matt was determined to see me as little as possible.

From Kat: "As if it wasn't enough trauma to my system, having to fly to Montreal"—my sister hated flying, but Nav had needed to get back to prepare for his exhibit—"then I get a shocker of a message from Mom. Wish I was there to give you a hug, sis. Guess all I can say is, there'll be lessons to be learned out of this. Be open to them, okay, Merilee?"

Lessons. I'd always been a decent student, but learning from a lecture or textbook was easy. What faced me this week was much harder.

From Jenna, on a crackly connection: "Hey, M, we made it to Bali. Mom left voice mail about you and Matt. Big stuff going on. Take care of *you*, okay, baby sis? And listen, you're on a cruise ship. You're going to Mexico. Have some fun, okay? And keep your eye on the open doors."

The open doors? What did she mean? Jenna had her own

philosophy of life, which made perfect sense to her and not so much to anyone else. As for fun, did she really expect . . .

No, wait. She was right. How was being miserable going to help me or Matt? I took a deep breath, then let it out slowly. Sunshine sparkled off the ocean, I had an appetite for the first time in days, my sisters were all being nice to me, and it was time to be shiny and new and open to having fun.

I sent quick texts to my sisters and mom. Then I put on a denim skirt and a tank top, and brushed on a touch of mascara and lip gloss. Now what? I was starving and I was alone. Alone, on a ship that carried, give or take, a thousand passengers, and God knows how many crew. I could order room service. . . . Ack! No, I wouldn't start this trip by being a wuss.

I did pick up the phone, though, and called the spa to book a massage and facial for later in the afternoon.

"Why not treat yourself to a mani-pedi?" the perky voice asked. "And how about an appointment in the hair salon?"

That was too much like what I'd planned for Saturday morning before the wedding. I was going to look forward, not dwell on the sad stuff. "No, thanks, just the massage and facial."

Remembering to take my key, I left the cabin to find a narrow corridor lined with doors on either side. I chose a direction, wondering if I'd ever find my way back.

When I found myself in a brightly lit atrium with gorgeous spiral staircases, I paused to gaze around, dazzled by the glamour. A neatly uniformed crew member paused, smiling, and asked if she could help me find something.

"Food," I replied.

"You mean lunch?" When I nodded, she said, "You've missed the last sitting for the buffet, but if you go up two decks you'll find a number of bars and restaurants. There's something to suit every taste."

I followed her directions, and wandered past a bar that

looked like my idea of a men's club, which didn't appeal to me. Then I saw a small restaurant called La Vie en Rose. This one fit my image of a French bistro to a T: pink-toned décor, roses on each table—not prim buds but sensually full blooms, a ballad sung in French by a woman, drifting on the air. Everything drew me in.

"Yes, just for one," I told the waitress, trying to remember if I'd ever in my life had anything more than coffee alone. Confident women like my mom and sisters dined out alone all the time. I could handle this.

The special last-minute cruise package included food anywhere on the ship, and nonalcoholic beverages, but unfortunately not booze. Still, my family had given me some money, saying they wanted me to enjoy myself and not worry about a few indulgences. My trip should start with a glass of wine, so I asked for a French chardonnay, then settled in to study the menu.

When my waitress returned with the wine, I ordered chicken and mushroom crepes, together with an endive salad. After living on a student budget, it was a total luxury to not have to think about prices.

I took a sip of wine and it went straight to my head—and to a stomach that hadn't tasted food in longer than I could remember. Hurriedly, I drank ice water, vowing not to drink more wine until my meal arrived.

Several other people were scattered around the small restaurant: mostly couples, but there was a family with three kids, and four middle-aged women laughing over a bottle of wine. No one else was on their own. Why hadn't I brought a magazine or a book?

I remembered something Mom had once told me. I'd been thinking about teaching in a classroom—I love kids and totally respect teachers, but the idea of standing in front of a class was scary—and asked her how she had the guts to argue a case in front of the judges of the Supreme Court of

Canada. She talked about preparation and practice, but also said, "You act the way you want to be. It's partly a performance. If you act assured, you'll feel more assured and they'll perceive you that way."

Okay, Mom, let's test this out. I straightened my back and crossed one leg over the other, acting the role of a poised woman who thoroughly enjoyed her own company. But what did I know about my own company? For the most part, when I'd been alone I'd been studying or thinking about Matt.

If I'm bored with myself, did Matt ever really find me special or was he just being nice?

Without thinking, I took another sip of wine and felt the potent punch of alcohol. I gulped water to dilute it. Jenna had said a woman needed to be independent, and I was still trying to figure that one out. So far, it wasn't much fun, yet she'd always made it look like a blast.

Impulsively, I hauled my cell phone out of my bag. The cost of calling Bali from a cruise ship made me shudder even as I dialed. But, really, she almost never answered her phone, so the chances of me running up that bill were—

"Jenna? Is that really you?"

"M? Like, seriously? I just got your text."

"How's Bali?"

"Oh, man, it's unbelievable. I was *born* to live here. It's so *me*."

"Ocean, sunshine, and hippie skirts?" I teased.

"Sarongs rather than hippie skirts, but yeah. It's the crack of dawn here and we're rounding up the team and getting organized, and can you believe, I'm already working? You'll notice my cell's charged and I actually answered. But enough about me. Tell me how it's going with Matt."

"Once I got on the ship, I crashed in bed and I've just gotten up. I haven't seen Matt, but we agreed we'd go our separate ways." It felt bizarre to say that. We'd always been so linked. Even if we weren't together, we knew exactly where the other person was.

"Sounds wise, sis. Must be hard on you, though."

"It is." I resisted slugging back more wine. "Jenna, you said it's important to be independent, right? And I guess now I am. All I ever wanted, before this, was to be half of M&M, but I'm not any longer. I'm this new Merilee and . . . I'm confused."

"Poor Merilee. I bet you are. You two have had the M&M *two halves of a whole* thing going on for so long, it's like neither of you's had a separate existence. And that's not good."

"It felt good. We were soul mates." I'd always figured finding your soul mate was the best thing in the world.

"Okay, soul mates are good, but you each still have to be self-sufficient. You don't want to marry someone because you can't imagine who you'd be without them."

She, Theresa, and Kat had been very much their own women before they hooked up with their special guys. Whereas I had no idea who I'd have been as a woman if I hadn't known Matt. "I guess that makes sense." I sighed. "So I suppose it's a good thing we broke up. Matt said that hanging on to our old relationship would be like having a security blanket."

"That's smart."

My brain agreed, even if my heart hurt. "Yeah." I glanced around the bistro again. "But here I am, trying to be independent, and it's not feeling like a lot of fun. You always made it look like fun."

"It's great."

"I need pointers," I confessed.

She chuckled. "Wow, the hippie free spirit advising the good girl. The earth's flipped on its axis."

"Pretty much." The new, shiny feeling I'd felt in my cabin

had given way to a gloomy one. I allowed myself one tiny sip of wine.

"Aw, M, I'm really sorry. But this'll all work out. The universe gives you what you need."

I rolled my eyes. How often had I heard that philosophy? Jenna was such an optimist, a trait that was both lovable and frustrating. "So far it's given me a French bistro and a glass of chardonnay, with crepes coming up."

"Excellent start."

"But I'm not having fun."

"You're whining."

She was right. "I'm entitled," I shot back.

"Yeah, you are. Okay, try living in the moment. Don't get all into your mind and obsess about whatever. Just enjoy the surroundings, the wine, the food when it comes."

The surroundings? The people eating with friends, family, and lovers just made me feel more lonely. Even the French chanteuse, when I translated her lyrics, was singing about lost love.

Jenna was going on. "Taste, look, smell, appreciate. Live, really live. Enjoy your own company, but when you feel like talking to someone, the world's full of interesting people. One'll turn up."

"Does this really work for you? The *universe will provide* thing?"

"Always does, though you have to be open to the messages it sends. Open doors, open roads, possibilities, opportunities. Sometimes you step through a door thinking it'll take you one place, and then find yourself somewhere completely different—and yet, that's the right place to be."

"O-kay," I said doubtfully.

"It got me Mark," she said smugly.

"Hard to argue with that."

"You going to be all right, sis?"

"I guess. I'll try out your advice."

"M, before you go . . ." Surprisingly, there was now a tentative note in her voice.

"I'm here, Jenna." The waitress brought a basket of French bread and I smiled my thanks.

"There's something I want to tell you," my sister said. "To tell the whole family. I didn't want to last week because I had some trust issues, and then Mark came, and you called off the wedding, then Kat and Nav were getting married and there wasn't time anyhow. But I've been thinking about it. We're doing better now, aren't we? All us sisters, and Mom and Dad. We're closer than we've ever been."

"We are." Even if I still felt like I was a pale shadow compared to their vibrant personalities. "What's this big secret?"

Chapter 5

Jenna didn't answer for a moment. Then, sounding unusually subdued, she said, "I told you my stupid first love story, right?"

"About the hot biker who turned out to be a jerk. Yeah, I'm really sorry." I tucked the phone between ear and shoulder so I could butter a slice of bread.

"There's more to the story."

I didn't hear anything more and, after chewing and swallowing, said, "Jenna? Have we lost the connection?"

"No, it's just hard. Confessing to how stupid I was. Anyhow, long story short, he gave me gonorrhea, I was too stupid to figure it out, and when I finally got to the hospital I had a PID and a ruptured abscess, and they operated and there was such bad scarring that I can't have kids."

Once she'd gotten going, the words—such incredibly unexpected words—had flown out in such a rush that it took me a moment to sort through them all. "You're infertile? Like I may be?"

"Yeah."

"Oh, my God. And you've been carrying around this secret since you were seventeen?" Bubbly Jenna had kept that inside her?

"Yeah."

"You always said you loved kids but didn't want any of your own," I said tentatively.

"Why want what you can't have?" she tossed off. Then, "But I do, Merilee. I really do. So I can identify with how awful you feel."

"Wow. You've blown me away with this. I'm so sorry, Jenna."

"I told Mark, on that long drive up the coast. We both want kids so we're talking about adopting. Which is something you can do, too, M. You know that, right?"

"I guess I just always figured Matt and I would create babies together, as soul mates. Since I got the diagnosis, I've been trying to get my head around the idea that it's not likely to happen, and now, well . . . Who knows what's even going to happen with him and me? If we don't get back together, I can't imagine being with anyone else. Oh, Jenna, it's just all too much. You know?"

"I know, sis, and things will sort themselves out in time. I'm just saying it's something to keep in mind down the road. You'd make a fantastic mom and I'm betting that's what the universe has in store for you."

Oh, Jenna. "I'd like to believe that." And that those kids had a wonderful father who loved them, and me, with all his heart. But that was way, way down the road. "Thanks, sis. For the advice, and for sharing your secret. You're going to tell the rest of the family?"

"Yeah. And thanks for not saying I was a total idiot to not take better care of myself."

"Hey, you were seventeen and in love."

"Wanna bet Mom doesn't see it that way?" she said ruefully.

We said good-bye and I hung up smiling, feeling closer to her than ever before.

My meal arrived, and I dug in. Following my sister's advice, I focused on the taste. Oh, wow, this was great. I didn't know much about fine cuisine, what with my and Matt's student budgets, and the fact that my parents were so busy with their jobs that dinners were hit-and-miss at home. A creamy French sauce with herbs was a treat. I savored every mouthful, concentrating on the food and nothing else. When I took an occasional sip of chardonnay, its crisp, slightly citrus flavor was perfect with the rich food.

Oh, yeah, I could turn into a serious foodie. I enjoyed cooking basic meals myself when I had time, and baking cookies, but I'd never experimented with anything fancy. Hmm, I'd noticed that cooking classes were offered on the *Diamond Star*. Maybe I'd try them out.

The waitress refilled my water glass. "How is everything?"

"Delicious." Jenna had said that if you wanted to talk to someone, a person would turn up. An idea occurred to me. "*Parlez-vous Français?*"

"*Mais oui. Et vous?*"

"*Oui.*" In French, I told her that I was Canadian, studying to be a middle-grade teacher, and that French would be part of the curriculum. I said I'd love to practice, and she gave me a smiling, "*Bien sûr.*" Carrying on in that language, she said, "Enjoy your meal. But be sure and save room for dessert. Ours are magnificent, particularly the Grand Marnier crème brulée, the Alsatian pear tart, and the chocolate mousse."

I stifled another moan. Chocolate was my weakness. At this rate, by the end of the week I'd have not only gained back the weight I lost, I'd be on the road to getting fat.

For the next little while, I gave myself up to the pure pleasure of enjoying good food. I didn't usually pay this much attention to what I was eating because I was either involved in conversation or studying while I ate, but thanks to Jenna I was really getting into this.

I had finished my crepe and sliced into the last leaf of endive served in a rich lemony sauce, when a couple of men walked into the bistro. At least twice my age, they were both hefty and had flushed faces and loud voices. I guessed they'd come from a bar or the casino.

"We need a good steak," one said to my waitress.

"Certainly, sir. We have Steak Diane and steak with green peppercorn sauce."

"Nah, not that girlie crap. A man's steak, rare enough it's still mooing."

"Yeah," the other guy put in, "with fries and a mess of onion rings."

"I think you might find the food at Delrays more to your liking," the waitress said politely. "They serve sixteen-ounce steaks with onion rings and fries."

"That's more like it," the first man said. "Point us in the right direction, doll." He reached toward her with the obvious intention of groping her butt, but she deftly sidestepped and told him how to find the restaurant.

As the two men turned to leave, they noticed me and one nudged the other. "Hey, here's a pretty girl all on her own."

I gazed at them warily.

"What d'you say, doll?" the other said, leering at me. "Bet you'd like some company, and some real food." He gestured disdainfully toward my half-finished lettuce leaf. "You come along with us and we'll buy you a steak."

If Matt had been here, they wouldn't have come near me. The joys of being single. If this was one of Jenna's open doors, it was one I intended to slam shut. "How kind," I said flatly, "but I just ate a delicious meal and I'm perfectly happy with my own company." Oddly, I realized those words were true, at least for the moment.

When the two men left, the waitress came over. Still speaking French, she said, "Sorry about that. Notice the wedding rings? I hate to think what their poor wives are doing."

"Getting a much-needed break," I said dryly.

She laughed. "Now, how about that dessert?"

"I can't resist the mousse."

"You'll love it. And coffee? A *café au lait*, perhaps?"

"Why not?"

And after I finished, I'd put on my bathing suit, slather on sunscreen, and nap on a lounge chair until it was time for my spa appointment. It would all be quite perfect—if my real life wasn't a total mess. But right now, I wasn't going to think about that.

When the waitress brought the mousse, I tasted it and moaned. "That's pure bliss." It was dark, decadently rich, and there was a hint of something—maybe coffee or coffee liqueur in it.

She grinned. "Didn't I tell you?"

Then she turned to greet a new customer, a pretty brunette two or three years older than me, wearing white shorts and a stylish pink top.

"Yes, it's just me," the newcomer said, "and I'm dying for a glass of merlot and something chocolate."

The waitress seated her near me. "Here's the wine list. As for the chocolate, I highly recommend the mousse." She glanced in my direction.

"I'll second her recommendation," I said, sliding my spoon into it again.

"Thanks, then that's what I'll have."

When the waitress had gone, the brunette studied me for a moment, then said, "Feel like joining up? Just tell me if you don't. I'll try not to cry into my wine."

Another open door, this one way more appealing. I grinned. "That would be nice." And not just because I wasn't used to being alone. I liked her style.

"Cool." She came over to sit across from me. "Hi, I'm Des, which is short for Desdemona. Blame my mom, she's nuts for Shakespeare."

"I'm Merilee. No particular significance, they just liked the name." With some difficulty, I stopped myself from digging back into my mousse. I could hold off until hers came.

"Are you on this cruise alone?"

"Sort of, but not exactly. I'm sharing a room with, uh, someone I know." Not my husband, not my fiancé, not even my boyfriend. A wave of sadness threatened to swamp me, and I fought it off by waving a hand. "Long story. How about you?"

"With my granny."

"Really?"

"Yeah. I adore her to pieces." Her wine came and she took a sip, then grinned approval.

"Me, too, with my gran. Sadly, she has Alzheimer's now."

"That's so sad. I'm really sorry. I'm so lucky Granny's healthy and has all her marbles."

"Where is she now?"

"In the casino. She loves the slots. I don't. So, you know, it's not like she and I have to be bonded at the hip, right?"

"Right."

"Same with you and your roomie?"

"Yeah. Not bonded at the hip." Not bonded at all anymore. But I was supposed to be living in the moment, so I gave her a quick smile. "How come you're traveling with your grandmother?"

"She won a cruise and, sweetie that she is, invited me along."

Her mousse arrived and we both dug in, eating and chatting about ourselves and our families, casual getting-to-know-you stuff. She and her grandmother were from San Diego. Des managed a women's clothing store and her granny was retired but did a lot of volunteer work. Granny was widowed and Des was, as she put it, happily single. I felt kind of shabby not even mentioning Matt, but I didn't want to get into the whole complicated story.

Enjoying chatting with Des, I realized that, while I had female friends, I didn't spend a lot of time alone with them. Mostly, it had been me and Matt hanging out with them and their boyfriends. A few girls had e-mailed or left voice mails in the past few days, but I hadn't responded. I wasn't so close to any of them that I'd wanted to talk about what was going on with Matt and me, or maybe I just felt too embarrassed and uncertain. They'd never been the ones I'd shared real confidences with. That had been Matt.

With a sigh of pleasure, Des shoved away her empty mousse bowl. "I'd best get back to Granny."

Too bad. I'd happily have spent the rest of the day with Des. "Have fun," I said. "I'm going to lie in the sun, then I have a spa appointment."

"Hope I'll run into you again."

"Me, too. And I'd like to meet your granny." I half-hoped she'd invite me to join them. Much as I'd love to lie out in the sun, I still felt awkward about being alone. But Jenna had said I needed to be more self-sufficient and she was probably right.

Des and I rose, thanked our waitress, then strolled out together. "Hey," Des said, "you figured out your costume for the ball tomorrow night?"

"No, I haven't." When we'd planned the trip, Matt and I had said we'd go to the costume shop onboard and pick out complementary costumes. Now, did I even want to go to the ball? This was a whole new world, one I'd initiated.

"Granny and I are going to the costume rental place tomorrow morning. Want to meet up with us? We can give each other advice. Bring your roomie, too, if you want."

"Uh, I don't think my roomie would be interested, but that sounds good to me."

We agreed on a time, then I headed back to the cabin. No Matt, but he'd left a note on cruise ship stationery: *I see you're up. Hope you're feeling better and having a good time.* No mention of what he'd been doing.

A roommate type of note without even a signature. No little drawing of two overlapping circles with smiley faces, the M&M symbol we'd been using since we were kids.

Below his note, I scrawled: *Yes, thanks, I'm feeling better. I needed the sleep.*

I fiddled with the pen, not knowing whether to say any more. Finally, I added: *Hope you're having fun, too. See you around.* My hand automatically wanted to make our M&M symbol, but I stopped myself.

Sunshine poured into the unfamiliar room and, with the taste of chocolate on my tongue, I told myself that coming on the cruise was a good idea. If I had to figure out who the new Merilee was, it would have been harder back in the house I'd grown up in, with my parents around and everything totally familiar. Probably the same was true for Matt.

What was he doing anyhow? Who was he with? Did he miss me at all?

Where would we be, at the end of this cruise? Where would *I* be? Who would I be? Did I know myself at all, this person who was now Merilee, rather than one M of M&M?

A thought struck me. There'd been three certainties in my life: my family, Matt, and my career plans. Now my family was going through big changes—good ones, but major. Matt and I were no longer M&M. So, what about my career? Did I even still want to teach school? It was something I thought I'd known since junior high, and Matt had said he wanted to be a teacher, too. But was that still true? It wasn't too late to change. We'd only finished third year university. There was still fourth year, then the twelve-month programs to get our B.Ed. degrees.

I shook my head vigorously. Of course I wanted to teach.

I loved children, and thought teaching them was one of the most important jobs in the world. Was I going to question absolutely everything I believed? Yeah, probably.

Including my resistance to the thought of adoption. Thinking about my phone conversation with Jenna, I shook my head wonderingly. She'd sure given me a lot to reflect on. I really hoped no one in the family gave her a hard time when she revealed her long-held secret.

Outside the window, sunshine beckoned. What was I doing inside when I could be out there relaxing in the heat, maybe taking a nap? I smoothed on sunscreen and changed into my bikini, the modest pale blue one I'd been wearing for two years. A shoulder strap promptly snapped and I groaned, then dug out a safety pin for a temporary fix.

Jenna's comments about messages from the universe popped into my mind, making me chuckle. The universe was clearly saying I should buy a new suit. Quickly, I pulled on a cover-up, and piled sunglasses and a magazine into a book bag. I added my cell, too, so I could set the alarm and make sure I didn't doze past my spa appointment. Then I headed for a swimwear boutique I'd passed earlier.

I tried on three suits. Two were much like my old one— boring!—while the teal-blue string bikini was more daring and flashy. I squared my shoulders and thrust out my chest, a little embarrassed by how I looked, but liking it. This suit, definitely. If I was going to find the new Merilee, I had to break out of all my ruts.

I made my way up to the Lido Deck to find the pool. The sight that greeted me made me stop and heave a sigh of pleasure. This was exactly what I needed. Sunshine sparkled off bright blue water, people lazed on lounge chairs in bathing suits and shorts, and colored paper parasols sprouted out of fruity drinks. A waterslide reminded me of fun times with Matt and our friends at waterslide parks.

As my gaze skimmed over the passengers, I wasn't sure

whether I wanted him to be there or not. He wasn't, and I told myself that was a good thing. I'd do my best to live in the moment the way Jenna had recommended rather than dwell on the past or angst about the future.

The moment I plopped down on a chair and pulled off my cover-up, a cute Asian guy about my age appeared. He wore a white uniform, carried a tray of empty drink glasses balanced on one hand, and flashed a white grin. "Good afternoon, miss. Can I bring you a drink? A snack?"

"What are the drinks with paper umbrellas?"

He grinned. "Figured you for the type who'd like a girlie drink. They're a *Diamond Star* specialty, mixed fruit juices and Mexican coconut rum liqueur. Or, of course, there's always a classic margarita."

"I'll have one of the fruity ones."

"Want a snack as well?"

"No, thanks. I just finished a very rich late lunch."

"Oh, yeah?" He shifted the tray to his other hand. "Which restaurant?"

"La Vie en Rose. The food was delicious."

"Trust me, all the food on the *Diamond Star* is delicious. Everyone gains ten pounds." His gaze cruised my body and, with an internal start, I realized there was a gleam of interest in his eyes. When I was with Matt, I wasn't tuned in to those kinds of looks from men, if I'd ever even received them. Matt's own expression was always warm and loving, but he hadn't looked at me as if I was . . . hot.

I wasn't hot. Or was I? Was the new Merilee? Maybe, in this bikini, she was. The waiter's scrutiny was flattering, but a little embarrassing and I tried not to blush. "I'm in trouble then, because I'm thinking of taking cooking lessons, too."

"You'll have fun. And if you can't indulge when you're on holiday, when can you?" Did he put special emphasis on the word *indulge?* "Speaking of which, I'd better go get your drink."

Hmm. For the first time it really dawned on me that men, men other than Matt, might be interested in me. That I might date.

It was too soon. Way, way too soon. But even if the time did come, did I even know how to date? Or want to? From what I heard from my girlfriends, it was all, like, "Is he really into me?" and "Will I have a date for the party?", and "What a loser, I can't believe I actually went out with him."

But if my big dream was to find that one perfect, forever, passionate romance—and if it turned out that Matt really wasn't it—I'd have to date.

And—ack!—so would he. My Matt, with some other girl. Being his attentive and caring self. Finding a girl who was more exciting than me, one who made him passionate. Matt making grand romantic gestures to another girl.

I couldn't stand it. But if we stayed broken up, eventually we'd both have to move on. I wanted him to be happy, which had to mean I wanted him to find someone he loved passionately. Maybe with time, that idea would hurt less.

I groaned. This was terrible. It was one thing to realize I was unhappy, but how did I figure out the path to happy? And how could I stop agonizing over this and enjoy the sunshine and live in the moment, the way Jenna said?

My waiter returned and handed me a peach-colored drink with a bright yellow paper parasol. "The guy over there says he'd like to buy this for you."

"Huh? Oh, really?" I glanced in the direction he indicated, and saw a cute, tanned blond in board shorts and sunglasses standing by the bar, a margarita in his hand. "Uh . . ." This had never happened to me before. What should I do?

The blond answered the question for me by heading over. "Hi, I'm Tony." He had an engaging smile.

"Merilee," I said automatically, as the waiter faded away.

"No one should be sitting alone with a drink on a sunny

afternoon like this." He shoved his sunglasses up on top of his head, and I saw his eyes were hazel, thickly lashed, and attractive with his fair hair.

If I sat alone, I'd continue to agonize. Better to talk to someone, the way I had with Des at lunch. "Then save me from that horrible fate," I said. As he laughed and pulled up a chair, I raised my drink glass. "And thanks for this."

He clicked his glass to mine and sat sideways on the chair so he faced me. "Thanks for brightening up my afternoon. What's a pretty girl like you doing alone on a Mexican Riviera cruise?"

"That's a very long story and"—I thought of Jenna—"and it's the past. Right now I'm living in the moment." I sipped the drink, enjoying the blend of coconut and fruit.

"I like your style, Merilee."

My style? Well, it was really my sister's, but all the same, cool.

"Have you been to Mexico before?" he asked. "Oh, wait, maybe I can't ask that. I mean, it's the past, too."

"That one's okay. No, I haven't. And it's my first time on a cruise ship. How about you?"

"Same. I'm from Colorado and—"

"Colorado? You look more like you're from California. Like you spend your days surfing." He was actually pretty hot, objectively speaking, but he didn't get my hormones in a buzz. Not that I'd ever really had that response to a guy. For me, arousal was slow to build. It took time, cuddling, emotional connection. Which I sure didn't want from this guy, or any guy, for the foreseeable future.

"Don't I wish." He stretched out on the lounge chair, settling in. "Colorado's as landlocked as they come. Anyhow, a buddy and I just finished undergrad and we're goofing off before we start our summer jobs. Then in the fall I'm starting law school. In Colorado."

"Not one in California by the beach?"

"Couldn't swing it financially."

"Too bad." Should I tell him my mom was a lawyer? I was so used to being with a man I totally trusted, but I'd just met Tony. How much personal information should I give out? And was he hustling me, or just being friendly? How would I know, so I could give the right signals? This was all so complicated.

"Are you in college?" he asked. "Or working?"

It was called making conversation, I told myself. People did it every day without obsessing over it. "I'm an undergrad. I'm going to be a teacher."

For a few minutes we chatted easily about school and the careers we were planning. It was a lot like my conversation with Des, and I relaxed, taking an occasional sip of my drink and enjoying the warm caress of the sun on my skin. The heat, the alcohol, the big meal I'd eaten, they were all combining to make me feel drowsy.

"You realize there's a pool over there," Tony said. "Or are you one of those girls who"—he paused, then said more slowly, with a sparkle in his eye—"doesn't like getting wet?"

I liked swimming. But there was something about that sparkle that made me look for a hidden meaning in his words. Was that a sexual innuendo? If it was, I sure wasn't going to respond.

Searching for words he couldn't misinterpret, I said, "I could use a swim. The *sun* is pretty warm." By emphasizing the word *sun*, I hoped he'd realize I was saying that I wasn't overheating because of him.

"Then let's have a swim." Humor kinked the corners of his mouth and I figured the message had been received.

When he rose and extended his hand to help me out of my lounge chair, I took it. No tingle. No buzz. Just a firm, warm hand. Of course it was too soon to be feeling attracted to another guy, but would it ever happen? Maybe the problem in my relationship with Matt was me. Maybe I was incapable of the kind of passion my sisters had discovered. Or maybe it would take me another ten years to find it.

Live in the moment, Jenna's voice chided in my head. I refocused. I was twenty-one and on holiday. Sunshine, a swimming pool, companionship. *What's not to enjoy?*

When I went down the ladder at the side of the pool and the water's coolness nipped my overheated skin, I squealed and stopped partway.

"Sissy," Tony teased, entering the pool far more quickly and splashing water up onto my chest.

"Bully," I teased back, making him laugh. Then I plunged forward into the water, ducking below the surface and getting the shock over with in one go.

Putting my feet on the bottom, I stood and shook my soaking wet hair so that drops sprayed in his face. "That feels great!" So invigorating, counteracting the effects of alcohol and sun. And of the past days' gloom.

"Want to try the waterslide?" I asked him. "Or are you too *sissy?*"

Again, he laughed. "Yeah, I like your style, Merilee. Let's go slide."

We got out of the pool, then climbed the steps to the top of the slide. "Who goes first?" I asked.

"You do."

I climbed into the channel of the slide, bracing myself and hanging on to the edges as I got settled. Before I realized what he was doing, Tony was climbing in behind me, nudging my legs toward the center so he could sandwich my lower body with his own legs. Tanned, toned legs. Bumpier knees than Matt's, and the hair on his legs was a bit thicker and lighter in color.

A stranger, holding me in the vee of his legs. Both of us wearing only bathing suits. It was intimate, too intimate. "I don't—" I started, just as he said, "Let's go!" and gave a forceful push that sent us catapulting down the slide.

Sheer excitement took over. I leaned back to increase our speed and whooped along with him. Seconds later we shot out into the pool.

When we surfaced, he caught me in an unexpected hug. "Fun, isn't it? Let's go again."

Uncomfortable with the physical contact, I freed myself and gazed up at him, still unsure of what he wanted. "I need to get going soon. I have a massage appointment."

"Cancel it." He gave me a knowing grin. "I'm pretty good with my hands."

If I'd had any doubts before, now I knew for sure. "Look, I'm sorry if I've given the wrong signals. I'm not into, uh . . ."

"Oh, come on, it's a cruise. It's all about hooking up."

What a jerk. "Not for me," I said stiffly, and turned away.

Chapter 6

This was what true betrayal tasted like. Matt strode from the pool area with a sour taste in his mouth, feeling like he'd been kicked in the gut. Locked in his mind were images of the girl he'd always loved, the one he'd been going to marry three days ago, laughing and playing with another guy. Going down a waterslide with their bodies locked together, then hugging, naked but for wet bathing suits.

His hands had fisted and he'd wanted to dive into the pool and punch the guy out. Then he'd remembered his mother saying, "Violence is never a solution. A strong man never resorts to it." He was a better man than his father. And so he'd left, acid churning in his gut.

As he hurried back to the cabin, the images spooled in his mind and he couldn't turn them off. When he'd first seen the honey-haired blonde walking toward the pool, she'd caught his eye because she was so pretty. He'd thought she looked like Merilee. Then he'd realized it was her, but in the kind of skimpy bikini he'd never seen her wear before.

She hadn't noticed him. She'd only had eyes for the fair-haired guy in board shorts.

Hard to believe that earlier today he'd been concerned about her, thinking how exhausted she must have been to sleep almost twenty-four hours. When he'd seen she'd finally risen, he'd even left a note saying he hoped she had a good time.

He'd meant getting a massage or relaxing in the sun, not picking up some fucking stranger. No wonder she'd broken up with him. She'd been champing at the bit, wanting her freedom, all too ready to hook up with someone else. Shit, he must've bored her to tears. Why had she even agreed to set the wedding date? Had she felt sorry for him—then, as the date approached, realized she couldn't go through with it?

"Shit," he muttered under his breath.

When a gray-haired woman passing in the corridor gave an outraged, "Really!" he mumbled an apology.

He unlocked the door to the cabin and thrust it open, then went into the shower and stood under the spray, bathing suit and all, hoping chilly water would cool his temper. Finally, shivering, he turned off the water and dried himself sketchily. Towel wrapped around his waist, he stepped into the cabin where the note on the bureau drew his attention. Merilee's rounded feminine handwriting telling him to have fun.

Damn it, he would. If she wasn't wasting any time, nor would he. So far since he'd boarded the *Diamond Star*, he'd tried out the exercise facilities and had a beer or two with some other guys. It had never occurred to him to seek female company.

But now he would. No way was he going near the pool, so where else were girls likely to hang out? He glanced at the time. Almost six o'clock. Cocktails? Quickly, he threw on some clothes.

Anger still a sour taste in his mouth, he went to check out the bars. A pub-style English one didn't have any likely prospects, so he went into a Mexican one that had a younger crowd. He'd never cruised a bar before, and felt awkward. At a couple of tables, kids his age, both male and female, hoisted bottles of beers with wedges of lime and munched chips with salsa.

He didn't see any girls on their own, just a woman with black hair sitting at the bar with an almost-finished drink that looked like a margarita. She was pretty hot, in white shorts and fancy sandals that showed off great legs, but definitely in her thirties. When she saw him, she shifted position, straightening and turning toward him, and he saw very full breasts barely confined in a tight black sleeveless top. He tore his gaze away to see her smile, her lips glossy and red.

"Hey there, handsome. You on your own, too?" Red-tipped fingers patted the bar stool beside her in clear invitation.

"Uh . . . no, I'm supposed to be meeting a friend. But, uh, thanks." Could he sound any dorkier?

Her lips curved in amusement and he had the feeling she saw right through him. "You could have a seat until your friend shows up."

She wasn't his usual type—he tended to like more natural-looking girls—but she really was pretty, with glossy wings of hair, arched eyebrows, and big green-gray eyes made more dramatic with makeup. What the hell. She was the only female who was by herself, so why not?

"Yeah, maybe I'll do that," he said, sliding onto the adjoining stool. "Can I buy you another drink?"

"I'd like that."

He wasn't much for hard liquor and normally would have ordered a beer, but now he said to the bartender, "Two margaritas, please."

"I'm Trina," the woman said, extending a hand.

"Matt. Nice to meet you." He took her hand and she squeezed his in what sure wasn't a handshake. Her thumb stroked his palm and a pulse of sexual awareness throbbed through him, disconcerting him so that he eased his hand away. He was a guy so, sure, he looked at women; he got aroused by women. But he'd always resisted those feelings because he was with Merilee, the girl he loved.

Now, he wasn't. If he wanted to get turned on, he could. Without guilt.

And so could Merilee, damn her.

Their drinks arrived and he raised his glass to Trina. "Cheers."

"Cheers." She touched her glass to his, then recrossed her legs. Her movements were slow, deliberate, and had the sensual grace of a cat. "Tell me about yourself, Matt. What do you do?"

Did she think he was older than he was? "I'm in university." He fudged a little. "Studying to be a teacher."

"Not just a pretty face," she said, and he almost choked on his first sip of his margarita.

"That's good," she went on. "I like a man with substance." Her hand dropped to his arm and her fingers danced across his skin in a touch that was light, yet erotic. "So, Matt, are you going to forget about your *friend* and let me seduce you?"

His eyes almost bugged out. Man, she was right out there. When she said *friend*, he knew she meant the imaginary friend he'd said he was meeting, but her words made him think of Merilee. Merilee, who'd already found herself a new guy and was letting him fondle her near-naked body. From somewhere, words came to him. "Sometimes a man likes to do the seducing."

Her smile widened. "I won't say no to that."

She was a sure thing. He could have sex with her. He'd only ever had sex with Merilee. But she was gone now. Maybe finding all that *excitement* she'd been missing. He was pretty sure Trina would show him some excitement. But was he ready for that? For superficial sex with a stranger? What self-respecting woman would do this?

He gazed into her wide, clear eyes. "Why, Trina?"

He hoped she wouldn't be offended, and the kink of her mouth said she wasn't. "Why you, or why at all?"

"Both."

"Why you is obvious. You're young, fit, attractive. We'd show each other a good time."

The certainty in her voice made his dick stir.

"Why at all?" she went on. "D'you know, not many men ask that?"

No surprise that she'd done this before. No surprise, he guessed, that most guys didn't care why.

"You do have substance, Matt. And believe it or not, so do I. For eleven months of the year, I have a very responsible job. I work my butt off, and there's not much time for play. Not much time for being a woman."

"Hard to believe." He gestured toward her, so sultry and glamorous.

"Thank you. But normally my hair's up in a knot, I'm wearing a lab coat, and I spend my time with microscopes, not people." She waved a hand gracefully. "Don't ask; that's all I'll say about my job."

"So, when the twelfth month comes around . . ."

A mischievous smile lit her red mouth. "I make up for it." The smile was so irresistible, he had to smile back.

"I go wild," she said.

"I've never met anyone like you. You don't want to get married, have kids?"

Her eyebrows lifted. "You assume I have that option."

"Look at you. Gorgeous, and you're obviously smart to have that job. I'm sure lots of guys would have offered that option."

"Thank you again. I like you, Matt. You're good for my ego. And yes, you're right. If I wanted that life, I could have it. But it would mean less focus on my work, and I love what I'm doing. I'm going to make a difference in the world."

She reminded him of Merilee's dad, a scientist researching genetic links to cancer. Except Dr. James Fallon had made room in his life for a wife and family. For Matt, while he wanted a meaningful career, people were what counted most. He'd always longed for a big family, a cheerful, bustling home.

Something that, with Merilee, he might not have had.

"Do you think that's unnatural for a woman?" she asked.

"Unnatural? People have different paths, right? Sounds like you're living the life you want to. And with your determination, I bet you will make a difference in the world."

"D'you know, you are totally adorable." She leaned forward to press a kiss to his cheek, and some subtle but sultry scent filled his nostrils.

"I, uh . . ."

She chuckled. "How about you? Are you living the life you want to?"

He shook his head. "My life's kind of a mess right now."

"Ah. And that's why you're here, sitting beside me."

"I guess. I mean, not that you're not great company," he hurried to add.

"Maybe you need to do what I'm doing, and go wild for a while."

The idea was tempting. Trina was about as much temptation as a guy like him could imagine. And yet . . . "I don't think that's me," he said, half pissed at himself for rejecting an opportunity like this. "At least not yet. I was with someone for a long time, and we just split up."

"You're not over her yet."

That was for sure. Would he ever be? "I guess not."

"I could make you forget her." Her eyes were compelling. "For at least a little space in time."

She could. He had no doubt. "But after, I don't think I'd like myself much."

Trina raised her glass toward him. "Definite substance, and I do like you. If you don't mind my asking, did you break up with her, or her with you?"

He was the one who'd officially broken up, but he'd never have done it if Merilee hadn't called off the wedding. "She started it."

"I think she's crazy."

Feeling mellow and sleepy after a luxurious massage and facial, I had strolled slowly in the direction of the cabin, gazing into shops and restaurants. The catchy Mexican music drifting out of Maria's Cantina had made me pause to glance inside, looking forward to going ashore in Puerto Vallarta the day after tomorrow. My attention was caught by a man at the Cantina's bar, lounging on a stool, deep in conversation with a striking brunette. He reminded me of Matt. No, he *was* Matt.

I had frozen, gaping in the window as he talked to a woman with long, bare, shapely legs and very full breasts almost exploding out of a low-cut black top. A woman, not a girl. She was well over thirty, maybe nearing forty. And sexy. Very sexy, in that way some older women have, that no girl can possibly compete with.

The bitch. Stunned, I had watched as she leaned over and planted a kiss on Matt's cheek. A cougar, stalking my man.

Except he wasn't my man any longer, and maybe he was stalking her. The woman definitely didn't look *boring*.

When she raised her glass to toast him, I huffed and turned away. Seemed as if Matt wasn't having the slightest bit of trouble getting over me. Who'd have guessed he was a guy like Tony who'd hook up with a total stranger?

All the relaxing effect of the massage had disappeared during the five minutes I'd stood outside the cantina window. Now I just felt depressed. And tired. I wasn't the least bit hungry, and the idea of going to a buffet banquet dinner by myself made me want to cry.

Enough. I'd followed Jenna's advice for hours. Now I deserved a rest. I was even going to take a sleeping pill because I did *not* want to know when—or if—Matt returned tonight.

Tuesday after lunch, Matt headed back to the cabin to get his exercise stuff, planning to head to the fitness club and work off some of the calories he'd been packing in. So far today, he'd managed to avoid Merilee. In fact, he'd yet to speak to her since they'd come aboard on Sunday. Last night, after chatting awhile longer with Trina, then joining a table of passengers for the incredible buffet dinner, he'd returned to the cabin to find her asleep. Had she been with that blond guy or not?

Unable to get that thought out of his mind, he'd tossed for a good part of the night, then finally fallen into a sound sleep. Sound enough that he slept in, and when he woke, she was gone. No note. So he hadn't left one either. After all, what could he say? *Have fun with your new boyfriend?* Hell, no.

Even if she wasn't sleeping with the guy, the idea that she was already seeing someone else pissed him off. She could've at least waited until after the cruise.

Now, returning to the cabin distracted by his own thoughts, he opened the door and started to go in, then stopped dead. Someone was there, and it wasn't Merilee. Nor the chambermaid. No, this was a stranger, and a very sexy one from what he could see of her back view. As he studied her, arousal quickened his body.

She was clad in a skimpy dress with a fringed hem that clung to a seductively curvy butt. The dress was the color of tea with loads of milk, which should have been boring but definitely wasn't, especially because it was close to the color of her skin. But for the fringe and the sequins that sparkled all over the fabric, he could almost imagine she was naked.

Below the dress, long, shapely legs led down to very high-heeled sandals. Above it were pretty shoulders, bare but for two tiny sparkly straps, a slender neck, and short, tousled blond hair a couple of shades lighter than Merilee's much longer curls. In her hair, she wore some kind of glittery tiara thing. Clearly, she hadn't seen him come in because she didn't turn around, just kept gazing in the mirror as she fiddled with dangly, sparkly earrings.

Somehow, he'd entered the wrong room. He should back out quietly before she noticed he was there, yet he couldn't peel his gaze off her, nor halt the thick pulse of arousal. If she was this hot from the back, what was the front view like?

Still staring, he fumbled behind him for the door handle. Rather than grasping it, he managed to bang his elbow against the door.

She whipped around, eyes huge. "Oh!"

His own eyes just about fell out of his head. Her features were delicate like Merilee's, but her lips were lush and shiny red, dramatic eye makeup made her sophisticated and sultry, and rosy color highlighted her cheekbones. The dress was cut low enough that he could see the upper curves of pert breasts and the cleavage between. Hot. Another woman who wasn't his usual type, but very, very hot. Like a performer from some sexy Las Vegas nightclub act. She must be one of the ship's entertainers.

And he was getting an erection. Thank God he was wearing baggy cargo shorts. He peeled his gaze away from her breasts and turned back toward the door. "Excuse me," he blurted out. "I must be in the wrong room."

"What are you talking about?" she snapped.

That voice was totally familiar. "Merilee?" He swung around and took a closer look, trying to see past the makeup and trappings. Sure, Merilee had a good body, a pretty face, but her style was "girl next door" not "siren." And the hair . . . "Is that a wig?"

The color on her cheeks deepened, a real flush underneath the makeup. Self-consciously, she plucked at a few strands. "No, I got mine cut. And highlighted. I wanted something different."

"Oh, yeah?" he snapped, understanding now. "New hair, makeup, slutty clothes, all for your new boyfriend?"

Her mouth gaped. "What? What are you talking about?"

"That guy at the pool. I saw you."

"Like you can talk," she shot back. "I saw you with that cougar in the cantina."

"She's not—" he started, about to deny there was any-thing going on with him and Trina. But if Merilee had a boyfriend, why shouldn't he have a girlfriend? "So what?"

"So nothing! If our relationship mattered so little to you that you can just go out and hook up with someone else, then I'm totally glad I didn't marry you." Her words were angry, but moisture gathered in those made-up eyes and her voice quavered on a note of hurt.

Her words and her tone defused his anger. "I didn't," he said quietly, not wanting to keep deceiving her, even if it salved his pride. "She kind of came on to me, but we just talked. She's actually really nice, and smart. But what about the guy? You're saying you didn't . . ."

She shook her head vigorously. "No, he turned out to be a jerk. And I never, you know, intended anything with him. I was just trying to relax and live in the moment, which is something Jenna said I should do. But he wanted . . . Any-how, I told him nothing was going to happen and I'm sure he picked someone else up five minutes later."

"Oh. Well, I guess . . . I mean, we're both free now, but . . ." It was too soon to even think about getting involved, and his experience with Trina had told him he wasn't the kind for a meaningless hookup. He'd have said Merilee wasn't either, but he didn't know her anymore. She didn't even look like herself. "I can't get over the way you look. The hair, and those clothes."

"You know it's the costume ball tonight, don't you?"

"Oh, yeah, right." Now he felt like an idiot. He hadn't paid much attention, figuring that if he went he'd just wear jeans and a tee and go as a college student. "That's quite the outfit."

"You really think it's slutty?"

He wasn't about to tell her he found it sexy as hell. "Nah, I guess not. But who are you supposed to be?"

"A flapper. Like in *Chicago*? When I saw it in the costume boutique, it reminded me of the dresses Renée Zellweger and Catherine Zeta-Jones wore."

Usually on Friday or Saturday night, if they weren't out with friends, they'd have a movie-and-pizza night at his garage apartment. She always paid way more attention to the names of the actors. "Who?"

"You know, Roxie and Velma, the two girls who murdered their guys."

He winced. Was there symbolism to this? Wryly, he said, "You called off the wedding. You don't have to murder me, too."

A surprised laugh jolted out of her. "Oh, Matt, that's not what I meant. Just, it's a cute dress. I went to the costume boutique this morning with Des and Micky and—"

She'd gone hunting for costumes with two guys? Gay or straight? "Des and Micky?"

"Desdemona, my new friend, and her granny."

Okay, they were women. "Her grandmother's called Micky?"

"Short for Michaela. Anyhow"—she drew that word out, rolling her eyes—"they said my hair was wrong for the dress, so we went to the salon together and, well, this is what happened."

"Uh-huh." Hearing Merilee's familiar voice come out of the heavily made-up face threw him, to say the least. But she really did look sexy. His growing hard-on definitely approved. He thrust his fists into his shorts pockets, hoping she wouldn't see the effect she had on him.

Uncertainty flickered on her face. "You don't like it. Is it my haircut?"

He'd always loved her thick, wavy, honey-gold hair, but the new cut worked with the tiara and dress. "It just takes some getting used to. You don't look like you."

She grinned. "That's kind of the idea of a costume ball."

"Yeah, I guess." And he'd planned to go looking exactly like himself. Maybe he should rethink that one. Merilee was hyped up about going as some flapper performer who'd offed her lover. She'd never been interested in acting or role play, so he didn't really get it, but perhaps it was the influence of these new friends of hers.

He remembered something Trina had said last night before they went their separate ways. "A tip from a friend. You're a great-looking guy, but you're not making the most of it." When he'd asked what she meant, she'd suggested he see a good hairstylist and invest in some trendier clothes.

Matt was a bit of a jock, not for the sake of competition but for physical action and the opportunity to, for once, hang out in a testosterone-laden environment. So he spent a lot of time changing into and out of sports clothes, jumping in the shower, rushing to the next activity. He'd never paid much attention to his appearance and Merilee had never complained.

He'd laughed and told Trina that trendy wasn't his style, but she'd leaned close and breathed in his ear, "As with so many things in life, you never know until you try." Then she'd chuckled and moved on to find a man to go wild with.

Merilee was facing the mirror again, staring at her reflection as if she was as bemused by her new appearance as he was. "They made me up at the salon, and now I need to take it all off because I'm dying for a nap, then there's dinner. Des said she'd help me do my makeup before the ball. I'll be getting ready in their cabin, so you can have this one to yourself." She leaned forward, peering at her reflection. The movement made her curvy butt thrust in his direction and the fringed skirt ride even higher up her thighs.

Man, he was seriously horny. He enjoyed sex with Merilee, but for them it had always been gentle and sweet. Now he felt a near-overwhelming urge to jump her bones. Trina probably would have loved it, but Matt knew that wasn't the way to treat a good girl.

It was kind of nice, talking to Merilee like this—almost like friends—but no way could he hang around here while she took off her makeup and that dress. What was she wearing under it? Sure couldn't be much.

"Have a good nap." His voice came out hoarse. "I'm going to, uh . . . See you later." Hurriedly, he backed out of the room and whipped the door shut before he did something stupid.

And there he was in the hall without his exercise stuff. Maybe he should go to the costume place, too, and find something for tonight. Or maybe he should take Trina's advice. He was being the same old Matt, and that was the guy who'd bored Merilee. Maybe he'd even bored himself.

No way was he going to the costume ball as his same old self.

After Matt left the cabin, I removed the flapper clothes, pondering his stunned expression. He hadn't even recognized me and there'd been an intense kind of heat in his eyes.

Almost like he was turned on. Turned on when he thought I was someone else. That sure wasn't flattering. Had he ever looked at the real me that way? But maybe I'd misread him, and it was pure surprise.

I slipped a sleep tee over my head and began taking off my makeup. It was good that we'd cleared the air, and I shouldn't feel so glad he hadn't slept with that cougar. How strange that he'd seen me with Tony, and I'd seen him with Trina. Tony and Trina, hey, they'd be T&T. The two of them should hook up. Or maybe they already had.

Yawning, I climbed between the sheets. What luxury, being able to nap whenever I was tired, but would I ever get caught up on sleep? Or maybe it was the ocean air, the stress, all the new activities that were wearing me out. This morning I'd taken a cooking lesson, then for lunch the class had eaten the scrumptious Italian meal we'd prepared.

I remembered to set my alarm so I'd be on time to meet up with Des and Micky. It'd be fun getting ready for the ball together.

Would Matt go? What would he wear?

He always looked good, whether he wore casual university stuff, shorts and a tee, or a shirt and pants like he wore for his summer job at his uncle's company.

Good, yes, but no Bradley Cooper.

Though when he'd been washing the car . . . With that image in my mind, I hugged the pillow to me. Oh, yeah, the car-washing guy had been pretty hot.

Chapter 7

Several hours later, I entered the *Diamond Star*'s ballroom. The room was spectacular, romantically lit by glinting chandeliers. They cast a flattering light on costumes that might otherwise look tacky, and I noted everything from Teletubbies to ballerinas to Spiderman. Most faces were hidden behind masks.

I was so grateful to walk in with two companions. Des was dressed as Eve, straight out of the Garden of Eden, in a flesh-colored body suit and three strategically placed fig leaves. Micky, the seventy-something granny, was a dominatrix in black leather, cracking her whip with gusto. They both looked fabulous, and the three of us were getting our share of admiring looks from men of all ages.

My flapper dress wasn't much briefer than a sundress, but it had a sexy, sophisticated *look at me* vibe that made me self-conscious. I had to force myself not to keep yanking the skirt down or peering at my chest to make sure my breasts hadn't escaped. My mask was firmly in place, a sparkly champagne-colored one that matched the sequined dress and dramatically framed my heavily made-up eyes. When I'd had my hair cut, I'd also had my fingernails and toenails painted bright red and they matched my new lipstick. But for the mask and heavy makeup, and the support of Des and Micky, I'd never have had the guts to venture out in public looking like this.

Glancing around the room, I noted a couple of bars, then studied the dance floor, where a number of costumed people moved to a live band playing "New York, New York." Oldies music, but not bad. Dancing. Would I? It would be weird to dance with someone who wasn't Matt, one of our friends, or my dad at the occasional wedding.

"What was that guy thinking?" Des whispered, drawing my attention away from the dance floor to a guy passing in front of us: a Spiderman who was anything but buff.

"I think I saw him in a Speedo by the pool earlier," Micky said. "You'd think with assets like his, he'd do better hiding rather than displaying them."

The three of us spluttered with laughter, then Micky's eyes widened and she pointed across the room with her whip. "Now there's a man who's worth looking at. Who do you figure he is? Clark Gable or Cary Grant?"

Des and I both turned to look. The silver-haired man, maybe ten years younger than Micky, wore a tux and a simple black mask.

"Or a man who couldn't be bothered finding a costume and just wore his tux," Des said disparagingly. "Yeah, he looks debonair, Granny, but he isn't getting into the mood of things."

"Then he needs to be whipped into shape," Micky said, and with a crack of her whip, sauntered across the room, leaving Des and I to dissolve in giggles.

I wondered if Matt was there, and if so whether he'd gotten into the mood of things. I glanced from a sailor to a firefighter to a pointy-eared Vulcan.

"Now," Des purred, "there's a guy who could whip me into shape any day."

"Which one?"

"Over by the bar. The pirate standing with the redhead in the evening dress—another lame costume—who's she supposed to be anyhow?—and the hot Asian girl in the harem costume."

I glanced over to where she was looking and had to agree. This pirate was no Johnny Depp with girly eye makeup; he had a way more masculine, Orlando Bloom kind of vibe. He had the build and presence to carry off a flowing, long-sleeved white shirt, the front open to showcase a lean, muscled chest. The shirt was topped by a battered leather vest and tied at the waist with some kind of sash. Black pants hugged muscular thighs, and tall leather boots plus a knife scabbard at his waist heightened the impression of power, of danger. Long, curly black hair fell past his shoulders, held back from his face by a dark bandanna. His jaw had sexy stubble, and a black mask slashed across his face. "Oh, yeah, totally hot," I confirmed.

We weren't the only ones who thought so. The two girls, both quite stunning, were flirting like crazy. Oddly, the pirate seemed a bit uncomfortable. Or maybe that was part of his act. Rough, unsophisticated. Not the kind of guy to make cocktail chat with a woman; he'd just sling her over his shoulder and carry her off.

Not that I was into rape fantasies, that was for sure. It was just that his brand of raw masculinity was potent. The kind of thing I'd only seen in the movies, or read about in romance novels. Was he just as sexy without the costume? Probably not. What man was?

He glanced away from the two pretty, animated faces, his gaze scanning the room and, I thought, stopping on Des and me. Before I could be sure, two guys came up to us, one in a Zorro costume complete with black hat and cape, and the other dressed as Elvis—the young Elvis, when he was seriously hot. Neither had the potent vibe of the pirate, but they both did have the build and attitude to carry off the costumes.

"Can we buy you ladies a drink?" Elvis asked.

Des glanced at me. I knew I wouldn't hook up with either of them, but there was nothing wrong with a little socializing so I gave a tiny shrug, letting her make the decision.

"Great," Des said with a smile.

The two men flanked us, Elvis beside her and Zorro on my right, and steered us toward a bar—the one across the room from the pirate and his groupies.

"What will you have, lovely *señorita*?" Zorro asked me, speaking with a super-phony Spanish accent.

Des ordered a margarita, but after my experience at the pool with Tony, I figured it was safer to avoid alcohol so I said, "Same, but make it a virgin." The guys both went with Mexican beer.

"You girls traveling together?" Elvis asked as we moved away from the bar.

"No," Des said, "we met on the ship and hit it off. How about you two?"

"We both work on the *Diamond Star*," Elvis said. "I'm an activities director. My name's Larry, and I'm doing grad studies in parks and recreation at California State."

"I'm Ray." Zorro had dropped the accent. "I'm a personal trainer, working in the fitness club." He flashed a smile. "Haven't seen either of you there."

"I've been doing more lazing than exercising," I said. "Oh, and learning how to cook Italian food. I'm Merilee, and my friend is Des."

The four of us chatted for a while, and the guys were easy company. Then Ray said, "How about a dance, Mary Lee?"

I didn't bother to correct him because what did it matter? "Sure." I loved to dance.

He took my hand and I realized that his hands and the

strong-jawed face below his mask were the only parts of his body that weren't covered snugly in black. The music was a catchy old Shania Twain number: "Man! I Feel Like a Woman!"

Ray found us a place on the floor, let go of my hand, and we both began to dance. Fringe flicked my legs and the sequined dress shimmied across my skin. As I got into the music, I really did feel like a woman. Ray's appreciative smile told me I was looking good.

He did, too: He not only had a great body, he knew what to do with it. He was fun to dance with, but I didn't feel any chemistry. I'd bet a lot of other women would, though.

He worked on the ship. How many women did he dance with on each cruise? How many did he assist at the fitness center? It was probably against cruise ship lines policy for employees to sleep with passengers, but I'd bet it happened all the time.

Was he another Tony, just out for the next hookup? Was he assuming it would be me? Should I let him know it wouldn't? Oh, yeah, this stuff was complicated.

But I didn't want to think about dating and all its complications. Tonight, I wanted to relax and dance. The number ended and the next began: "Billie Jean," the original Michael Jackson one. We kept dancing.

"Must be hard figuring out music for such a mixed group," I said.

"They play a mix of everything, and keep an eye on the crowd. If the older folks pack it in early, they play more rap and hip hop. But often it's the silver hairs who shut the place down, and they want a lot of romantic oldies."

"Pretty sweet, to think of couples who've been together for decades, dancing to the songs they fell in love to." It made me think that Matt and I had never had a song because we'd begun loving each other at the age of seven.

"Such a romantic," Ray teased. "Maybe I shouldn't burst your bubble."

His comment drew me back to the present. "What d'you mean?"

"Some of the ones hanging around until the end are single ladies—widowed, divorced, or never married—dancing with escorts."

"Escorts?"

"At that age, single ladies way outnumber the guys. Some older men—decent looking, personable, good dancers—get free trips if they'll serve as escorts. The guy dances with the lady, accompanies her on shore excursions, plays cards." He grinned. "Does whatever the two of them agree on."

Shocked, I said, "*Whatever*? You don't mean . . . ?"

"Sex? Of course not." He gave an exaggerated wink. "Nah, never happens." He moved closer and lowered his voice suggestively. "Just like it never does between crew and passengers." His hand slid down my bare arm, then he caught my hand in his and squeezed. Crowding me with his body, he said, "Seems to me, if a man and woman are attracted and available, isn't it up to them where it goes?"

I swallowed and took a step back, pulling my hand free from Ray's and bumping into another dancer. Ack, my partner definitely was another Tony. Was sex the only thing on these guys' minds? "Look, I don't want you to think—" The music stopped and my last words came out too loud, so I promptly shut my mouth.

"My dance," a male voice said in a low voice that was almost a growl.

I jumped, and saw that the pirate I'd been ogling earlier stood beside me, holding out his hand. "I, uh . . ." I turned to Ray, who shrugged and turned away, no doubt hunting easier prey.

As the next number started, the pirate grabbed my hand

and towed me across the dance floor away from Ray. Where was he taking me? And what was up with all this hand grabbing?

Yet, somehow his hand, with its warm, determined strength, felt different—much better—than Ray's. "You shouldn't have done that," I protested halfheartedly, heart racing from being swept away like this. I hated pushy men. Didn't I? Matt was always so considerate. And yet the racing beat of my heart was more pleasure than annoyance.

We'd crossed over to a less packed patch of dance floor when he stopped, facing me and still holding my hand. Music was playing again, this time something Latin with a provocative beat, maybe salsa.

"I don't know how to dance to this," I admitted. The only formal dance I'd ever learned was the foxtrot, to dance occasionally at weddings.

"Make it up."

Was his voice always so low and growly or was it part of his act? It sent strange tingles through me, in a way Zorro hadn't. He released my hand and stared down at me. In this dim light, I couldn't really see his eyes, which made him mysterious and exciting. Was he just another guy on the make? But if so, why hadn't he chosen the redhead or the Asian girl in the harem costume? They'd looked pretty available to me.

Given his commanding ways, it surprised me that he didn't grab me and lead. He'd asked me to dance. He must know how. Still, he didn't touch me and was obviously waiting for me.

My heart still raced pleasantly and the rhythm of the music called out to me. If ever there was a time to live in the moment . . . Feeling liberated by my costume and mask, and the fact the pirate and I hadn't even exchanged names, I began to move, letting my hips sway the way the beat demanded.

He began to dance, too, in a masculine version of what I was doing. At first, he seemed a little awkward, probably getting a feel for those pirate boots, but then he really got into it. The man had excellent moves.

Though our bodies didn't touch, somehow dancing with him to this music made me even more aware of the way my sequined dress shimmied over my skin, the fringe caressing my thighs, and the top sliding across my naked breasts, teasing the nipples and making them harden. The sexy dress, the disguise of makeup and mask, the seductive music, and the dashing pirate with his take-charge manner all combined to make me cut loose even more. After all, if I looked like Roxie, the showgirl, I should act like her.

I remembered what Des said when we were choosing costumes in the shop. *If you got it, girl, flaunt it!*

And so I flaunted, in a way I'd never had the guts or even the inclination to do before. And the pirate flaunted back, his own movements growing more blatant. So sensual that, yes, they made me think of sex. Dancing with Ray in his Zorro costume had been fun until he got pushy, but this was a whole different thing.

It was only because of the dance, the music, I told myself as the tune changed, one Latin number replaced by another. Latin dance was supposed to be sensual. People danced this way all the time, with sexy confidence and flair. But I never had, and the pirate and I weren't dancing the formal steps; we were creating something of our own that felt almost . . . erotic. Arousing. My nipples were taut and aching and a warm, tantalizing pulse beat between my thighs.

Not that I'd ever do anything about it. Not now, when Matt and I had just broken up. Still, it was amazing to feel so sexually aware. It wasn't like me at all. If I'd been drinking, I'd blame it on the booze.

Like that night when Matt and I'd been drinking, joking around, and he'd tied my hands with my scarf and spanked me. It had shocked me, not because I was scared—I knew Matt was nothing like his father, and he'd never really hurt me—but because it was so out of character for him. Then a hot rush of unexpected pleasure made me cry out. Matt immediately stopped, saying he didn't know what had come over him, begging my forgiveness, and asking me to try to forget it ever happened. He'd so clearly thought I should be appalled that I hadn't dared admit I'd been turned on. I wanted Matt to love and respect me, not think I was a skank.

Matt . . . Why was I thinking about Matt when I was supposed to just enjoy the moment?

The pirate called me back into the moment by moving closer, his hands brushing my bare arms in a slow, deliberate slide that made my skin tingle, sent heat rushing through my veins, and speeded the pulse in my sex. Someone behind me bumped into me, hard. Thrown off balance, I stumbled forward, beginning to fall. Strong hands caught my upper arms, rescuing me. Holding me, steadying me.

He made me feel safe, and at the same time turned on.

And that made me feel guilty, yet intrigued. I'd never thought of dance as arousing. It was just a fun activity shared with friends. But tonight, it was like the most exquisite foreplay. I should walk away, but I couldn't. This was the kind of excitement I'd craved and I was going to savor this moment.

His hands moved from my upper arms to my shoulders, then in a slow caress down my bare back, and then over the dress to my waist. Oh, my. My heart raced faster than the music and my cheeks burned. Was this part of finding the new Merilee? She liked to dress up and dance with a hot guy? Well, not just any hot guy, but an anonymous pirate with very smooth moves.

Solely in the interests of research, I let him ease me closer, his hands firm and warm on my lower back. He'd feel every wriggle of my waist and hips, and feel the muscles shift in my butt, which was naked but for a tiny strip of thong—the kind of underwear I rarely wore at home.

A thong that, between my legs, was damp with more than sweat. The only man I'd ever had sex with, ever even kissed, was Matt. I'd never wanted to be with anyone else. Now, though, my body throbbed with a need I barely understood. Not that I'd do anything about it, not beyond dancing.

But now I knew it was possible to feel this way. Some day, when Matt and I had each moved on in our lives, I'd find this again with someone.

Leading now, the pirate synched our motions so our bodies moved in harmony, forward and back, side to side, brushing teasingly, temptingly.

Tentatively, I raised my arms to clasp my hands behind his neck, under those midnight curls of hair, to rest on flesh that burned as warm as my cheeks. He was tall, but not quite as tall as Matt, or maybe it was just my heels that made him seem shorter. Usually, I wore flats or sandals.

Against my forearms, the leather of his vest was hard and rough, a sensual abrasion. His chest, bared almost to his waist by the flowing pirate shirt, was firmly muscled and lightly glossed with sweat. I felt the crazy impulse to lick it.

He moved even closer, or maybe I did. The vest that covered him to mid-thigh was bulky and hard between us. How much better this would feel if he took it off and wore only the loose shirt and those leg-hugging black pants. I wanted to be closer, to rub against him, to feel him respond and grow hard. To—

"No!" On a quick gasp, I lowered my hands and pushed against his chest.

"What's wrong?" he said in that growly voice.

"This. I'm sorry, I know it's just a dance, but I . . ."

"What?"

"I have a . . ."

"Boyfriend?"

"N-no. But this isn't, I mean, it doesn't feel . . ."

"Good?"

Of course, and that was the problem.

We'd stopped moving and stood still among the other dancers. He hadn't let go of me, but gripped my hips firmly. Then he said, "Merilee."

"Wh-what?" I hadn't told him my name. Then, in my mind, I heard him again. Speaking not in a growly voice now, but—"Matt?" I gaped up in disbelief.

"Good costume, eh?"

There was an edge in his voice, but I didn't try to analyze it. Stunned, I could only stare at him. This was Matt? I'd never imagined he would choose a pirate costume. He wasn't exactly a dashing, *take no prisoners* kind of guy. But then, I wasn't exactly a racy flapper either. How could I not have realized it was him? Of course, the lights weren't bright and I couldn't see anything of him but his jaw—unshaven, which wasn't like him—and the exposed portion of his chest. His very sexy chest.

"You really didn't guess it was me?" he asked, sounding annoyed.

He'd tricked me, deceived me. He'd cut in on Zorro and got me to make a fool of myself. "Ooh! How dare you!" I stalked away, weaving through dancers until I reached the edge of the floor, then hurrying toward the door.

I needed air. Fresh, cold air. What had he been thinking? Why had he done that to me?

He was behind me. I heard him, but even if I hadn't, I'd have sensed him. He gave off a kind of energy I'd never felt before.

When we were out in the spectacular atrium, all gold and glittery, I turned. "Stop following me!"

"No."

Trying to ignore him, I headed outside, where I let out a

gasp of surprise. The starry canopy of sky took my breath away and the night air raised goose bumps, which was probably why there were so few people around.

"What's your issue?" Matt demanded, stepping in front of me.

"You deceived me."

"You should have recognized me," he snapped back.

"You didn't recognize me when you saw me in the cabin in the flapper costume."

For a moment, he looked disconcerted, then he came back with, "You were dancing all sexy with that asshole."

"He wasn't—" Okay, he kind of was an asshole. But maybe I'd led a sheltered life, thinking a guy could actually respect a woman, not just want to hustle her into bed.

"Come here." He grabbed my hand and steered me across the deck. His touch was harder, more urgent than usual. Again my heart raced in that not unpleasant way.

I'd felt safe with him on the dance floor when he stopped me from falling and steadied me. Matt always made me feel safe, looked after, cared about. But I'd also felt aroused. Yes, Matt and I had good sex, but normally I was slow to respond. I didn't get aroused by dancing, by looking, by touching with our clothes on.

I shouldn't get aroused by being pulled along behind him and yet tonight, despite the chill air that raised goose bumps, something warm pulsed beneath my skin.

When we'd reached an out-of-the-way spot, he released my hand. He peeled off his vest and tossed it on a deck chair. He was too hot, out here in the chill night air? Then he stripped off his sash. Good God, was he going to strip? I found myself wishing he would.

But he stopped there, and faced me, wearing the flowing pirate shirt and snug-fitting pants.

We needed to talk. I wanted to know what was going on. "Matt, I—" I started.

"Let's dance." He silenced me by drawing me into his arms and holding me tight against him.

Dance? There was no music. But it didn't matter. What did was the firm heat of his body, banishing my goose bumps and sending a different kind of shiver through me as he clasped my butt and pulled me to him.

Maybe we didn't need to talk, not this very minute. My arms lifted of their own volition and wrapped around him. He felt different, not the same old Matt. Of course, his body hadn't changed, but, as we began to slow dance, there was a new tension between us. His touch wasn't the usual casual, gentle one. It was a little rougher, almost demanding. As if . . . as if we weren't M&M but a dashing pirate and a sexy flapper he couldn't resist and had to claim for his own.

And he felt so different. The fabric of the shirt under my hands was silkier than his normal tees and cotton shirts, sliding sensually over the solid muscles beneath as they shifted constantly in the dance. In the light of moon and stars, the white shirt glowed dimly, the open front a frame for solid pecs and a dusting of golden-brown hair. Unable to resist, I leaned closer, catching the scent of something spicy I didn't recognize, then leaned my cheek against the firm, warm skin of his upper chest.

One of Matt's hands still curved around my butt, but the other slid up and down my bare back, warming me and making me shiver at the same time. He tugged me even closer so the fronts of our bodies touched, all the way down.

I gave a soft gasp. A firm erection pressed against the front of those body-hugging pants. Because the fabric was so soft compared to jeans, I could really, really feel that rigid length against my belly. Oh, God, did it ever feel good. I slid my hands down his back and curved them around his butt cheeks, so taut and strong as he shifted from foot to foot.

His hips thrust against me as we shuffled in place, and mine swiveled restlessly, wanting more of him. A slow burn of arousal throbbed through me, centering in a needy ache between my legs.

Dimly, I was aware of a couple wandering past us, their voices hushed and tender. They made me aware we were dirty dancing in public, yet our costumes made me bold. M&M would never have done this—they were far too conventional—but the pirate and the flapper were exciting, daring.

"Merilee." Matt's voice was rough.

I raised my head from his chest and looked up, seeing his masked face, the long, black curls secured by a dark bandanna. The stubble on his jaw was so unlike Matt, though his mouth, at least, was familiar. But not when it took mine with forceful passion. This wasn't the way Matt and I kissed. It wasn't full of respect and affection. It was demanding and fierce, like he was desperate for me.

It sent sparks licking through me, and I answered back, eager for more. A pleasantly yeasty hint of beer on his breath, the soft rasp of stubble, the wet heat of his mouth— I was feeling a little desperate myself.

He plowed his hands through my new short hair and I heard the tiara hit the deck. He held my head exactly where he wanted it, and his tongue thrust into my mouth, forcing mine to either retreat or mate with it.

I joined in—had I ever kissed him this way before?—until both of us were panting for breath. My nipples ached for his touch; dampness moistened my thighs; I wanted to climb his body so I could rub my needy sex against the ridge that distended his pants.

His hands stroked firmly down my back, then slid under my short skirt. When he cupped the bare flesh of my butt, he groaned into my mouth and his hips jerked against me.

We were no longer even trying to dance, just kissing urgently, bodies plastered against each other. With our masks on, my makeup, his wig, and this rare intensity between us, it was almost like making out with a total stranger. Yet I knew I was safe.

He nipped my lower lip, a totally un-Matt thing to do, and that dart of pain sent quivers of resonance to my breasts and my sex.

Then one big hand curved around the bottom of my butt and his middle finger tracked my thong between my legs, pressing the soaking wet silk against the swollen skin beneath.

My breath caught, then I whimpered against his mouth when he stroked back and forth along the crotch of my thong. I closed my eyes, concentrating on the sensations. The tip of his finger brushed my clit and my body trembled, my breath coming in quick, shallow pants as he kept doing it, a little more firmly now. Had I ever felt so aroused?

I'd figured I wasn't a highly sexual being, though I enjoyed sex and especially the cuddling and intimacy of being so close to the man I loved. But now, standing on the deck of a cruise ship where any of the thousand passengers and crew could go by at any moment, my nerve endings had all sprung to life as if something new, sensual, and primal inside me had awakened.

His big hand cupped my crotch from behind, he'd found his way under my thong to slick, bare flesh, and his finger circled my clit relentlessly. As a climax built inside me, I squirmed against him, needing release.

He groaned. "God, you're sexy. You drive me wild."

Me? I drove him wild? He'd never said that before. And he was driving me wild, too. Panting, I felt the delicious tension inside me, the firm press of his finger, and then everything came together and I came in quick surges of pleasure. My legs trembled, but his hands held me up as spasms rocked me.

Gradually, my eyes flickered open and, dazed, I stared at him. At Matt. My ex-fiancé. Ex-boyfriend.

Oh, God, what were we doing? A rush of a whole different kind of awareness sent a chill though me and, though it almost killed me to do it, I eased away, forcing him to let go of me. "Matt, we need to—"

"Get some privacy." He grabbed my hand. "Come to the cabin. I want you."

"No." I tugged my hand free and wrapped both arms around myself, body still tingling from orgasm. "We can't. If we make love, it'll just set us back into the same pattern."

I heard him swallow, saw his throat ripple. Through his mask, his eyes glittered fiercely. "Is *this* the same pattern? Is *this* our fucking rut?" The words grated out of him. Then he lifted his hand to his face, the hand that had a minute earlier been pressed between my legs, and he stuck his finger in his mouth. Staring straight into my eyes, he sucked it. The finger that was damp with my sex juices.

I'd never seen him do something so blatantly erotic. Shock and another powerful jolt of arousal made me tremble even harder. I wanted him, too. I wanted him to take me.

But this was so confusing. Matt, but not Matt. Matt acting so out of character, so . . . raw. Where was this coming from? And where was my own shameless behavior coming from? The last time we'd been anything like this, we'd both been drunk. Tonight, I'd had no alcohol and, though I'd tasted beer on Matt's breath, he'd danced with perfect coordination.

If it wasn't alcohol, was there a spell on these costumes?

Shivering from tension, utterly bewildered and, I realized, suddenly exhausted, I was sure of only one thing. "We can't do this. I don't know what it'd mean and I'm not ready for it."

"Shit."

He rarely swore, at least around me, and there was a barely banked *something* in him that scared me a little. Would he force me? Pirates did that.

No, underneath the costume, he was still Matt. He'd never force a woman. But he'd proven he could be powerful and persuasive, and right now I couldn't deal with that. "I really can't do this, Matt. I need to go to the cabin." Even my voice trembled. "Can you wait fifteen minutes? Give me a chance to have a shower and get into bed?" I didn't say the word *alone*, but I figured my tone and body language were pretty clear.

They must have been because his hands fisted, then slowly he stretched out his fingers. I could see the tension in them. "Go," he growled.

Not willing to test his control—or my own—I rushed away. Only when I was halfway to the room did I realize I'd forgotten to retrieve my rented tiara.

Matt stared after Merilee, who was almost running away from him. He curled and stretched his tense fingers again, not sure what had just happened. He was desperate for her, and he'd thought she felt the same.

The pirate clothes had freed something inside him, just like the sight of her in that sexy outfit had, and the way she'd danced with that man in the Zorro costume. Just dancing. Probably nothing more to it than with that guy at the pool. But she'd looked sexy and uninhibited, shaking her booty in that sparkly little dress, and this time he'd given in to the very primitive, possessive male jealousy that heated his blood.

Nah, so he hadn't exactly been the polite, considerate guy that his mom and Merilee had trained him to be. But he hadn't been rough, and he'd thought M was really getting into it. Man, the way she'd squirmed against his hand, and came for him . . .

He groaned. He needed to come. Bad. He'd wanted to drag her to the cabin and explode inside her.

Not tender. Not gentle. Not the way he'd always tried to

be as a lover. When they'd both been virgins, Merilee had been shy about their bodies, nervous about sex. He'd taken it slow, although waiting had almost killed him. He'd jacked off so often he was scared he might wear his dick out before it ever got inside her.

He sure as hell needed to jack off now, but he shared a cabin with her. Right now she was in the shower, her soft, naked curves under cascading water. They'd never showered together. In his apartment, the stall was barely big enough for him alone, and at her place it seemed weird because it was her parents' house. They made love in her bed, with the door closed, keeping quiet.

He wanted to fuck her in the shower, up against the wall, until they both screamed out.

But that wasn't Merilee. She wasn't that kind of girl. She'd just proven it by running away. Yeah, she'd made the excuse of not wanting to fall back into old patterns, but she had to know tonight was something new.

Matt picked up the vest and sash he'd tossed aside, but didn't put them on. His still-aching erection needed cold. His boot kicked something and he bent to pick up the tiara he'd knocked from her hair.

She'd been into it. No one could have faked that. Was it her own out-of-character reaction that had scared her?

The wig and bandanna were itchy, so he pulled them off and ran his hands through his newly cut hair. It wasn't much shorter than before, but it did look different. He'd gone to the ship's salon and, feeling self-conscious, asked the female stylist to give him a more trendy cut that'd still be easy to look after. He'd bought new clothes, too. He wasn't stuck in any old rut.

He began to walk along the deck. His body was cooling now, his erection subsiding. As his lust faded, he began to think more analytically. Were new haircuts and a bit of dress up really enough to change things between him and Merilee?

One night of excitement, then tomorrow . . . yeah, they'd both probably start out kind of embarrassed, then it probably would be same old, same old.

So she'd been right to call a halt before things went any further. Did this mean there was no hope for them?

He halted abruptly. Wait a minute. They'd broken up. Yet here he was, still wondering if they might have a future.

Slowly, he started off again. It made sense, he guessed. For fourteen years, *future* had meant Merilee. That was a pattern he couldn't easily break. And the woman he'd fooled around with tonight was one he couldn't easily get out of his mind.

He wished there was someone he could talk to about this stuff. He knew what his guy friends would say: If one girl doesn't work out, move on to the next. They could be so immature.

Was Merilee asleep yet? He hated that they were sharing a cabin. He really didn't want to talk to her about this shit until he'd sorted it out in his own mind, but he didn't have a clue as to how to do that.

Oh, hell, enough of this shit. In the morning, the ship would be in Puerto Vallarta and he was going to let loose and have some fun—without Merilee around to complicate things.

Chapter 8

I had hurried through my shower and into my sleep tee and panties, then slid between the sheets, not wanting Matt to catch me half-naked.

Maybe he and I should talk about what had happened tonight, but I didn't know what to say. In the old days I'd thought I could tell him anything, but everything was different now. We'd broken up, but we'd kissed; we'd made out more passionately than ever before. Matt was different, more forceful. Exciting. But that was some strange fluke. He'd seen me in that costume, not looking like boring old me, seen that other guys found me attractive, and it had roused some kind of spark that hadn't existed before. But it wasn't real.

Reality was the way we'd always been together, and I didn't see that changing.

When I set the alarm on my cell so I'd be up in plenty of time to go ashore in Puerto Vallarta, I saw I'd missed a call. I retrieved the message and heard Kat saying she wondered how I was doing and hoped everything was going okay.

Okay? No, that wasn't how things were going. Suddenly, I really wanted to talk to my sister. Matt wasn't back, so maybe he'd stopped off in a bar. Maybe he'd gone looking for another girl, one who wouldn't run away from him. I heaved a noisy sigh, then dialed my sister's number.

Her phone rang several times before she said, "Hello? Hello?"

"Kat, it's Merilee."

"Merilee? Is something wrong?"

"Wrong? No, not really, just—"

In the background I heard Nav's voice, sleepy sounding, asking what was going on.

"Ack!" I smacked my palm against my forehead. "I forgot you were back in Montreal." Where it was several hours later than here. "Damn, it's the middle of the night, isn't it? I'm so sorry."

"And you should be," she said, but teasingly. "It's okay, I'm awake now. Let me throw on a robe and go into the other room, then I'll call you back."

"Thanks."

She hung up and I waited impatiently, yawning from tiredness but too distraught to sleep. A minute or two later my phone rang. "How are things going?" she asked.

"Confusing." I curled on my side, the phone cradled between my head and a pillow. "Since we came aboard, Matt and I have been avoiding each other. Each doing our own thing."

"Makes sense. How's that been?"

"Some good, some not so. Honestly, are guys only interested in sex?"

Kat gave a quick laugh. "Well, you're a pretty blonde and it's a cruise ship. You know how to say *no*, right?" Then, with a tone of concern, "No one's seriously harassing you, are they?"

"No, it's just that they go, like, 'Hi, what's your name.' Then there's two minutes of chit-chat, then they're trying to hustle you into bed. But it's okay, I can handle it."

"Being with Matt, you haven't had to deal with this stuff before. It's a good learning experience."

"Not a fun one, though."

"Yeah. But you said there's some good stuff happening? Like what?"

This part was easy. Smiling into the phone, I enthused, "I took a cooking lesson and loved it, and I got my hair cut and it's really different but I like it. And I met this girl Des, who's traveling with her granny Micky. They're both cool. Micky kind of reminds me of Gran before she got Alz, though she's, well, sometimes she can be a little outrageous." I thought of white-haired Micky, the dominatrix, cracking her whip.

"Good stuff, sis."

"Tonight, there was a costume ball. Des and Micky talked me into this flapper costume, like Roxie in *Chicago*."

"Woohoo. Doesn't sound like you, though."

"Maybe it is. I don't know. It was fun. And Matt, he came as a pirate."

"You're kidding. With reams of eye makeup like Johnny Depp?"

"No. Think more Orlando Bloom. He was actually . . . hot. Black wig and a bandanna, shirt open down his chest, tight black pants, high boots,"

"Matt? Our Matt?"

"Hard to believe, eh? But he carried it off. Can you believe, at first I didn't even recognize him?"

"You didn't? That is hard to believe." Then she laughed. "No, I guess it's not. I didn't recognize Nav on the train, either."

"Nav? Oh, right, you said he played those stranger roles, and used them to seduce you."

"Yeah, and when he first appeared on the train, he actually convinced me he was a Bollywood producer. And he wasn't even wearing a wig or fancy costume."

I'd told Matt a bit about what Nav had done on the train.

Tonight, had he been trying to seduce me? But he was the one who'd broken up. It made no sense that he'd danced with me, kissed me, wanted to make love. It wasn't like he hadn't known it was me in that Roxie costume.

I let out a long sigh. "Kat, I really didn't recognize him, and he asked me to dance. It was Latin music, with that real sensual beat. I'd never danced to anything like that before. It was fun and . . . sexy. Then I realized it was him, and I was mad that he'd deceived me and I stormed away. He followed me on deck and . . . somehow we were slow-dancing, even though there was no music. We kissed, and, you know, went at it hot and heavy." Hotter and heavier than ever before. In public. I couldn't tell her he'd brought me to climax with his hand.

"Merilee, really?" she broke in. "You're back together already? I mean, I love Matt, but—"

"We're not," I hurried to say, pressing my free hand to my burning cheek. "I stopped it because I was so confused. Even though I was, uh, really into it, it felt like we were rushing into something. We broke up because we both figured we were in a rut. It was comfortable, we both wanted more. If we get back together . . . well, nothing will have changed, will it?"

"Fourteen years is a long pattern to break," she said slowly. "It's going to take more than a couple of days of being apart, and one hot make-out session."

"So I'm right?" I clutched the phone tighter, not sure what I wanted her to say. "We should cool it? Jenna said we both needed to be independent."

"I agree. You have to know who you are as a person to know if you've found the right person for you."

How about that? For once my sisters agreed on something. "I've really only known myself as half of M&M. So now I need to figure out who Merilee really is. The Merilee who is—or at least should be—an independent person."

"Exactly."

"How do I do it? How do I figure out who the new Merilee is?"

"You're already doing it. Trying out the haircut, having fun with the costume, taking a cooking lesson. Making new friends." She chuckled. "Rejecting jerks who come on to you."

"I'm getting to be good at that. What about Matt, though? You're saying I should avoid him?"

"Not necessarily. But don't center your life on him or spend all your time with him. If you do get together, don't do the same old things you always did."

"Tonight we didn't," I said wryly, "and look where that got us."

"But you had the sense to know where to draw the line. And I think maybe tonight was a good thing. The costumes tossed both of you out of your rut. Out of your comfort zone. Being thrown isn't necessarily bad. Use it; think about it, about how you felt and why."

"I'm not so big on introspection."

She gave a soft laugh. "Believe me, nor was I. Nav dragged—or maybe seduced—me into it. But, Merilee, it really is important. You need to know yourself—your insecurities and fears, your hopes and dreams and goals."

That seemed like a lot to figure out. Before, my hopes and dreams and goals had centered around Matt. And my fear had been that I wouldn't be loved. Now, if Matt and I didn't get back together—

Thankfully, Kat's voice broke into that thought. "It's great that you've made new friends," she said. "It's good to have friends of your own, not just couple friends. But don't just use them for, uh, distraction, to keep you from feeling alone or keep you from thinking about your feelings."

I frowned in puzzlement. "You've always had tons of friends."

"Yeah. I'm outgoing and I like people, and friends gave me validation that I didn't get from Mom and Dad. But being so busy and popular kept me from figuring out my issues and dealing with them."

That was a huge amount to take in. About Kat, and the parallels I could see—like how my relationship with Matt had given me the love and acceptance I'd wanted but never truly felt from my family. "Wow," I breathed. "And here I always thought you had it so together, Kat."

"Had you fooled," she joked. "Myself, too. That's what I'm saying: You have to look below the surface. I did this summer, and so did Theresa and Jenna."

"You're right," I realized. And it had brought all of us sisters closer together.

I missed them. "I feel so alone here," I confessed softly. "Trying to be independent is hard when I've always been half of a couple."

"I'm sure it is. But you can do this. When you decided to go on the cruise, you thought you'd be doing it alone. Some instinct told you that was better for you than staying at home. Believe in that instinct. You'll learn a lot this week, and yeah, sometimes it'll be lonely, but that's life."

Since I was seven, I'd almost never felt lonely. I'd never had to make decisions on my own. No wonder this was tough.

"And, sis," she went on, "you're twenty-one and you're on the Mexican Riviera. Have some fun, too. Promise?"

Now there was a concept. "I will. Thanks, Kat. And apologize to Nav for me, okay? I didn't mean to wake you both up." I was about to hang up, when I thought to ask, "Have you talked to Jenna recently?"

She let out a low whistle. "Oh, yeah. Big stuff, eh? She said that after she talked to you, she called all of us. I can't believe she kept all that locked up inside since she was seventeen. It's terrible that she felt she couldn't tell us."

"I know. I'm so glad she finally did. Mark's been really good for her."

"She's done a lot of growing up. You know, I wouldn't have seen her as a mom before. Too irresponsible. But now I can."

"Me, too." And I really hoped it happened for Jenna. Almost as much as I hoped it happened for me.

After we said good night, I turned off the light. No Matt yet. Had he gone back to the costume ball, or to a bar? Found more pretty girls to gush all over him? Maybe another one to kiss in the moonlight—a girl who wouldn't run away?

Huffing out a sigh, I rolled over and tried to get comfortable. Enough obsessing about Matt. I was independent Merilee and, like my sisters, I had some growing up to do. In the morning, we'd go ashore at Puerto Vallarta for the day. I'd set foot on Mexican soil for the first time, and I was definitely going to have fun.

The *Diamond Star* offered all sorts of excursions. Des and Micky were touring the town and a botanical garden and had invited me to join them. I'd been planning on it, but now I reconsidered. I'd seen another excursion that intrigued me, but it was kind of scary and I'd be doing it on my own. . . .

It was another open door. I could step through it and maybe I'd have fun. Or be scared shitless.

I slept so soundly, the next thing I heard was the insistent buzz of my alarm going into panic mode, telling me I'd missed its first gentle beeps. I flicked it off and glanced around the cabin. No Matt. Rumpled bedding said he'd been and gone. I wouldn't think about where he'd been last night and what time he'd come in.

He'd be going snorkeling this morning. He was a good swimmer. Good at all athletic stuff, actually.

Seeing colorful fish would be fun, and if we'd been on our honeymoon I'd have loved going with him. But today I was being independent. Besides, I didn't want to run into him. I felt too weird about what had happened between us last night.

I jumped out of bed and gazed out the window. It was exciting to see the harbor and another cruise ship, and know I was in Mexico. Early morning sun shone in a cloudless sky and I couldn't wait to get out into it.

Quickly, I dressed in shorts, a light summer top, and, as the excursion instructions had suggested, sturdy sandals with rubber soles. I studied my reflection. I'd been tempted to shop for new clothes on the cruise ship, but figured it'd be more fun to buy things in Mexico. Even so, my new hairstyle made me look more fun and stylish. I gathered the rest of my stuff and left the room.

Stopping at the buffet, I picked up a blueberry muffin and coffee. Excited and nervous, I managed to choke down half the muffin. Then I went to join the other passengers who were disembarking.

When I got on shore, I heard a woman calling, "Canopy ziplining over here." I followed her voice as I pushed through other passengers hunting for their own excursions. A fit blonde in the *Diamond Star* uniform stood at the center of a dozen or so passengers, together with a sturdy young Mexican man in shorts and a red T-shirt with ZIP THE CANOPY on it.

"Have you done this before?" I asked the forty-something couple next to me.

"In Costa Rica," the woman said with a grin. "It's a blast. Your first time?"

"It is. I'm a little terrified."

"Ah, a zip virgin." She winked. "Bet you a glass of tequila that you'll be hooked."

"It's an adrenaline rush," her husband said. "And you can't beat the scenery."

"Yeah, right. I'll probably have my eyes closed in sheer terror."

"There's nothing to worry about," the woman said, and started to talk about safety harnesses.

As I listened, desperate to be reassured, I watched other passengers disembark and head in various directions. Some distance away, a guy and girl stood facing each other, laughing and talking, probably trying to decide which excursion to go on. A twinge of envy made me keep watching. She had long dark hair and looked casual and comfortable in cargo shorts and a loose navy tank top layered over a white one. He was dressed classier, in a stylish short-sleeved blue shirt and khaki shorts that showed off great legs, and his dirty-blond hair was fashionably cut. He was actually pretty hot. Lucky girl, being with a guy like that. I envied their obvious coupledom.

I shifted a couple of steps over, so that the happy pair were hidden behind the woman and her husband who were still recounting their ziplining experiences.

A few minutes later, I was listening so intently I barely noticed when someone came up beside me.

"Merilee?" a disbelieving voice said.

I turned. "Matt?" My eyes widened at the sight of him and the brunette, the pretty girl in cargo shorts. That was Matt I'd been watching earlier?

As I remembered what we'd done on deck last night, it felt like my entire body was one big blush. He'd made me come with his hand, then he'd licked his finger. And I'd run away.

Trying to ignore the flood of hot embarrassment, I studied him, intrigued. No, he wasn't wearing a pirate wig this time, but he wasn't the same old Matt either. He was close enough now that I could take in the details of the flattering new haircut, and the way the denim blue of his shirt matched his eyes. He hadn't shaven and the sexy stubble was longer than last night, darker than his sun-streaked hair, the same shade as his eyebrows and lashes. He looked . . . maybe he did look like Bradley Cooper, with his lean, strong features and build.

And he was here with a girl. Jealousy tightened my body.

Had he picked her up after I ran away last night? Had they . . . no, he wouldn't have spent the night with her. Would he? His bed had been slept in. Or at least messed up.

We'd broken up and last night I'd said no to sex. I was supposed to be independent, and it was his business whom he slept with. I refused to be jealous and childish.

But why had I worn my boring old shorts and top rather than bought something new, flattering, sexy? Not, of course, that I wanted to win him back or anything. It was just female pride, making me want to compare favorably to the brunette.

I was too upset and confused to find words. All I could do was gape at Matt and his pretty companion.

He was gaping back. "You're going ziplining?"

That note of skepticism in his voice snapped me out of my daze and made me stick my chin out. "Why not?"

"I didn't think you were into that kind of thing."

He really did think I was totally boring. Running away from him last night had probably confirmed it for him. "What kind of thing?" I snapped. "Having fun?"

"Uh, not this kind of fun. I mean, I didn't think you'd think this was fun."

The brunette and the older couple were staring curiously at the two of us.

I glanced at the couple and said airily, "A friend from home, Matt Townsend. And I'm Merilee Fallon."

"Colleen and Dan Withers," the woman said.

I gazed pointedly at Matt and the brunette.

"And this is Mandy," he said. Then, to her, "I don't know your last name."

Her smile had a knowing curl. "Mandy Jacobs." She met my gaze levelly. "Matt and I met at the breakfast buffet and we realized we were both going ziplining."

Or had she seen a cute guy and decided to get friendly by going wherever he went? I wasn't the least bit thrilled with the idea of spending hours with him and Mandy. Oh, God, they were another M&M. "I figured you'd go snorkeling," I said accusingly to Matt.

"I wanted to try ziplining. This is the only shore stop where it's offered." Clearly, he wasn't going to change his mind.

I was tempted to hurry away and catch up with Des and Micky, but that would be wimpy. "Me, too. I've just been hearing how addictive it is."

"Uh"—Colleen Withers broke in tentatively—"if you want to try it, everyone's heading out."

I realized that the group, which now numbered two or three dozen, was being herded away. Colleen and Dan hurried after them, with her casting curious glances over her shoulder.

Without a word, I strode after them toward a dock with several small and medium-sized boats.

From behind me, I heard whispers, but I refused to turn around. I did hear Matt say, "No, of course not."

A few minutes later, as the group boarded a bare-bones craft with lots of seats, he and Mandy joined us. She went to sit with Colleen and Dan, saying brightly, "You've been ziplining before, too? Whereabouts?"

Matt came up beside me. "Honest, we just met at breakfast, so we walked off the ship together."

"If you think I'm jealous—" I started, then realized it was hard to deny after the way I'd been acting. "Okay, maybe I was, but I thought you'd been with her last night. After . . . you know."

"I'd never do that." He might be the updated version of Matt, but his blue eyes held the old familiar sincerity.

"Sorry," I said softly. "I'm so confused and emotional."

"Me, too. And Merilee, I was jealous last night when you were dancing with that guy."

He was? That was actually kind of cool. Never before had he said he was jealous. Of course, I'd never done a thing to make him feel that way.

Automatically, we took seats side by side. When the boat cast off and began to speed across the bay, I realized what we'd done. After fourteen years, habits were ingrained. That didn't mean they were smart. I leaned closer and said, "Matt, I—" Then that same spicy scent I'd noticed last night distracted me. "What's that smell?"

"Smell? What smell?"

"Like spice. Not cinnamon . . ." I inhaled deeply. No, not cooking spice. Something masculine, a touch exotic as it drifted on a clean ocean breeze. Exotic? Now there was a word I'd never before applied to Matt. The scent made me want to lean closer, to brush my nose against his skin, to lick—

"It's soap." His words broke my sensual reverie. "Sandalwood. Kari at the hair salon gave me a free sample."

"Huh." I hadn't received a sample of anything, and I wasn't on first-name terms with the woman who'd cut my hair.

"I kind of like the smell," he said.

"So do I," I admitted. "But what's up with the stubble? Are you growing a beard?"

He shrugged, looking embarrassed. "No. The first couple of days, I didn't feel like shaving. Then Kari said the stubble looked good, made me look older and, uh . . ."

Sexier. "She did, did she?"

"You don't like it?"

"It's different. And the haircut." I sighed and told him the truth. "But they look good, Matt." The urge to brush my cheek against his was hard to resist. Last night, when we'd kissed, I'd noticed that the stubble was like a slightly rough caress. Tingles rippled through me at the memory of those kisses, of his hand between my legs, of the climax that shuddered through me. I suppressed a shiver of arousal and felt my cheeks flood with color again.

"I like your hair, too," he said, jolting me out of my thoughts. "Took me a while to get used to it, but it's sassy."

"Sassy?" No one had ever called me sassy before.

"Yeah. I always think of you as sweet and really feminine, but now you look kind of, uh . . . sassy."

"Thanks. I like that." If I looked sassy, maybe I could *be* sassy. The flapper was sassy; I could try to channel her the way I'd done on the dance floor.

"What were you going to say before?" he asked.

I thought back to when I'd first leaned toward him and got distracted by the scent of sandalwood. "I chose ziplining because it sounded fun and different, and I want to do some things on my own. But here we are, sitting side by side. . . ." It was so familiar. And a couple of times, I'd started to call him "M," then stopped myself. That was our old nickname, the soul mates' one. He hadn't used it either, though once or twice he'd stumbled over my name and I'd wondered.

He studied me. "Yeah. We don't want to fall back into our rut, do we?" The edge in his voice suggested he was referring to the way I'd run off last night.

I wasn't going to apologize for saying no to sex when it hadn't felt right—or had felt, scarily, both too right and too wrong all at the same time. "No. I'm used to relying on you. I need to be more self-sufficient."

He sighed. "Me, too. And yeah, I'm used to being the guy you rely on."

I realized something. "It's not just me you've done that

for. It's your mom, too. That thing about being the man of the house."

He shrugged. "I like helping people, making them happy."

"That's great, but Matt, your mom and I should both be more independent. And you should have a life of your own."

His mouth twisted. "Sometimes it's just easier to do what someone else wants."

Easier. Hmm. "But it's kind of lazy. You need to think for yourself. Often I felt this, uh, pressure to figure out what we should do. You hardly ever suggested anything." My cheeks warmed again and I lowered my voice even further. "Last night, you were different. More of a take-charge guy. It was cool." And a total turn-on. I'd never guessed I'd find that kind of man so appealing.

"Cool? I scared you off."

"*You* didn't. Where we were heading did. I got kind of carried away, then realized it wasn't such a good idea."

"It felt like a good idea at the time." His tone held a hint of challenge, and so did the intense gleam in his eyes.

It wasn't like Matt to challenge me, and a shiver—the good kind—made me suck in a breath.

"I'm not the only one who acted different," he said. "I'd never seen you dance like that. Never seen you act so—" He, too, took a deep breath and didn't finish the sentence. What word was he thinking? *Uninhibited*? *Sexy*? *Slutty*? He let out the breath. "It was like that costume brought out something in you I hadn't seen before."

I swallowed. "Both our costumes. We weren't Merilee and Matt, we were a pirate and a flapper." I studied his face, familiar and yet more mature with the new haircut that emphasized his strong features and great eyes, the movie star stubble on his jaw. Such simple things. Yet they made me see him differently and made me . . . aware. Attracted. I thought he felt it, too, but I didn't know if it was me who turned him on, or the memory of a slutty flapper.

Whatever the cause, there was a sexual charge in the air between us.

"Why did you do it?" I asked. "The costume, the haircut, the new clothes?"

"I saw you in that flapper dress, having fun with it. After that, I didn't want to just, you know, be the same old me."

"You weren't." I'd fallen in love with the same old Matt, yet in the end I'd had doubts about marrying him. Now, I felt a buzzy sexual awareness of the man beside me. What did this mean? I was tempted to explore it. . . .

The boat engine cut out and I realized we'd reached shore. I glanced around, noting some expensive-looking waterfront homes. When the other passengers rose, chattering excitedly, Matt and I also got to our feet.

"You're right," he said decisively. "We both need to be more independent. So I guess this is where we each go our own way."

I came down to earth with a thud, remembering that this had been my original plan. Of course, I'd stick with it. "Yes. So, you, uh, have fun today." He'd last a whole minute on his own, then Mandy'd latch on to him again, and there would go his *independence*. I got in line to disembark and he held back, letting me get ahead.

When our group was divided in half to travel in rugged yellow 4x4s with bench seating in the back, I chose one group and he went with the other. No surprise, Mandy chose his group.

My fellow passengers spent the fifteen-minute trip introducing ourselves and exclaiming at the scenery as we drove through a picturesque town and then into the forest. People shared ziplining stories. About half of them had tried it before—and survived, which was reassuring.

After the truck ride, we transferred to mules. Riding a mule was another first for me, this one a little uncomfortable but not scary. As my animal plodded serenely in line along a trail through tall trees, I took Jenna's advice to live in the moment. Forcing aside my anxiety about whizzing through the jungle on a cable, and my jealousy over Mandy, I focused on enjoying my surroundings. Everything was lush, green, and on a grand scale like a British Columbia forest. But the trees and shrubs were so different, more like a jungle. Bananas hung in bunches under fringed palmlike leaves, and I knew I'd remember this the next time I sliced one onto my granola back home.

The air had the kind of balminess we only experienced at home in August, and the scent was kind of jungly, not the crisp evergreen one I was used to. This was a terrific introduction to Mexico, one only a few dozen of the *Diamond Star*'s passengers would experience.

We arrived at our destination and dismounted. Then guides in red T-shirts got us into harnesses, helmets, and gloves. My muscles tensed with anxiety as we learned how to grip the line, position our bodies, signal the guides, and— most important of all—brake.

"But if you get going too fast and can't slow down enough, don't worry," our instructor, an attractive young Mexican woman named Paloma said. "There's always a guide on the platform below and we'll catch you when you come in."

After practicing and asking questions, a dozen or so of us climbed up to the first platform, a large, sturdy one that held us all, partially shaded by branches above our heads. A zipline stretched an awfully long distance across the jungle and slightly down to another tall tree with a much smaller platform.

One of the male guides hooked himself onto the line, explaining everything carefully. Then, with a whoop, he swung out into space and, hanging suspended, zipped down the narrow cable. Paloma gave a running commentary as he demonstrated all the things we'd been taught, until he arrived safely on the other side and waved a hand at us.

"Who's next?" Paloma asked.

Colleen and Dan rushed to volunteer. I stood back, hugging my arms around myself nervously, while a few other people took their turns. Two had trouble braking, but the male guide was strong and sturdy and caught them easily. One woman braked too soon and had to be pulled in to the platform.

A girl about my age who was there with her boyfriend muttered, "I can't do this. I'm not good at heights. I want to go back."

The guy scowled. "Shit, Chris, you're such a wimp. I'm not letting you ruin this." He stepped to the edge of the platform next, and was soon whipping through space, yelling like Tarzan.

Wondering why anyone would date a guy like him, I stepped next to Chris. "I'm nervous, too. But they're not going to let us get hurt"—I crossed my fingers behind my back—"and it does look like fun."

"I guess." She shot me a rueful gaze from under heavily mascaraed lashes. "But I'd rather be shopping for jewelry."

"You can do that later. This is a once-in-a-lifetime experience."

Her mouth twisted with a touch of humor. "Just hope it's not the last in my lifetime. But okay, I'll do it if you will. You go next."

I'd got myself into that one. Cautiously, I stepped toward the edge of the platform. "My turn." I took a deep breath and tried to concentrate as Paloma gave me a quick last-minute briefing.

The cable, impossibly narrow, stretched across a huge expanse of space above green tops of trees. But I couldn't fall;

I was securely harnessed and I'd be hooked onto that cable with an extremely sturdy-looking hook. Sometimes, in life, you just had to take a risk.

Firmly gripping the line that held me onto the cable, I stepped out into space and began to glide. Many of the others had whooped or cheered, but I was too overcome to even breathe. I couldn't look down, couldn't look up, and was barely aware of the brush of warm air on my face. My sole focus was on the platform ahead, which was rapidly growing closer. Brake. I had to brake. Gingerly, I did, then harder, and a moment later I was standing on shaky legs atop the platform.

The male guide slapped me on the back. "You did great. Fun, isn't it?"

Fun? I had no idea, only that I could breathe again. But next time I'd pay more attention. I turned and waved encouragingly to Chris, back on the big platform.

I wondered how Matt was enjoying ziplining—and Mandy's company.

Chapter 9

From the beginning, Matt loved ziplining. He was strong, coordinated, and not the slightest bit nervous. Now his group of a dozen only had three or four more zips left, and he wished they could start all over again. Whipping through the canopy of trees was a total adrenaline rush. In his life, he'd had few of those.

Maybe when he got back home, he'd take up something like rock climbing that was outdoorsy and kind of rugged and exciting. Talking to Merilee on the boat this morning had made him realize something: He wanted to be more like the pirate. A guy could have a little edge without turning into a violent asshole like his dad.

Mandy, the girl he'd met at breakfast, hurtled through the air toward the platform. She'd told him she was on the cruise with a couple of girlfriends, but they were into shopping rather than adventure.

She landed, laughing with pleasure. "What a buzz. I love to fly."

Together they headed for the ladder from the platform to the ground. "Yeah," he agreed, struck by a memory. "When I was a kid, I made model planes and zoomed them around my bedroom imagining I was the pilot." He let her take the ladder first.

"And now?" Her voice came up to him as he started down. "Still want to be a pilot?"

"I'm going to teach high school." He landed on the ground beside her.

"A valuable job." She studied him with big chocolate-brown eyes. "Definitely feet on the ground, though. I guess people's dreams change."

"My mom hated the pilot idea. I'm an only kid; she's a single mom. She figured it was dangerous." He shrugged. It had been a kid's dream. When Merilee said she wanted to be a teacher and he'd make a great one, too, that had sounded good to him.

"Hate to say this," Mandy said, "but has your mom heard of Columbine? Schools aren't exactly safe places either. Nowhere is really safe these days. Seems to me, you need to follow your passion."

Was he following Merilee's passion rather than his own? This was the kind of thing he needed to think about. "How about you? What's your passion?"

A sparkle lit her eyes. "Am I only allowed one?"

She was flirting a little, the way she had been since they'd met. He hadn't figured out whether she really meant it or if it was just her personality. If he was ready to think about dating, he'd probably like to go out with Mandy. But Merilee was still too much on his mind, especially after last night. "Uh, I guess everyone's allowed as many as they want. But I meant for your career."

"Eco-tourism."

"Seriously? That sounds like fun."

"Doesn't it?" She flashed a big smile. "Being outside and active, enjoying the environment without hurting it. Introducing people to activities like ziplining, wilderness kayaking, hiking."

"Rock climbing."

"Yeah, like that. Being paid to have fun. Seems to me that's what a job should be."

"It should." That was how Merilee felt about teaching. Fun, because she loved kids, and meaningful, because she believed it was one of the most important jobs in the world. He agreed it was meaningful work, but for him it didn't sound like a barrel of laughs. He'd enjoy it, but now that he was thinking about this, there were probably jobs he'd like better. If he could figure out what they were.

"Merilee thinks you should be a teacher?"

He'd told her the two of them had been seriously involved and had recently broken up. "She does."

"You gotta do it for you, not for her."

"I know that." Why hadn't he thought this through before? Jesus, he really didn't have a mind of his own.

She chuckled. "Your life is way too complicated. Ought to live free and easy, the way I do."

"Tempting." Yet not really. Yeah, maybe it'd be fun to have an adventurous career and a casual relationship with a girl like her, but only for a little while. One thing he did know about himself was that he liked stability and long-term relationships. Security, love, family.

"Yeah, right," she teased. "Hey, our group's leaving us behind."

All morning, feeling the adrenaline rush of ziplining, he'd wondered how Merilee was making out. If he waited for her group, would she be annoyed or glad? The pirate wouldn't waffle; he'd do what he wanted. "You go on."

Mandy shook her head tolerantly. "You got it bad, dude."

One of their guides joined them. "Time to go."

"Think I'll wait for the next group," Matt told him. "I have a friend in it."

"Sure. They'll be here in a few minutes. Just don't wander off and get lost."

After the guide and Mandy had gone, Matt climbed back up the steps to enjoy the view from the platform. He felt almost like a bird up here under the canopy of a tall jungle tree. Soon he saw the next group begin to arrive on a high platform on the other side of a gulley, and a guide zipped across on the line.

"Get left behind, *amigo*?" the Mexican man asked.

"Decided to wait for a friend. She's—"

He broke off when he saw Merilee on the other platform. It was too far to make out her expression, but when he waved, she waved back enthusiastically.

A moment later she was hooked to the cable and whizzing toward him faster than he'd have believed possible. Her whoops of excitement made him grin. She braked when she got near, but still had some momentum when she landed on the platform, stumbling a couple of steps, then flinging her arms around him. Face flushed and glowing, she cried, "Isn't this amazing?"

"I love it." He hugged her tight, so glad now that he'd listened to the pirate. Merilee felt great in his arms, warm and firm, familiar yet somehow fresh and new. A zipliner, full of energy and elation. The sexy dancer he'd made out with on deck last night.

The guide said, "Hey, *amigos*, I need to unhook the lady."

Laughing, Merilee pulled out of his arms. After she'd been unhooked, they headed for the ladder. When they reached the ground, she said, "You waited for me."

"Wanted to see how you were doing."

"I'm glad. This is so special and I want to share it with"— she ducked her helmeted head, then lifted it again—"someone special."

"Me, too." He gazed at her a moment, then, on the pirate's urging, took her hand. "We proved we can be on our own. Now let's spend some time together."

"I'd like that." In the depths of her blue eyes he saw the

same uncertainty and vulnerability he was feeling. It was easier to hurl yourself into space on a zipline than to figure out what your heart truly wanted.

Above their heads, someone else from the *Diamond Star* whipped through the air and landed, then another. Matt and Merilee let go of each other's hand to descend the ladder.

Standing surrounded by tall, unfamiliar trees, he said, "We've broken up, but we still care about each other. We can be friends now. Right?"

"I'd like that." Then she added, with a snippy edge, "If you're sure your new girlfriend won't mind."

He and Merilee might be just friends, but that didn't stop him from liking her jealousy. But friends were honest, and he did care for her, so he said, "Mandy's not a girlfriend. I'm not ready for that yet."

Her face softened. "Me either."

Other zipliners joined them, enthusing about their experiences. When everyone had climbed down, the group moved along the trail to the next platform.

Merilee scrambled up the ladder and Matt was right behind her, admiring the flex of her calves and the curves of her butt filling out her shorts. He'd always found her attractive, but that flapper costume and the haircut had got him paying attention in a new way.

Had he been taking her for granted, he wondered as a guide hooked her up to the cable? A few days ago, he'd thought of their relationship as a cruise ship steaming happily along its appointed route. But now that he thought about it, that wasn't very exciting. It dawned on him that he, and maybe Merilee too, had been letting their relationship drift like it was on autopilot rather than really paying attention.

Well, now he was paying attention and he sure couldn't take this Merilee for granted. Not the one who flashed him a brilliant smile before she flung herself off the platform and into the air. This Merilee was pretty darned irresistible. A flapper, a sexy dancer, a zipliner. Were any of these the real her, or just roles she was trying on for size?

Who would Merilee turn out to be?

He realized he couldn't wait to find out. The prospect was just as intriguing as figuring out who Matt was going to be.

He climbed into the harness next and whipped down the line, over a surging river, to join her on the next platform.

After they'd climbed down, he asked, "What are you doing when we get back from this excursion? Going into town?"

"Oh, yeah!" she said eagerly. "I can't wait to see Puerto Vallarta, and I want to shop for clothes and gifts. How about you?"

"Figured I'd explore the town, too. What do you think? Should we stick with the independence thing?"

"I don't know." The eagerness was replaced by uncertainty. "This is confusing."

She'd said she liked the pirate's take-charge approach. "Let's go in together and have lunch," he said. "We'll talk then, and decide what we want to do."

The group finished the zipline excursion with another mule ride, then returned to the *Diamond Star* to clean up and change. When they reached their cabin, Merilee was yawning. "I can't believe I'm so tired. Guess that's more fresh air and exercise than I've had in a while."

Though Matt was pumped from the excursion and eager to get into Puerto Vallarta, he worried about her. She did look exhausted. "Why don't you take a nap?"

"I could really use one." She sighed. "Bummer. I hate being like this. If you want to go ahead into town . . ."

"No, I'll wait for you. We have lots of time." It was true. Tonight, the ship wouldn't leave until eleven.

He went to take a shower, and when he came out she was

sound asleep, curled up facing away from him. He gazed at her, feeling tender and protective. She'd always seemed so small, so feminine, with a touch of vulnerability. All he'd ever wanted to do was look after her.

But she was twenty-one now, and she'd proven in the last couple of days that she had a mind of her own and did just fine looking after herself. Somehow that made her even more appealing.

What was going on with the two of them? As he dressed he wished, again, that there was someone he could talk to. His buddies were fine for playing sports or drinking beer with, but not so hot when it came to discussing relationships. He didn't have a dad, older brother, uncle, or granddad. It had been just him and his mom, and while she was great, sometimes a guy wanted a male perspective.

He felt a twinge of guilt. This week, he'd kind of shut his mom out.

When he'd checked his cell after the flight on Sunday, he'd found a text from her, reminding him to tell her when he'd arrived safely. Rather than text, he'd called her when Merilee was in the ladies' room. He'd said he was fine and told her that Merilee had come, too, and that they'd broken up. She'd been stunned for about two seconds, then started to offer advice.

He'd broken in. "Mom, please don't be hurt, but this week I don't want to be your little boy or the man of the house. I need some space. I want to figure things out on my own, and I'm not going to keep reporting in. Okay?"

She'd been quiet for a long moment, then said, in a rather tight voice, "Gotcha. Just let me know if you need anything."

No, he wasn't going to call his mom, nor any of his friends.

He left Merilee a note that he'd be on deck, and picked up *Thunder Struck*, the book he'd brought with him and tried to read on the plane. Then, he hadn't been able to concentrate. Would he have any better luck now? The book was written by Theresa's new guy, Australian author Damien Black. Matt had gone with the Fallons to Damien's reading and signing, and he'd been hooked on the excerpt Damien read. He'd been about to buy the book when Theresa stopped him. "Save your money for the honeymoon," she said, and bought the set of three thrillers for him.

Damien had seemed like a pretty cool guy, though he'd gone off on his book tour before Matt had a chance to get to know him. No way he could call Damien for advice; the guy would think he was crazy.

Kat's husband, though . . . He'd gotten to know him better and figured he was a good guy. Even when Nav had been excited out of his mind about suddenly getting married, he'd found the time to call Matt on Friday. He'd said he was sorry about how things had worked out, and thanked Matt for being so generous about the wedding.

If Nav and Kat had been off on a honeymoon, Matt never would have bothered them. But because their wedding had been so unexpected, they'd flown back to Montreal so Nav could prepare for his first big photography exhibit.

Mind made up, Matt went out on deck, taking his cell and the book. The ship was almost deserted since most passengers were ashore, so privacy wasn't an issue. In his cell, he'd stored the numbers of all of Merilee's family. Now, leaning against the rail, he dialed Kat's cell.

"Hey, it's Matt. Uh, congratulations. I'm sorry I didn't make it to the wedding but, you know . . ."

"I totally understand. Matt, I heard about you and Merilee. Is everything okay? Is Merilee all right?"

"Yeah, she's fine. She's getting some rest and seems to be having fun."

"I really am sorry about you two. I always thought you were meant for each other, but you guys know best."

He didn't know a damned thing, and he wasn't sure Merilee did either. "How about you? Must be tough not getting a honeymoon."

"We'll do it later. We have to get married again, in India, for Nav's family. We'll plan a honeymoon after that."

"Good. Uh, Kat, the reason I'm calling is, can I get Nav's phone number?"

"Nav's?"

Embarrassed, he stared at the cruise ship docked beside theirs and confessed, "I could use a guy to talk to. Think he'd mind?"

"Of course not. And in fact, he's right here. I've taken a few more days off work and I'm at his place, helping him work on his exhibit. I'll give him the phone and disappear for a while so you two can talk guy talk."

A moment later, he heard Nav's voice. "Hi, Matt. Kat says you want to talk?"

"Yeah. This is kind of weird, but I could use a guy's opinion. Not one of my goofball friends, but someone older. Is that okay or—"

"Of course," Nav said in his classy English accent.

Matt leaned back in the deck chair, trying to force tense muscles to relax. "So the thing is, Merilee and I have been a couple since we were little kids. Our relationship, well, it got kind of routine. And that's not what either of us want for the future."

"Hmm. Do you see any hope of it changing?"

An image flashed into his mind. "Last night, there was a costume ball. I went as a pirate and she went as a flapper and it was like . . . like we were different people. It was, uh, exciting." He remembered something Merilee had told him about Nav and Kat's train trip. "Didn't you do some role-play thing or something with Kat?"

"Yeah. She'd stuck me in the buddy trap," he said wryly. "I needed to make her see me differently, so I played stranger on a train. Sure, she knew it was me, but it let her play along so we could test things out without endangering the friendship."

"Hmm. We can't exactly play pirate and flapper all the time."

"No, but the costumes, the roles, are just a tool. Our relationship had formed a certain pattern—a routine, as you said about you and Merilee. The role play broke us out of our pattern."

"I hear you." That steamy make-out session last night was sure a breakout. "But how do you keep from falling back into the same old rut?"

"You have to see yourselves, and each other, differently," Nav said.

"Like, she has this cute new haircut and looks really sassy, and she went ziplining?"

"Okay, that's seeing her, or at least the more superficial stuff. It's a start. Now, how about seeing you?"

"How d'you mean?" Idly, Matt watched as a tour bus delivered a group of tourists, most carrying green shopping bags. He figured they'd been on an excursion and were returning to dump their loot before heading off somewhere else. "Seeing me?"

"Figuring out who you really are, what makes you tick. Kat and I each had some hangups and stuff we needed to deal with. We were both kind of crippling our lives because of them. We each had to take a hard look inside. And we're older than you and Merilee. Trust me, you still have stuff to learn and growing to do. So do I. You learn more about yourself all the time."

Matt frowned. "Not so much. Seems like I've been pretty much the same guy for the last fourteen years." Ever since his parents had divorced, his mom had brought him to Vancouver, and his life had stabilized. Ever since he'd met Merilee. "And she's been the same girl." At least she had until she called off the wedding. Since then, sometimes he didn't even recognize her.

"And that's not working for you," Nav said quietly, but firmly. "Or you'd have been the couple exchanging rings on Saturday."

"I guess." It pretty much had been working for him, or at least he'd thought it had. Merilee was the one who'd had the big problem with their comfortable routine. Now, maybe he had to agree she'd had a point.

"Matt," Nav went on more slowly, "I like both you and Merilee. I want the best for both of you."

"Thanks. I'm sorry if I'm putting you in an awkward position. I mean, being married to Merilee's sister . . ." That aspect hadn't dawned on Matt before.

"Not a problem. My advice would be the same to each of you. If you were married, I'd say you should focus on your relationship. Like on what's wrong and how to improve it. But you've broken up. Now the focus needs to be on each of you as individuals. And you say you haven't changed in more than a decade?" He paused, then added quietly, "That's not good, my friend."

"I guess maybe it isn't."

"Take some time. Figure out who you are. What scares you, what excites you. What your goals and dreams are." He paused again. "I don't know if this would work for you . . ."

"What?"

"Kat and I figured a lot of this out by talking to each other. It sounds to me like you and Merilee haven't done a lot of talking about the deep stuff."

"I don't think either of us knew we had any deep stuff," he said ruefully. In some ways, they really were stuck back at the age of seven.

"You do. Trust me on this. You both have passions and dreams, you have values and ideals, you have interests and opinions. You just need to figure out what they are."

As Nav had spoken the words, at first Matt had felt intimidated, but then he realized he did know some of this stuff about himself. Like, one of his values was to care about people and be a man they could rely on. "Okay, I hear you. So you're saying we each need to find ourselves, but maybe we can do it by talking to each other?"

"Maybe. But not, like, joined at the hip. You need to do separate things, too. You have to have some different interests, activities, and friends, or you're just like . . . mirror images of each other, and that's not healthy."

"Mirror images. Is that the same thing as soul mates? We always figured we were soul mates."

"No, it's not the same thing. Soul mates are different and complement each other, which is a wonderful thing. Mirror images are the same as each other; they don't stimulate each other, challenge each other, make each other better."

"Huh. Thanks, Nav. You've given me some good stuff to think about." He knew his brain would be mulling this over in the next few days. "Wish you were here, man. I'd buy you a beer."

"Call anytime."

Yeah, he'd mull this over in time, but right now Matt's brain hurt and he needed a break. He opened Damien's book and found that the writing drew him in. He was quickly absorbed in the adventures of an Aboriginal Australian police officer who got secret assistance from creator spirits from the Dreamtime.

"Matt?"

Merilee's voice made him raise his head. He let out a low whistle. With her short, tousled hair and a figure-hugging, candy-pink sundress, he almost didn't recognize her. "You look great." Great enough that he wanted to touch the bare skin revealed by the dress, and kiss her pretty pink lips. They'd agreed to hang out just as friends, and he could see it was going to be tough sticking to that.

She tugged self-consciously at a skinny shoulder strap, almost as if she felt the heat of his gaze. "It's Des's dress. When she wore it yesterday, I admired it, and she loaned it to me. I need to get some new summer clothes."

He hoped she'd get more outfits like this dress. Even if she was just a friend, he could sure enjoy looking at her. "Let me run back to the cabin and get rid of the book. I'll be right back."

When he returned a couple of minutes later, she was standing by the railing, gazing ashore. She turned an excited face to him. "Puerto Vallarta. I can't believe we're really here."

"You're feeling rested?"

"And eager to go. The nap did the trick. Thanks, Matt, for being so understanding."

"You're welcome." Yes, being caring and understanding was one of his values, and something he had no intention of changing. He liked it when Merilee appreciated that quality in him.

As they went ashore, she said, "You were reading Damien's book? How is it?"

"Fantastic."

"Theresa says he loves what he does. He used to be a journalist, but he wanted to be his own boss and he liked making up stories rather than being confined by facts."

"She loves what she does, too, right?" The statistics Theresa spouted were pretty dull, but her passion always shone through.

"Oh, yeah. It's like a mission with her, helping aboriginal peoples. Kind of like me with teaching kids."

"I know you've felt that way for a long time," he said as he hailed one of the waiting taxis for the short ride to town. Remembering what Nav had said about the deep stuff, he said with some surprise, "But I don't really know what it means to you. Why it's so important."

They climbed into the shabby backseat. "D'you remember when I made up my mind about teaching?" she asked.

He peeled his gaze off her bare, lightly tanned legs, revealed up to mid-thigh in her sundress. Legs he'd seen a million times, but today they looked sexier. Those legs had gone ziplining, they'd dirty danced in a flapper dress. Normally, it was habit to touch Merilee: to clasp her hand or rest a hand on her leg. The fact that they'd broken up and were trying to be friends—that he could look but not touch—made him particularly aware of her.

Even when he focused on her face, her eyes seemed wider and bluer, her lips pinker and fuller. He cleared his throat. "When you made up your mind? Seems to me you always wanted to teach."

"Well, at least since we had Ms. Green in fourth grade. She was so terrific. She made a difference in lots of kids' lives. Then a few years later Jenna came home for a visit, and she'd been working with autistic kids. We talked about how important children are, and how they should be given every possible opportunity. That's when I knew for sure it was what I wanted to do."

"You'll be a fantastic teacher, Merilee."

"So will you."

Should he say something about his doubts? Nav said they had to talk about the deep stuff.

Merilee peered out the window and gave a little bounce. "We're here. This is so cool!"

The taxi crawled down a street clogged with traffic and jaywalking pedestrians. The scene was lively and cheerful, and very different from Vancouver. "Very cool," he agreed.

Under the bright sun, white-washed walls dazzled his eyes, contrasting with vividly painted doors and trim. The shops and restaurants that lined the streets were generally low, only one to three stories, and while most were made of painted plaster, a few walls were red brick or stone. Wrought-iron railings and louvered wooden shutters added a decorative touch to the higher stories. Fringed palms rustled like fans and tropical plants sported vivid blooms.

People were everywhere. Tourists in casual summer clothes mingled with Mexicans, who often wore more traditional white cotton clothing. The women's dresses and blouses, as well as some of the men's shirts, were embroidered with flowers and patterns.

He and Merilee piled out of the taxi, eager to be a part of the bustling scene. "Food?" he asked. His stomach told him it had been a lot of hours since the big buffet breakfast he'd eaten.

"Yes. One of the sidewalk places, so we can feel the sun and watch everyone go by."

"How about that one?" He pointed across the street to a busy outdoor patio with bright pink and red flowers tumbling from hanging baskets.

"Great."

As they walked over, she said, "D'you want a real meal?"

He was about to say, "Whatever you want," but remembered the pirate. Consideration was good, but a guy could take it too far. "I'd rather get something quick—maybe nachos—and then explore."

"Good idea. I'm so glad we get the evening ashore. I'd hate to have to rush back to the ship on our first night in Mexico."

Once they were seated, Matt told their waiter, "Nachos with the works." He ordered a beer and Merilee went with Coke.

After he'd taken a first long swallow of beer, he said something he knew he had to. He only hoped it didn't spoil the holiday mood. "What you said in the taxi about me making a great teacher? Well, I'm not sure that's what I want to be."

Her eyes squinted in disbelief. "But, Matt, that's what you always said."

"Actually, you said it. When you were so keen on teaching, I said it was an important job, and somehow that ended up with us saying that I should be one."

She gave a quick head shake, her eyes narrowed. "You're not saying I railroaded you into a teaching career?"

"No, of course not." Jeez, he might be considerate but he wasn't a doormat. "But you were keen on it, on us doing it together, and it was fun making plans. It's not like I had anything else in mind, so it was easy to go along. Mom was happy, too." And relieved he'd given up on the childhood dream of being a pilot.

She frowned. "You can't plan your future based on what someone else wants."

"I guess I'm figuring that out." Which he might not have if they'd gotten married. He studied her warily. She'd loved the idea of them having the same dream, and said it was another thing that proved they were soul mates. "Are you mad?"

Her frown was still there. "Well, yeah. Why didn't you say something?"

"I meant, are you mad I have doubts about being a teacher?"

She rubbed her hands across her cheeks. "Not mad. A little disappointed, maybe." She dropped her hands. "I'm more mad that you had doubts and never said anything. It's like you lied to me."

He shook his head vigorously. "I didn't really have doubts. It sounded good to me. You made it sound good. Your enthusiasm kind of carried over. I've only just realized that it may not be my thing. And that it's good when a person has passion for their career, like you and Theresa and Damien do." And Mandy, too, though he knew not to bring her name up.

She studied him, eyebrows pulled together in what looked more like puzzlement than a frown. "You said you didn't have anything else in mind. You're saying you honestly never felt drawn to any particular career? You're good with people. Like, you're always helping our friends settle their arguments. You get them to see both sides. You could be a counselor or a mediator."

"I guess." He did like helping people be happy and get along, but that was just part of who he was. It wasn't a career passion. He'd never—no, wait. "There was one thing, back when I was a kid. I wanted to be a pilot. Not for the big jumbo jets that fly internationally, but smaller planes. Like the seaplanes that fly up the coast into more remote places." That sounded way more exciting and challenging than piloting giant sky-buses.

Her blue eyes lit up. "I remember. You built model planes and pretended you were flying them." She grinned. "You had this tiny plane and said you'd fly me to Paris."

He chuckled. "Okay, not so realistic. But I could fly you to Victoria, Seattle, San Francisco, if I had my license."

"Are you serious about this?"

"I didn't even remember it until today." With Mandy. "I don't know. I've never even been in one of those planes."

"Why did you give up on the idea when you were young?"

"Oh, Mom worried. Thought it was too dangerous. You know how she is."

"Yeah. Adele's perfected that *you're all I have* thing. I remember when she didn't even want you to get your driver's license because she said there are so many crazy drivers out there."

"And we pointed out I'd be more protected from them in a car than on a bicycle."

They shared a laugh. Then she said, "I bet that, like driving, flying's not as dangerous as she thinks."

He repeated Mandy's point. "And it's not like schools are

safe either. Violence, weapons, drugs. Some kids are pretty disturbed."

"If you were a pilot, you'd be careful," she said with certainty. "You pay attention to detail, you do things thoroughly."

"Thanks," he said. Yeah, it felt good to be appreciated. And he liked the enthusiasm that filled him when he thought about flying. "You know, I'm going to check into it when we get back. See what it takes to be a pilot."

She nodded. "You should."

This was good, really good. Talking to her so openly, having her say nice things about him, enjoying the light in her clear blue eyes and the expressiveness of her pink lips. Her very kissable lips. Maybe this *just friends* thing was crazy. They'd both made a few changes; they were talking; and he was more attracted to her than ever before.

Their waiter broke into his thoughts by delivering a giant plate of nachos. Melted cheese, black beans, guacamole, sour cream and, of course, salsa. His stomach growled and he dug in eagerly.

Merilee did, too. "Mmm, good. A million calories, but who cares? That's one good thing about losing weight—I can eat anything I want until I gain it back." She popped a finger into her mouth and sucked gooey cheese off it.

His dick pulsed. He'd never thought of eating nachos—or eating anything—as sexy before.

"I'm glad you told me, Matt," she said.

Told her what? Had he said that out loud, about how she was turning him on?

"Honesty's important to me, and of course you shouldn't be a teacher if it's not something you're passionate about." She loaded a cheese-coated tortilla chip with goodies, popped it into her mouth, and made *mmm-mmm* sounds as she chewed.

"Uh, yeah." Now Merilee, he could be passionate about. Especially if she'd make sounds like that in bed.

"And I like it when you're decisive, Matt. A person should know what they want and go after it."

The only thing he'd ever really wanted was Merilee, and right now he wanted her in a surprisingly down and dirty way. A way that, given how she'd run from him last night, would offend her.

He forced his mind off sex and back to communication. "You want honesty? Here's the thing. If I'm not decisive, it's because I see lots of good alternatives and I usually don't really care which one wins out. Like, what's it matter if we have pizza or Chinese for dinner? Or nachos? What's the big deal whether we watch an action movie or a romantic comedy? It's all good."

He took another swallow of beer, starting to get a little worked up about defending himself. "And I like making people happy. What's so wrong with that?"

"Nothing. It's a good quality. So's being flexible. But don't you ever really care about anything?"

Care? Wounded, he said, "You. My mom. My friends."

"Okay, yes, I know that. But—"

"But what?"

Chapter 10

I'd told Matt I wanted him to be honest. How honest should I be with him? I didn't want to hurt his feelings, but this felt important. I swallowed, then said softly, "You're easygoing. Mostly that's good, but it's like nothing touches you really deeply. You don't get passionate about things."

"I don't understand what you're saying," he said stiffly.

"Like, when I was having all those really bad periods. You were so sweet about looking after me, so sympathetic, and you said I should talk to my doctor. When I told you that Mom and the three-pack said pain was normal, you backed down. Until finally last fall, when I was in total agony, you went all take charge and pretty much dragged me to the doctor."

Poor Matt, he looked so baffled. "Uh, are you saying that was good or bad? I mean, I know a guy shouldn't push a woman around, but I was really worried, and I was right to be because—"

"Matt." I held up a hand. "What you did was good. Yeah, you shouldn't be a bully, but you got passionate and you acted on it. That was strong, decisive, and pretty exciting."

Still looking confused, he said, "Are you saying I should have done that years ago?"

If he had, I'd have been spared years of pain. But then I should've had the brains to go myself, rather than listen to the women in my family. "I'm saying . . ." I sighed, remembering how, when I'd gone to his apartment last Thursday to talk to him about my doubts, I'd hoped he'd fight for me. "Do you care enough about anything that you'd fight for it?"

"I'd fight to save you if someone threatened you," he answered promptly.

He would. I was positive, and that meant a lot to me. "Thank you. But does it take something so drastic? Like, would you"—did I have the guts to ask this?—"fight to win someone if you really, really loved them?"

He frowned. "You mean fight some other guy?"

"No, I mean . . ." I took a long swallow of Coke, wishing I'd ordered something alcoholic. How to explain this? Matt was practical, not a romantic, so was there any hope he'd understand? Or would he just think I was foolish?

We'd agreed that, for now, we were just friends, so why was I even bothering?

Because my heart couldn't give up on us completely. And what we were doing today—being honest, baring our souls—was important. I took a deep breath and, despite feeling fragile and vulnerable, said, "When I told you I had doubts about the wedding, you didn't yell or cry or argue. You didn't sweep me up in your arms and make mad, passionate love to me, tell me I was the most important thing in the world to you, and beg me to marry you."

He cocked his head, looking confused again. "You wanted me to try and change your mind?"

That wasn't the point. He *so* wasn't getting it. Frustrated, I said, "I wanted you to care!"

He scowled. "Jeez, Merilee, I've loved you for fourteen years. You know I damned well care." His voice had risen and he glanced around.

I did, too, noting a few people staring at us. How to explain what I meant? Keeping my voice low, I said, "I know, but—"

"Look," he broke in impatiently, "you said you had doubts, and I heard you. You have to decide who you want to be with. Marriage is for life, and I'm not going to try to persuade you into something you're not sure about. Not with arguments, tears, or sex."

I read the sincerity on his face. What he said made sense, yet my feelings were legitimate, too.

"Besides," he said, slowing down, "you made me realize I had some doubts, too, that I hadn't really acknowledged to myself."

He had? So somehow I'd railroaded him into a relationship, the way I had into a career? Had anything between us been real? Hurt, I struggled for words.

He beat me to it. "Much as it shattered me, I knew you were right. We weren't ready to get married."

"Shattered you?" That was a big word. A strong, passionate feeling. Did he really mean it? And how could I be mad that he'd realized he had doubts when I felt the same way myself?

"Yeah. Life as I knew it, the future as I'd envisioned it, was over," he said heavily.

"Oh, Matt. Yes, that's exactly it."

"I'm trying to cope." He sighed, looking much older than twenty-one. "I listen to what you say and I'm doing what I can to figure things out."

I reached past the almost-full plate of nachos to touch his hand. "Me, too. It's all we can do."

"It's hard."

"Yeah. Kat gave me some advice I've been trying to follow. She said I should do lots of things, with and without you, then think about how I feel and why I feel that way. I've been trying. You, too, right?"

"Yeah. That's a pretty good description of what I've been doing. And, you know, thinking about the big stuff: dreams and values, interests and, uh, opinions and stuff."

That was pretty darned insightful. Really, that was what it came down to, bottom line. "So let's both keep doing it, and we'll keep talking. And being honest. Okay?"

His face lightened and he squeezed my hand. "Yeah."

We gazed into each other's eyes for a long moment, and I wondered where on earth we were heading. As individuals, and as a couple.

Our waiter paused by our table. "You don't like the nachos, *amigos*?"

"They're great," I hurried to assure him, and Matt nodded agreement.

When he'd gone, Matt released my hand. "Merilee, this stuff we're talking about is important. But let's spend some time enjoying Mexico, too. We have nachos, sunshine, a whole town to explore. D'you want to—" He broke off, then started again. "I'd like to do that with you. What do you say?"

He'd stated his wish rather than asked me, and I liked it. I also liked the idea of roaming this foreign town with him. "Sounds perfect."

With renewed appetites, we dug into the nachos. After, for the next couple of hours, we played tourist, laughing and snapping pictures of each other, trying on clothes and giant sombreros, browsing through stores and stores full of silver jewelry, and wandering through the market.

Matt replaced his beat-up old wallet with one made of tooled leather. I found a silver pendant with a stone the exact color of my gran's eyes. It was easy and fun, like the way we'd always been together. But not exactly the same.

Underneath that ease, I felt a different awareness. Of me, and of him, even though we'd said we were just friends. I tried on clothes that were brighter and more trendy than my usual practical student wardrobe, and he watched, encouraging me to be even bolder. His blue eyes held a distinct gleam, the gleam of a man appreciating an attractive woman, that made my pulse speed.

Then, when his sunglasses broke, I helped him choose new ones—designer knockoffs. When I said, "Wow, they make you look like a movie star," I meant it. I'd always been proud to be with him, but now he was the kind of guy that girls turned to look at. It made me want to hook my hand possessively through his arm, but I resisted. What message would that send? What message did I want it to send?

All I knew, on this sunny afternoon, was that there was no one I'd rather be with.

Finally, laden with packages, we flopped down on a bench to take a breather.

Matt turned to me. "I've been thinking."

"About?"

"Us. We've broken up, right?"

My eyes widened in surprise behind my sunglasses. When I'd been musing about how much I enjoyed being with him, his mind had sure been on a different track. "Yes," I said softly, an ache in my heart.

"So we can date."

The ache tightened like a fist. "I . . . Yes, I guess so. I mean . . ." I really didn't want to see him getting friendly with another girl, but of course one day it would happen. Just please not this week, with Mandy or Trina or any of the other women I knew would be delighted to be with him.

"What if I want to date you?"

"Wh-what?" I gaped at him.

"No assumptions, no 'are we or aren't we getting back together?' Something fresh. The guy in the movie star glasses dating the sassy girl in the pink sundress, the one he met ziplining this morning."

"Met? You mean you want us to pretend we only met today?"

"It might be fun."

"That's like what Nav and Kat did on the train. Remember, I told you?"

Something twitched his lips for a moment. "Oh, yeah, maybe you did mention something. So, what do you think?"

Last night, it had been the pirate and the flapper. Now it was the guy who looked like Bradley Cooper and the sassy girl in pink. A thrill of excitement rippled through me. "Let's do it."

He took off his sunglasses and hooked them in the neck of his shirt. Blue eyes dancing, he said, "So, lady in pink, will you dine with me tonight?"

I took off my own sunglasses. "It would be my pleasure."

For a moment we just stared at each other and sparks darted between us—as if this really was a first date with a sexy guy I was attracted to. This was going to be one interesting evening.

"Where will we go?" I asked. I pointed to a restaurant across the street, its bright turquoise-and-red awning sporting a frog logo. Lively music filtered out the open door. "Des said Señor Frog's is a popular place."

He glanced at it, then shook his head. "No. That's the kind of place I go back home with my friends. This is Mexico. Let's find somewhere less touristy and more Mexican." He snapped his fingers. "Remember that restaurant on one of the backstreets, up on a second-floor patio? In among some private homes?"

"I do." I remembered commenting about all the wonderful flowers. "It looked lovely. But will we ever find it again?"

He rolled his eyes and I smiled. I'd yet to see Matt get lost. Except, of course, this wasn't *Matt*, it was the guy I'd met this morning.

It seemed he shared Matt's sense of direction, though, because ten minutes later we were walking up whitewashed steps to a patio that overlooked the town and the harbor. Pots of flowering plants were everywhere, the tables were beautifully set with embroidered tablecloths and napkins, and candles danced in ceramic holders. Half the tables were occupied, some by Caucasians and others by Mexicans. People weren't formally dressed, but they weren't in the typical tourist T-shirts either. I was glad for Des's sundress, and Matt fit right in with his new clothes, haircut, and sunglasses.

The gracious middle-aged Mexican hostess must have approved of us because she showed us to a wonderful table. Right beside an iron railing twined with vivid purple bougainvillea, it looked over town and the harbor where, beyond the fringe of palms, the sun was sinking in an orangey-pink sky. I sighed with pleasure. "This is wonderful. It's our first night in Mexico," I told her.

Her smile widened. "You have come to the right place to enjoy it, *señorita*. We will make sure you have a wonderful meal, to accompany the sunset. Now, perhaps a cocktail or a glass of wine or sangria to start?"

"Sangria?" I asked. "Red wine with sliced fruit?"

"We have red or white. A little club soda to make it light and refreshing. If you prefer a stronger version, we add brandy."

"That sounds good. The red for me, please. Without brandy."

"Let's get a pitcher," Matt said.

Knowing we were behaving like total tourists but not caring, we snapped pictures of the restaurant and the sunset.

The woman returned with a pitcher and matching wineglasses made of heavy Mexican blown glass with blue rims. Inside the pitcher, slices of orange and lemon floated in red wine, and when she poured, ice cubes clinked.

With a graceful hand, she beckoned toward Matt, who held the camera. "Give it to me and I'll take a picture of the two of you."

He handed the camera over. Then we leaned across the table toward each other and smiled as she clicked two or three times.

After, she left us alone with menus, and we picked up our glasses and clicked them together. "To being here tonight," he said. "I'm glad I met you this morning."

I smiled. So he really did intend to play this game. "I'm glad, too." I took a sip of sangria. "Mmm, this is nice."

He tasted, too, and agreed. Then we both opened menus. "Not enchiladas or tacos," he said. "Not the same things I'd eat back home."

"I like those things," I protested, but I studied the menu with interest. "I don't know what half these dishes are, but they sound intriguing."

"Let's ask our hostess to choose a meal for us." He beckoned the woman over. "*Señora,* we're looking for something traditionally Mexican. What would you recommend?"

She smiled approvingly. "You should start with tortilla soup, a spicy tomato soup with crispy strips of fried tortilla on top. Squeeze a little lime in it."

Matt glanced at me and I nodded. "That sounds great. And then?"

The woman went on. "Chicken *mole,* which is with a sauce of chocolate, chili peppers, and other spices. I know that sounds odd, but it's a wonderful combination. And also *huachinango*—you call it red snapper—freshly caught today, in a chili tomato sauce. Then, for dessert . . . Well, perhaps *tres leches,* a rich cake of milk and eggs. Or *buñuelos,* or flan. We will see when the time comes. *Sí?*"

"*Sí*," I agreed, "to all of it. Does that sound good to you, Matt?"

"Can't wait. Thank you," he told the woman.

"It will all be delicious. This I can promise," she said with another smile.

When she'd gone, I said, "That was a good idea, asking her."

"When in doubt, ask an expert."

"Some guys get their egos all tied up in knots and refuse to ask for directions or ask advice."

He shrugged. "Yeah, I don't get that. No one knows everything. What's the big deal about asking someone else?"

"It's only a big deal to a guy with no self-confidence, and it makes them look stupid." Matt, thank heavens, wasn't like that at all. It was one of the many things I'd always loved about him.

It had become habit to touch him; it was something I'd done a hundred times a day. Now my fingers almost itched with the desire to stroke his face, check out the softness of his stubble, drift over cheekbones that looked more pronounced thanks to his haircut.

A pretty young waitress arrived, looking enough like our older hostess that she had to be a relative, and served our soup. It was great—spicy, but not too spicy—and a few squeezes of lime made it even better. While we ate, we watched the sun disappear and chatted casually about the things we'd done today. I'd always found Matt easy to talk to, but had probably never told him.

So I'd tell the new guy on this first date. "You're good to talk to. Some of my girlfriends say their boyfriends' idea of communication is either grunts or sports talk. You listen, and you talk."

"Probably comes of being an only child, with a single parent mom. She trained me." His lips kinked in a wry grin. "So did my girlfriend."

In so many ways, I'd been so lucky to have him. Now, seeing him in the light of the setting sun looking movie star handsome, I tried to remember why that hadn't been enough for me.

The waitress cleared our empty soup bowls and brought out plates with the red snapper and chicken. "You're sharing, Mama tells me?"

"We are," Matt said, and I thought of how we'd shared food ever since grade two, when I usually had ham and cheese sandwiches and he had PB&J or tuna fish.

She put the laden platters in the middle of the table, and empty plates in front of each of us. We served ourselves, tasted, and dug in eagerly.

"Nothing against enchiladas," Matt said, "but this food's a whole different thing."

"I love chocolate, but who'd have guessed it went with chicken?" I glanced up from my meal. "I took an Italian cooking lesson on the cruise ship and really loved it. It inspired me to buy a cookbook with recipes from all over the world. I'll have to see if this one's in it."

He tilted his head, looking surprised. "You like to cook?"

"I've never done much." As he well knew. "Aside from chocolate chip cookies for my boyfriend," I added teasingly. "Cooking's never been a big thing around my house. Everybody's always too busy with other things. But I think it's relaxing and creative, and I love eating the finished product."

"Be sure and let me know if you need a taster."

"I'll do that."

A burst of laughter made me look up to see two gray-haired couples in animated conversation with the hostess as she seated them. The patio was almost full now, and everyone was older than us. Now that the sun had set, the dancing candles made the scene mellow and romantic. This place would have been perfect for our honeymoon. I almost wanted to pretend, just for tonight, that nothing had changed between us. I wanted to twine my fingers through Matt's, have him lean across the table and give me a kiss.

But if nothing had changed, it would have been a comfortable peck, not a deep, sensual kiss. And right now, gazing at the handsome man across the table, I was more in the mood for the latter. This first-date thing—especially with a guy who was so hot, interesting, and confident—was turning out to be fun. "I'm glad you chose this restaurant," I said. "It's so elegant and grown-up."

"Not the kind of place you usually go?"

I chuckled. "No. That'd be the pub with a bunch of friends."

He tilted his head and studied me. "How come you and your boyfriend didn't do this? Have dinner, just the two of you, someplace nice?"

Why hadn't we? Honestly, it really hadn't occurred to me, and I guessed it hadn't to him either. "Budget? Students can't afford places like this."

He reflected, then shook his head. "No, it's about priorities. That's something Mom taught me, because we've always lived on a tight budget. Funds may be limited, but you choose how to spend them. If you can buy pizza, rent videos, go to the pub with friends, put gas in cars, you can afford an occasional dinner out instead."

"I guess." Yet we never had.

"Me and my girlfriend, we've hung out with this group of kids for years. And they're great. Lots of fun. But maybe we're all kind of stuck back in high school. I mean, how do you grow up if nothing changes?"

"You're pretty smart." I studied him. "My boyfriend and I saw each other almost every day for fourteen years. We got older, but it didn't feel like growing up because it was so gradual. And like you said, nothing really changed." We'd been in a comfortable rut and it hadn't occurred to either one of us to break out.

He nodded. "And when it does, it's a shock. It makes you think differently. Which can be good."

"It can." This week, he'd turned into a more mature, more sophisticated, sexier guy. Did he think the same about me? He'd called me sassy. Sassy was good. He'd invited me—the new me—on a date.

We both ate in silence for a couple of minutes, then he said, "Maybe it's a process. Either you get really set in your ways or you keep, uh, exploring ideas and options."

"And that's way more interesting. But also scary. I mean, if you keep changing, how do you know that anything's going to last? That you're going to like the same job, or love the same person?"

"I don't know. People who get married must believe they're going to stay in love."

Our gazes met across the table. Once, I'd been so sure we would. The thing I'd wanted most in life was to love and be loved, and feel secure in that love. Now, I had no idea if it would ever happen.

We both looked away and, in silence, finished our dinner.

When we settled back in our chairs, he said, "It's been an unusual first date."

"I don't even know what a first date's supposed to be like," I mused. "I've never been on one."

He chuckled. "Me, either. So we get to make it up as we go. And right now, I'm just thinking how pretty you look and what a great evening it's been. And that"—he reached across the table and caught my hand—"I want to do this."

We linked fingers. I was in a foreign country and had no idea what the future held, but his hand was warm and strong. He'd always had wonderful hands, so capable and sure. Now, though, I felt something more than the comfort of familiarity. There was also a buzz of awareness and sensuality that made me long to feel those hands stroke me toward passion.

"What do you want for dessert?" he asked.

Your hands, taking my clothes off, making me feel sexy and desirable, bringing me to climax the way you did out on deck. When I spoke, my voice came out a little choked. "I'm too full to hold another bite. But you have something."

He shook his head. "I have something else in mind. We have an hour before we need to get back to the boat. How about a stroll on the Malecon, that promenade down by the beach?"

It sounded romantic. "I'd love to walk. To see Mexico at night."

We paid our bill, then said good night to the waitress and also to the hostess, who said, "I hope you'll come back one day."

"I hope so, too," I told her.

As we started down the stairs from the patio, Matt again took my hand. We strolled that way through town, a current of awareness running between us. It was so strong, he had to feel it, too. But neither of us said anything about it, just commented on the children who were still running around at this time of night, the music pouring from the clubs, the liveliness of town on this dark, balmy evening. It was so foreign and exotic, from the rustle of palm leaves to the softness of the air to the street vendors selling jewelry, small paintings, and snacks.

We weren't the only ones who'd come to wander along the Malecon. It was almost a parade, with about equal numbers of tourists and Mexicans of all ages. The ocean was serene and there was almost no breeze. When Matt put his arm around me and drew me closer, I went eagerly, nestling against him and putting my arm around his waist.

Kat had said it was okay to spend time with Matt, but that I should think about how I felt, and why. Now, something felt different, even though we'd walked this way so often. His new shorts rode low on his hips and, under his shirt, I was aware of warm skin and the flex of muscles as he walked. His fingers toyed with the strap of my sundress and caressed my shoulder, making me very aware I was braless under the dress. My nipples perked to attention, less from the chill air than from his attention.

How did I feel? More aware of him. Being with him felt special. Not like a comfortable routine.

Why? Was it being in Mexico? Dining out like real adults? The new clothes? The way we'd both enjoyed ziplining? The realization that other girls, pretty, vivacious ones like Mandy, found him attractive? The memory of the outrageous way we'd behaved on the deck of the *Diamond Star*? The way we'd talked, each sharing more about our thoughts and feelings than we'd done before? The first-date game we'd played and maybe still were playing?

What did this mean, for me as an individual and for us as a couple—or, no longer a couple?

We wandered along under tall, evenly spaced palms, then came to a stop in front of a huge statue of a seahorse with a child riding it. "Really, seahorses are tiny," I said. "But what a great way to spark a kid's imagination. I'll remember this for when I'm teaching."

"And I'll remember this." Gently, but firmly, he tugged me around to stand in front of him, then cupped my face in both his hands and kissed me.

It wasn't last night's fiery kiss fueled by the sexy dance. Instead, it was slow, almost sultry, tasting of chocolate and spice. Lazy, yet relentless in the way he stroked my tongue with his, overcoming any objections I perhaps should have had, and making me respond. A Mexican kiss, different from any kiss we'd ever shared before. Or maybe, I'd kissed him so often, I'd forgotten to pay attention.

Tonight, he didn't let me forget. He nipped my bottom lip, making me squeak with surprise. It should have hurt—it did hurt—yet it sent an achy tingle surging straight to my sex.

Still holding my face as if to ensure I didn't escape, he moved closer so the fronts of our bodies brushed. Against my belly, I felt him harden. A whimper of need escaped me.

Shocked at myself, I put my hands on his shoulders and pushed him away. "No. What are you thinking? There are people all around us."

Expression enigmatic, he said, "Such a good girl."

It didn't exactly sound like a compliment, but I couldn't believe Matt really wanted to make out in public. We'd always held hands, maybe exchanged a little kiss, but we'd agreed that getting carried away with PDAs was tacky.

He took my hand again and pulled me along to walk beside him. My nipples, painfully hard, rubbed against the fabric of my dress. I cast a surreptitious glance down and saw that the untucked front of his shirt concealed his erection. We were decent. Barely. I was glad that the diffuse light on the Malecon, coming from the moon and scattered street lamps, wasn't bright.

"Merilee," he said, "do you like sex?"

Chapter 11

"What?" I jerked to a stop, pulled my hand from Matt's, and stared up at him. "What kind of question is that?"

"An honest one. Because I don't know for sure."

"Of course, I do." I glanced around, hoping no one was in earshot, and lowered my voice. "How could you ask that? We've been lovers for years. You know I like sleeping with you."

"I know you like sleeping with me," he echoed my words. "Curling up with your head on my shoulder and my arm around you, or lying on your side with me spooning you from behind. Drifting into sleep together. Waking together and getting ready for a new day. But I don't know about the sex part. You're so . . . quiet."

My eyebrows flew up. "Quiet? You want a girl who screams? Matt, half the time we're at my house with my parents just upstairs."

"And half the time we're in my apartment where no one can hear us."

I shook my head in disbelief. "You aren't seriously saying you want me to scream like a, a . . ."

"A woman who's having an earth-shaking orgasm?"

My mouth fell open and heat surged to my cheeks. I was glad of the darkness that would hide my flush. I turned away from him and began to walk again. Under my breath, I said, "I have orgasms. Can we not talk about this here?"

"Where, then? Back in the cabin? With our two separate beds?"

Or not at all. I wasn't as uninhibited as my sisters, who for the past week had been discussing the places they'd had sex and their guys' techniques. Still, those girl-talk sessions were one of the things that had made me realize something was lacking for me, with Matt. Or maybe it was just lacking *in* me.

To be fair to both of us, I had to have the guts to discuss this.

We were walking past a statue of a man and woman seated side by side, a sense of intimacy between them. "Let's sit," I suggested.

We found a bench facing the ocean, with our backs to the town and the people strolling by. Deliberately, I sat with a couple of inches of space separating us. I didn't touch Matt or look at him when I said in a low voice, "I enjoy sex with you. But to be completely honest, I'm not sure I'm a very sexy woman."

After a moment, he said, "When we hit our teens, you were shy about sex. I respected that." I heard him swallow. "I tried not to push you, to take things at a pace you were comfortable with, but . . . are you saying it's never been really good for you?" Pain edged his voice.

"Good? Yes, of course. But . . . Matt, be honest. Has it been great for you? Like, rock your world great?" Like in the romantic movies I loved? "So great that it completely satisfied you? That you never looked at another girl and, you know, lusted after her and wondered what it'd be like to have sex with her?"

"Sure, I look at other girls. I've been attracted to them.

Wondered. That's in a guy's nature. It's basic biology. But I'd never act on it. I don't want sex to be basic biology. For me, it's about love and respect." He swallowed again. "You've wondered what it'd be like with other guys?"

"Mmm, not really. I've been attracted, like to actors. And remember our Psych 101 prof, Dr. Mackie? Oh, man."

"Dr. Mackie." He sounded offended. "You're kidding."

I waved a hand. "It was silly. Lots of girls had a crush on him. He had that long, wavy black hair, a wetsuit and surfboard in his office. His lectures were so interesting and he was so animated, like he obviously loved what he was doing."

"He was a good teacher," Matt said, and his grudging tone made me grin.

"He was, and if you did teach high school you'd have loads of girls with crushes on you." I gave a quick laugh. "Which is definitely *not* a reason to do it."

He snapped his fingers. "Damn. It was sounding good to me."

We were quiet a minute, then he said, "You're saying you were attracted to men like him, but you didn't wonder about sex with them?"

"Not really. There was no emotional connection. You said you don't *want* sex to be basic biology. For me, it isn't. I need to know someone if I'm going to feel emotional intimacy. Probably to love them. I don't even know, Matt. I've never wanted to go to bed with anyone else." I gazed out at the dark ocean and the night sky dotted with stars, and sighed. "Maybe I am kind of . . . undersexed. Though," I mused, "Theresa said she was like that after she and her ex-husband broke up. She figured she had no sex drive. Then she met Damien."

Matt drew in a noisy breath, then let it out. "Shit, Merilee. With me you don't have a sex drive? Is that what you're saying?" He turned to face me, expression bitter and hurt in the moonlight. "That somewhere out there, there's a guy who'll . . . awaken your sex drive? Hell, maybe I'm just a crappy lover."

"That's not true. You're considerate and gentle." And I was probably crazy to wish that sometimes he wasn't so gentle. "And no, it's not that I don't have *any* sex drive. It's just kind of predictable. Like on Friday nights, we'll watch a movie and cuddle up, maybe drink a glass of wine, neck a little, and yeah, I want to make love with you. But it's, uh, kind of comfortable and relaxed, not a burning need." Voice barely above a whisper, I went on. "Though last night, when we were kissing, that was really hot. And the dancing was sexy. Arousing."

"You really got into it." He studied me appraisingly. "Did the pirate turn you on?"

From my very first sight of him, and then when we danced, it was unbelievable. "Oh, yeah."

"Before you knew it was me?"

Oops. He reminded me of my mom in cross-examination mode. "Uh, yeah, I guess."

"And the Zorro?"

I shook my head. "No, it was different. He was attractive and fun to dance with, and he did start to flirt with me, but I didn't, you know, respond to him. I wasn't aroused."

"Why with the pirate then?"

"I don't know." Again, I thought back. "He was dashing. Exciting, mysterious, sensual."

"Were you disappointed that it was me? Did you want to hook up with someone else?"

Ack, he was relentless.

"Merilee, we said we'd be honest."

"Okay, I thought about it. Briefly. I've only ever been with you. I was curious. But I knew I wasn't ready to be with someone else." I wanted to touch his hand, but wasn't sure I should. "Are you mad?"

"Mad that you were turned on by me when you didn't know it was me?" He gave a ragged laugh. "Shit, I'm jealous of myself. How's that for confusing?"

"Everything's so confusing."

He tipped his head back, maybe looking at the stars, maybe thinking. When he straightened, he said, "We've only ever been with each other. We learned about sex together. It's always been good, but not exactly, uh, adventurous."

"No." We sure didn't do the things my sisters had talked about. Kama Sutra positions? Sex on a public beach? Did I really want to? Did he? "Do you want to be more adventurous?" I asked hesitantly.

He rubbed a hand over his jaw. "Okay, the thought's crossed my mind. But I was afraid if I suggested something, you'd think I was a perv. You're so sweet and wholesome. I don't want to insult you by asking you to act like . . . To do something that's . . ."

Oh, my God, what had he been thinking about? Tying me up and spanking me again? Was that the kind of sex he really craved? And if so . . . Yeah, it had turned me on in a weird, surprising way, but was it what I wanted? "Like what?" I asked cautiously.

"Sex in the shower?" he said.

Like Jenna and her guy, when he brought her car to her. "You think *that's* pervy?" To me, it sounded like fun.

"No, but we've never done it."

"Your shower's too small and you know I'm really careful about what we do at my parents' house. It was weird enough asking them if you could stay over. I don't want them hearing . . . stuff like the shower and wondering what's going on."

"We're at the house lots of times when they're both at work. You don't have to have sex just at night. Remember?"

When we'd first started fooling around, we'd done it at my house after school. But when we turned eighteen and graduated from high school, we'd decided to be up front about it with my parents and his mom. So then he'd stay over at my place and once we fixed up his garage apartment I stayed over there. Maybe it had seemed grown-up to have sex at night, in bed. Then it had become our routine. But he'd never suggested anything else. "Matt, if you wanted to make love during the day, in the shower, why didn't you tell me?"

"I didn't know if you'd like it."

I gave a frustrated huff. "This is what I mean about you not taking the lead. You could've at least asked."

He scowled. "Okay, while we're at it, I'd like to have sex in other places, like maybe outside in the middle of the night, or on the kitchen counter."

The kitchen counter? Where people prepared food? But then my buttoned-up sister Theresa had done it in an airplane bathroom and boasted afterward. "What else?" I asked, wondering how I'd ever imagined Matt was happy with boring old me.

"Uh, well, every guy likes it when his girl goes down on him, but the first couple times we tried you didn't like it, so . . ." He shrugged.

I liked his penis. It was warm and smooth, firm and beautifully shaped. Yeah, I'd kind of gagged when I'd gone down on him, but I'd been awkward, self-conscious. And when he'd groaned and exploded in my mouth, taking me by surprise, I'd almost choked. But I could try again.

"And different positions would be fun," he said. "Like doggy style."

I'd wondered about that, too. "You should have said something."

"I know not all girls like that kind of stuff, and you're so sweet and kind of old-fashioned. In a good way," he quickly added. "You're not like those slutty girls who do guys at parties. You're not into drugs. You're always happy to be the designated driver. I really like all that stuff. So I didn't want to suggest something crude."

And I'd never wanted to suggest anything kinky because I'd wanted him to respect and love me, not think of me like one of those slutty girls. "I'm an old-fashioned good girl," I said, disgruntled with him and myself. "How totally boring."

"I didn't say that."

"It's kind of true, though," I admitted. "Remember, I told you I got some weird stuff at the stagette?"

"Vaginal balls," he said promptly. Oh, yeah, he remembered. I was learning a lot about Matt tonight.

"And his and her leopard-print thong underwear, edible massage oil, a dildo—"

"What? You're kidding."

"It all made me blush. Kat gave me this totally gorgeous black silk and lace teddy—not slutty at all, just really sensual—and even it made me squirm." I hardly ever wore thongs, either, because the whole naked butt thing made me feel self-conscious.

He moved closer, so his shoulder touched mine. "That's too bad that you were uncomfortable at your own stagette. But, Merilee, you get to be any kind of girl you want. If those things bother you, toss them out. If you'd rather wear cotton panties than leopard thongs, there's nothing wrong with that."

"But it's not very exciting. Maybe that's been our problem, Matt. I'm just not very exciting."

He didn't rush to deny it. After a moment, he rested his hand on my leg below the hem of my short dress. Making little circles with his fingers, he said, "You were exciting in that flapper dress when we danced and kissed. Really exciting. It seemed to me you were into it."

I had been. I was also into the rub of his fingertips over my bare skin, reminding me of how sensual I'd been feeling before we started this conversation about my inadequacies. "Maybe it was the costume. And at first not knowing the pirate was you. It wasn't you judging Merilee for acting a little wild. It was two strangers, so I could do whatever I wanted."

"You can do whatever you want with me. Especially if it's sexy. You think I'm going to complain?"

"But if I'd ever . . . like, shown up at your place in a leopard thong and asked you to do me from behind, your opinion of me would have changed." I'd wanted, more than anything in the world, to have him love me. I'd never have done anything to jeopardize that love and I'd believed that, in order to keep it, I had to be the sweet girl he'd first fallen for.

His hand had jerked to a halt on my leg. "Shit," he growled. "You just gave me an instant hard-on, saying that."

"I did?"

"Jesus, yeah."

"Wow. That's cool. But I don't want you to think of me as a slut, I want you to respect me."

He groaned. "I respected you for fourteen years. You think I'd lose that respect if you'd gone crazy in bed?"

I nodded. "Yeah, maybe. Be honest, Matt. That time, the one we both promised we'd forget, when you, uh, spanked me—" Just remembering made me hot.

He groaned again. "I never, ever meant to hurt you. When I heard you cry out, I was so ashamed."

Was that why he'd seemed so shocked? Even though it was embarrassing, I had to confess. "You didn't hurt me," I whispered. "Well, you did, a little, but when I cried out, it wasn't just pain. I was t-turned on."

His jaw dropped. "You were?"

I wrapped my arms across my chest. "You see, you're shocked. Sweet Merilee shouldn't be turned on by being spanked. If I'd told you, your opinion of me would have changed."

Slowly, he said, "It might have. You're right. It doesn't fit the image I've always had of you."

"I know."

His fingers started making those slow, sensual circles on my lower thigh again, sending pulses of awareness tingling up my leg to my sex.

"But now, we're not the same people," he said. "Not the M&M who got engaged. We can see ourselves and each other differently."

"You're right. That's what we've been doing today, isn't it?"

"And last night, wearing those costumes."

He gazed at me steadily, his eyes dark in the diffuse light. "So let's try seeing each other differently when it comes to sex. Let's ditch some of the hang-ups and start fresh. Today, I met a girl named Merilee and asked her on a date. She's pretty and sexy and she turns me on."

I did? I liked that. I also liked that he was suggesting we return to the role play. "The feeling's mutual," I told him. "This guy I met today is pretty hot."

He leaned toward me and I met his lips eagerly. The kiss went deep and hard, fast, until we finally broke apart, panting for breath.

He grabbed my hand and pulled it toward him, then stopped, holding it in mid-air. "I want to put your hand on my dick."

In public? I took a breath. People were strolling by behind us, but we had our backs to them. "I'd like to touch your . . . dick." I'd probably never said that word before. Normally, I avoided using any term for his penis. *Dick* was so raw, so sexy. I liked saying it. Deliberately, I pulled our joined hands down so my palm and fingers curved around the bulge in his shorts.

He jerked. And when I firmed my grip and stroked him, he groaned. "That feels so good."

"For me, too." My nipples were hard again and my sex pulsed with a sweet ache. Being a little daring was arousing. "I wish . . ." I swallowed, pushing myself further out of my comfort zone. "I wish I could go down on you right here, right now."

He jerked again. "Jesus, don't say that. You'll make me come."

"Just with words?"

"No, with imagining it. You bent over me, your lips closing around—No, I can't even think it or I'll explode." He grabbed my hand and pulled it away, breathing hard.

The sense of sexual power that filled me was new. Being naughty was fun. "I have a cabin on the *Diamond Star*," I said, continuing to pretend we'd just met. "We'll open the window to let in the night air and you can sit on the edge of the bed. I'll kneel in front of you and unzip your shorts and—"

He leaped to his feet, grabbed my hand, and pulled me up. "Oh, yeah. Let's go."

Fortunately, there were lots of taxis on the street, and one whipped us back to the cruise ship terminal. We weren't the only ones arriving at the last minute. Passengers laughed and called out to each other, some unsteady on their feet, clearly having hit the tequila pretty hard. We rushed past them. My heart raced with excitement, with nerves, and I had trouble catching my breath. I tried hard to hang on to the role play, to force away any doubts about my own sexuality. I'd promised him a blow job, and I'd deliver.

Matt hurried me down the narrow corridor to our room, holding my hand tightly. Inside, he dropped his shopping bags, tossed mine aside, then backed me against the door. Caging me in with his hands on either side of my shoulders, he kissed me.

He took my mouth hungrily, without finesse, as if he couldn't get enough of me. Matt, yet not Matt, the same as when he'd played pirate. His tongue plunged between my lips, making me gasp, and as he thrust in and out, sexual heat flooded through me.

I moaned, kissing him back, throwing my arms around him. I went up on my toes, pressing the front of my body against his and rocking my hips so the ridge of his erection ground against the needy ache between my legs. Normally, I was slow to arouse, but tonight foreplay was the last thing on my mind. The urgency of his kiss, the jerky way he thrust against me, told me he felt the same.

I almost never initiated sex. But tonight I was the new Merilee, so I reached between us to undo his shorts. As I did, he slid the zipper of my dress down my back. By the time I'd freed his dick and wrapped my hand around it, my dress was sliding off my shoulders, to be trapped between us.

He pulled away, hurriedly stripping off his clothes. I stepped out of my dress and tossed it on a chair, then turned, wearing only brief pink panties.

He was naked, fully aroused, every muscle in his body taut. "Off," he said, hooking one hand in the side of my panties and yanking them down my hips.

I'd barely stepped out of them when he caught me in his arms, lifting me easily. He carried me the few short steps to my bed and, rather than placing me down gently, almost tossed me onto it. Then he surged down on top of me, his chest crushing my breasts, his legs spreading mine, his erection pressing painfully against my pelvic bone. If he really had been a stranger, I'd have felt intimidated. But underneath the role play I knew this was Matt and he'd never hurt me. His unusual forcefulness, reminding me of the pirate, was a turn-on.

My sex swelled and moistened, ready for him when he reached down to part my folds.

A moment later, he plunged in hard and fast, filling me, shocking me, but in a good way.

When I gasped, he paused. "You okay?"

"Mmm-hmm." I'd never been vocal during sex. Nor had Matt.

He surprised me again, saying, "Wrap your legs around me," as he wormed his arms under my body.

"What?" Automatically, I did as he said.

Somehow, he maneuvered our bodies on the small bed, and seconds later he was on bottom, with me astride him.

"Ride me," he grated out. We hadn't turned on the lights, but nor had we pulled the curtains. Light from the ship terminal filtered in and I could see the flush across his cheeks, the brilliance of his blue eyes.

"I . . ." I liked being on bottom. It was safe there. I didn't feel self-conscious, didn't have to decide what to do next. I could leave everything to him. Now he was changing things, demanding I stop being the shy good girl and become the new Merilee.

His big hands caught my hips, holding firmly. "You're beautiful, Merilee."

I heard honesty in his voice and saw it on his face. It gave me courage. Tentatively, I began to ride his shaft, lifting up a little, then coming down. As I found my balance, I set a slow rhythm that sent quivers of arousal rippling through me.

There was an advantage to this position. I could see him. Not just his face, but his lean, muscled torso, the sprinkling of dark gold curls on his chest, the gleam of sweat on his skin. He really was pretty spectacular, and sexy. His intent gaze told me I was, too.

I ran a hand through my new hair—my sassy hair—and arched my back so my breasts thrust out. My body tingled inside from the delicious pressure, the wet, hot slip-slide.

My nipples were tight and achy. Daringly, I ran a hand down my neck, across my upper chest, and to my breast. When I took my nipple between my thumb and finger, he groaned and his hips jerked.

I'd been controlling the pace, but now he took over, hips pumping hard and fast. One hand still held my hip, but the other reached down to where our bodies joined and his thumb brushed my clit, making me gasp with pleasure.

He rubbed gently, the motion intensifying every sexual sensation that rippled through me.

Pressure built inside me as orgasm gathered, fueled by so many sensations. His dick thrust into my core, his thumb circled and pressed relentlessly, his breath rasped and his chest heaved. The nipple I squeezed tingled with something on the border of pleasure and pain. A ripe, primal scent filled the air and my thighs were damp with my juices.

Messy sex, vigorous sex. Not good-girl sex.

Everything came together, and I cried out as an amazing climax rocked through me. Moments later my body rocked again as he jerked hard in his own orgasm.

For long minutes, neither of us spoke, bodies heaving as we caught our breath.

Muscles turning to jelly, I slid down to lie atop him. "Wow," I breathed.

"Oh, yeah. *That* was very hot."

What did it mean, though? We'd broken up and were pretending to be strangers, but we'd had, quite possibly, the best sex of our entire relationship. The best *sex*. Not tender lovemaking. I missed the deep, certain emotional connection we'd always shared. But how could it be there for us when neither of us knew where our relationship was headed?

For fourteen years, my life had been all about certainty, and now it was all about confusion.

Needing a couple of minutes' privacy, I unstuck my sweaty body from his to head for the bathroom. Glancing out the window, I said, "The ship's underway." In the morning, we'd be in Mazatlan.

In the bathroom, I splashed cold water on my face. Already, the cruise was half over. Matt and I had come a long way, but not far enough to decide anything. Should we talk? Feeling indecisive, I opened the bathroom door.

He didn't notice. He'd pushed the beds together, not asking me if it was okay, and I liked his new decisiveness. As I watched, he smoothed one of the top sheets to cover both single beds, then did the same with the light bedspread. He moved easily, unself-conscious in his nakedness, fit and gorgeous. How had I taken this body, this man, for granted? Now, just watching him made my breath quicken and a pulse throb in my sex.

I took a deep breath. No, this wasn't the time for more talk, or for worrying about what this meant. I'd take a page from my sister Jenna's book, and go with the flow. She'd talked about open doors, so I shoved the bathroom door wider and said, "Shower, anyone?"

He looked up with a pleased smile. "Can't resist that offer."

When he joined me, I reached behind the shower curtain to get the water running. Getting back into the role play, I said, "I hope you're flattered. You're the first guy I've invited into the shower."

"Very flattered. And you're my first, too. Except in fantasies."

Adjusting the water temperature, I glanced over my shoulder. "Fantasies? Care to share?"

"Well, there's one where a girl—one who looks exactly like you, in fact—is in the shower alone. Under the spray, facing the taps."

He had sexual fantasies about me. Excited and a little nervous, I slipped behind the shower curtain and stood in the spray. Water sluiced through my hair, then down over my breasts, stimulating my sensitive nipples. It streamed over my belly, then in a sensual caress between my legs, rinsing away the stickiness.

I closed my eyes and lifted my face to the spray, and heard the shower curtain slide along the rail.

"You don't know I'm here until I touch you," he said. His hands came down on my shoulders, making me jump. "So at first you're startled."

"Or scared to death," I said, nervous again, "if you're striving for realism." I wasn't ready to be tied up or spanked; I'd need a lot more alcohol to get over those inhibitions.

"Fantasy, remember? Then you turn and see that it's me."

Reassured, I turned toward him and faked surprise. "Matt, it's you. I'm glad you're here." It was hard to imagine a girl who wouldn't be thrilled to have this hot young guy join her in the shower.

He stepped closer until the spray, coming over my shoulders, pelted his chest and shoulders. Then he put his arms around me to cup my butt-cheeks in both hands, tipped his head down, and kissed me, taking his time about it. The kiss was as steamy as the hot, moist air curling around us, and a slow burn crept through my body, building toward ignition.

His hands slid up and down my back possessively under the hard, hot spray of water. He caressed, massaged, fondled, owning my body and stroking sensation deep into me with each touch. Arousal tingled and throbbed through me, tightening my nipples and swelling my sex.

He had kissed me so many times before. Why, now, did his kisses seem different? Was it just because of the role play?

I realized the answer. Before, he'd treated me like the girl he'd grown up with. Now, he was treating me like a woman. And I was responding like one, with a sexuality I'd never known was in me. In the last couple of days, we'd stopped being kids and become woman and man, and the game we were playing tonight allowed us to express that.

His swollen dick pressed against my belly and I wriggled

sensuously against it, craving more. Craving him inside me. But not yet. Inspiration struck. Whatever his shower fantasy might be, maybe I could top it. I eased my mouth from his, then put my hands on his shoulders and shifted our positions so that now he had his back to the spray. "Close your eyes," I said, and he obeyed.

I reached for the soap, choosing his bar of sandalwood rather than the herbal, cruise lines one. "It's a shower. We're supposed to get clean." I lathered both hands, releasing that spicy, exotic scent into the humid air, then caught his shaft between my palms.

He sucked in air in a startled gasp, and opened his eyes. "Oh, yeah. Nice."

I slid my slippery hands up and down, twining them around him, teasing every inch of him, circling under and around the silky crown. Feeling him like this in my hands made my sex quiver, wanting his hardness there.

He braced himself with a hand against the shower wall, and we both stared down, watching as I lathered him with suds, pumped, caressed.

"Shit, that's good, Merilee."

I tightened my grip, guessing that any minute now he'd stop me. The old Matt always did when he got close to coming. He said it was selfish of him to climax alone. This time, when he gasped, "Okay, enough, you gotta stop," I obeyed.

But only to sink down on the hard floor of the tub. Time to make my promise come true. I captured his dick again, made sure it was rinsed free of soap, then closed my lips over the head and took as much of him into my mouth as I could.

His fingers wove through my hair. Panting for breath, he said, "You don't have to."

"I want to." And I did. His flesh was hot, hard, and smooth, smelling of soap and spice. In the steamy shower, I could almost imagine we were in a tropical jungle under a waterfall. I ran my tongue over him tentatively, then more firmly when he gave an approving moan.

Before, when I'd tried this, he'd almost choked me, perhaps because I was inexperienced and he was over-eager. Now he held still as I explored with lips and tongue, my wet fingers stroking the base of his shaft and curving over his firm balls. This intimate touch thickened my own blood with arousal.

Despite the steady thrum of the shower, I heard him panting for breath. "I won't come," he said raggedly. His fingers were warm against my scalp under my wet hair, but they never tried to guide my head, so I didn't feel trapped.

I could stop now, and we'd go to bed and make love. My needy body would have what it wanted. But this was good, too. I liked it and I wanted to take him all the way. I slid my mouth free of him. "I'm gonna make you come." Then I sucked him back in.

He drew a shuddering breath and began to thrust, just a little. He never forced himself deep into my throat, just slid back and forth against my fingers and the suction of my lips. I clenched my thighs together as my sex pulsed, imagining him thrusting inside me.

He pumped a little faster and I firmed my grip on his shaft and ran my tongue around the head of his dick.

Then he groaned, "God, Merilee," jerked, and flooded my mouth with hot liquid. Automatically, I swallowed. His come was thicker and saltier than the water of the shower, but not at all unpleasant.

He groaned again, then eased free of my mouth and slumped down to kneel in front of me on the floor of the tub. "Wow. Now that was a fantasy." Both of us kneeling, he kissed me gently, brushing his tongue inside my mouth, no doubt tasting himself. "Thank you."

"You're welcome."

"How was it for you?"

"Good. Really good, Matt. So different than before."

Using the soap holder for leverage, he pulled himself to his feet, then held out a hand and helped me up, too. He kept his back to the shower spray, sheltering me from it. Our gazes held, his blue eyes so familiar. We could pretend we were on a first date, but never could I have felt so safe with a stranger. And yet, oddly, I might never have been so uninhibited without that pretense. Strange . . .

The thought drifted away as he tipped his head and kissed me again. Then he said, "Now it's my turn to wash you. I think I'll start with . . ."

"Let me guess." My sex throbbed at the idea.

"Your hair." He picked up the small bottle of cruise ship shampoo and poured some into his palm.

"My hair?"

"Call me kinky, but I've fantasized about shampooing your hair."

"You do have some strange fantasies."

But when his soapy fingers slid into my hair to caress and massage my scalp, I sighed with pleasure. It was sensual more than sexy, but it sure felt wonderful. A minty scent rose in the air and my scalp tingled. He tipped my head carefully back to rinse, guiding the water so it didn't run down my face.

When he poured more shampoo into his hand, I said, "My hair's not exactly dirty."

"Different hair this time."

And his hand went straight to the vee between my legs.

Chapter 12

If this was a sex dream, Matt hoped it'd go on forever. This Merilee was amazing—uninhibited and erotic like the old one had never been. Always before, with her, he'd felt like a boy, one who'd grown up beside her and never quite turned into a man. Tonight, he definitely felt like a man.

When his fingers smoothed soap into the curls of her pubic hair, he touched her with firm pressure, not tentatively. Earlier, she'd said maybe she had a low sex drive, but that sure wasn't true now. This Merilee was a woman, no longer a girl who was nervous about her sexuality.

He slid his fingers through the curls as he'd done on her head, caressing the tender skin beneath and gently massaging her mound. When he slipped his hand between her legs, she gave a soft gasp, then gripped his shoulders and widened her stance to give him better access.

He toyed with the soft, slightly swollen folds of skin and flirted a soapy finger across her clit, then away again. Warm water swirled the soap away. He eased a finger inside her, then another, and felt the welcoming grip of her steamy hot channel.

"Mmm," she murmured, "mmm-hmm."

Good sounds, sensual sounds of pleasure, even better than

the ones she'd made eating those nachos. Even though he'd had two potent orgasms in the last fifteen minutes, arousal stirred in him again. He pumped his fingers in and out, swirling them a little.

She squeezed around him, her breath coming in little pants now. Her fingers dug into his shoulders and her eyes were closed, like she was focused on the sensations inside her body. Normally, it took a long time to arouse her, but tonight was different.

Before, she'd been so shy that he'd never felt free to explore the way he wanted to, and now he loved getting to know her beautiful body, and loved her responsiveness. He teased her clit with his thumb and she shuddered.

He really wished she'd be more vocal. "Feel good?" he asked, needing to be sure he wasn't hurting her.

"Oh, yeah," she said on a breathy exhale.

So he did it again, and again, and now she whimpered. What did a whimper mean?

His uncertainty reminded him of how badly he'd misread her signals the night he'd gotten drunk and carried away, and spanked her. When she'd cried out, he thought it was pain and protest. Instead, it had been arousal. If he'd known that, what might have happened between them?

The blood in his dick surged at the thought. No, he definitely didn't want to hurt her, but it would be exciting to find out how far they each wanted to go. He knew it was a lot further than he'd ever imagined.

Still pumping his fingers in and out of her pussy, he stroked her clit again, circling it, rubbing.

She cried out, high and uncontrolled, a cry that resonated in his own core and tightened his balls.

Her body rocked, spasming against his fingers as she came. Her fingers bit into his shoulders and he guessed her legs had grown weak and she was using his strength to keep her on her feet.

Her legs might be weak, but he was rock hard with urgency. He couldn't get enough of this woman.

When she'd stopped quivering, he eased his fingers out of her, but kept his hand pressed gently against her for a long moment, just holding her. Then he turned to shut off the shower.

He hadn't realized how noisy the water had been until the sound was gone.

She looked up at him, her wet face rosy, her expression a little stunned. "Wow."

Abandoning the first date game, he said, "We should have done this long ago."

Her brow furrowed. "I'm sorry if—"

"No." He pressed a finger to her lips. "I held back, too. Maybe neither of us was ready." There was something else he wanted to do, something she'd always been shy about. He sensed this was the right time.

He slid back the shower curtain, grabbed a towel, and rubbed it lightly over her shoulders.

"Give that to me." She took it and began to towel her hair.

He dried himself quickly, tossed the damp towel over the shower rail, and watched as she finished her own more thorough process by putting her feet, one by one, on the edge of the tub. A good girl, drying between her toes. A sexy woman, her curvy butt sticking out as she bent down. Oh, yeah, he wanted to make love to her that way, too.

When she was done, he took her towel, tossed it haphazardly over the rail, then hoisted her up in his arms. This time, she didn't squeak, just purred, "I could get used to this."

He laid her down on one of the now-joined beds, and she stretched luxuriously. "My body feels like it's humming with pleasure." She shot a glance at his erection. "I hope you're going to make good use of that."

"That's the plan." He lay beside her and kissed her softly. "But first . . ." He kissed her again, but when she curled toward him and tried to put an arm around him, he slipped away.

He eased lower down the bed and caressed her breasts, so round and soft and perfect. The areolas were a delicate pink and the nipples, which budded under his touch, a deeper rose. When he sucked a nipple into his mouth, she caught her breath. He increased the suction and swirled his tongue around the little bud, and the rise and fall of her chest quickened.

He moved to her other breast, then trailed kisses down the center of her body. When he reached the delicate nest of curls, her legs pressed together, stopping him from going farther.

She always resisted this. The few times she'd given in, her body had been so tense he knew it hadn't been good for her. Tonight, with her muscles and her inhibitions relaxed from the shower and two orgasms, he wanted to pleasure her. "Let me taste you, sweetheart." He trailed his tongue along the crease at the top of one thigh and pressed soft kisses into the tender inner flesh of her thigh.

Her legs eased apart a little, and he slid his tongue between them to find the engorged bud of her clit.

She gave a soft, breathy gasp.

Yes, she was aroused, even if she still felt shy about doing this. He teased her clit until she gasped again, twisted to evade his insistent tongue, but finally spread her legs. The cabin was dark now, the only light coming from a glimmer of moonlight out the window. He longed to turn on the bedside lamp but feared it would rouse her inhibitions.

Instead, he explored by touch, by taste, by scent. She was moist and lush, sweet and spicy, feminine and mysterious. He read her response in the dew that slipped from her body, the tiny sighs and gasps, the restless squirm of her hips.

His aching dick urged him to plunge deep into her, but instead he eased two fingers into her as he'd done in the shower, and swirled, and sucked her clit.

Merilee's head thrashed on the pillow and her hips tilted to give him better access. Her body was taut with a tension that, this time, he knew for sure was the right kind. He strummed her bud again and she cried out, "Matt!" and her body surged in climax.

When the spasms began to fade, he couldn't hold back any longer. He moved between her spread legs and thrust hard into her still quivering core.

Her internal ripples undid him, and he pumped fast, surging quickly to climax.

Then, exhausted, he collapsed on top of her. He barely had the energy to roll, taking her with him so they were both on their sides.

Her eyes were closed, her face relaxed in the dim light. "Mmm," she murmured, the sound like the purr of a drowsy, contented cat. "Very nice."

A deep sense of tenderness and love filled him. He'd always loved her. They'd been kids together, then adolescents, then teens. Tonight, they were man and woman. Not engaged, not even officially boyfriend and girlfriend. Lovers, taking the first step toward the future.

He shouldn't get ahead of himself. They still had lots to learn, individually and together. Merilee had called off their wedding, and she'd been right. Before he thought about getting serious again—being vulnerable again—he needed to know things had really changed and that they were both completely sure.

But tonight gave him hope that, somewhere down the road, they really might have a future.

I drifted up from the depths of sleep, aware of something warm and bright on my face. I blinked, then slammed my eyes shut again and moved my head out of a slanting ray of sunshine. Then, more slowly, I again opened my eyes.

Matt lay beside me, sleeping the way he always did, flat

on his back with his limbs spread out. As I'd done so many times before, I moved over to cuddle against him, my head on his warm, firm shoulder. Even in his sleep, his arm came around me, holding me close.

So much for two separate beds. They'd served their purpose, and now . . . Hmm. Where did we go from here?

He stirred, turned his head, opened his eyes, and smiled. "Hey, you. Did I just have the best fantasy ever, or was that for real?"

"I have no idea what you're talking about," I teased.

"I could show you," he offered, a twinkle in his blue eyes. "A shower was involved, and—" He broke off, a startled expression on his face.

"What?"

"We didn't use birth control."

"Oh! I never thought . . ." I'd been on the pill for years, but had gone off last month. Our desire to have kids was one of the reasons we'd moved up the wedding. When the doctor had said I'd likely have trouble conceiving, we figured it was better to start trying right away. But now . . .

"Me either." He sat up in bed and ran a hand through his tousled hair. "But I guess we do need to think about it. I should buy some condoms."

I settled back against my pillow. "I suppose." We hadn't used condoms since we were sixteen and I'd gone on the pill. "The odds are really slim"—I'd be lucky if I ever, in my life, managed to get pregnant—"but all the same . . ."

"After what we've gone through in the last week, this sure isn't the right time. If we do decide we have a future together, it needs to be a real decision. Not something that's forced on us."

He was totally right, so why did it feel like a rejection? Of me, of a child we'd create together, of the future we'd once planned? "No, it shouldn't."

"Which means no intercourse this morning." He slid

down again and pulled me close so I felt his erection against my thigh. He kinked an eyebrow. "But after last night, we both know there are other ways of making love." A big hand cupped my butt and squeezed.

Had that really been us, last night? Now I felt inhibited again and unsure of where we should go from here. We were us, in the bright light of day. Not the pirate and the flapper; not the couple who'd pretended to be on a first date last night. I shook my head and pulled slightly away. "I want a shower and breakfast before going ashore."

"Aw, come on, sweetheart. We'll make it a quickie."

"I'm not in the mood for a quickie."

He gave a resigned sigh. "Can't blame a guy for trying. Okay, I'll pick up condoms today." He winked. "Just in case you're in the mood later."

He said it like it was a sure thing. But for me to get in the mood, I'd need . . . something from Matt. Passion? Sexiness? Another game I could opt into? Or some assurance he really loved me and was thinking about the future, too? Right now, I didn't even know.

I didn't know anything. Hesitantly, I asked, "What were you thinking of doing today? Should we spend time together or keep working on our independence?" Usually, I'd been the one who picked our activities, but that was part of the old pattern we needed to break.

"Figured I'd go scuba diving."

"What? You don't dive." Nor was he waiting for me to make the decisions, which was great, except it made me feel kind of shut out.

"A lesson's included. At first I figured on going snorkeling because it'd be really cool to see tropical fish. Then I thought, why not take this one-hour lesson and I can go deeper, see more." His face shone with excitement and it seemed he'd forgotten all about morning sex.

I was a little miffed, but mostly concerned. "A one-hour course? Is that safe?"

"Guess I'll find out."

When I frowned, he said, "Come on, Merilee, they run these lessons every day. It has to be safe or they couldn't do it."

"I guess." And if it wasn't, he'd pull out. Matt was a responsible guy. I nodded. "Yeah, you're right. I bet you'll be great at it, and you'll have a blast."

"Thanks. I'm kind of stoked."

More stoked about diving than about spending the day with me.

"How about you?" he asked. "What do you figure on doing?"

Obviously not dating a "stranger." But no, I told myself, this was good. Doing things separately, things we each enjoyed. Matt having an opinion of his own and being decisive. "I'll take the city tour," I told him. "Mazatlan's so big; there's so much to see. An Old Town, a huge market like a bigger version of the one in Puerto Vallarta, the tourist zone, and I definitely want to walk on the beach."

"Cool." He swung out of bed and headed for the bathroom. "I'll be out in three minutes, then it's all yours." The door closed and a moment later, I heard the shower start.

If I'd been last night's Merilee, I'd have surprised him in there. But I wasn't, and he wasn't last night's Matt. Great sex definitely didn't solve all our problems.

I rose and pulled on a long T-shirt, then went to the window and peered out at the sunny ocean. Soon we'd be in Mazatlan and I'd have a day to explore. It would be fun; I'd live in the moment, enjoy myself, and not worry about me and Matt.

When he came out of the bathroom, looking sexy with his freshly combed hair and a towel wrapped around his waist, I ignored the temptation and hurried past him to get ready.

His words followed me. "I'll be gone by the time you get out, so have a great day."

"You, too." An insecure part of me wondered if Mandy was going diving.

"How about getting together for dinner later? We can share our adventures."

I swung around, relief and pleasure making me smile. "I'd like that." And because we were going our separate ways, we'd have lots to share.

In the shower, of course, I remembered everything Matt and I had done there. He was buying condoms. He expected we'd have sex again, but he wasn't ready to have a baby with me. So we were . . . what? Dating?

Well, that was up to me just as much as to him.

I came out of the bathroom to find Matt gone. I should dress and get ready to go ashore. To be independent.

Independent. Right now I just felt lonely. Always before, I'd had someone to talk to when I had a problem. It had rarely been my family or my girlfriends; it had been Matt. Now, Matt *was* the problem. Or I was. Or the two of us were.

I glanced at my cell on the desk, a connection to the world back home. In the last two weeks, my family had grown closer. Even since we'd all gone our separate ways on Sunday, there'd been voice mails and texts flying back and forth. Short messages asking how everyone was; little updates on what was going on in everyone's life. Support for Jenna, now that she'd told us about her infertility.

In the past years, a month could go by without my sisters and I being in touch, or my mom and I talking about anything of significance, even though we lived in the same house. Now we were connected in a new way, and I sure hoped it would continue.

I'd talked to Jenna and Kat since I'd boarded the *Diamond Star*, and now I felt an urge to hear my oldest sister's voice and get her perspective. Theresa was in Manhattan with Damien on his book tour. I dialed, fearing I'd get voice mail, but she answered. "Merilee? How are you? Is everything okay?"

"I'm fine. Can you talk?"

"I can. Damien's a guest on a radio talk show and I'm walking around Manhattan playing tourist. What's up?"

I plunked down in a chair to get comfy. "I'm confused. So I thought I'd ask my big sister, because you're always, uh, decisive." Actually, she tended to be a know-it-all, but right now that was okay. If she had a magic answer, I'd be grateful.

"Tell me what's going on."

I filled her in on what Matt and I had been doing, right up to this morning and the condom discussion. "I don't know where things stand. I don't know what I want."

She let out a low whistle. "And I thought Damien and I had a wild ride. That's a lot to think about." She paused. "This is pretty new for you, isn't it? I mean, you've never really analyzed your relationship before. It was just *there*."

"I haven't analyzed *anything* before. I've just tried to be the good girl."

"And you are. Up until calling off the wedding, which I know you had to do, you've never caused anyone a bit of trouble."

I slumped back in my chair. "For all the good it did me."

"Excuse me?"

Outside the window, I saw that we were docking. It would've been fun to watch from out on deck, but right now I'd rather talk to my sister. "I was the afterthought kid. Not planned, not wanted, so—"

"Of course, you were wanted," she said crisply. "Mom and Dad wouldn't have had you if they didn't want you. Same with me. Yes, we were unplanned, but they didn't have an abortion."

"Okay, you're right. But I came along eight years after

Jenna, and the family was a unit. Mom and Dad and the three-pack. And you three all had your *things*, you know? Like you being the brainiac, and Kat the sociable one, and Jenna the free spirit who loved butterflies and hated rules."

"That's true. But what are you saying?"

I rubbed my forehead, remembering what it had been like. "There wasn't a place for me. Half the time, it was like no one even noticed I was there. I thought that if I was really, really good, if I was sweet and nice all the time, I'd be . . . accepted into the family. L-loved." My voice quavered.

"Of course, you were loved."

"I know. I do know that." At least I sort of did. "But I never really felt seen. Then I met Matt, and it was the first time I felt like someone saw *me* and liked *me*."

She didn't say anything for a moment, and when she spoke, she sounded unusually subdued. "I'm sorry, Merilee. I never realized all this and I'm sorry the family wasn't there for you. But when you and Matt became friends, you were so bonded. I guess . . ." She paused for a long moment. "You being with Matt, it made it even easier to assume everything was okay with you."

"And it was. But . . ." What was I trying to say? I nibbled the edge of one red fingernail. As a kid, I'd chewed my fingernails until Matt got me to stop.

"But you based your identity on being Matt's soul mate. We never encouraged you to find out who you were, what you liked, what you wanted. I'm sorry about that. But it's not too late. You're doing that now. I'm glad you had the sense to realize all of this, when the rest of us were blind to it."

"Me, too, but it's hard."

"It's really good, what you and Matt are doing. Getting in touch with who you are as individuals. And realize, too, that you're going to keep changing."

"How do you mean?"

"Life's about change. If you get too fixed in a rut—like

you did with Matt and I did with my job—it's not good. You need to be flexible and open."

I rose and paced across the small cabin. "But if we keep changing, then how can you know that anything's going to last? That you're going to"—I glanced at the rumpled bed— "love the same person?"

She laughed softly. "Hey, M, I'm new to this myself. I'm grappling with the same things you are. Like, how do I know if Damien and I will be forever?"

"Well?" It was so weird to think of my brilliant, successful older sister going through the same uncertainties as me.

I heard her take a breath. Then she said, "I think we will. We share the same values and we trust and respect each other. We have a deep emotional connection, great sex, and we're both strong but also flexible. We learn from each other and from the world around us." She was sounding lecture-ish again, obviously hitting her stride. "We'll keep growing and changing, and I think we can do that together rather than having it separate us. Merilee, it's trying new things, learning new things, that keeps life—and us—fresh and interesting."

I smiled. She did have the magic answer, and she'd provided it without being too obnoxiously know-it-all. "You may say you're grappling, but it sounds to me like you've figured it all out. I'm happy for you, Theresa." And envious.

She gave a soft laugh. "Me, too. And it's all because of you. Same with Kat and Jenna."

"You've lost me." And I was tired. The weariness that had been dogging me since my surgery had returned, so I moved from the chair to the bed and stretched out.

"You weren't there Saturday night when Jenna's guy Mark was talking about chaos theory."

"Chaos theory?" I grinned, imagining Jenna's hot scientist going into lecture mode. He could be even more professorial than Theresa, but the cute thing was that Jenna found it sexy.

"Chaos theory is the idea that a tiny change in one part of a system can cause huge and unpredictable consequences in another part. Like if a butterfly flutters its wings in Brazil, it can cause a tornado in Texas."

"Oh, yeah, I've heard that. But what's that got to do with anything?" Was my brain just really tired, or was my sister not making sense?

"According to Mark, you're the butterfly. Your wing-flutter was announcing your wedding. That sent the three-pack home from various parts of the world, and along the way our paths intersected with those of three men who broke us out of our ruts and—"

"You all fell in love." I remembered how I'd thought that I had passed my luck in love along to them. "You girls owe me big-time."

"We do. But that wedding announcement broke you and Matt out of your rut, too. When suddenly the actual day was there—"

"Yes," I interrupted, "it put things in sharp focus. Seeing you and Kat and Jenna come home, your excitement and passion, it kind of shone a light on my relationship with Matt and made me realize something was missing." That was what I'd told Matt when I'd called off the wedding.

"Theresa, thanks," I said. "I should go now. There's a shore excursion in Mazatlan." My body was urging me to curl up and pull the covers over me, but no way would I miss the opportunity to see Mexico.

"Me in Manhattan and you in Mazatlan. Jenna off in Indonesia and Kat in Montreal being a married lady. Big happenings in all our lives."

For the first time, I actually felt like one of the gang. No longer the baby sister at home, now I was a world traveler, too. An adult. An equal. And because of me, they'd all found love.

Had I shared my luck in love with them, or had I given it away?

Chapter 13

In the early afternoon, I slumped gratefully in a chair at a restaurant in Mazatlan's Old Town, across from Des and her grandmother Micky. "This is good," I said, "this is very good." I'd been on my feet all morning, wandering the huge block of market stalls at the *mercado*, visiting a cathedral and park, then exploring Old Town with its picturesque streets, galleries, and shops, and ending with a glimpse inside the Angela Peralta Theatre. Mazatlan was so big and foreign, impressive but overwhelming. Though I'd loved every moment, I was beat.

"A margarita will make it even better," Micky said, slipping her feet out of sturdy sandals and wriggling her toes. Despite being a little gnarled, they were painted with hot pink polish to match her T-shirt.

We were at an outdoor table at one of the half dozen or so restaurants along the sides of a large, attractive square called *Plaza Machado*. A patio umbrella provided shade, and we'd heaped the spare chair with the bags we'd collected at the *mercado*. Incongruously, the music coming out the open doors and windows was sixties, seventies, and eighties pop. The kind of music my mom used to play in the kitchen when we were kids. When I was tiny, we all used to dance to it. I'd almost forgotten. There had been good times, times I'd felt included.

Right now, I was happy that Des and Micky had included me in their lunch plans. Though we'd been on the same sightseeing excursion, I'd wandered around on my own, choosing the things I wanted to see. But now, tired and hungry, it was good to be with my new friends rather than join one of the other groups of passengers who clustered around tables at half a dozen other sidewalk restaurants.

When a Mexican waiter asked what we'd like to drink, Micky promptly said, "A margarita. You girls, too?"

"Definitely," Des said.

If I drank alcohol, I'd put my head on the table and go to sleep right now. "Yes, but make mine a virgin. And I need food." I'd missed breakfast because of my phone call with Theresa, and though I'd snacked on a pastry at the *mercado*, that was ages ago.

I studied the menu and decided on a spicy shrimp dish. Des ordered the same thing and Micky went with a local fish specialty. Then we all sat back with our drinks.

"We were surprised to see you alone today," Des said. "What happened to that hottie from yesterday?"

"What?"

Micky grinned knowingly. "Didn't think you saw us. You two were all wrapped up in each other, laughing and trying on sunglasses."

"Spill." Des leaned forward with her elbows on the table. "Who is he? And where is he today?"

"He's . . ." How to explain my relationship with Matt, when the two of us didn't even understand it? So far, all I'd told my new friends was that I wasn't currently in a relationship, which was technically true.

"And is he as hot as he looks?" Micky asked with relish. "He reminds me of a boy I dated back when I was in college. Ve-ry se-xy." She drew the syllables out.

He was. Even though it had taken me until this cruise to see it.

"That's for sure," Des said. "And, by the way, if you're finished with him, mind if I have a shot at him?" She made an exaggerated pleading face. "Pretty please?"

"Stand in line, girl," Micky joked.

"You two kill me." Often, they were more like sisters than grandmother and granddaughter. I wished I was the girl they thought I was, having a hot fling with a sexy stranger, rather than boring old Merilee trying to figure out what I was doing with my life.

Well, of course, last night Matt and I had pretended we were strangers on a first date. An urge to continue the naughtiness caught me up. "I'm not finished with him. He's scuba diving today."

"He's a diver? Very cool," Des said.

Rather than tell them he was just taking his first lesson, I said, "It is, isn't it? Bet he's terrific in the water." I knew he was. "He's so fit and agile."

"Ooh, agile's good," Des said. "Just how *agile* is he, Merilee? Did you check out his horizontal moves?"

Memories flooded me: the heated urgency of his kiss when he caged me against the door, the way he tossed me onto the bed and plunged into me hard and fast. . . . A wicked grin took over my lips and words popped out. "Not until I'd checked out his vertical ones. Against the door, then in the shower." Then I clapped my hand over my mouth, appalled, feeling color flood my face and chest. Mortified, I stared at Des's silver-haired granny. "Ack! Micky, I'm sorry, that was—"

"Old doesn't mean dead," she cut in sharply. "I've still got some pretty good moves of my own, young lady. Don't insult me by treating me like I'm over the hill."

"Uh, okay, if you're sure." My own gran, before the

Alzheimer's, had been smart and willing to discuss almost anything, but we'd sure never talked about her sex life. "Anyhow, his name's Matt and he's the pirate from the costume ball."

Des snapped her fingers. "Of course, he is. I should have known, the way you two were dancing together. Merilee, you totally surprise me. When I first saw you, you looked kind of, you know, wholesome. Not like you'd be into a shipboard fling with a total stranger."

She was exactly right. "I'm exploring my wild side."

Micky studied me over the rim of her margarita glass, her faded blue eyes serious for once. "You're being careful, right?"

Okay, so we hadn't used condoms, but STDs weren't an issue and my chances of getting pregnant were really low. Avoiding a direct answer, I said, "I may only be twenty-one but don't insult me by treating me like I'm a baby."

She made a pistol of her hand and fired at me. "Good one. Okay, we're both hot babes who know how to look out for ourselves."

"You're getting together with him later?" Des asked.

"For dinner."

"You've got yourself a real shipboard romance," Micky said with gusto.

"I guess so." I hadn't told any actual lies, but I was starting to feel bad about deceiving them. I made a pathetic bad girl.

"What about after?" Micky asked as our lunches arrived.

I cut a plump shrimp in half, popped it in my mouth, then took a hasty sip of my virgin margarita. "Mmm, good shrimp, but they're spicy. Uh, after the cruise? I don't know. We haven't got that far." More truth.

"You seem to me like a girl with a big heart," she said. "Just watch you don't give it to a man who won't be around for the long term." Then she laughed. "And there I go again, giving advice. I'll shut up and eat now." She suited words to action and attacked her fish with gusto.

As I ate my shrimp, I thought about her words. I'd given my heart to Matt long ago and I knew that he was a man who, if he made a promise—like "until death do us part"— would honor it. He'd been ready to make that promise. I was the one who'd pulled back. And now neither of us knew where we stood. But one thing I did know: No matter how I might pretend to Des and Micky that I was having a light-hearted fling, my heart was very much involved.

After lunch, our group went to see cliff divers climb craggy rocks, mount a forty-five-foot high platform, and dive with power, grace, and precision among crashing waves into a tiny space of clear water. I watched two men, then couldn't look any longer. "That's terrifying. My nerves can't take it."

"People have been doing it for decades," a guide said. "They're all very careful."

"Like your scuba diver," Des said. "If a person knows what they're doing, it's not all that dangerous."

It was true. I knew Matt wouldn't do anything foolish. He might like the thrill of scuba diving or ziplining, but he wasn't reckless. Still facing away from the cliff edge, I asked, "Are the divers finished yet?"

"Unfortunately," Micky said. "I could watch them all day."

"Time to go shopping," Des said. "Golden Zone, here we come."

In the popular tourist area, as I wandered on my own from shop to shop, I thought how different Mazatlan was from Puerto Vallarta. Much bigger, with so many different things: the picturesque and rather distinguished Old Town, the huge, colorful *mercado*, the boringly "normal" department stores and appliance stores, and the gaudier tourist zone with tons of jewelry stores, souvenir shops, and restaurants.

My feet were dragging again, and each store was looking like the last. Time to visit the beach before I had to head back to the bus and return to the ship. Tonight, dinner was aboard—and I'd be dining with Matt. That thought excited me and made me anxious. Every time we were together, things between us were different. Tonight, we'd have lots to talk about and that was good. But would we have romance, passion? Would we play games? Would we make love?

I walked through one of the big hotels, admiring the Mexican tile and mosaics, then out past a bright turquoise swimming pool and down a couple of steps to the sand. Beach vendors clustered there, selling jewelry, fresh fruit, straw hats, sunglasses, brightly colored sarongs, and T-shirts. Their displays charmed me.

An older Mexican man with a gap-toothed smile opened a jewelry case in front of me and I glanced inside. Silver hoops with brightly colored parrots caught my fancy. Usually, I wore little jewelry and nothing as dramatic as these, but they were fun, and matched a sundress I'd bought, and I wanted them. Too wimpy to bargain, I paid the twenty dollars he asked for them. An independent woman, buying my own souvenir.

Being on my own was fine and I was glad I'd proved to myself I could do it. Still, I missed Matt. I was in a foreign place, taking off my sandals to walk on a long stretch of pale sand beach beside a vivid blue ocean, and I wanted to share this with him. I figured that wasn't a bad thing, wanting to share special things with someone you cared about. It was a quite different thing than being dependent on someone else.

I walked at the very edge of the water, splashing my toes in the gentle waves that lapped onto the sand. The beach was busy with little kids, parents, lovers, and lots of elderly people with very tanned skin, almost everyone but me in a bathing suit. Tomorrow, I wanted to swim in the ocean. I couldn't leave Mexico without doing that.

But for now, exhaustion had caught up with me again and my feet dragged as I headed back to find the bus. Des and Micky were already aboard, along with most of the others. I took an empty seat, leaned my head back, and closed my eyes.

The bus got underway. I couldn't wait to get back to the cabin, climb under the covers, and have a nap. It would be good if Matt wasn't back yet. I didn't want to be a bore, but I sure wasn't in the mood for sex play. In fact, I was feeling a little nauseous with the bounce and sway of the bus over the uneven streets, and the smell of exhaust fumes coming in the windows. The feeling got worse and I swallowed, telling myself we were almost there.

When we arrived at the cruise ship terminal, I hurried off the bus. Having solid ground under my feet and fresh air against my face made me feel a little better. All the same, I headed straight to my cabin, just wanting to be alone.

And I was. No Matt. The two beds were made up together again, as we'd left them. I started to set down the bags containing my purchases, and my stomach lurched.

Thank God the bathroom was only steps away. Seconds later, I was on the floor in front of the toilet, losing my lunch.

Food poisoning. Those shrimp—oh, no, not going to even think about shrimp. I heaved again, then flushed the toilet and sat back on my heels.

A minute or two later I felt steady enough to pull myself to my feet and brush my teeth. My face was pale and sweaty and I still felt yucky, but my stomach was a little steadier. Bed, or stay by the toilet?

I was hovering there, holding on to the bathroom counter, when the door of the cabin flew open and Matt came in.

"Hey, Merilee, I'm glad you're here. Gotta tell you about the diving. It was fantastic."

Bursting with energy, he came toward me, then stopped. "Hey, are you okay?"

"No. I ate something"—bile rose again and I swallowed hard—"that disagreed with me."

"Aw, sweetheart, I'm sorry. Let's get you into bed. Or do you need . . ." He gestured toward the toilet.

I realized the bathroom must stink. Great. Really sexy and appealing. Not that I cared much at the moment. "I think bed will be okay."

Gently, he scooped me up, carried me to the bed, and eased me down on the edge. He pulled the covers aside, then bent to take off my sandals. From his own bag, he pulled a T-shirt. "Clean," he told me as he unbuttoned my blouse and took it off, and then my bra. He slipped the tee over my head and I huddled inside its well-worn softness. "Lie back."

I obeyed, and he unfastened my denim skirt and eased it over my hips. Then he tucked the covers around me. "Want an aspirin? Advil? Tums?"

I was feeling a bit better, and his solicitousness made me attempt a smile. "You take such good care of me." He always had. He even kept a heating pad at his place for the times I was there during my period, suffering from cramps. "Just a little water. Maybe. I'm not sure I want to put anything in my stomach yet."

"I could get ginger ale or club soda."

"Thanks, but I think I'll nap and see how I feel when I wake up."

He went to the bathroom and returned with water and a warm washcloth, which he smoothed gently over my face. It felt like heaven. Then he kissed my forehead. "I'll be here if you need anything."

"You always have been," I murmured, closing my eyes and refusing to think what life would be like if he wasn't.

Matt gazed down at Merilee as she shifted position to curl on her side, sighed softly, then fell asleep.

When he'd come back to the cabin, he'd been bursting with the excitement of the dive trip, eager to see her and find out how her day had been, and hopeful that they'd soon make use of the package of condoms he'd purchased. At the sight of her so pale and shaky, all those thoughts had fled his mind.

Color was returning to her cheeks, thank God. Her breathing was slow and steady.

Not wanting to leave her, he called room service and, in a low voice, ordered both ginger ale and club soda, and a Coke for himself.

Should he ask the ship's doctor to come? If Merilee had food poisoning, that could be serious. Or maybe it was the Montezuma's revenge tummy bug that people warned about. Or perhaps she'd just overdone it today, or had a touch of sunstroke.

He sighed. Was he fussing too much? He tended to. But he only had two people in his life who he loved: Merilee and his mom. He wasn't about to let anything happen to either of them.

Rather than risk the room service waiter's knock rousing Merilee, he opened the door and waited near it, then took the soft drink cans with a murmured, "Thanks."

He went into the bathroom, closed the door, and took a quick shower. Then he pulled on a pair of shorts, popped open the Coke, and settled on the other side of the bed, pillows behind his back, to read Damien's book.

Merilee slept without moving for about an hour, then shifted and her eyes fluttered open. Her gaze settled on him. "Matt?"

He smoothed her short, tousled hair. "How do you feel?"

She stretched gingerly. "Okay. Good, actually. Horrible taste in my mouth, I'm really thirsty, and I'm actually hungry." A happy smile flashed. "Whew. Whatever it was, it seems to be out of my system now."

"Hope so." Relieved, he told her, "I got ginger ale and club soda. Want something?"

"Thanks. Let me brush my teeth, then I'll see." Cautiously she slid out from between the sheets and got to her feet, then went into the bathroom.

Water ran, then she came out again. "I really do feel fine. I'll take that ginger ale, and I need a shower. Then let's go for dinner. I can't wait to hear about the scuba diving. Obviously you came back safely."

He handed her the can. "Did you worry about me?"

She shook her head. "No, not really."

Not that he'd wanted her to be upset, but it kind of stung that she hadn't worried.

"I knew you'd be careful," she went on, sipping ginger ale. "You may like doing some exciting things, but you're not going to be stupid."

"Oh." Well, that sounded better. And she was right; it wasn't in his nature to be reckless.

"Was Mandy there?" she asked casually.

He stifled a grin. "Yeah, she went diving, but she was with the other group. The experienced divers."

"Figures she'd be *experienced*." The twinkle in her eye said she was teasing. Then, eying his bare chest appreciatively, she said, "You picked up some sun."

"After the dive trip, a group of us went for beer and burgers. Then I hung out on the beach, went swimming, just relaxed."

"It looks good on you." She swept her gaze over him, ending up focusing on his face. "You're turning into a pretty interesting man, Matt Townsend." She handed him the now-empty can and headed back to the bathroom.

In the doorway, she paused and cast a flirtatious glance over her shoulder. "And a sexy one." An impish smile lit her face. "Hmm. What do you figure we're supposed to do with Ben Wa balls?" And on that note, she disappeared into the bathroom and closed the door firmly behind her.

She was thinking about playing with vaginal balls? His dick twitched. He only had a vague idea of how to use the balls, but just the name was sexy. Even sexier was the idea that Merilee, who'd been embarrassed by the stagette gift, now wanted to experiment. Talk about turning into an interesting person!

Half an hour later, he and Merilee headed for the dining room, her arm linked through his as they walked down the corridor from their room.

He wore beige chinos the salesgirl had recommended and a casually styled white Mexican shirt he and Merilee had bought in Puerto Vallarta. Merilee, who'd kicked him out of the cabin while she got dressed, looked vibrant and beautiful in a new sundress patterned in shades of blue, dangly hoop earrings with parrots, and high-heeled sandals that showcased her shapely legs.

The dress showcased the rest of her. The skirt was kind of floaty and swirly and the top was fitted, with little straps. Under the dress straps were thin black ones, so he knew she was wearing a bra. One that plumped her breasts up so that soft upper curves and cleavage were enough on display to tantalize him.

"You look really sexy," he told her.

"I told you about that teddy Kat gave me?"

"Uh, yeah, but I'm not sure what a teddy is." The word made him think of teddy bears, but when she'd mentioned it before she'd talked about black silk and lace, so he figured it was lingerie. He touched a finger to the straps at her shoulder. "You're wearing it?"

"I am. It's one-piece lingerie. This one has a built-in bra of lace and silk, then below that it's black lace with bands of embroidered silk. The bottom part is"—she broke off to smile at a man coming toward them in the hallway.

Matt tried to picture the garment. It sure sounded sexy. And what was the bottom part?

Merilee kept quiet as the man passed them, then leaned close to Matt and whispered, "A thong."

His pulse speeded. "You're wearing a thong under that skirt?" He swallowed. "You mean your butt's totally bare?"

"Why don't you find out?"

"Oh, jeez." Did she mean, lift her skirt and—No, of course not. They were stepping out into the sparkly atrium, where dozens of other passengers were heading in various directions. He put his arm around her, spreading his fingers so they spanned from the dip of her waist to the upper swell of her butt. Under the filmy skirt, he felt warm, firm flesh.

She put her arm around him, too, moving so close that their hips brushed each other. "This skirt's so light and so full, it feels sensual as it drifts across my skin. And I feel daring, like I'm almost naked."

The girl he'd known had never talked this way, so sexually open and teasing, especially not in public. Oh, yeah, she was growing up, and growing up *hot*. His dick, rising behind his fly, was definitely into this. "You're sure you're hungry?" He'd rather get her alone and flip up that skirt.

Slanting a gleaming look up at him, she said, "Starving." She ran the tip of her tongue around pink-glossed lips. "For dinner first, but afterward . . ."

He slid his hand in caressing circles around her hip and the top of her butt, wishing there weren't so many people around. "Please tell me you don't want to go to the show."

"Show? Oh, that's right, there's a Las Vegas show, isn't

there? I'm sure it would be fun, but . . ." She tossed him a flirtatious grin. "I'm hoping we can think up some fun of our own."

"Count on it." A black teddy, a thong, vaginal balls . . . He had no appetite for anything but Merilee.

But here they were, walking into the formal dining room, and delicious scents made him rethink that. Okay, he could eat. But quickly.

The scene was straight out of a cruise ship brochure. Sparkling light glinted off crystal glasses and polished silverware, and flowers decorated every table. A tuxedoed maitre d' stepped up to them.

"We'd like to dine alone," Matt told him firmly. When he'd been on his own, he'd been happy to join a large table of other passengers, but not tonight.

"Of course, sir." The man led them past noisy tables of eight or more, to a quieter area with tables for four and for two. With a flourish, he indicated an empty table. "A romantic spot. A waiter will be with you in a moment to take your drink order."

They thanked him as they sat, then Merilee said, "White wine or red?"

Though she was clearly feeling fine now, he remembered how sick she'd been. "Is wine a good idea? Maybe you should go easy on your tummy."

A frown creased her brow and she pressed a hand to her stomach. "I feel great, but you're probably right. I'll stick with ginger ale."

He'd just finished placing an order for two ginger ales when a pretty brunette a few years older than them and an attractive white-haired woman came over to the table.

"Hi, you two," Merilee said, smiling. "Matt, meet my friends Micky"—she indicated the older woman—"and Des."

It dawned on him that they'd been the sexy Eve and—oh,

my God, the black leather dom—he'd seen Merilee with at the costume ball. Trying to banish that image from his brain, he rose and shook their hands. "I'm glad to meet you. Merilee's talked about you."

"You too, pirate man." There was a mischievous twinkle in the older woman's eye that made him wonder what Merilee had been saying.

"We saw you come in," Micky went on, "and just had to get an introduction."

"And no, thanks," Des chimed in, "but we won't join you, not that you're inviting us."

"Um . . ." Was he supposed to?

She chuckled. "I'm teasing. Of course, you two want to be alone."

Merilee gazed up at the younger woman. "How are you feeling, Des?"

"Fine. Why?"

Merilee touched her stomach again. "I'm fine now, but I ate something that disagreed with me. I thought it might have been the shrimp."

"Oh, poor you. Too bad. But no, I'm totally fine."

"Me, too," Micky said. "But didn't you say you bought pastry in the market?"

"Maybe that was it."

"Poor Merilee," the older woman said. "You take it easy tonight, okay? Nothing too rich or spicy."

The dom was being maternal. He had the feeling this was one interesting woman.

"Yes, Mom," Merilee said teasingly. "Matt's already been lecturing me."

"Good for him." Micky nodded approvingly as the waiter delivered the ginger ale. "I see you're in good hands." She touched Merilee's shoulder. "Have a lovely evening."

"We will. You two as well."

"We should be so lucky," Micky murmured.

Matt laughed softly. "Nice to meet you both." After they left, he reached over to take Merilee's hand. "I see why you like them."

"I wish they lived in Vancouver. That's the tough thing with a holiday like this—you meet terrific people, then each go your separate ways. Speaking of which"—she squeezed his hand—"they think you're a shipboard fling."

In the act of drinking ginger ale, he almost choked. "What?"

"I didn't want to share all our private stuff and . . ." She made a mock-apologetic face. "Okay, I was kind of a bad girl. They jumped to the conclusion and I didn't actually lie. I just had fun going along with it. It's like, you know, trying on the flapper role, or us playing first date."

He stared at her in wonder. "You really do have a naughty streak. I like it."

"So do I. I never got to be—or let myself be—naughty at home. I was too busy trying to be the good girl."

"Trying? I thought that came naturally."

"After a while. But let's face it, no kid's that good. I just really wanted people to love me."

Astonished, he stared at her. "Merilee, you're the most lovable person I know."

"That's so sweet." She beamed at him. "But honestly, did anyone see the real me?" She shook her head, setting the parrot earrings bouncing. "I mean, I don't even know who the real me is."

"I do." He ran his thumb over the back of her hand. "Oh, sure, you may wear red nail polish, change your hair, go zip-lining, and act a little naughty. That stuff's fun." And sexy. "But the basic you will always be the same."

"And who's that?" she said with apparently genuine curiosity.

"A girl—woman—who's sweet and loving, who's crazy about kids, who puts spiders outside rather than harm them." A woman who was totally lovable.

She gave a little smile, then said softly, "That's nice, but my sisters have always been so impressive. Mom and Dad, too, of course. I've always felt I can't measure up."

"Measure up? You're all different. And you're the nicest. You brighten up every room you're in."

The smile spread to her eyes and she beamed at him. "Thank you, Matt. I think that's the nicest thing anyone's ever said to me."

He smiled back at her, then her stomach rumbled loudly, making them both laugh. "Time for dinner," he said, gesturing toward the laden buffet tables.

She rose eagerly and he walked behind her, thinking how pretty she looked in that dress, and imagining the teddy-clad body beneath. Unable to resist touching her, he touched his hand lightly to her lower back.

"Everything looks and smells so yummy," she said.

Merilee certainly did, but her words drew his attention to the enticing array of food. "Yeah, it does." With what he had in mind for the rest of the night, they'd both better fuel up.

She reached over to serve herself some paella.

"Maybe you shouldn't," he said. "It looks pretty spicy."

She paused, then glanced up. "Matt, please don't treat me like a baby. I'm grown up and I can look after myself."

Hurt, he said, "Fine." She hadn't objected when he'd looked after her when she was sick, and always before she'd seemed to appreciate his consideration. If she thought he treated her like a baby, why hadn't she said so?

Maybe for the same reason that, those times when she wanted to see a movie and he'd planned on going for a run, he hadn't told her. It was like a white lie—not one hundred percent honest, but done for the right reasons. How many things had they each held inside for the sake of getting along? Perhaps that hadn't been the smartest thing to do.

Which meant he should be glad she'd spoken up now, and he shouldn't get miffed.

"Sorry," he said. "I know you're a grown-up." He snuck a squeeze of her butt. "Believe me, I know."

Her smile flashed, and when she dished out some lobster thermidor, which looked awfully rich for a sensitive stomach, he kept his mouth shut.

They filled their plates with a bit of this, a bit of that, then returned to the table and dug in. "Tell me about the scuba diving," she said.

"I wish you could have been there. So many fish, incredible colors, and some very weird shapes." As she listened and asked questions, he told her about the lesson in a swimming pool outside the dive shop, then the boat trip to an island offshore, and the diving.

"You didn't feel nervous?"

"Excited, but you need to control your breathing or you use up the oxygen too fast. I've swum all my life so it came pretty naturally."

"I believe it. You're a great swimmer."

"Thanks. So how was your day?"

"Great. I'll tell you all about it, but let's get dessert."

He groaned. "I thought *we* were dessert." All evening, he'd been aroused by imagining her in the lingerie she'd described. He couldn't wait to get her alone, flip up her skirt, maybe try out those Ben Wa balls.

"We're for *après* dessert. Matt, there's chocolate on that buffet table. Loads of chocolate goodies."

He didn't have a hope in hell of winning out over chocolate. "Okay, we'll have dessert."

They made their way to the dessert buffet, where she oohed more noisily than she did in bed, and loaded her plate. It was on the tip of his tongue to again warn her to watch what she ate, but he refrained.

They returned to the table to find their waiter hovering to

ask if they wanted a drink. They both chose coffee, which he served promptly, steaming and smelling delicious.

As they made their way through samples of several desserts—the Black Forest chocolate cherry cake laden with whipped cream winning both their votes as the best—Merilee described how she'd explored the Old Town and tourist zone, then walked on the beach.

He listened, and everything about her—her animation, the sensual way she savored those desserts, the golden gleam of her hair under the chandeliers, the soft upper curves of her breasts as she leaned toward him—aroused him. As did the idea of that teddy she wore, and what he intended to do with her when they were alone.

Finally, she shoved aside her dessert plate with only a few mouthfuls of food remaining. She settled back in her chair and stretched her hand toward his. "It was good doing things on my own, but I missed you."

He clasped her hand warmly. "Me, too."

"I wish I'd had a chance for a swim. Tomorrow, for sure. I really want to swim in the ocean here."

Tomorrow, they'd be at Cabo San Lucas. From there the ship would cruise back to the terminal outside Los Angeles, and they'd fly home. Yeah, much as he'd enjoyed the diving, he'd missed spending time with Merilee. "Want to spend the day together tomorrow? It's our last chance to see Mexico together, and we'll make sure we go swimming."

She gave a happy smile. "I'd like that." Then she patted her tummy. "Though I shouldn't have eaten so much if I'm going to look good in my new bikini."

"I saw you in that bikini. It's hot." He remembered it well: little scraps of vivid greenish-blue material held together with ties at the hips, back, and neck. Simple little ties that could easily be undone. The thought made his dick stir. His pants were getting tight and he was damned impatient to be alone with her.

"It's as daring as I'm gonna get," she said. "No thong bikinis for me."

He leaned across the table and said quietly, "Thong underwear, though." Which he couldn't wait to see.

"And here I thought you'd forgotten."

"Not for one second." And now, finally, dessert was over. They'd head back to the room and he'd strip that dress off her, or maybe just hoist the back up—

Chapter 14

Merilee's voice broke into his fantasies. "I did mention one of the stagette gifts was leopard-print thong undies for you, right?"

That shattered the fantasy. "Jeez, no way am I wearing a thong."

"Coward." She sat up straight. "If I can, why can't you?"

"It's . . . they're . . . they look stupid on guys."

"Ah, so you've seen a lot of guys wearing them?"

"A few. In change rooms." He grimaced, and lowered his voice even further. "A guy's junk's dangling around in a goofy pouch, and his butt's hanging out."

Her lips twisted together like she was fighting a grin. "My butt's hanging out and you don't think that's stupid. And what's wrong with having your, uh, junk in a pouch?" Color rose to her cheeks. "You have nice junk."

"Gee, thanks." The fact that she thought so made him swell again, and he wished he could adjust himself. "But, like, what if a guy gets hard? There's no place for it to go."

"The leopard thong isn't all that tiny. Why don't we try it out? I'll wear the female version if you wear the male one. How about tomorrow, when we go into Cabo?"

Her in a leopard thong, he could definitely go for. But she

couldn't be serious about his wearing one. "Tell me you're joking."

She shook her head, lips pressed together, eyes gleaming. "Nope. After all, we don't want to be boring, do we?"

He groaned. Maybe there was something to be said for the old Merilee. The sweet, slightly shy one. Yet, his growing erection voted for this one.

"It'll be sexy," she said breezily. "You'll like the bare butt thing once you get used to it. And just think, if I hook my hand in the back pocket of your shorts, the only thing between my fingers and your naked skin will be one little layer of cotton."

Okay, she was winning her argument. "That erection thing's gonna be an issue," he told her. "In fact, just talking about it . . ." He shifted, trying to ease the increasing pressure against the fly of his chinos.

"Ah-ha, you're starting to see things my way."

"Not yet. You could be way more persuasive if we were alone together. You need to demonstrate the benefit of the bare butt thing."

"Demonstrate?" A mischievous expression lit her face. "What did you have in mind?"

The dining room was busy, noisy, and no one was seated too close. All the same, he lowered his voice even further and leaned across the table. She was into being naughty? Hell, he was the pirate. He could out-naughty her. "When we walk down that long, narrow corridor to our room, I want to slide my hand under your skirt and caress your backside."

Her hand jerked inside his clasp, but she didn't pull away.

"Then I want to run my fingers down the line of the thong." As he spoke, he raised his free hand and trailed his fingers softly down the side of her face, barely touching her skin. "Between your cheeks and then between your thighs." He brushed the pad of his thumb against her parted lips. "And I want to feel you get wet for me."

"Matt!" It was a halfhearted protest, the glitter in her eyes giving her away.

His dick was rock hard now, his breathing fast and shallow, not just from imagining doing those things to her, but from talking this way in a public place to Merilee.

Her free hand rested on the table and he caught it so he held both of her hands with both of his. Firmly, so she couldn't move away. "As soon as we're inside, I want you to grab onto the back of the chair and bend over, and I'm going to hoist your skirt, shove aside your thong, and"—he echoed her words from last night, the ones that had stuck in his mind and kept him on the edge of arousal ever since—"do you from behind."

She stared, unspeaking. Had he gone too far? Then she swallowed and breathed one word. "Okay."

He pressed a quick, hard kiss across her lips, then surged to his feet. He hadn't tucked in the summer-weight white shirt, and hoped it'd conceal the substantial bulge in his pants. "Let's go."

She came to her feet more slowly, and put her hand in his. "I've never seen this side of you before. I like it, Matt."

"Good." It wasn't that he hadn't fantasized about stuff like this. He'd just figured a gentleman wouldn't act on those fantasies. But if Merilee liked it, he had lots more where this came from.

They hurried across the dining room, then made their way through the ship, where people in everything from shorts to evening dress wandered around. Finally, they were in the corridor leading to their room, and it was empty.

He stopped and, when she looked up at him questioningly, he pulled her to him and kissed her. Beautiful, sexy, sweet, naughty Merilee. With his lips, his tongue, his body, he told her she was all of those things. Rocking his hips against hers, he pressed his erection against her, imagining the black lace teddy under her filmy dress and the warm, soft curves beneath it.

She squirmed against him and her breath sighed in quick pants against his face as her tongue tangled with his.

He slipped both hands under her floaty skirt and cupped her firm cheeks.

She gave a little gasp as he dug his fingers into them, pulling her even closer so he could grind against her. Damn, she was hot. He wanted to take her, right here and now.

She liked a guy who was decisive? Fine. Enough kissing. He thrust her away and turned her to face down the corridor again. Still empty, thank God. "Walk."

When she did, he walked at her side, reaching under her skirt again and curving his hand around her butt, feeling silky flesh and the alternating tightening and stretch of her muscles.

"If anyone comes . . ." she warned under her breath, her face rosy pink.

"It'll be us coming, and soon," he promised. He slid two fingers along the thin band of her thong as it bisected her bottom, tracing the line up and down.

She slowed her pace. "That feels . . . sexy."

"How about this?" He stroked between her legs, pressing the silky thong against her flesh. In a moment the fabric dampened, giving him his answer.

She gave a little wriggle and said breathlessly, "I can't walk when you do that."

"Yes, you can." Each time he rubbed the silk, it grew wetter. "I want you nice and ready for me. Once we get inside that room, there's not gonna be any foreplay."

"Tell me again what you're going to do," she whispered.

How about that? This stuff turned her on as much as it did him. "Bend you over, lift your skirt, shove aside your thong, and do you, fast and hard."

"Oh, yeah. That's what I want."

They'd reached the door of their room. Not letting go of

her, he used his free hand to remove the room key from his pocket, open the door, and click on the light. He slammed the door behind them. Guiding her with his hand between her legs, he shoved her a little roughly toward the chair by the window. Finally, he let go. "Bend over. Hold the back of the chair."

When she did, he flipped her skirt up, revealing two perfect, creamy curves framed by the black thong bottom of her teddy. He was so damn excited, he could barely undo his pants, free his throbbing dick, and get himself sheathed. Then he paused. Could he push her a little further? "What do you want, Merilee?"

"You," she breathed. "Now." She almost undid him when she tilted up, legs spread, offering herself.

He fought for control. "What do you want me to do? This?" He jerked aside the thin strip of black. Her lush pink folds were swollen and glistened with moisture

"Yes."

"What else?" Gently he spread those silky folds and lodged the tip of his erection at the entrance to her passage. With his pants and underwear down around his ankles—but who gave a damn?—he gripped her hips in both hands. and used every ounce of control to not move. "Tell me what you want."

Her body tensed, then after a long moment, she spoke. Voice breathy, just a whisper, she said, "I want you to do me, to take me from behind. Hard and fast and now."

Oh, yeah, now she was talking. He took a deep breath, gathering himself, then surged inside her.

She said, "Oh!" in a kind of gasp.

"Okay?"

"Oh, yes."

The way she was holding onto the chair as he drove into her repeatedly, there wasn't much she could do but receive his thrusts. He felt strong and powerful, looming over her as she bent in submission, arching her back and thrusting out her butt. Last night, he'd put her on top, in control, and now it was his turn.

But was she enjoying this? She'd gone quiet again. But then, so had he except for his ragged breathing and moans of pleasure. Maybe she wasn't the only one who could be more vocal in bed. So he told her exactly what he was thinking. "Damn, Merilee, you feel great."

He pulled out a few inches, then surged back in, staring in fascination at where their bodies joined. The twin curves of her butt were so full and firm, so smooth and pale-skinned, so totally feminine, and his shaft seemed so primitive and masculine. "Seeing my dick go in and out of you, man, but that's sexy."

Was this angle giving her everything she needed? He leaned over her, holding her with one arm around her waist, and kissed the nape of her neck. "How's it feel for you?"

"G-good," she said breathlessly.

He reached around and stroked her smooth belly, letting his fingers drift down into her soft curls, but no farther. "Can I make it feel better? Tell me."

Her body trembled. "Touch me, Matt."

The need to climax was building as he pumped into her. He fought it back, loving how her inhibitions were breaking down. "Where?" Again he stroked through her pubic hair.

"My . . . my c-clit," she whispered.

"Oh, yeah, sweetheart." He caressed the swollen bud.

She writhed against his hand, whimpering needily.

He pressed, squeezed gently. "You're so hot, you drive me crazy, M." The timid girl he'd lost his virginity with had sure grown up.

She cried out, body pulsing against him in climax.

Freed of the need to hold back, he let his own orgasm surge through him and into her.

When its force was spent, he sagged against her, weak-kneed, as she leaned on the sturdy chair. Finally, he eased out of her, took off the condom, and helped her straighten.

Her skirt flipped down again and she stood, her back to him, staring out the window. "You okay?" he asked.

Slowly, she turned, and he saw flushed cheeks and wide eyes. "I'm great. That was amazing. But I can't believe we did it with the lights on, no curtains pulled."

"There's nothing out there but the ocean." The ship had been underway for hours.

"I guess. Still, it's kind of kinky." A grin began to grow. "Not that there's anything wrong with kinky."

He chuckled and dropped a kiss on her nose. "Glad you feel that way." He stepped out of his pants and boxer briefs, then began to unbutton his shirt. "Speaking of which, want to figure out what Ben Wa balls do?"

"Y-yes," she said tentatively.

A thought struck him. "Why did you bring the stagette stuff? Were you figuring we'd, uh . . . ?" *What? Get back together? Have sex?*

She shook her head. "I forgot I had it. When I packed for, you know, the honeymoon, I tucked the gifts into this separate compartment in the bottom of my suitcase. Then I unpacked my bag and I was pretty emotional. Saturday night, I repacked it again in a hurry, when I decided to come on the cruise. Anyhow, all through that, I forgot they were there."

Probably she'd forgotten because they'd embarrassed her. He was so glad she was getting over that—and he was going to help her. "Let me see the balls."

Still dressed, she fumbled around in a dresser drawer, then handed him a package, unopened.

Through the plastic cover, he saw two gold balls, each maybe an inch and a half across, joined together with a cord. Those went up inside her, where he'd just been?

I watched Matt as he studied the package that had embarrassed me so much last week, and now kind of intrigued me. "Go ahead. Open it. I'm guessing they won't bite."

The wonderful thing about exploring my naughty side with Matt was that I totally trusted him. Whether he was the pirate, a "first date," or the edgier, sexier version of the guy I'd always known, I knew he'd never hurt me and never force me to do anything I didn't want to.

He peeled open the plastic covering and removed the balls, dangling them in the air by the cord. They swung hypnotically. If they'd been metal, they would have clanked together, but they were made of some synthetic substance. Each ball had a smaller one jiggling inside it. Duotone balls, the package called them.

"I read the back of the package," I told him. "Apparently they're great for strengthening internal muscles."

"Uh-huh. So that's what you want to do now? Exercises?"

"No, I'm just saying they have a, uh, legitimate use."

A brow cocked teasingly. "Sex isn't legitimate?"

"The girl who gave them to me said they come in handy when she's between boyfriends, too. She says she, uh . . ."

"Come on, don't leave me hanging."

Knowing my cheeks were bright pink, I said, "She puts them inside and sits on one of those big exercise balls, then she rocks. Back and forth and side to side. They shift around, bump against each other, and she has an orgasm."

"Seriously? One of our friends?" He cocked that brow again, then quickly held up his hand. "Don't tell me. I don't want to know."

"Don't worry, I'm not telling."

"Okay, that's what *she* does, but in case you haven't noticed, you do have a guy in the room." Teasingly, he added, "It's not good for my ego to know a couple of little gold balls can replace me." He dropped his hand so the Ben Wa balls dangled beside his growing erection. They really did look tiny next to him. And it was his swelling dick, not the balls, that made my insides quiver.

Still, I wasn't going to back out on playing naughty. "I want both. You and them." I held out a cupped hand and he dropped the balls into it. Then I kicked off my high-heeled sandals and headed for the bathroom.

"Hey!"

"Give me a minute." I closed the door, wanting privacy to insert these for the first time. It'd be too embarrassing if I put them in and they fell right out again.

I washed them in hot, soapy water, then rinsed away the soap. Curving my body slightly, I slid the drenched crotch of my thong aside and gingerly nudged one golden ball inside my channel, then the other, making sure not to lose the pull-string. They didn't hurt; I just felt a little . . . full. Tightening my muscles to hold them in, I straightened and gazed in the mirror.

Hmm. I looked exactly the same as before. A flushed, tousle-haired blonde in a flirty little dress, with parrot earrings dangling from my ears. I could go out in public like this and—assuming I didn't make any sudden moves and lose the balls—no one would ever know. I could go out for dinner with Matt, and halfway through tell him about the balls. I gave my reflection a wicked grin. Oh, no, I wasn't the boring old Merilee any longer.

Demurely, walking carefully, I left the bathroom. Inside me, the balls shifted with each movement, and I squeezed against them. I imagined my internal muscles getting stronger, and flexing against Matt's dick as he thrust in and out. Whether it was the balls themselves, or my own sexy thoughts, I was getting turned on.

"Well?" he demanded. His cheeks were flushed, too, and he was fully erect now.

Gorgeously, powerfully erect. Very sexy, but would he ever fit inside me along with those balls?

"Merilee? Did you put them in?"

"They're in and they feel, uh, odd, but sensual."

"Think there's room in there for me, too?"

"I was just wondering about that."

"Hey." He touched my cheek. "If it doesn't work, that's okay. You know I'd never hurt you."

I took a deep breath and put my hand over his. "I know. I'm just a little nervous."

"Let's see what we can do about that." He kissed me gently, with just one tantalizing lick of his tongue into my mouth, then said, "Turn around."

Was he going to flip my skirt up again? But no, when I presented my back, he slid the zipper of my dress down, following it with kisses and licks. When he reached the dip at the base of my spine, I shifted restlessly, wanting more. Then, realizing he'd distracted me from gripping the balls, I quickly clenched my muscles again. "Stop. I'm going to lose these balls."

He moved away and my dress fell to the floor. Cautiously, I stepped free of the fabric.

"Sure like the rear view," he said. "Now turn around and let me see the front."

Wearing the black teddy, I turned to face him.

"Oh, yeah, that's nice. Really nice. Even better than I imagined. God, you're sexy." His cheeks were flushed and a wicked gleam sparked in his eyes. "Sit on the edge of the bed and rock like you're on an exercise ball."

"I—"

"Do it. And tell me how it feels."

A shiver of arousal rippled through me. Self-consciously, I moved over to sit on the edge of the bed. Squeezing my thighs together, I rocked a little. Oh, my, that really was arousing.

"Tell me," he demanded.

"It's like everything's in motion inside me. The little balls inside the bigger ones, the bigger ones bouncing off each other and rubbing against me. Vibrations pulsing in every direction."

Standing a couple of feet away, gaze intent, he asked, "Is it a turn-on?"

"Yeah." I could even imagine climaxing this way, especially if I reached down and rubbed my clit.

He caught his erection in one hand and stroked himself.

My eyes widened and my breath quickened. He'd never done that in front of me before. "That's a turn-on, too," I admitted.

"I want to be inside you. I want to feel all those vibrations."

I lay back on the bed. "I want to feel you. But let's take this slow and easy, okay?"

"If it hurts, tell me." He sheathed himself, then came down on top of me, easing between my legs as I spread them a little. His fingers eased the crotch of my thong aside again and his dick nudged gently, opening me and slipping inside.

The balls shifted, making room, and I gasped.

He stopped. "Okay?"

"Yes, it's just . . . weird. Not bad, but strange."

"Yeah. Me, too. I've never felt anything like that." Slowly, he eased farther in, and I'd never felt so full. Then, in tiny motions, he began to slide in and out, and each motion set the balls to rocking.

"Oh!" I put my arms around him and clung, my focus internal, swept away by sensation. It wasn't like when he teased my clit and everything kind of gathered and focused; the feelings were more diffuse. But just as sexy. I felt like we were rocking together toward climax.

"Feels really good," he panted. "How about you?"

"Oh, yeah." I arched my back, feeling my taut nipples brush against his chest, the lace of the teddy a soft, stimulating abrasion between our bodies.

His lips met mine, and his tongue thrust inside in the same slow, relentless, seductive pace. And now my focus wasn't just on my own internal sensations, but on him as well. Matt, my best friend for fourteen years, and now my amazingly sexy playmate.

I sucked his tongue, teased it, felt the gentle scrub of his beard stubble against my chin. We gazed into each other's eyes and I felt the same emotional connection that had always existed between us.

Inside me, pressure built. *Rock me, M. Rock me, take me, take us both where we want to go.*

As if he'd heard my silent chant, he did exactly that, until our bodies clenched and we shuddered together in a sweet explosion.

The aftershocks trembled through me for a long time as Matt lay, breathing hard, atop me.

Finally, he eased out of me. He rested a gentle hand on my mound. "Want to leave the balls in?"

I groaned. "No way. I have no muscles left."

He tugged the string and another series of tiny shocks rippled as the balls slid, one by one, down my channel and out.

When he dealt with them and the condom, I peeled off the teddy.

He lay down again and pulled me close. I curled on my side and snuggled into him, my head in the curve of his shoulder, my arm and thigh thrown across him. He was so hard, so masculine; how had I not noticed when his body turned into a man's?

My own body felt soft and melty and blissfully satisfied, and yet . . . Tonight, I'd shed inhibitions and opened myself to Matt more than ever before, and I'd felt not just the arousal but the emotion between us. And yet we weren't really a couple. We were using condoms, both unsure what the future held.

Tonight, I realized, had been one of those open doors

Jenna talked about. Matt and I had both stepped through, and we were on a new journey. Time would tell where it took us. For now, I'd try to live in the moment.

I slid my hand across his lean belly and down to cup his dick. "You realize I'll have to tell my sisters about this."

He jerked. "What?"

"They were sharing all these sexy stories—sex on the plane, sex on the beach, Kama Sutra sex—and I was totally left out."

"I know you and your sisters are competitive, but about your sex lives?"

"It's not so much that we're competitive as we're just so thrilled to be with such hot guys."

He snorted. "You're competitive."

"Okay, so what if I am? You measure up just fine, Mr. Townsend, compared to their guys." I gave his dick a gentle squeeze. "Why shouldn't I boast?"

"You and your friends get furious when guys talk about the girls they've slept with," he pointed out.

I thought about that for a moment, then shrugged. "Double standard. What can I say?"

We lay quietly for a few minutes, and I thought about something Theresa had said. "What do you know about chaos theory?"

"Uh, Merilee, it's almost midnight, I've just had fantasy-type sex"—he dropped a kiss on the top of my head—"and I'm beat. You want to talk chaos theory?"

My own fantasies were about lovemaking. Not that I was knocking kinky sex, but I wanted to do it with someone I loved, who loved me back.

I pulled away slightly so I could see his face. That stubble sure made him look older, edgier, and I liked it. "I was talking to Theresa earlier," I told him. "She said Jenna's scientist guy had this chaos theory about me and my sisters. When I phoned to say we were getting married and they needed to come home, it set them off on paths they'd never otherwise have taken. Their paths crossed those of three guys. And because of me, all my sisters found love." And Matt and I had broken up and started out on new paths. Tonight, I felt hopeful that our journey would bring us back together, stronger and better than before.

"That's cool. But . . ." He was quiet a moment. "Because of all that stuff, you called off the wedding. That's pretty ironic, when you think about it."

Ironic. And a bunch of other things, some great and some not so great. "It's been good for us, though. Painful, but good. Would either of us ever have gone ziplining, would you have tried scuba diving, would we have given ourselves makeovers or—"

"Tried Ben Wa balls," he broke in. He gave a quick laugh, then stretched, all those glorious muscles flexing and shifting. "Hey, d'you remember when I was ten or eleven and I had pains in my legs? Mom said they were growing pains, and that growing up could hurt. That's kind of like what we're going through."

"It's better than not growing."

"Yeah. Even if it's all a little unsettling."

I curled up again, head nestled in the curve of his shoulder. Here we were, cuddled up together in way that was oh, so familiar, after having had sex that was wilder than anything I'd imagined. Yes, it was unsettling.

When we were seven, we'd recognized each other as soul mates. Was that still true? When—how—would we figure this out?

He yawned and stroked my shoulder. "You wore me out, sweetheart. Let's get a good sleep. Then we'll have fun in Cabo tomorrow."

Going to sleep together, waking up together, spending the day together. These all felt like very good steps on our journey. But, just to make sure we didn't fall back into any boring old rut, I said, "Yes, lots of fun. In our leopard-print thongs."

I smiled against his chest as he groaned.

I woke to the warmth of a hard male body spooning me and sunshine warming my face. Again, we'd forgotten to pull the curtains. A glance at the clock told me we should get a move on if we wanted to have breakfast before we left the ship.

The thought of breakfast sent an unexpected quiver of nausea through my stomach. Followed by another stronger one—and then I was out of bed and running to the bathroom.

Hanging over the toilet, heaving, I cursed myself for having eaten so much last night.

Matt knocked on the locked door. "Merilee?"

"Go away." I flushed, and sank down on the cool floor. "Leave me alone."

"M, let me in. Let me help."

"No, I—" I broke off, needing to throw up again. When finally no more came up, I flushed and dragged myself up to sit on the closed toilet seat. My stomach was settling, thank God. "Give me a minute," I said hoarsely. "I'm feeling better."

Shakily, I rose to wash my face and brush my teeth, then opened the door to find Matt, naked, leaning against the wall beside it. "I think I'm okay now," I told him.

Before I could move toward the bed, he hoisted me and carried me the few steps. It was like a rerun of yesterday as he tucked me in and brought me a can of leftover ginger ale. "I'm going to call the doctor."

"No, wait." Sitting up in bed, I sipped the drink cautiously, relieved that the nausea was fading.

"Food poisoning can be serious."

"It can't be food poisoning, not twice in a row. I just ate

too much last night when my tummy was still sensitive. So, fine, say 'I told you so.'"

"You wouldn't listen to me last night, so listen to me now. I want you to see a doctor."

Now that was just silly. "For eating too much rich and spicy food after a bout of food poisoning? Matt, I'm already feeling much better. And you're wearing me out, arguing like this."

He frowned as I said, "Let me lie down for a little while. You have a shower, get some breakfast, then come back and let's see how I feel."

"I'm not leaving you alone when you're sick."

I sighed. He was sweet, but I just wanted to doze until I felt better. "Then shower and call room service, but please don't order anything that smells like food." I sank down in the bed and pulled the covers high on my shoulders. "No doctor. Please?"

"Okay," he said grudgingly. He brushed a kiss across my forehead before I turned away, putting my back to the light from the window.

I heard him go into the bathroom, heard the shower start, then I was dead to the world.

I woke again to sunshine and didn't move, assessing how my tummy felt. No quivers, no roiling. Slowly, I turned over. Matt sat in the chair—mmm, nice, wearing shorts but no shirt—absorbed in Damien's book. On the little table beside him was a tray. I sat up, seeing the remnants of breakfast: an empty yogurt container, a cereal box, fruit, a slice of toast, and an empty juice glass.

My stomach gurgled, from hunger now. But this time, I wouldn't rush things. Small portions, bland food.

I slid out of bed and he raised his head. "I'm starting the morning over," I told him. "Forget all about what happened earlier, okay?" How gross for him to wake to the sound of me puking.

"How do you feel?"

"Much, much better, and in need of a shower." I went into the bathroom, energy returning with each step. An invigorating shower finished my rejuvenation. I flicked a comb through my damp hair, brushed on a touch of makeup, and wrapped a towel around myself.

He was still in the chair, still shirtless and looking very appealing, when I went out. As I walked over, he put the book aside.

I perched on his lap and put my arms around his neck. "Good morning, sexy guy."

He hugged me and gave me a quick kiss. "Get dressed and we'll go to the medical clinic. I found out where it is."

Caring was great; overprotective, not so much. "Don't be such a worry wart. I'm fine." I flipped the towel open and flashed him. "See?"

His gaze dropped to my breasts, then slowly returned to my face. "Don't joke about it. You were really sick. You should see a doctor or at least a nurse, and stay in bed."

Okay, so I'd been silly last night and overdone it with that buffet. I was still a grown-up and I'd make my own decisions. I wrapped the towel tight again, and gestured out the window. "We're in Cabo San Lucas. I want to go ashore. Stop telling me what to do."

"I'm just trying to look after you since you don't seem to want to look after yourself."

"It's patronizing. It's my job to look after me."

"Great job you've been doing." He scowled up at me.

I scowled back. Then I said, "What are we doing? We never fight like this."

"You're right." His eyebrows pulled together. "Because I always give in to make you happy."

"Then do it now."

He shook his head. "You said I was wimpy. You wanted decisive, take charge."

"Not always. Not when I'm right."

Our annoyed gazes caught and held. Humor sparked in his eyes and I realized what I'd said. A moment later, we were both chuckling.

"Guess we still have some things to work on," he said.

Clearly, that was true. With a sense of discovery, I said, "And maybe we have to agree that sometimes it's okay to disagree. Arguing isn't the end of the world."

"No, but I don't like it." He paused, then said, "Okay, I have to admit that talking about things is better than keeping quiet when we're pissed off."

"You're right." Again I dropped down to sit on his lap, and twined my arms around him. "And honestly, I feel great. Starving, but great." I reached for one of the leftover pieces of toast, took a couple of nibbles, then waited to see how my tummy dealt with it. "See? I just overdid it last night. Today, I'll be careful. I promise." I took another few bites. "You want to go into Cabo, don't you?"

" 'Course I do. Although . . ." He toyed with the top edge of the towel where I'd twisted one end under the other to hold it up.

Tempting, very tempting. But today was our last chance to explore Mexico together. I captured his hand and held it away from the towel. "Well, I want to go into town. I'll even promise you can tell me what I'm allowed to eat. Okay?" I touched my forehead to his and peered deep into his eyes.

"Well, okay."

"And in exchange . . ." I popped up from his lap, went over to the dresser, and opened a drawer. "I get to tell you"—I spun around, his-and-her leopard-print thongs in my hand—"what to wear."

Chapter 15

Matt held up his hands, palms toward me in protest. "You're not serious."

"No, I'm fun. Kinky and fun. And you like it." I flipped the *his* thong at him. "Strip and put this on. I want to see how it looks."

His lips were beginning to curve. "You first."

"No problem." I let the towel drop and turned my back to him. I bent down, lower than I really needed to, and stepped into the thong, taking longer than I really needed to. Still bent down, I flicked a glance over my shoulder. "So far, so good?"

"Jesus, Merilee."

"I'll take that as a yes."

Grinning to myself, I tugged the thong into place, then slipped a finger under the back strap, lifting it away from my body, then letting it slide back into place. Then I turned to face him.

"And now we're gonna test how good these things are at containing an erection," he said.

Sure enough, when he dropped his shorts, a lovely hard-on distended the front of his boxer briefs. He peeled off his underwear and his erection popped free. He ran a hand over it. "Sure you don't want to stay here and fool around?"

"You'll do anything to get out of wearing a thong," I teased. He did make my mouth—and other, female parts—water, but Cabo was out there, waiting. "Put it on."

With a grimace, he stepped into the thong and pulled it up, forcing his swollen shaft into the skimpy fabric. On a lot of men, the underwear would have looked ridiculous, but he had the body to carry it off.

I said happily, "Oh, yes, I'm going to be thinking about that all day, and looking forward to taking that thing off when we get back this afternoon."

He didn't go study his reflection, just yanked up his shorts and put on a summer shirt we'd picked out together in Puerto Vallarta.

I studied my own wardrobe selections, torn between my denim mini and a pair of shorts. "What do you think we'll be doing?"

"Maybe take a whale-watching tour? And go swimming." He tossed his bathing suit on the bed, along with a towel. "And let me guess, you want to shop."

"What can I say? I'm female."

"Been noticing that." He winked. "We should have time to do it all. If you hurry up and get dressed." He whacked my bare backside with his palm, not hard enough to hurt, but enough to make a slapping sound.

A tingle spread through me. Maybe one day we'd try that spanking thing again. . . .

With a bland roll in my stomach to serve as breakfast, I strolled along the harbor in navy shorts and a turquoise top, taking note of restaurants and shops to check out later. His hand holding mine loosely, a tote with our stuff for the day over his other shoulder, Matt seemed more interested in the dozens of pleasure craft docked in the bay. We were headed toward the area where whale-watching tours departed.

"I'm glad we're spending the day together," I said, swinging our joined hands, savoring his company on this perfect day.

He squeezed my hand. "Me, too. In fact—"

"Do you think—" At the same moment, I started to ask if he thought we'd really see whales. We both broke off with a laugh.

"You go first," he said, considerate as always.

Gazing up at him, with the Mexican sun on our shoulders, a revelation hit me: Of course, Matt was my soul mate. I'd always loved him, and now, in my heart, I was sure it was the forever kind of love. He might not be a man who made grand romantic gestures, but he'd shown me fire and passion, and the ability to tease and play. He'd wear a leopard thong if I goaded him into it, and later today I'd make sure he didn't regret it. Add all that to his consideration and reliability, and he was the perfect man.

The reason my sisters had all that drama and excitement with their guys was because their relationships were brand new. Matt's and mine, the thrilling combination of old and new that we were building, was even better.

How totally weird that I'd had to call off the wedding for us both to take our feelings to a deeper and more exciting level. Or maybe I was jumping to conclusions. Matt was the one who'd said we should break up. Now he was clearly enjoying our sex life and I knew he still cared about me, but what was he thinking about our future?

Forget my trivial question about the whales; I had a more important one. "How do you see things going when we get home?" Was he ready to get back together as a real couple rather than just hang out as friends and lovers?

"Uh . . ." He studied me for a moment, then glanced away,

as if he was thinking about it. "I guess we need to keep doing what we've been doing this week, right? I mean, we can't be bonded at the hip again. We have to keep figuring out who we are as individuals. I think that's actually strengthening our relationship."

Hmm. It wasn't the declaration of love I'd hoped for, but what he said was true. "Yes, it is. In fact, I remember something Jenna said. People have to be independent, so when they give their love, they know it's out of want rather than need." I didn't exactly mean it as a hint, but it was definitely an opening for him to say he loved me.

Instead, he glanced toward the boats again, then back at me. "I guess that's true. So we need to do that, to find our independence. But we'll still do things together, too, right?"

Do things together? Trying to hide my hurt, I said off-handedly, "Oh, sure."

"Okay. Good," he said, sounding less than certain. "So we'll just take things easy rather than rush into anything."

"I guess that's what happened this year," I admitted. "When I got my diagnosis and we found out I'd have problems getting pregnant, we rushed into something we weren't ready for." If I hadn't been ready to get married last week, how could my heart feel so sure now? Matt clearly didn't feel that way.

"People said we were awfully young to be taking such a big step, and I guess we proved them right." He sighed.

"Yeah. Bummer, eh?" I was still twenty-one, but I felt years older than the girl I'd been last week.

"We always said we'd get married, then we kind of drifted into it, setting the date without really thinking."

"I know."

"Marriage is big, Merilee. It's a life-long commitment. A person needs to be absolutely sure."

"I know." Both people needed to be absolutely sure. And

they needed to believe that the other person loved them totally and forever. Which Matt clearly didn't. Tears moistened my eyes and I blinked furiously behind my sunglasses,
trying to hold them back.

I wouldn't give up hope. We were doing well. We had
walked through an open door, and we were on a journey. It
was, as Theresa had said, a bit of a wild ride. Matt was traveling the road more slowly than I was, but maybe we'd both
reach the same destination. Together.

"Enough serious stuff," he said. "Let's go see some whales."

I realized we'd reached the ticket booth for the whale-
watching tour.

As we joined a couple dozen other tourists and got fitted
out with bright orange-red life vests, the excitement in the
air proved contagious. Soon our sturdy open boat was zip-
ping across the dark ocean, the breeze cool on my cheeks
and bare arms. Matt put his arm around my shoulders and I
leaned into his warm, strong body.

The sharp-eyed guide yelled, "Over there!"

Before my wide eyes, a giant whale breached. Its huge
bulk rose in a graceful arc, then splashed down again, water
flying every which way. Thrilled, I grabbed Matt's hand, and
he squeezed mine.

The whale jumped again. Another joined it as our boat
moved closer. We all grabbed cameras and clicked away. Flying drops of water splashed us, making us squeal. Again,
tears rose to my eyes, but this time they were good ones,
elicited by the majesty and joy of these gentle monsters, and
by sharing this experience with the man I loved.

Eventually, the whales went on their way and the boat
turned back to Cabo. I leaned my head on Matt's shoulder
and said with satisfaction, "Now that was perfect."

He put his arm around me. "It was. It is."

* * *

Now this, Matt thought, was the opposite of perfect. Standing outside a closed door labeled *Damas*, listening to the sound of retching inside.

He and Merilee had returned from whale watching and had lunch at a restaurant on the harbor where she had, with token grumbling, eaten only a grilled cheese sandwich. After, they'd walked toward the group of big hotels along the beach, figuring they could change into bathing suits in a restroom and go swimming.

Strolling along the beach, Matt had splashed his feet in the edge of the ocean, looking forward to that swim. Looking forward to seeing Merilee in that string-tied bikini, and teasing her that he'd untie it.

Then he'd heard her strained voice. "I'm not feeling so well."

One glance at her pale, sweaty face confirmed that. "Let's get you into a hotel, out of the sun."

They speeded their pace, up the beach toward the closest hotel. A few steps took them into the pool area and he saw side-by-side doors marked *Damas* and *Caballeros*.

Hand over her mouth, she sprinted to the ladies' room.

He was about to follow when a woman came out and shot him a nasty look. So he stood there, listening to the muffled sounds of Merilee throwing up. Had she caught that tummy bug the passengers called Montezuma's revenge?

Maybe it would pass on its own, but this time he wasn't giving her an option. She was going to see the doctor as soon as they returned to the ship.

He heard the toilet flush, and no more retching sounds.

A middle-aged woman with bleached blond hair and sun-leathered skin started to open the restroom door and he said, "My girlfriend's in there. She wasn't feeling well. Would you mind seeing if there's anything I can do?"

"You bet, hon," she said.

A moment later, from behind the closed door, he heard female voices. The blonde stuck her head out the door. "She's feeling better. Just wants to sit down for a few minutes and make sure."

"Thanks. I appreciate it."

"Sun and margaritas," she said. "Happens to the best of us."

"She wasn't drinking." He hadn't let her. "Maybe it's Montezuma's revenge."

She wrinkled her nose. "Yeah, that happens to the best of us, too. Dontcha just love Mexico?" On that note, she disappeared back inside.

Keeping an eye on the door, he hurried over to a poolside bar and bought a glass of ginger ale, then returned to wait for Merilee.

Perhaps five minutes later, she emerged, looking shaky, the hair around her face damp. "I'd kill for toothpaste."

He put an arm around her and guided her to a chair in the shade, then handed her the glass.

She gave him a fragile, grateful smile, and sipped.

"As soon as you feel better," he said, "we're going back to the ship and you're seeing the doctor."

She sighed. "Maybe you're right. I must have some kind of bug. Perhaps I need antibiotics. Damn. I really wanted to go swimming."

So had he. With her.

She lay back in the lounge chair, her eyes closed, and he sat beside her, watching tourists enjoying the pool. He sure hoped nothing was seriously wrong with Merilee. She'd been so run-down, never really giving herself a chance to recover from her surgery.

After ten minutes or so, she said, "Hey there."

He turned to see that the color had returned to her cheeks. "How are you feeling?"

"Better. We could still go swimming."

He shook his head. "Nope. We're going back to the

boat." He stood and reached down a hand to help her rise. When they got there, she was going to the doctor. This time, he wasn't giving her a choice.

She sighed as she let him pull her to her feet. "You're right."

Keeping an arm around her, he guided her into the hotel, then out the other side where taxis were waiting. "Cruise ship terminal," he told the driver.

Beside him, Merilee sighed. "This isn't how I wanted to end our last day in Mexico."

"Nothing about this trip's been exactly what we expected, has it?" he said ruefully.

In the confines of the tiny examination room, feeling absolutely fine now, I recited my symptoms to the ship's doctor, a chic, petite brunette with a French accent. "You must get lots of people with tummy upsets," I said. "I probably just need to take some Pepto-Bismol, right?"

Dr. Lasseur smiled. "Hold on, I'm the doctor so let me do my job. And yes, there are lots of tummy problems. Everything from overeating to food poisoning to Montezuma's revenge—which, by the way, I doubt you have because there's no diarrhea. There are also more serious conditions. Sometimes nausea is associated with appendicitis or a heart attack."

"You don't think—"

"No, no," she said reassuringly. "I am only explaining that I want to be thorough and not make assumptions. So, I will take a medical history and examine you. Please change into a gown, and I'll be back in a minute."

I put on one of the ridiculous paper gowns, then she asked me a series of questions.

"My only health issue," I told her, "is endometriosis." I told her about my surgery.

"How have you felt since then?"

"Tired and run-down, but that's partly because I needed to make up course work at university."

She took my blood pressure. "Have you been taking iron supplements?"

"No."

"Your blood pressure is a little low. When was your last period?"

"I don't exactly remember. I've been so busy I haven't paid attention."

"You aren't on birth control pills?"

"No, I stopped taking them a few weeks ago, so I guess that's why my period's kind of erratic. We're—we *were*—hoping to get pregnant." And now Matt was using condoms.

I answered more questions and endured some poking and prodding, including an internal exam which I thought was pretty excessive for a stomach bug. Still, I respected her thoroughness. Next, she asked me to go into a tiny bathroom and provide a urine sample.

When I gave her the little cup, she said, "You can get dressed now. Wait for me in the exam room."

A few minutes later, Dr. Lasseur joined me again. "The good news is, while you're a little run-down, you're healthy."

"Just take some Pepto?" I could have saved myself a fifteen minute exam.

"No, take these." She took a small bottle from the pocket of her white jacket and held it toward me. "I hope this isn't bad news."

Puzzled, I took the bottle from her and read the label. Prenatal vitamins?

Prenatal vitamins?! I almost dropped them in my shock. "I'm pregnant?"

She leaned against the counter and nodded. "I did two urine tests, both highly reliable, and they're positive. It's very early days, so as soon as you get home, you need to see your doctor. They'll do a blood test and—"

"I'm pregnant?" As the news sank in, a wave of joy rushed through my body, catapulting me off the chair. Tears gushing, I gave her a giant hug.

She squeezed back, smiling. "It's good news then?"

"The best!" I grinned through the flood of tears. "I've always wanted children, and I was so worried I'd never get pregnant." Oh, my God, I was pregnant! Just wait until I told Matt!

But . . . The energy suddenly drained from my body and I collapsed back on the chair.

The doctor studied me with concern. "You said you *were* trying. Something happened between you and the father?"

Trying to blink back more tears, I took the tissue she handed me. "We were going to get married, but, uh, we decided we weren't ready yet." He'd said we should use condoms because we didn't want to be forced into a future together."

"You're young," she said. "Is he?"

I gazed across at her. "Yes. My age."

"Marriage and a family, they're big decisions at any age." Solemn-eyed, she went on. "You know you have options, Merilee."

Options? If I told Matt I was pregnant, he'd marry me. No question. But he'd be doing it out of his sense of responsibility and loyalty, maybe out of love for the baby, not because he knew he wanted to spend his life with me. Tears kept seeping down my cheeks.

"You are less than a month along, yes?" she said, passing over more tissues.

"Yes." Then it dawned on me what she meant about options. "Abortion? No! No way. This is my baby, the baby I've always wanted. Whatever happens with Matt, I'm having my baby. And keeping her. Him."

She nodded. "Do you have someone back home you can talk to about this? You'll need support."

"My family." I gave a wavery smile, glad to be able to say something I hadn't been sure of until recently. "They'll all support me. Whatever I decide." They'd noisily share opinions and advice, because that was the Fallon way—and they'd stand by me, because they loved me. Now I understood that I didn't always have to be good, I didn't have to knuckle under and go along with what they wanted. They'd love me just because I was me: Merilee Fallon.

"That's wonderful. And perhaps things will work out with the father. Even if you don't marry, it's good when a child has two loving parents who are involved in his or her life."

I swiped at a fresh wave of tears. "Yes, and Matt will want that. But . . ." I gazed at her, feeling inexplicably close to the petite, dark-haired Frenchwoman. In this small, sterile cubicle, she must hear so many people's confessions, their dreams and fears. "I love him. And, of course, I want him to love our child and be involved in her—his—life, but I don't want him marrying me just because I'm pregnant."

"It's not the best start, is it?" she said gently.

I shook my head. "When you marry, it should be out of want, not need or obligation. If I marry him, I want to be absolutely sure he loves me, too, and wants to be with me for the rest of his life."

A soft smile lit her face. "You're young, but mature, I think."

Mature? No one had ever seen me that way before. It sounded good.

"You'll find your path, Merilee. The right one for you and your baby." She held out a hand. "Congratulations, Mom."

In a flash, the joy returned. Oh, yes, that was what counted most. I was going to have a baby. I reached out to shake her hand. "Thank you. Thank you for giving me the best news of my life." A thought struck me and I asked, "What's your first name, Dr. Lasseur?"

"Danielle. Why do you ask?"

Danielle, or Daniel for a boy. I liked them both. "I've been thinking about baby names all my life. Right now, yours is on top of the list."

She touched a hand to her heart in a graceful, very French gesture. "I am honored. Now, for a few minutes, we must be practical. You have the vitamins and should start taking them right away. You must build up your own health, to best look after your baby."

"Oh, I just thought." Horrified, I said, "I've been drinking. Not much, but some alcohol. And coffee. D'you think—"

"It's very unlikely that'll cause a problem. But stop now, yes?"

"Absolutely."

"As for the nausea, the vitamins I've given you contain things like ginger that will help."

"That would be very nice."

"The traditional things like nibbling saltines and drinking ginger ale help, too. Make sure you stay hydrated."

I nodded, taking it all in. *I'm pregnant!* My hand rested on my tummy. *Hello, baby, I'm your mom.*

"You're hormonal, so don't be surprised if your emotions are all over the place."

"Tell me about it," I said wryly.

"If you have any problems before the end of the cruise, come see me."

Slowly, I got to my feet. Matt was outside. What was I going to tell him?

She touched my shoulder gently. "Good luck. You're going to make a lovely mother."

"Thank you, Dr. Lasseur."

"You might want to wash your face before you leave."

"Yes. Yes, please." I again went into the little bathroom,

where I splashed cold water on my face, trying to banish the signs of my tears. Then, feet dragging with uncertainty, I walked toward the closed door that led out to the waiting room. To Matt. My baby's father.

My baby. I still could hardly believe it. I had that shiny, new feeling again, brave and vulnerable all at the same time. My future had begun. I knew it was going to hold a baby. But what else?

I stared at the closed door. Jenna said open doors meant opportunities. How many times had I imagined telling Matt I was pregnant? Imagined us holding hands as we watched the first ultrasound?

I stuffed the vitamin bottle deep inside my purse. No, I wasn't going to tell him. I wanted him to decide how he felt about me, not be influenced by the baby. Then I opened the door and stepped through.

Matt, sitting in the waiting room along with a flushed, overweight man, rose quickly and came to take my hands. "How are you? You were in there so long." He guided me to the door.

Thoughts in turmoil, I forced a smile as we stepped out into the corridor. "Dr. Lasseur is thorough. She wanted to make sure I didn't have appendicitis or a heart problem." As his eyes widened, I held up a hand. "Which I don't. I'm perfectly healthy. Just a little run-down."

"Why've you been throwing up?"

Had I ever out-and-out lied to him before? Not that I could remember, and it made my heart ache. "Probably I did have food poisoning that first day, and now my system's sensitive. I may still feel a bit off, but it should improve." I sure hoped the ginger in those vitamins worked.

Today was Friday. Tomorrow we'd be at sea, then we'd disembark Sunday and fly back to Vancouver. Once I was home, it would be easier to keep my secret.

How long would it take until Matt knew how he felt

about me? And what if, in the end, he didn't want to get back together as anything other than friends? I had to believe that, whatever else happened, we'd at least always be friends.

"What do you want to do now?" he asked, squeezing my hand gently. "Take a nap? Go for dinner?"

Confused and emotional, I wanted to be alone with my baby. I wanted to phone my family. And yet it wouldn't be fair to tell them before I told Matt. I stifled a groan.

"Merilee, are you okay?"

"Just tired. I do need a nap. Then I'll probably get something light from room service."

"Okay, we'll stay in the cabin tonight."

"No." I couldn't be alone with him, not right now. "There's no reason for you to stay. I'm just going to doze. Then maybe I'll read your book, the one Damien wrote. It looks really good. You go and enjoy that delicious buffet dinner." Oh, man, I was babbling.

When he started to protest, I said, striving for a light tone, "Not joined at the hip, remember? Independent? And you don't have to worry about me because the doctor gave me a clean bill of health."

Matt forced a smile. "I hear you." Did being independent mean he couldn't be concerned about her and want to be with her when she wasn't feeling well? Or was she really saying she wanted to be alone? People needed time on their own. Not that Merilee'd ever seemed to before, but it was probably part of her finding her independence.

"Thanks," she said absently, her mind obviously somewhere else. Maybe looking forward to that quiet time alone.

When they entered the cabin, she kicked off her sandals, then peeled off her shorts, leaving her shirt on, and climbed into bed. There, she settled on her side with her back to him.

He took off his own shorts and stripped off the ridiculous

leopard thong, the one he'd intended to make her pay—in the very best way—for forcing him to wear. Not feeling like dressing up tonight, he chose jeans and a Mexican tee that Merilee had said matched his eyes. Quietly, he let himself out of the room.

As he strolled through the ship's enormous atrium, all golden and glittery, he passed other passengers, sun-flushed, most of them dressed up. If he went to the fancy buffet, he'd be sitting at a table full of animated tourists and he wasn't in the mood. Instead, he headed for a sports bar where he could find a game to watch and a couple of guys to drink with.

He passed a French bistro called La Vie en Rose, romantically lit, with music drifting out. Definitely not a guy place.

Except he was supposed to be trying new things, being independent. Hanging out in a sports bar was the kind of thing he did with his buddies back home.

It wouldn't kill him, a little French food and music in some girlie place. If it was nice, and if Merilee was feeling better tomorrow, maybe he'd bring her here for their last dinner aboard.

He was pretty fluent in French and his brain automatically translated the lyrics of the music from the restaurant. How about that, it actually had the restaurant's title in it. The song was about seeing the world as all rosy-hued when you were in love.

It was true. He'd thought his life was terrific up until last Thursday night when Merilee pulled the plug on their wedding. She'd shattered him and turned his world on its head. Since then . . . well, life sure hadn't been boring. Mostly, he felt good about how the two of them were doing, but he was wary about feeling too good. Wary about letting himself be vulnerable.

He tuned into the lyrics again. Man, that was one sappy love song, but it went along with the pale pink tablecloths, the sparkling crystal, the candles. Trying to ignore the fact that most of the people in the restaurant were in pairs, he smiled at the pretty, brown-haired waitress who came toward him. His mind still working in French, he greeted her with, "*Bonsoir, mademoiselle.*"

"*Bonsoir, monsieur. Comment allez-vous ce soir?*" She went on in that language, asking him if he wanted a table for one.

He squared his shoulders and said yes, deciding to keep speaking in French. Then—because what did he know about French food and wine?—he asked her for recommendations. That strategy had worked out great at the restaurant in Puerto Vallarta. When she described the *boeuf bourguignon*, he chose that, and also a glass of the red wine she said would go best with it.

Then he sat, sipping wine, feeling weird. When he was alone in his garage apartment, he either studied or watched a game or TV show, maybe read a book. He never sat doing nothing. *Try new things*, he reminded himself.

His immediate reaction to ziplining and scuba diving had been, *What a blast*. Dinner alone in a French restaurant? Not so much. Definitely outside his comfort zone. But he'd stick it out. Hopefully, at least the food would be good.

Interestingly, as he sipped wine and listened to the music, he found himself relaxing. It was actually kind of peaceful doing nothing. He could think, or not think. And when his dinner arrived, he really tasted it.

The waitress came by to ask how he liked it, and when she offered another glass of wine, he accepted. From time to time, she dropped by to chat for a few minutes, not coming on to him, just being nice. Her name was Jamie and she wasn't French, but had majored in the language in college. She came from the Midwest and was working to earn money for an extended trip to France.

He told her that he wasn't on the cruise alone, but his friend wasn't feeling well tonight.

"I'm glad you came here," she said. "It's nice to have someone to talk to. Everyone else"—she gestured with her head—"is all wrapped up in each other." Sure enough, there was a lot of hand-holding, eye-gazing, and intense conversations going on at the other tables.

Maybe tomorrow, he and Merilee would be doing that. "I'm glad I came here, too," he said honestly.

"You're a rare man. Much more interesting than those guys with their beers and shots in the sports bar."

He didn't tell her that he'd almost been one of them. "Thanks."

When Matt made it back to the cabin after a very leisurely dinner—including a dessert of Grand Marnier crepes the waitress talked him into—he found the lights out and Merilee sound asleep. He slid off his sandals and moved silently across the room to the bathroom.

As he brushed his teeth, he looked forward to tomorrow. He sure hoped she felt better, because he really wanted to take her to that restaurant. It would be more grown-up than the big fancy buffet. Maybe they'd even drink French champagne. He really wanted this cruise to end on a high note. He wanted to believe that, sometime down the road when they both figured things out, they really would be walking down the aisle together.

Maybe he shouldn't have had that third glass of wine. He, like that French singer, was getting all sappy and sentimental and seeing the world in rosy hues.

Absentmindedly putting his toothbrush down, he knocked against Merilee's purse, which was sitting on the bathroom counter. It fell to the floor with a crash, stuff cascading out of it. "Damn," he muttered, hoping he hadn't woken her.

Gingerly—because what guy wanted to mess with a girl's stuff?—he began to collect the spilled items and put them back in. Nail file, lip gloss, breath mints, bottle of pills . . . Pills? He held the bottle up to take a closer look.

Prenatal vitamins? Oh, she must have started taking those when she went off birth control in hopes of getting pregnant. Though it was strange she hadn't told him.

He was about to toss the bottle back in her purse when the bathroom door opened and Merilee, shielding her eyes against the bright light, stood there in an oversized T-shirt. "Matt, are you okay? I heard—" She broke off, eyes widening, an expression of total shock on her face as she stared at the bottle in his hand.

She yanked it away from him, screeching, "What are you doing going through my purse?"

Chapter 16

Huh? Merilee never yelled. Why was she going postal over his finding her vitamins? "I wasn't. I knocked it off the counter accidentally and—" He broke off. She'd been throwing up and had resisted seeing the doctor. Women took prenatal vitamins when they were pregnant, as well as when they were trying to get pregnant.

"You're pregnant?" Even as he spoke the words, he knew he was crazy. She'd have told him the moment she found out.

Her guilty expression said it was true.

Anger surged through him and he grabbed her by the shoulders. "You're pregnant and you didn't tell me? Is that why you called off the wedding? You found out you were pregnant and—what? You weren't sure you wanted to have a baby with me? Jesus, Merilee!" It had hurt when she pulled the plug on the wedding, but this betrayal was ten times worse.

"No!" She wrenched free of his hands. "Stop it, Matt, don't get so upset. The doctor just told me. She gave me the vitamins."

And that made it better? "Why didn't you tell me? What the hell? I'm the father." For a moment, he wondered if that was true. She'd been acting so strangely, who knew what was going on with her? But no, he did know that much: She'd never cheat on a guy.

"I was going to. It was just such a shock and—"

"Shit, yeah." They'd talked for years about having a baby, about how excited they'd be when they found out the news. Then, with her medical condition, they'd wondered if it would ever happen. "Yeah, a shock, but jeez, this is what we wanted. How could you not tell me?"

Her blue eyes were dark with worry and another horrible thought struck him. "You still want the baby, don't you?" he asked.

"Yes! Yes, of course I do."

Relief weakened his knees. Of course, she wanted their baby. He took a few deep breaths until he could speak more calmly "Why didn't you tell me? Did you think I wouldn't want it, now that we, you know, kind of broke up and are trying to figure things out?" Of course. That must be it.

Quickly, he assured her, "I do. Definitely." Their baby. How could he not want it? "We'll set another wedding date whenever you want."

Still standing in the doorway, she shook her head vigorously. "No, we won't. Damn it, Matt, this is what I *didn't* want happening."

He gaped at her. Once, he'd been so sure he knew Merilee like she was his other half. "You don't want to get married?"

"No, I—"

Hurt and anger rushed through him again and he cut her off. "You don't want to get married, you didn't tell me you were pregnant. Were you ever going to tell me?"

Defiantly, she stared back at him. "Of course. But not for a while."

"A while? A *while*?" He ground the words out.

"We both need time to think, to see where things—"

"Think? What the hell's to think about? We're having a baby." Once, he'd figured those would be joyous words. A child created from their love, one they'd raise together. He fisted his hands on his hips. "You're not keeping my child from me." His dad had been the worst kind of parent, and Matt was determined to be the best he could possibly be.

"Jesus, Matt." Her eyes spit fire. "I never said that. Just that I need some time—"

"*You* need? How about what I need? *I* need a woman who's honest with me, who doesn't shut me out like I don't count." Anger vibrated through him, tightening every muscle.

She stuck her own hands on her hips and glared. "When have I ever done that?"

"Hah! You decide to call off the wedding. You don't even tell me I'm going to be a father. Shit." He wanted to hit something. Not her, he'd never hit her, but he wanted to strike out.

The way his dad used to.

Without another word, he strode out of the bathroom and out of the cabin, pissed off that the heavy door refused to slam behind him.

After Matt had gone, I huddled in bed, shivering despite the comforter I'd wrapped around me.

I stuck my hand out from my nest of covers and picked up my cell. I needed to talk to someone. Like Dr. Lasseur had said, twenty-one wasn't all that old. Not so old I couldn't call the one person in the world I wanted right now.

When she answered the phone, her voice brisk, I wailed, "Mom," and began to cry.

"Merilee, honey, what's wrong?"

"I, I . . ." I hiccupped, then let it out. "I'm pregnant."

"Oh, my gosh. Really? I . . . don't know what to say." But, Mom being Mom, that didn't last for more than a second. "You're crying. You're not happy? Or Matt's upset about it?"

"I *am* happy, I'm thrilled." I brushed tears off my cheeks and shoved another pillow under my head. "I just found out this afternoon, and I didn't tell Matt, but he found out anyway and he's furious."

"You didn't tell him?"

"I knew how he'd react. He'd want to get married."

"Ah. And you don't want to. So this time on the cruise hasn't brought you closer together?"

"Yes, yes, it has. It's been wonderful."

A pause. "Then I'm not seeing the problem."

"Oh, Mom, I love him so much. We've both come a long way in just a few days, learning to be independent, but also really connecting in, uh, new ways." Ways that sometimes involved Ben Wa balls, though I wasn't about to tell her that. "I'd marry him tomorrow if he felt the same way."

"Matt's always loved you."

"I know. But it may not be the right kind of love, and he's not sure about the future."

"You're losing me, Merilee. You just said he would want—does want?—to get married."

Well, he had, before he stormed out without saying where he was going or when he'd be back. *If* he'd be back. Matt was even-tempered; he didn't get mad, much less furious like he'd been tonight. Was this fight the final straw that would destroy our relationship?

"Merilee?"

I sniffled. "He said he wants us to get married, but it's for the wrong reasons. Because of the baby, not because he wants to spend his life with me. That's not how it should be. It wouldn't be good for any of us. Oh, Mom, I couldn't bear living like that."

"That doesn't sound like Matt."

"He's not the same Matt. I'm not the same me. And it's

good, mostly. But before he found out, he said we should use birth control so we wouldn't be forced into something. And he said marriage is a really big thing and we shouldn't rush. I know he doesn't really want to marry me. And then when he found out I was pregnant and hadn't told him, he was furious and we had a horrible fight. And we *never* fight."

"I'm sure he was stunned, hurt, upset. And you're emotional and your hormones are going crazy. Fights happen, dear. He'll calm down and the two of you will talk. He's not going to be mad at you forever."

I'd have said that was true of the old Matt, but the new one was edgier, more confident, more decisive. "I hope," I said. "But Mom, I don't want us to get married because of the baby. I want to know that Matt really, really loves me and wants to commit to me for life."

I sighed and tugged the covers more tightly around my shoulders. "That's what I decided in the doctor's office. Maybe I handled things badly, not telling him. But I do think my decision's the right one." I waited for her judgment. Maybe she'd say I was being selfish, and we should get married for the sake of the baby.

When she didn't say anything, I said, "Mom, are you still there?"

"Yes."

"What do you think? Am I crazy?"

"I think you've thought things through and made a sound decision."

"Really? Are you okay? You don't sound like yourself."

She gave a soft chuckle. "I'm fine. And I don't think you handled it badly, not wanting to tell Matt. That was a Catch-22 situation with no good answer. Yes, he deserves to know, but I understand that you'd like him to decide about you and him independently of the baby."

"Thanks, Mom."

"You're being very mature about this. I'm proud of you."

Wow. I smiled a little. "Mature? I cried all over you, long distance."

"Adults cry, too. And I'm glad you called me. For what it's worth, Merilee, if I'd gotten pregnant before your dad and I married, I'd have felt the same way you do."

My mom was the smartest woman I knew, so it meant a lot to hear her say that. "Thanks."

"Are you going to tell your sisters that you're pregnant?"

I leaned back against the pillows, a wave of tiredness hitting me. "Now that Matt knows, there's no reason to keep it a secret. But I think I'll wait until I'm home, rather than call from the ship." It'd give me more time to reflect, and maybe Matt would come back and we'd talk, rather than fight.

"My lips are sealed."

"What about Dad? Is he there? Did I wake you both up?"

"No, I'm in my office and he's working in his. I want to tell him about the baby. That's all right?"

"Sure."

"Merilee?"

"Yes?"

"You're going to have a beautiful baby, and you'll be a wonderful mother."

"Thanks." I realized she'd never mentioned the possibility of abortion. It proved how well she knew me.

"I promise you I'll do better as a grandma than I did as a mother," she said firmly.

Yeah, she hadn't been perfect and I knew I'd do things differently. But she'd been there, she'd done her best, and always in my heart I'd known she loved me. "Mom, the only person I wanted to talk to tonight was you."

There was a small sound. An intake of breath? A sniffle? "That means the world to me. I love you, honey."

"I love you, too." A grin twitched my lips. "Grandma." I hung up, thinking how odd—in a totally nice way—that conversation had been. I'd expected her to tell me what to do. If she'd said I should apologize to Matt and marry him, would I have done it?

No. I'd made my decision and it was the right one. But I hated that Matt was hurt and mad. I hated that he'd stormed off into the night. When he came back, I had to do a better job of explaining.

If he came back.

I smothered a yawn. He would, and I'd wait up for him, and we'd talk.

Matt woke to find Merilee curled up facing him, her breath warm against his neck. Asleep. One of his arms rested across her hip, holding her there. In their sleep, they'd come together as they so often did.

Last night he'd spent a couple of hours outside on the chilly deck, trying to sort things through. He'd let himself be vulnerable again, and again she'd shattered him. That was the raw emotion that made him want to punch something.

And yet, when she'd called off the wedding, she'd had reasons. Ones that, in the end, had made sense. Maybe she did this time, too, if he gave her time to share them.

He'd returned to the cabin and there she'd been, sound asleep, propped up on pillows with the light on like she'd tried to wait up for him.

She'd looked so pretty, so sweet. He had gazed down at her, marveling. She was carrying their child. Their relationship was messed up, but that one truth remained, and it was a whopper.

He was going to be a dad. That wasn't a decision like whether to be a teacher or a pilot, or even whether to marry or not: It was a fact. It would shape the entire rest of his life. This was huge, but it didn't scare him. Well, a little, because it'd scare any sane guy, but mostly it thrilled and awed him. He didn't worry that he had a rotten paternal role model to draw on; his dad had shown him exactly how *not* to behave.

No, he wouldn't let Merilee shut him out of his son or daughter's life. Surely, she wouldn't. Yesterday, she'd been emotional. Irrational.

As if she sensed his attention, she stirred and her lashes fluttered. Then her eyes opened. When she first saw him, her expression was sweet and loving. Then her eyes narrowed and her facial muscles tensed. She was remembering. "Matt," she said tentatively. "You came back."

"You thought I wouldn't?" What kind of guy did she take him for?

"No, I did, I hoped, but . . ."

She had. She'd actually thought he might abandon her. After fourteen years, how could she think that? Fresh anger stirred. He thrust himself to a sitting position, about to ream her out, when she went pale.

With an intent, inwardly-focused expression on her face, she rolled slowly onto her back, pressing a hand to her stomach.

Morning sickness. Gruffly, he said, "Are you okay?"

She closed her eyes and he saw lines of strain at the corners.

"There's ginger ale in the bedside table," she murmured, as if speaking loudly would make the nausea worse. "Could you open one for me?"

He jumped out of bed naked, came around to her side of the bed, and took a can from the drawer. In there, she had several more cans and a package of saltine crackers, which he took out as well.

He poured ginger ale into a glass, then sat beside her on the bed. Automatically, he slid an arm under her shoulders to lift her so she could drink.

She took a sip, paused, then another. "Ginger's supposed to be good for nausea," she said in that same soft voice. "And so are the vitamins. Sure hope so."

"I got the crackers, too. Do you want—"

"No!" she yelped. "Keep them away from me."

After a moment, she sipped again. "Thanks, Matt. I'm feeling a bit better. Maybe I'll try a cracker—in a day or so." Then she waved a hand. "Just kidding."

Maybe they were in the middle of a fight, but she was the woman he'd always loved and she was carrying his child. "I'm sorry you feel so bad. But it's worth it, though. Right? You're having a baby." When the doctor had told her she might never conceive, she'd been shattered.

"Easy for you to say," she grumbled, then her lips curved at the corners. "Yeah, I could be sick for nine months straight, and it'd be worth it."

Part of him was still mad and worried, but he wasn't going to push her when she was feeling shitty. Instead, he kept his arm around her as she took slow sips. Then, finally, she said, "I might try a cracker."

When he handed her one, her gaze raked him. "You're naked."

"Oh. Yeah." Did that bother her? He got up and pulled on a pair of boxer briefs while she nibbled the cracker, then reached for another. Color slowly returned to her cheeks.

When he came to sit beside her again, she said, "I was an unplanned baby. I never believed my parents—or my sisters—wanted me. But this baby"—she rested her hand on her flat stomach—"will always know it's wanted."

"By me, too, Merilee." Unable to resist, he rested his hand atop hers. One day, he'd touch her body and feel the baby kick. If she let him. Oh, damn, he couldn't keep quiet. "We could be a family. It's what we always wanted. Was last night just jitters or hormones or something? I really think we should get married."

She winced. Fighting another surge of nausea?

"Sorry," he said guiltily. "I shouldn't be talking to you about this when you're not feeling well."

"No, I really don't feel up to it. Give me a little while. Then yes, we need to talk."

He nodded, rose, and walked over to the window to shift the curtains aside and glance out. "We're on the ocean and it's another sunny day."

"How about I meet you on deck at that coffee shop that has outside tables? Say in an hour?"

She wanted to meet in public. So he couldn't get carried away and fight with her? What was she going to say that would get him so upset? "Fine," he said curtly, whisking the heavy fabric back across the window to shut out the sun.

Quickly, he put on workout gear and gathered a change of clothes. "I'm going to the fitness club. I'll shower and dress there." And try to work off some of the pent-up mix of hurt, anger, and uncertainty.

When he walked toward the coffee shop and saw Merilee sitting at a table eating a breakfast sandwich, she was a different person than the wan girl he'd left in bed. Her skin glowed with a golden tan, her white shorts and yellow tank were dynamite, and that sassy haircut definitely suited her.

A tentative smile quivered on her lips as he approached. "Why don't you get something to eat?" she suggested.

Despite feeling anxious, he was starving after a vigorous workout. "Okay. Want anything else?" A near-empty bowl of fruit salad sat on the table.

She held up an empty mug. "I want coffee, but I can't have it. How about another ginger tea? Thanks."

He got himself a couple of breakfast sandwiches, a coffee, and an orange juice, and brought them and her tea to the table. Sitting down across from her, he said, "Well. Our lives are going to change. We need to talk about that."

She nodded. "I'm sorry for not telling you."

He chewed and swallowed. "I don't get it. Why didn't

you? Tell me you're not going to try to shut me out of the baby's life."

"Of course not."

Relief flooded him. "Good."

Her lashes drifted down, then up. "It hurt that you thought I might. But I know the way I acted hurt you, too. And I did want to tell you, Matt. I was so happy about being pregnant, but things are confusing, too. Between you and me."

He finished another bite. "They don't have to be. We can do what we always planned to. Get married and have a baby." Why was she making this so complicated?

She shook her head. "The old plan is the one that wasn't working. The rut."

"Yeah, but we've both changed. We won't fall back into the rut."

"Maybe not," she conceded.

He finished the first sandwich and took a long swallow of juice. "Then what's the problem?"

"Yesterday you said we shouldn't rush things."

"Well, yeah, but now you're pregnant." And he loved her, loved their baby. Didn't she feel the same way? "I want this, Merilee. You and our son or daughter."

Her eyes lit momentarily when he said that, then the worried look reappeared. "I knew that as soon as you found out, you'd want us to get married."

"What's so wrong with that?" Exasperation colored his voice. He took a deep breath and tried to stay calm. Fighting wasn't going to help. Merilee was always practical, so he'd give her a reasoned argument. "Be practical here. A baby should have two parents. We're both going to love it, look after it, raise it. It's crazy to do that separately. What are we going to do, shuffle the poor kid back and forth? That's not fair to any of us."

"Fair?" Her mouth tightened. "It's not fair to be forced into something we're not sure about. I'm just barely pregnant. We have months and months to think about this."

She was shoving him away again. Okay, he could be overprotective, but damn it, if she was pregnant, he wanted to go through it with her. To look after her when she was sick, to shop for a crib, to talk about names. To see their baby moving around on an ultrasound screen.

He was pissed off. Hurt. But he'd do his best to see her side. If she needed time, he could give it to her. Days, weeks, maybe even a month or two. Surely by then she'd know. They'd both know, absolutely and forever, and then they'd get married.

Or she'd have decided that the instinct that led her to call off the wedding was right. That she didn't want to spend the rest of her life with him.

Matt shoved aside the second sandwich, no longer hungry. "Fine, I hear you. We'll take some time."

She nodded, not even looking happy that she'd won.

"But tell me what it is we're waiting for."

She clasped her china tea mug between both hands as if she were cold. "Yesterday morning, you said marriage is a big thing and both people need to be absolutely sure."

He nodded. He was sure. She wasn't. That was the bottom line.

"We need to be sure," she went on, "that we're both getting married because we really, really love each other and want to spend our lives together. Not just because of the baby. Otherwise, it's not fair to any of us."

He stared at her earnest face as her words sank in. She was right. Much as he wanted them to be married and raise their child together, he didn't want her doing it unless she truly loved him. And he needed to be absolutely sure, too. He thought he was, but . . . "How do we know?" he asked quietly.

"I . . . don't know." Doubt pinched her face.

He was going to be a dad, and it wasn't anything like the way he'd imagined it. Suddenly, he couldn't sit here with her any longer. He couldn't talk about this anymore. He was too hurt and frustrated, too confused and pissed off.

He rose abruptly, the feet of his chair scraping the deck. "I'm going to go take a martial arts class." When he'd seen it in the event calendar, it had appealed to him. Now he welcomed the opportunity to do something purely physical and work off some tension.

"Martial arts?" she said disbelievingly. Her chin went up. "Well, I'm going to take another cooking lesson."

I stared after Matt, heart sinking and tears rising to my eyes.

What had I hoped for from him? Was I still the same naïve girl as last week, hoping that he'd fight for me, that he'd make that grand romantic gesture? That when I'd said we needed to take time and be sure, he wouldn't agree, but would somehow persuade me he did love me: truly, madly, deeply, passionately, and forever?

Why should I feel so shattered that he didn't even want to spend the last day with me? We'd agreed we needed more independence.

We'd agreed on everything, damn it, and it was stupid that I had to blink back tears. Was I extra emotional these days because of what was going on with us, or because of pregnancy hormones? Both, probably.

Matt was right that we needed to be practical, and I was right that he shouldn't marry me out of duty. That wouldn't be good for any of the three of us. Of course, we needed to take time and be sure of whatever decision we made. If we made a mistake, we could hurt our child.

But what if he decided he didn't love me in the right way, the forever way? Yes, he'd be there for our baby, but how could I stand watching him eventually fall for someone else? Commit to someone else, marry her, have babies with her, too? The child in my belly could have half-brothers or half-sisters, and—

"Ack!" I muttered aloud. What had happened to me? I'd always been an optimist, not a pessimist.

Worrying couldn't be good for the baby. I needed to be more Zen, the way Jenna was. I took a slow, deep breath, then let it out. She'd say that the universe would provide what the baby and I needed. I would do my best to believe that. Perhaps it was marriage to Matt; perhaps it wasn't. Either way, I'd love my baby and I'd be fine.

Feeling more at peace, I rested my hand on my tummy. "Hey, you in there, it's just you and me today. D'you want to learn how to cook?"

It had been a good day, I told myself firmly as I headed back to the cabin in the late afternoon.

I'd learned to cook chicken *mole*, had a massage, then joined Des and Micky for tapas and drinks—I'd gone with ginger ale, my new favorite—at a poolside bar. We'd all said how we could get used to this decadent life, but in my heart I knew that luxury and frittering away my time wasn't the real me. At least not for more than a day or two every now and then. Every day, I was learning new things about myself.

They'd teased me about my dashing pirate, but when I'd said things were complicated, they backed off. I hadn't told them I was pregnant. Our friendship was too new. It was good, though. We'd chatted for hours by the pool, and all said we wanted to keep in touch and exchanged e-mail addresses.

They had invited me to join them for dinner, the extra-fancy last night buffet. When I'd thanked them and said I wasn't sure yet, they'd exchanged knowing glances. "If you're on your own, come look for us," Des had said.

Probably, I would be on my own. Matt hadn't said anything about dinner. Given the weirdness between us right now, I could see why he hadn't. Tomorrow, we'd travel back to Vancouver together. When we'd come a week ago, we'd spent the trip in awkward silence. What a bummer to think that tomorrow would likely be a repeat performance.

What would happen when we were back home? Was our relationship destined, or doomed?

So much for the good mood I'd been trying to cultivate. Now, as I opened the cabin door, I felt depressed. And ready for a nap. At least I hadn't thrown up all day. There'd been a little nausea here and there, but nothing crucial. Those prenatal vitamins were magic.

The cabin was empty, but an envelope lay on my side of the bed. In Matt's bold, scrawly handwriting, it was addressed to Ms. Merilee Fallon.

My heart clutched. What did Matt need to say that he couldn't tell me to my face? Had he decided he wanted the breakup to be permanent?

My hand trembled as I reached for the envelope and ripped open the seal. I pulled out a card, the kind with a photograph stuck on it. This picture was of a courtyard patio with a table and two chairs, and a hanging basket cascading with blooms. On the table were two wineglasses. Warm light gave the scene a romantic golden glow. Surely a card like this couldn't contain bad news.

I took another breath, then opened it. My eyebrows rose in astonished pleasure. It was an invitation. Not in fancy calligraphy, but in messy handwriting, which made it even more special. I smiled as I read it.

Matt Townsend requests the pleasure of Merilee Fallon's company for dinner at La Vie en Rose tonight at 7:00.

Charmed, unable to really believe it, I read it again. He'd gotten over being mad. He wanted to have dinner together.

La Vie en Rose was the French bistro where I'd eaten my very first meal on my own. It was delightful, but not the kind of place I'd picture Matt at. He was more the "beer in the pub" kind of guy. Or at least that's who the old Matt had been. The new one had chosen that wonderful ocean-view restaurant in Puerto Vallarta.

And he'd picked a French restaurant for our last night on the *Diamond Star*. Not the groaning buffet table with the noisy crowd of holidayers, but a quiet, charming, and yes, romantic place. Wow. From down in the dumps, I swung up to ecstatic.

It felt like he was giving us another second chance, another fresh start. Almost as if he was wooing me, but Matt had never had to do that because from the day we'd met, I'd been a sure thing.

But he wasn't a sure thing anymore, and I wanted to impress him.

My tiredness fled. I was going on a date with the man I loved, and I would look amazingly beautiful. If there was one time in my life when extravagant spending was called for, this was it.

On the bottom of the card, I wrote,

Merilee Fallon accepts with pleasure!

Then I picked up my purse and headed out to shop my heart out.

Chapter 17

At seven o'clock, I approached La Vie en Rose. My heart skittered with excitement and nerves—kind of crazy, considering I'd known Matt for fourteen years, but I didn't know what was going on. Last night, he'd been furious; this morning, we'd kind of been at odds. Now he'd issued a formal invitation to . . . was this a *date*? The choice of an intimate French restaurant with *pink* décor . . . How many times this week had Matt surprised me?

I hoped that I'd surprise him, too, in the gauzy blue-and-gold dress that floated over a form-fitting gold slip. It had cried out to me, and the salesclerk had said it was flirtatious and classy. When I'd told her it was a special occasion, she'd said, "He'll so totally fall for you in this."

We'd added sparkly blue earrings that looked like sapphires, and gold sandals that were all straps and heels. She'd refused to let me carry my old all-purpose purse and given me an incredible deal on a tiny gold clutch.

I scanned the front of the restaurant. A number of tables were occupied, but no Matt. The place looked wonderful at night: candles flickering, light sparkling off crystal, and pink roses that had gone beyond full to overblown, reminding me of a woman who'd been sexed to blissful satiation. No question the effect was intentional, and it matched perfectly with the soulful French ballad that was playing.

The waitress who'd looked after me last time came forward with a smile, and automatically I greeted her in French. "Hello again."

"Hello. It's good to see you. I'm glad you're spending your last night here. A table for one?"

"No, this time I'm joining someone."

Her face lit. "You're Merilee, Matt's girl. I should have guessed."

"How could you have guessed?"

"You're perfect together."

"You know Matt?"

"He had dinner here last night and we got talking."

My Matt? I couldn't stop myself from asking, "Oh? Who was he with?"

She chuckled. "Don't worry, he was alone."

Matt had dinner in a French bistro by himself?

"You're a lucky girl, dating such a handsome, interesting guy."

"I totally agree."

She led me through the restaurant, past tables of diners having a good time, then gestured. "Our most romantic table."

"Oh, nice!" It was a curved banquette, cozy and intimate, with a dancing candle and a small vase of roses on the table. And Matt.

The Matt who stood to greet me stole my breath. He wore new clothes again and looked more sophisticated than I'd ever seen him. Slim-fitting black pants showed off his long legs and lean hips. His stylish pale blue shirt had a slim line, emphasizing that classic male shape of broad shoulders, firm chest, and narrow waist. The sleeves were rolled casually up his strong, tanned forearms, yet he wore a tie. A tie striped with black, cream, and the same light blue as the shirt—and his eyes.

"You look great," I exclaimed, just as he said, "You look amazing." We both laughed, then he reached for my hand and helped me slide into the banquette. It was the first time we'd touched today, except for when he'd supported me as I sipped ginger ale. I squeezed his fingers quickly, then let go, unsure of what we were both doing. The way he was dressed—Matt *never* wore black pants—this had to be a date, didn't it?

We sat with maybe a foot of space between us, not quite side by side, yet not across from each other either.

The waitress said, in French, "I'll be back in a moment."

"You'll bring our drinks, Jamie?" Matt asked, also in French.

She assured him she would, and hurried away.

He turned to me, and still speaking in French, said, "I hope you like the restaurant."

He knew the waitress's name and he was speaking French to me. Still off balance, I responded in the same language. "I do. In fact, I had lunch here on . . . I guess it was Monday."

Looking a little chagrined, he said, "I didn't know that. I just found it last night."

"So, uh, Jamie said. I'm surprised."

"I was trying something outside my comfort zone. I liked it, and it made me think of you."

Flattered, I said, "It's perfect. What a great way to spend our last night aboard." I gazed into those gorgeous denim-blue eyes framed by thick mink lashes. The restaurant was called La Vie en Rose, and tonight I wanted to keep my world rosy and hopeful. "Let's make a pact that we won't argue, okay? I know we have a lot of things to think about, to talk about, but tonight let's just be . . . mellow."

His lips quirked in a rueful expression. "I'm not sure I can promise mellow, but I sure hope we won't argue."

I was about to ask what he meant when Jamie returned to put two flute glasses and a silver bucket on the table. From the bucket, she drew a bottle that had the distinctive champagne shape. Matt had ordered champagne? How totally sweet, and how I hated to say, "Sorry, I'm not drinking tonight."

She rotated the bottle to show me the label. "De-alcoholized?"

I grinned with delight. "In that case, absolutely." I touched Matt's bare forearm, so firm and warm. "Thank you."

When Jamie had poured sparkling wine into our two glasses, she left us alone again.

Matt said, "I figured we needed champagne." He lifted his glass. "To you and our baby."

I lifted my own. "No, to us and our baby." I clicked my glass against his and, holding each other's gazes, we both drank the toast. I knew it was a promise, too—that whatever happened between us, we'd both always be there for our child.

"You're a good man, Matt Townsend," I said softly.

He looked pleased and surprised. "*Merci.*"

"By the way, why are we speaking French?" We used to practice French together when we did homework, but we'd never used it in conversation.

He shrugged. "Seems fitting. And kind of fun. Don't you want to?"

"It is fun." Fun. Oh, yes, this evening was off to a great start. "Yes, let's. You have some good ideas, you know?"

"I hope so," he muttered under his breath. Then he indicated the closed menus. "Want to check out the menu or ask Jamie for recommendations?"

"Let's ask her."

He beckoned her over, and she said that her personal favorites were bouillabaisse, veal in chanterelle mushroom

sauce, braised rabbit, rack of lamb, and *boeuf bourguignon.*
"Which Matt had last night," she finished.

"It was great," he said. "What appeals to you, Merilee?"

"I'm not big on veal and I'm not eating a bunny, but I love seafood and lamb, so I'm torn between the rack of lamb and the bouillabaisse—if the chef can make it without shrimp." I knew now that I hadn't been poisoned by shrimp, but all the same my tummy didn't want to contemplate them. I smiled at Jamie. "And of course chocolate mousse for dessert."

"I might change your mind on that," she said. "Tonight we also have chocolate soufflé."

"Yes," I said promptly. "One of those."

She and Matt both laughed, then she said, "And yes, we can do the bouillabaisse without shrimp."

Matt said to me, "If you feel like splitting, we could have the lamb and the bouillabaisse. They sound good to me, too."

Splitting a meal. We used to do it automatically. I liked that he wanted to, and I liked that he'd asked. These were excellent signs. "I'd love to. Start with seafood and move on to lamb?"

He agreed, and Jamie took our unopened menus and left us alone.

Matt studied me, looking a bit nervous.

His expression sent anxiety skittering through me, and I tried to shove it away. "This is wonderful," I said quickly. "Everything. The formal invitation, this restaurant, the pseudo champagne. I love it."

"That's good."

Trying to relax, I settled back on the comfy bench seat and had another sip of wine. It might not be real champagne, and I could have used a little alcohol right now, but it tasted good all the same. Trying to keep things casual and easy, I said, "Tell me what you've been doing all day."

Something flickered on his face, a bit of an "I've got a secret" expression that roused my anxiety again. "I went shopping," he said.

"I love the clothes. Your new look is terrific."

"Thanks to a great salesgirl. When we're back home, I hope you'll help me out."

Another good sign. "Be glad to." I studied him, comparing tonight's Matt to last week's. Of course, he had the same face and body, the same strong features, wonderful eyes, thick lashes and eyebrows. Did a haircut and more stylish clothes really make so much difference? Or had they just been the trigger to make me view him with fresh eyes, not the same eyes that had seen him almost every day since we were seven? Maybe it was a little of both.

"You really don't look like Bradley Cooper," I decided.

"Huh? Who?"

"The actor in *The Hangover*?"

"Oh. Which one?"

"The cutest."

"And I don't look like him?" He sounded puzzled and a little insulted. "Did someone say I did?"

"My girlfriends back home. But you don't."

"You said that already." Now there was definite huffiness in his voice.

I grinned. "Nope. You're better looking."

"Oh." He cocked his head and studied me. "Seriously?"

"Definitely."

His lips curved. "Okay then."

Curious, I said, "Have you ever thought I looked like an actress?"

"No." Maybe realizing that wasn't enough of an answer, he went on. "I've never compared you to anyone. You were always just Merilee, the prettiest girl I'd ever seen."

"Aw, that's so sweet."

He caught my hand in his, and I thought there really was

nothing nicer than the two of us being linked that way. An appreciative smile lit his face. "And now you're the most beautiful woman I've ever seen."

"Oh, Matt." Those crazy hormones, bringing quick tears to my eyes.

Jamie's arrival gave me an opportunity to surreptitiously blink them back. She slid a small plate down between us, with some delectable looking treats arranged artistically. "A few *amuse-bouches*," she said, "to hold you until dinner comes."

"*Amuse-bouches*?" I asked, unfamiliar with the term. Translated literally, it meant "mouth-amusers."

"Palate teasers," she said in English, topping up our flute glasses. "You have miniature onion tarts, olive tapenade, salmon mousse." She switched back to French. "And of course, rounds of toasted baguette. Enjoy."

We thanked her, and when she'd gone Matt let go of my hand and reached over to stroke his thumb across my lips, a soft tug, a gentle friction that sent delicious shivers through me. "I have ideas for amusing your mouth," he said in French.

A date. It really, for sure, was a date. He wouldn't say something like that if he was still mad at me. Relieved beyond belief, I opened my lips and sucked the tip of his thumb into my mouth.

A sharp intake of breath told me I definitely had his attention. I scraped his thumb gently with my teeth and swirled my tongue around the firm pad at the top. As I imagined doing the same to his dick, arousal pulsed in my sex.

"You know you're making me hard."

"That was my goal," I admitted.

"Tease."

I released his thumb. "Isn't a tease a girl who doesn't intend to follow through?"

"And now you've made me harder." His eyes gleamed with humor as well as arousal. "Watch out, or we won't end up eating dinner."

"No way. I'm starving." I touched my stomach. "I'm eating for two." The moment I said it, I wondered if my comment would spoil the mood. Before, every time we'd talked about the baby, we'd ended up getting upset.

But Matt chuckled easily. "That baby weighs less than an ounce."

"All the more reason to feed her."

"You want a girl?" he asked, spreading salmon mousse on a toasted round of thinly sliced baguette. Rather than handing it to me, he held it toward my mouth.

Letting my lips brush his fingers, I nibbled. "Mmm, good."

As he took a bite himself, I said, "I don't care if it's a boy or a girl. Healthy, that's all that matters." Happy that we were talking so easily, I dared ask, "How about you?"

"The same. But we have to call it something, don't we? *It* doesn't sound right. But if you keep calling it *her* and it's really a boy, you could give the poor kid a complex."

We were talking like happy parents. I loved it. "Then we'll alternate. Half the time it's *he* and half the time it's *she*."

He held a miniature onion tart to my lips.

Rather than try to nibble it, I tugged the whole thing into my mouth and bit down through flaky pastry into a creamy, oniony center. He chuckled and took one himself.

"So what else did you do today?" I asked. "Did you go to that lesson in"—I had no idea how to say *martial arts* in French, so said it in English.

"Yeah, and it was fun. I could get into that stuff."

"People beating up on each other?" We'd seen a few movies and they seemed pretty violent to me. "That doesn't sound like you." After his experience with his dad, he was antiviolence.

"No, that's not what it's about. Self-defense yes, and strength, power, technique. But it's a discipline. It's as much about concentration and self-control."

Yeah, that was a good fit for him. "Sounds cool. I think UBC has a club, don't they?"

"Several. I'll check them out in the fall."

Between us, we'd finished the appetizers, and he took my hand again. His grip was warm and steady, and it made my pulse jump. "How was your day?" he asked. "And how've you been feeling?"

"A little off every now and then, but nothing major. Love those vitamins. And my day was great." I'd started to tell him about the cooking lesson when Jamie presented us with a fragrant, steaming bowl of bouillabaisse and a basket with more rounds of bread.

We both dug in, savoring clams, mussels, and chunks of firm, sweet fish, and dipping bread in the rich, saffron-tinged broth. When we'd taken the edge off our appetites, I told him more about my cooking lesson and my newly discovered urge to reproduce delicious meals like the one we were eating.

When we'd finished every last drop of broth, Jamie cleared the dishes and served us with a beautifully presented rack of lamb garnished with rosemary and served with roasted potatoes and a selection of tiny, perfect vegetables.

"It's not just the recipe," I said. "The presentation makes it special, too." I glanced at Matt as something dawned on me. "That's something we were missing. We did lots of great things, but we let them become a habit. Like always ordering the same pizza from the same place. We could make pizza, try different toppings each time, have fun cooking together." Then, realizing I'd been getting carried away imagining us together, and he might not be ready for that, I hurriedly added, "I mean, if you'd be interested."

"I'd like that. I get what you mean about making things special." He touched my cheek. "You're special, M. You deserve special things."

My heart went mushy. "You haven't called me M much lately." I'd avoided using the nickname, too, because it felt like an intimate endearment.

One shoulder lifted and fell. "A few days ago you said that stuff about having no identity apart from being half of M&M. We needed to find Merilee and Matt. Well, we're doing that, and it's good. But I liked M&M, too. Can't people be individuals, and be soul mates, too?"

"Yes. Oh, yes." Did he still see me as his soul mate?

Humor lit his eyes. "We'd better not give the baby an M name though. Don't want the poor kid having identity issues, too."

Was he changing the subject? "What do you think of Danielle or Daniel?"

He considered. "They're good. Where did you get that idea?"

"It's the doctor's name."

He smiled. "I get it."

We ate lamb and worked on the fake champagne, chatting about this and that, our hands touching now and then. It was like old times, but it wasn't. I still felt totally comfortable with Matt, yet with a new awareness of both of us. A large part of that awareness was positive and exciting: We were man and woman, sexy lovers, soon-to-be parents. There were so many more intriguing levels and textures to our relationship than there'd been before. Yet I couldn't totally relax and enjoy because I kept wondering what he was thinking and where our relationship was heading.

I loved Matt. Always had; always would. I knew, for sure now, that I wanted this man for the rest of my life. Would he, in time, feel the same way? If he said he did, would I believe him?

If he didn't, could I stand it? Could I stand co-parenting with the man I loved with all my heart, knowing he didn't feel the same way? Stand seeing him find another girlfriend, fall in love, marry her, and start a family with her?

"Merilee, are you okay?"

I realized I'd stopped eating, my empty fork suspended in the air. "Yes, I'm fine. I'm great." This wasn't the time to worry about the future. I'd let tonight be rosy, an evening away from worries and stresses. Hadn't I decided to be more Zen?

I concentrated on all the delicious flavors of the food, then finally shoved my plate away and relaxed against the back of the banquette. "That was so good. I wonder if they'd share the recipe?"

"We can ask." He finished his own meal and lounged back, too, one arm along the top of the banquette, his fingers resting lightly on my shoulder.

"By the way," he said with an attempted casualness that didn't quite come off, "there's something I didn't tell you. Maybe now's a good time."

Wary again, I said, "Oh?"

"Yesterday, we never got a chance to try out those leopard-print thongs."

Whatever I might have expected, it wasn't that. "Because I got sick." I sighed. "Bummer."

"So I figured you deserved a second chance."

"A second—Wait, are you saying you're wearing the thong?" I glanced toward his crotch, draped with a pale pink dinner napkin.

"The things I do for you," he teased.

"You are? Really, M?" I sat up, alert now, remembering how sexy he'd looked in that skimpy thong.

His arm followed me, curling around my shoulder, fingers

caressing my skin lightly. "If you're a good girl and eat all your dessert, maybe I'll show you."

My body quivered with arousal and my heart sang. Tonight, we'd make love, and it would be the perfect end to this wonderful evening. "I should've ordered the chocolate mousse rather than the soufflé. We could have taken it back to the cabin, smeared it all over each other, and licked it off."

"Oh, man, I like that idea. Is it too late to change our order?"

I laughed. "Yes, but I promise I'll learn how to make mousse. Okay?"

"Make that your first recipe and I'll be happy."

Jamie came to clear away our plates. "I hope you're ready for dessert," she said, "because it'll be coming out of the oven any moment."

"Great," I said promptly, less because I was hungry than because I wanted to be alone with Matt and strip him down to that thong.

While we waited for our dessert, I slid closer to him so our thighs pressed together and his arm wrapped me tighter. How I hoped things would be this good when we got home.

I loved our friends and still wanted to hang out with them, and I loved sharing a movie and pizza at home with Matt, but how great it would be to have an occasional romantic evening like this, too. And to work our way through every single sex toy I received at the stagette—and then go shopping together for more.

To shop for baby stuff, too, and fix up a room, assemble a crib. I wanted all of that. And I also wanted to take cooking lessons, and for Matt to get into martial arts and maybe scuba diving. For each of us to go off on our own and do fun things, then come back together and share our excitement.

That was my dream, my wish. I could envision it so clearly. Needing to do something physical, I curled the fingers of one hand, symbolically cupping that wish, that vision of the future. Then I released my fingers to send it winging into the universe. Jenna had said the universe sent what we needed, and I hoped she was right.

What the universe responded with was chocolate soufflé, presented with a dramatic flourish by Jamie. It wasn't a bad start.

Matt and I dug in, taking turns feeding each other bites, teasing each other with sexy glances, licks, and sucks off the spoon, orgasmic moans of approval. The soufflé was sinfully rich, maybe the best dessert I'd ever tasted. As I ate, I imagined Matt, naked but for a thong. A thong that barely contained a massive erection that was mine, all mine. Decadent chocolate and sexy images, what a tantalizing combination.

I realized Matt was no longer matching me bite for bite. "You're so sweet," I purred, "letting me have more than my fair share."

"Huh? Oh, the soufflé."

He seemed distracted. Was his mind on sex, too? I couldn't fault him for that.

"I can't eat any more," I told him. "So we can go back to the cabin and—"

"No. Not yet."

Surprised, I studied his face. Suddenly, he was tense and anxious looking. What was the problem?

Abruptly, he slid out of his side of the booth. Oh, no, was it his turn to get sick?

But rather than rushing to the men's room, he came around to my side and captured my hand. Oh, now I got it. He was in a hurry to rush back to our room.

But, as I started to slide out of the booth, he stopped me. "No, come sit at the end of the seat."

Puzzled, I obeyed, swinging around so I was sitting facing out of the banquette toward him as he stood in front of me. In the background, I was aware that the music had changed and the song was now the restaurant's signature piece: "La Vie en Rose."

Matt reached into his pants pocket, then dropped down on one knee.

I gaped at him as he held out a small, black-velvet jewelry box, and my heart pounded so erratically I pressed a hand to my chest. Was this . . . ? No, it couldn't be.

"Merilee, I love you." His voice was strained. "I've always loved you, and every year I love you more." Now the strain was fading, and a glow lit his face. "I know it'll be like that for the rest of my life. I want you. Not because you're pregnant, but because of who you are, and who we are together. Because of the joy and passion you bring into my life. I really hope you feel the same way and that you'll do me the honor of being my wife." He flicked open the box.

I stared in wonder at a ring set with a Mexican fire opal, shooting sparks of turquoise, blue, and green in the candlelight. I'd admired the stones when Matt and I had gone shopping together. He'd paid attention.

A ring. He really was proposing. Down on one knee in a restaurant. Slowly, it was sinking in. Matt, my Matt, making that grand romantic gesture I'd always hoped for, saying words that made my heart sing.

I wanted to reach out and take everything he was offering, but how could I be sure he really meant it? "We said we shouldn't rush." My voice came out quick and breathy.

His blue gaze was piercing. "I thought about that a lot. And you know what? For me, this doesn't feel like rushing. It feels right. You want a guy who's decisive, who knows what he wants. Well, I want you, I want you badly, and I'm damn well going after you. You said we needed to be sure, and I am. You want a man who'll fight for you? Well, I will, Merilee, whatever I have to do, however long it takes, because I'm going to win you."

My heart beat a crazy rhythm inside my chest. "Matt, I—" I wanted to believe him. I wanted it so badly.

He caught my hand and gripped it firmly. "Look into my eyes, M. Look into my heart and tell me what you see. Then tell me—God, please tell me—you feel the same way."

I stared into eyes that were fierce in their sincerity, and I knew. Pure, blazing joy filled me. My eyes filled, and overflowed. "I love you, Matt, with all my heart. The boy you were, the man you've become, the incredible father you're going to be. Now and forever. Yes, I'll marry you."

His eyes were damp, too, as he took the ring from the box and slid it onto my finger. He stood and pulled me to my feet, and then I was in his arms and we kissed deeply, holding each other as if we'd never let go.

Dimly, I was aware of applause, and realized we'd just made a public spectacle of ourselves. I loved it.

Finally, we eased apart, smiling at each other.

"Let's go back to the cabin and be alone," Matt said.

"Oh, yes."

Arms around each other's waists, we turned to leave. The music was still playing, and dreamily I thought that now, finally, Matt and I had an *our song*.

Jamie rushed up with a bottle of the pseudo champagne we'd been drinking and a perfect pink rose. "Congratulations, and compliments of La Vie en Rose. You make a perfect couple."

"Thanks," I said, taking the flower. Then, with a grin at Matt, who tucked the bottle of wine under his arm, "We think so."

"You should have your honeymoon on the *Diamond Star*," she said.

Matt's eyes twinkled, my grin widened, then we both burst out laughing.

"Long story," he said to a puzzled-looking Jamie. "Thanks for making this evening so great."

"It's been my total pleasure."

How much had he told her? And had it been coincidence that the song "La Vie en Rose" had started playing as Matt got ready to propose? One day, I'd ask him.

As we strolled through the restaurant, I knew what people meant when they said they were walking on air. If his strong arm hadn't been around my waist, bliss might have floated me away.

When we were in the atrium, I held my left hand up and admired the sparkles in the fire opal. "When did you get this?"

"Today. I took that martial arts lesson and somehow it cleared the stress and confusion and helped me focus. By the time I'd showered afterward, I realized I was fed up with all the 'we should wait, there's no rush' stuff. I knew what I wanted, and I knew I was sure. So I went to the gift shop and chose a ring."

"You could have proposed without a ring. Last time, we agreed on no engagement ring."

"That was last time. This is now."

"We need the money," I said halfheartedly, because I really wanted to keep the ring. "Especially now there's a baby coming."

He stopped and turned to face me, his hands resting on my shoulders. "You know what our baby needs? To know how much Dad loves Mom."

My heart melted all over again as he kissed me.

A few minutes later, we walked on again.

"I know a diamond's the traditional thing," he said, "but I really like this stone. You'd admired fire opals in Mexico and I think the stone suits you better than a diamond. I mean, it's more like you."

Intrigued, I gazed up at him. "How do you mean?"

"It's so vivid. Lots of colors and sparkle as well as depth."

I had so envied Kat's diamond ring—but what made it

really special was that it had been Nav's ring, and he'd given it to her when he proposed. It was unique to them, like this one was unique to us. "I love it. It's exactly what I would have picked. And it'll always be a reminder of this trip, and how much we've both learned."

"And of finding out we're going to be parents."

As we walked down the corridor to our room, he said, "How are you feeling?"

"On top of the world."

"Good, because you know what?" He stopped at our door.

"I have no idea what."

"I've been wearing this stupid thong for three hours now and I'm ready to collect my reward."

Pink-tinted romance, fiery opal love, and leopard-thonged sex. What an amazing guy. I put my arms around him, slid my hands into his back pockets, and squeezed. "You know what Gran told me?"

"Tell me it wasn't to pinch my butt."

I giggled. "No, that'd be more like Micky. Gran said every woman deserves passion, and she asked if I'd found mine. And tonight, I know I have."

Epilogue

Two days later, I sat at the kitchen table back home. The conference phone rested in the center of the table, along with a vase of bright pink dahlias from the garden.

Beside me, holding my hand, was Matt.

Mom, who'd rushed home from work early, sat down across from us and kicked off her pumps. She rubbed her hands together. "This is going to be fun. James," she said impatiently to Dad, who was rummaging in the fridge, "what's holding you up?"

"Uh, I forgot what I went in here for."

She rolled her eyes. "If it's not under a microscope, the man can't see it."

"I can *see* perfectly well. I just forgot what I'm looking for."

"Milk," she said. "For your grandchild. Get used to it, you're going to be doing it a lot over the next years."

A couple of minutes later, he put a glass of milk in front of me, touched the top of my head in a brief caress, then went to sit beside Mom. He scrutinized her. "You're not under a microscope, but seems to me you look pretty good for a grandma."

"Oh, you." Smiling, she swatted him. "All right, everyone's here and hopefully the three-pack are all waiting for our call. Ready to do it, Merilee?"

I clasped Matt's hand tighter, he squeezed back, and I said, "Ready."

One by one, Mom dialed my sister's cells, and I heard their voices saying variations of "Hi, what's up?" and we all said hi back.

When everyone was on line, I said, "Matt and I have an announcement to make."

"*Déjà vu* all over again," Kat murmured, humor threading her voice. "Let me guess."

"Let her tell it," Theresa scolded.

"We're getting mar—" I started, then three sets of female squeals cut off the rest of it.

When the commotion died down, Theresa said, "You two are really sure?"

"We are," Matt and I said together.

"It took having a honeymoon for you to figure out you wanted to get married?" Jenna teased.

"Something like that," I agreed. "And some wise advice from all of my sisters."

"And from Nav," Matt said.

"Nav?" I stared quizzically at him. "You didn't tell me that."

"I'll fill you in later. Let's just say, I'm glad he'll be my brother-in-law."

"Me, too," said Kat. "Matt, you know we've always loved you. I'm so glad you and Merilee worked things out."

"It did take some work," I said. "And some fun," I added, leaning my shoulder against my fiancé's. "It's like we have a fresh start, and we know what we need to do."

"When's the wedding?" Theresa asked. "What do you need us to do?"

"Christmas. And you've already made that terrific wedding plan. Mom and Adele are going to help. What I need—

what I really want more than anything—is for you and your guys to be here. I know that'd be two trips to Vancouver in a year, and you're all really busy and—"

"Merilee," Theresa interrupted. "Of course, we'll be there. We're not going to miss seeing our baby sister get married."

"You bet we will," Jenna said.

"Oh, goodie, a train trip in winter," Kat said. "That'll be so romantic. I can't wait to tell Nav. Hot toddies and hot sex."

"I'm still here, girls," Dad said, and we all laughed.

"I have the most gorgeous ring," I said, holding up my hand for the millionth time to admire it. "Mexican fire opal."

They oohed and aahed and I promised to e-mail pictures. "I'm thinking those will be the wedding colors. Rich, bright blues, turquoises, and greens. You all look good in those colors."

"You'll get to wear that beautiful dress after all," Kat said.

I rested my ringed hand on my flat tummy. "No, I'm not wearing it."

"Bad karma?" Jenna asked.

"It's not that. But I picked it out when I was a girl. It's all frilly and lacy, like the wedding dresses I dreamed about as I was growing up. Well, now I'm grown, and I'm going to pick out something more mature." I smiled across the table at my mother. "Mom's promised to help, and we're going to get her a fabulous mother-of-the-bride dress, too."

I loved the new closeness between us, loved having a mom who'd rearrange her busy schedule to be with me while I broke the news to my sisters, and who wanted to shop for a wedding dress with me.

"We'll send pictures of bridesmaid dresses, too," I said, "so you can pick your own."

Kat cleared her throat. "Pardon me, but I'm a maid no more. Matron of honor, if you please."

Jenna gave a hoot. "Matron. It sounds so old and, you know, matronly."

"Wish you were here so I could sock you," Kat rejoined cheerfully, and again we all laughed. Even my dad.

Across the table, my gaze met his. He was so much the absentminded professor, yet he'd always been there for us and I knew how much he loved us. Still holding Matt's hand, I reached my free hand toward Dad. He caught it and held it. "This is good, Daddy," I said softly.

"It is, baby. Now go on, and tell them the rest of it."

Mom cradled her hand around both of ours. "Go on, Merilee."

"I have more news." I took a breath, gazed into Matt's warm blue eyes, and said, "That old wedding dress? It wouldn't fit anyhow. Matt and I are having a baby."

This time, the cries almost deafened me.

Then the eager questions began, my sisters' voices competing for attention. As I answered, I knew that I'd never before been so open with my sisters or my parents, and never had I felt such a warm sense of nonjudgmental support.

I realized tears of happiness were sliding down my cheeks.

Finally, the questions died down. Then Jenna said, "I wonder if it's catching?"

"Excuse me?" I said.

"Remember chaos theory? You're the butterfly, M. You were the one who always said you were lucky in love, and when you and Matt set the date and the three-pack traveled home, we all found love along the road."

"Airways," Theresa said.

"Train tracks," Kat put in. "She's right. You passed along your luck in love, so now what? When we come home at Christmas, are we all going to get pregnant—or in Jenna's case find a baby to adopt—en route?"

Mom and Dad exchanged a horrified glance. "Four grand-children all at once?" Mom said. "Oh, no, you're not doing that to us."

"If it happens," I said, "just bear something in mind, older sisters of mine."

"What's that?" Theresa asked.

"My baby's going to be the oldest."

We talked a little longer. Kat raved about the success of Nav's photography exhibit, Theresa talked about her and Damien's plans for a book they were writing together, and Jenna told us about how she was making a place for herself on Mark's coral reef restoration project.

When we all hung up, the kitchen seemed very silent.

Mom took Dad's hand. "Grandpa, our kids are out in the world building wonderful lives for themselves."

"It's a good day," he said. Rising, he kept hold of her hand. A look, some secret message, flew between them, and she got up, too. Together, they left the kitchen.

"They must have figured we'd like to be alone," I said to Matt.

"And they'd be right." He tugged me over to sit on his lap, and wrapped his arms around me. "I'm glad your family's so cool with this. Did you notice that no one's treating us like kids anymore?"

"Guess we're not the only ones who realize we've grown up, M."

He touched his forehead to mine and peered deep into my eyes. "Feel like doing something grown-up?"

"Such as? Buying paint for the apartment?"

We'd be moving into our own place soon. We loved the big windows and roominess, but the walls were dingy. We planned to paint before we set up the hand-me-down furniture our families were giving us.

"I was thinking about a shower," he said.

"Together?" I wriggled on his lap and felt him grow against my backside. Arousal sparked, and I rubbed against his hardness. "That's a sexy idea, but where?"

"Upstairs."

We never had. I hadn't wanted Mom and Dad to think— what? That my love and I had a hot sex life? Which, in fact, we hadn't. But now we did.

"Upstairs," I agreed, the thrill of it pulsing through my blood. Mom and Dad were likely talking in his office, and chances were they wouldn't even hear, but still I felt pleasantly naughty.

We hurried up the stairs and along the hallway, and were just about to enter the bathroom when, from the floor above, I heard a sound. A rushing kind of roar.

Matt stopped. "What's that?"

Wide-eyed, I stared at him. "Mom and Dad's shower. You don't think . . ."

His shoulders shook in a silent chuckle. "For their sake, I hope so. D'you still want—"

"No! Not here, not now." Of course, my parents had sex; they'd had four daughters. But no way did I want to think about it. Or, God forbid, hear it. Eeeww. "Let's go. Now."

"No shower," he agreed as we hurried back down the hall. "So, what does that leave? We could go parking at Spanish Banks."

"Mmm, nice idea," I said as we went down the steps. "Or there's that edible massage oil I got at the stagette. We haven't tried it out yet."

He opened the front door and ushered me out. "Or we could christen the kitchen counter at the new apartment."

As I rushed toward his car, he caught my hand and stopped me. Gazing deep into my eyes, he said, "I can't wait to spend the rest of my life with you, Merilee."

I realized we were standing in the exact same spot as

Jenna and her guy, when they'd made their romantic declarations. That had been the moment everything had come together for me, and I'd known I had to call off the wedding.

"When my sisters came home with their wonderful new loves," I told Matt, "I was envious. I wanted what they had." I smiled up at my amazing fiancé. "And now I've found something even better. M&M, the new and improved version."

He smiled and nodded. "The one with the lifetime warranty."

"Oh, yeah. I'd bet on that."

We leaned into each other and our lips touched, sealing the deal.

AUTHOR'S NOTE

It's hard to believe I've reached the end of the Wild Ride to Love series. With this book, baby sister, Merilee Fallon—the catalyst for her three older sisters' romances—finally gets her own happy ending.

I've loved spending time with the Fallon sisters and I hope my readers have, too. If you haven't read the previous books in my sexy "planes, trains, automobiles, and a cruise ship" series, I hope you'll look for them:

- Theresa's story (planes): *Sex Drive* (under the pen name Susan Lyons)
- Kat's story (trains): *Love, Unexpectedly*
- Jenna's story (automobiles): *His, Unexpectedly*

Writing books can be a bit of a wild ride in itself, and I'd like to give heartfelt thanks to my agent, Emily Sylvan Kim, my editor, Audrey LaFehr, and her assistant, Martin Biro, for their support on this journey.

As always, I couldn't have done it without my friends and critiquers Nazima Ali, Elizabeth Allan, and Michelle Hancock. Thank you for giving so generously of your time during a season when everyone was particularly busy and stressed out. I owe you, big-time!

I love sharing my stories with my readers and I love hearing from you. You can e-mail me at susan@susanlyons.ca, or contact me through my website at www.susanfox.ca where you'll also find excerpts, behind-the-scenes notes, recipes, a monthly contest, my newsletter, and other goodies.

If you enjoyed *Yours, Unexpectedly,* you won't want to miss Susan Fox's deliciously sexy and exciting romances, *Love, Unexpectedly* and *His, Unexpectedly.* Read on for a little taste of both of these terrific stories. Brava trade paperbacks on sale now!

Love, Unexpectedly

"What's new with me? Only everything!" Nav Bharani's neighbor Kat widened her chestnut brown eyes theatrically. She dropped her laundry basket in front of one of the half dozen washing machines in the basement laundry room of their apartment building, then hopped up on a dryer, clearly prioritizing gossip over chores.

Nav grinned and leaned back against his own washer, which was already churning his Saturday-morning laundry. "I saw you Wednesday night, Kat." She'd taken him to one of her girlfriends' to supply muscle, setting up a new bookcase and rearranging furniture. "*Everything* can't have changed in two days."

Though something major had happened in his own life yesterday. A breakthrough in his photography career. He was eager to tell Kat, but he'd listen to her news first.

She gave an eye roll. "Okay, *almost* everything. My baby sister's suddenly getting married."

Even in the crappy artificial light, with her reddish-brown curls a bed-head mess and pillow marks on one cheek, Kat was so damned pretty she made his heart ache.

"Merilee? I thought she and . . . what's his name? always intended to marry."

"Matt. Yeah, but they were talking next year, when they graduate from university. Now it's, like, *now*." She snapped her fingers.

"When's now?" he asked.

"Two weeks, today. Can you believe it?" She shook her head vigorously. "So now I have to take a couple weeks off and go to Vancouver to help put together a wedding on virtually no notice. The timing sucks. June's a really busy month at work." She was the PR director at Le Cachet, a boutique luxury hotel in Old Montreal—a job that made full use of her creativity, organizational skills, and outgoing personality.

"Too bad they didn't arrange their wedding to suit your workload," he teased.

"Oops. Self-centered bitch?"

"Only a little."

She sighed, her usual animation draining from her face. Lines of strain around her eyes and shadows under them told him she was upset about more than the inconvenience of taking time off work. Nav knew Kat well after two years. As well as she let anyone know her, and in every way but the one he wanted most: as her lover.

He dropped the teasing tone and touched her hand. "How do you feel about the wedding?"

"Thrilled to bits for Merilee. Of course." Her answer was prompt, but she stared down at their hands rather than meeting his eyes.

"Kat?"

Her head lifted, lips twisting. "Okay, I *am* happy for her, honestly, but I'm also green with envy. She's ten years younger. It should be me." She jumped to the floor, feet slapping the concrete like an exclamation mark.

That was what he'd guessed, as he knew she longed for marriage and kids. With someone other than him, unfortunately. But this wasn't the time to dwell on his heartache. His best friend was hurting.

He tried to help her see this rationally. "Your sister's been with this guy a long time, right?" Kat didn't talk much about her family—he knew she had some issues—but he'd heard a few snippets.

"Since grade two. And they always said they wanted to get married."

"So why keep waiting?"

She wrinkled her nose. "So I can do it first? Yeah, okay, that's a sucky reason. But I'm thirty-one and I want marriage and kids as badly as she does." She gave an exaggerated sniffle and then launched herself at him. "Damn, I need a hug."

His arms came up, circling her body, cuddling her close.

This was vintage Kat. She had no patience for what she called "all that angsty, self-analytical, pop-psych crap." If she was feeling crappy, she vented, then moved on.

Or so she said. Nav was dead certain it didn't work that easily. Not that he was a shrink or anything, only a friend who cared.

Cared too much for his own sanity. Now, embracing her, he used every ounce of self-control to resist pulling her tighter. To try not to register the firm, warm curves under the soft fabric of her sweats. To fight the arousal she'd so easily awakened in him since they'd met.

Did she feel the way his heart raced or was she too absorbed in her own misery? Nav wished he was wearing more clothing than thin running shorts and his old Cambridge rugby jersey, but he'd come to the laundry room straight from an early run.

Feeling her warmth, smelling her sleep-tousled scent, he thought back to his first sight of her.

He'd been moving into the building, grubby in his oldest jeans and a T-shirt with the sleeves ripped out as he wrestled his meager belongings out of the rental truck and into the small apartment. The door beside his had opened and he'd paused, curious to see his neighbor.

A lovely young woman in a figure-hugging sundress stepped into the hall. His photographer's eye had freeze-framed the moment. The tantalizing curves, the way the green of her dress complemented her auburn curls, the sparkle of interest in her brown eyes as they widened and she scanned him up and down.

As for the picture she saw—well, he must've made quite a sight with his bare arms hugging a tall pole lamp and a sandalwood statue of Ganesh, the elephant god. *Nani*, his mum's mother, had given him the figure when he was a kid, saying it would bless his living space.

The woman in the hallway gave him a bright smile. *"Bonjour, mon nouveau voisin,"* she greeted him as her new neighbor. *"Bienvenue. Je m'appelle* Kat Fallon."

Her name and the way she pronounced it told him that, despite her excellent Québécois accent, she was a native English speaker like Nav. He replied in that language. "Pleased to meet you, Kat. I'm Nav Bharani."

"Ooh, nice accent."

"Thanks." He'd grown up in England and had only been in Canada two years, mostly speaking French, so his English accent was pretty much intact.

His neighbor stretched out a hand, seeming not to care that the one he freed up in return was less than clean.

He felt a connection, a warm jolt of recognition that was sexual but way more than just that. A jolt that made him gaze at her face, memorizing every attractive feature and knowing, in his soul, that this woman was going to be important in his life.

He'd felt something similar when he'd unwrapped his first camera on his tenth birthday. A sense of revelation and certainty.

Already today, Ganesh had brought him luck.

Kat felt something special, too. He could tell by the flush that tinged her cheekbones, the way her hand lingered before separating from his. "Have you just moved from England, Nav?"

"No, I've been studying photography in Quebec City for a couple years, at Université Laval. Just graduated, and I thought I'd find more . . . *opportunities* in Montreal." He put deliberate emphasis on the word "opportunities," wondering if she'd respond to the hint of flirtation.

A grin hovered at the corners of her mouth. "Montreal is full of opportunity."

"When you wake up in the morning, you never know what the day will bring?"

She gave a rich chuckle. "Some days are better than others." Then she glanced at the elephant statue. "Who's your roommate?"

"Ganesh. Among other things, he's the Lord of Beginnings." Nav felt exhilarated, sensing that this light flirtation was the beginning of something special.

"Beginnings. Well, how about that."

"Some people believe that if you stroke his trunk, he'll bring you luck."

"Really?" Her hand lifted, then the elevator dinged and they both glanced toward it.

A man stepped out and strode toward them with a dazzlingly white smile. Tall and striking, he had strong features, highlighted hair that had been styled with a handful of product, and clothes that screamed, "I care way too much about how I look, and I have the money to indulge myself."

"Hey, babe," he said in English. He bent down to press a quick, hard kiss to Kat's lips, then, arm around her waist, glanced at Nav. "New neighbor?"

Well shit, she had a boyfriend. So, she hadn't been flirting?

Her cheeks flushed lightly. "Yes, Nav Bharani. And this is Jase Jackson." She glanced at the toothpaste commercial guy with an expression that was almost awestruck. "Nav, you've probably heard of Jase—he's one of the stars of *Back Streets*." She named a gritty Canadian TV drama filmed in Ontario and Quebec. Nav had caught an episode or two, but it hadn't hooked him, and he didn't remember the actor.

"Hey, man," Jase said, tightening his hold on Kat. Marking his territory.

"Hey."

"Jase," Kat said, "would you mind getting a bottle of water from my fridge? It's going to be hot out there."

When the other man had gone into the apartment, Nav said, "So, you two are . . . ?"

"A couple." Her dreamy gaze had followed the other man. "I'm crazy about him. He's amazing."

Well, hell. Despite that initial awareness between them, she hadn't been flirting, only being friendly to a new neighbor. So much for his sense of certainty. The woman was in love with someone else.

Nav, who could be a tiger on the rugby field but was pretty easygoing otherwise, had felt a primitive urge to punch out Actor Guy's lights.

Now, in the drab laundry room, hearing Kat sigh against his chest, he almost wished he'd done it. That rash act might have changed the dynamic between him and Kat.

Instead he'd accepted that she would, at most, be a friend and had concentrated on getting settled in his new home.

He'd just returned from a visit to New Delhi and a fight with his parents, who'd moved back to India when his dad's father died last year. In their eyes, he'd been a traitor when he'd rejected the business career they'd groomed him for and moved to Quebec City to study photography. Now that he'd graduated, his parents said it was time their only child got over his foolishness. He should take up a management role in the family company, either in New Delhi or London, and agree to an arranged marriage.

He'd said no on all counts and stuck to his guns about moving to Montreal to build a photography career.

Once there, he had started to check out work opportunities and begun to meet people. But he'd moved too slowly for Kat, at least when it came to making friends. She'd figured he was shy, taken him under her wing, kick-started his social life. Enjoying her company—besides, who could resist the driving force of a determined Kat Fallon?—he'd gone along.

But even as he dated other women, his feelings for Kat grew. He'd known it was futile. Though her relationship with Jase broke up, and she ogled Nav's muscles when he fixed her plumbing or helped her paint her apartment, she went for men like Actor Guy. Larger than life—at least on the surface. Often, they proved to be men who were more flash than substance, whose love affair was with their own ego, not their current girlfriend.

No way was Nav that kind of man. In the past, growing up in England with wealthy, successful, status-oriented parents, he'd had his fill of people like that.

Though Kat fell for other men, she'd become Nav's good buddy. The couple times he'd put the moves on her when she'd been between guys, she'd turned him down flat. She said he was a really good friend and she valued their friendship too much to risk losing it. Even though he sometimes saw the spark of attraction in her eyes, she refused to even acknowledge it, much less give in to it.

Now, standing with every luscious, tempting inch of her wrapped in his arms, he wondered if there was any hope that one day she'd blink those big brown eyes and realize the man she'd been looking for all her life was right next door.

She gave a gusty sigh and then pushed herself away. She stared up at him, but no, there was no moment of blinding revelation. Just a sniffle, a self-deprecating smile. "Okay," she said. "Five minutes is enough self-pity. Thanks for indulging me, Nav."

She turned away and opened two washing machines. Into one she tossed jeans and T-shirts. Into the other went tank tops, silky camisoles, lacy bras, brief panties, and thongs.

A gentleman would never imagine his friend and neighbor in a matching bright pink bra and panties, or a black lace thong. Nor would he fantasize about having hot laundry-room sex with her.

Glad that the loose running shorts and rugby shirt disguised his growing erection, he refocused on Kat's news. "So you're off to Vancouver." That was where she'd grown up, and where her youngest sister lived with their parents. "When are you leaving? Are you taking the train?" She hated to fly.

She flicked both washers on, then turned to him. "I plan to leave Monday. And yes, definitely the train. It's a great trip and I always meet fascinating people. It'll take my mind off my shitty love life."

"No problem getting time off?"

"My boss gave me major flack for leaving in June and not giving notice. Gee, you'd think I was indispensable." She flashed a grin, and this one did sparkle her eyes.

"I'm sure you are." He said it teasingly, but knew she was usually the center of the crowd, be it in her social life or at work.

"We sorted it out. My assistant can handle things. But it's going to be a crazy weekend. There's tons to organize at work, as well as laundry, dry cleaning, packing."

"Anything I can help with?"

"Could you look after the plants while I'm gone?"

"No problem." He'd done it before, along with playing home handyman for her and her friends. She in turn sewed on buttons, made the best Italian food he'd ever tasted—

she'd once dated a five-star chef—and shared popcorn and old movies.

"Thanks. You're a doll, Nav."

A *doll*. Also known as a wimp. As one of his friends said, he was stuck in the buddy trap.

Brushing away the depressing thought, he remembered his good news. "Hey, I have exciting news, too."

"Cool. Tell all."

"You know the Galerie Beau Soleil?"

"Yeah. Ritzy. Le Cachet buys art there."

"Well, maybe they can buy some of my photographs." He fought to suppress a smug smile, then let go and beamed.

"Nav!" She hugged him exuberantly, giving him another tantalizing sample of her curves. "You got an exhibit there?"

"Yeah, in three weeks." He scraped out a living doing freelance photography and selling stock photos, but his goal was to build a career as a fine art photographer. He wanted his photos to display his vision and perspective, and eventually to hang on the walls of upscale businesses, private collectors, and galleries.

This would be his first major exhibit of fine art photography. "They called yesterday. Someone had to cancel at the last minute, and they asked if I could fill in."

"That's fabulous." She gave him another squeeze, then stepped back. "This could be your big breakthrough."

"I know."

For a long moment, while washing machines chugged and whirred, they smiled at each other. Then she asked, "Do you have enough pieces for an exhibit?"

"I'll need a few new shots. Everything has to fit the theme."

"You already have a theme?"

"We're calling it 'Perspectives on Perspective.'" His photographs featured interesting lighting and unusual angles, and often incorporated reflections. They were accurate renditions of reality but from perspectives others rarely noticed. He liked shaking people up, making them think differently about things they saw every day.

"Ooh, how arty and highbrow. It's great. I am *so* happy for you. This is going to launch your career, I just know it. You're going to sell to hotels, office buildings, designer shops, private collectors." Her eyes glittered with enthusiasm. "And I'm going to be able to say 'I knew him when.' "

Nav chuckled. "Don't get ahead of yourself."

Kat hopped lithely up on the closest washer, catlike, living up to her nickname. Sitting cross-legged, she was roughly on eye level with him. "You're a fantastic photographer and you deserve this. You've made it happen, so believe in it. Don't dream small, Nav."

If only that would work when it came to winning Kat.

"Believe in how great you are." She frowned, as if an interesting thought had occurred to her, then stared at him with an expression of discovery. "You know, you really are a great guy."

It didn't sound as if she was still talking about his photography, but about him. Nav's heart stopped beating. Was this it? The moment he'd longed for? He gazed into her brown eyes, which were bright, almost excited. "I am?" Normally he had a fairly deep voice, but now it squeaked like an adolescent's.

Her eyes narrowed, with a calculating gleam. "You know how unlucky I've been with my love life. Well, my family blames it on me. They say I have the worst taste in men, that I'm some kind of jinx when it comes to relationships."

"Er . . ." Damn, she'd changed the subject. And this was one he'd best not comment on. Yes, of course she had crappy judgment when it came to dating. The actor, the international financier, the Olympic gold-medal skier, the NASCAR champ? They swept her off her feet but were completely wrong for her. It was no surprise to him when each glittery relationship ended, but Kat always seemed shocked. She hated to hear anyone criticize her taste in men.

"Merilee said I could bring a date to the wedding, then got in this dig about whether I was seeing anyone, or between losers. I'd really hate to show up alone."

He'd learned not to trust that gleam in her eyes, but couldn't figure out where she was heading. "You only just broke up with NASCAR Guy." Usually it took her two or three months before she fell for a new man. In the in-between time she hung out more with him, as she'd been doing recently.

Her lips curved. "I love how you say 'NASCAR Guy' in that posh Brit accent. Yeah, we split two weeks ago. But I think I may have found a great guy to take to the wedding."

Damn. His heart sank. "You've already met someone new? And you're going to take him as your date?"

"If he'll go." The gleam was downright wicked now. "What do you think?"

He figured a man would be crazy not to take any opportunity to spend time with her. But . . . "If you've only started dating, taking him to a wedding could seem like pressure. And what if you caught the bouquet?" If Nav was with her and she caught the damned thing, he'd tackle the minister before he could get away, and tie the knot then and there.

Not that Kat would let him. She'd say he'd gone out of his freaking mind.

"Oh, I don't think this guy would get the wrong idea." There was a laugh in her voice.

"No?"

She sprang off the washer, stepped toward him, and gripped the front of his rugby jersey with both hands, the brush of her knuckles through the worn blue-and-white-striped cotton making his heart race and his groin tighten. "What do you say, Nav?"

"Uh, to what?"

"To being my date for the wedding."

Hot blood surged through his veins. She was asking him to travel across the country and escort her to her sister's wedding?

Had she finally opened her eyes, opened her heart, and really seen him? Seen that he, Naveen Bharani, was the perfect man for her? The one who knew her perhaps better than she knew herself. Who loved her as much for her vulnerabilities and flaws as for her competence and strength, her generosity and sense of fun, those sparkling eyes, and the way her sexy curves filled out her Saturday-morning sweats.

"Me?" He lifted his hands and covered hers. "You want me to go?"

She nodded vigorously. "You're an up-and-coming photographer. Smart, creative." Face close to his, she added, eyes twinkling, "Hot, too. Your taste in clothes sucks, but if you'd let me work on you, you'd look good. And you're nice. Kind, generous, sweet."

Yes, he was all of those things, except sweet—another wimp word, like doll. But he was confused. She thought he was hot, which was definitely good. But something was missing. She wasn't gushing about how *amazing* he was and how *crazy* she was about him, the way she always did when she fell for a man. Her beautiful eyes were sharp and focused, not dreamy. Not filled with passion or new love. So . . . what was she saying?

He tightened his hands on hers. "Kat, I—"

"Will you do it? My family might even *approve* of you."

Suspicion tightened his throat. He forced words out. "So I'd be your token good guy, to prove you don't always date assholes."

"Ouch. But yes, that's the idea. I know it's a lot to ask, but please? Will you do it?"

He lifted his hands from hers and dropped them to his sides, bitter disappointment tightening them into fists.

Oblivious, she clenched his jersey tighter, eyes pleading with him. "It's only one weekend, and I'll pay your airfare and—"

"Oh, no, you won't." He twisted away abruptly, and her hands lost their grip on his shirt. Damn, there was only so much battering a guy's ego could take. "If I go, I'll pay my own way." The words grated out. He turned away and busied himself heaving laundry from his washer to a dryer, trying to calm down and think. What should he do?

Practicalities first. If he agreed, would it affect the exhibit? No, all she was asking for was a day or two. He could escort her, make nice with her family, play the role she'd assigned him. He'd get brownie points with Kat.

"Nav, I couldn't let you pay for the ticket. Not when you'd be doing me such a huge favor. So, will you? You're at least thinking about it?"

Of course he'd already accumulated a thousand brownie points, and where had that got him? Talking about *roles*, she'd cast him as the good bud two years ago and didn't show any signs of ever promoting him to leading man.

He was caught in freaking limbo.

The thing was, he was tired of being single. He wanted to share his life—to get married and start a family. Though he and his parents loved each other, his relationship with them had always been uneasy. As a kid, he'd wondered if he was adopted, he and his parents seemed such a mismatch.

He knew "family" should mean something different: a sense of warmth, belonging, acceptance, support. That's what he wanted to create with his wife and children.

His mum was on his case about an arranged marriage, sending him a photo and bio at least once a month, hoping to hook him. But Nav wanted a love match. He'd had an active dating life for more than ten years, but no matter how great the women were, none had ever made him feel the way he did for Kat. Damn her.

He bent to drag more clothes from the washer and, as he straightened, glanced at her. Had she been checking out his ass?

Cheeks coloring, she shifted her gaze to his face. "Please, Nav? Pretty please?" Her brows pulled together. "You can't imagine how much I *hate* the teasing." Her voice dropped. "The *poor Kat can't find a man* pity."

He understood how tough this wedding would be for her. Kat had tried so hard to find love, wanted it so badly, and always failed. Now she had to help her little sister plan her wedding and be happy for her, even though Kat's heart ached with envy. Having a good friend by her side, pretending to her family that she'd found a nice guy, would make things easier for her.

Yes, he was pissed that she wanted only friendship from him, but that was his problem. He shouldn't take his frustration and hurt out on her.

He clicked the dryer on and turned to face her. "When do you need to know?"

"No great rush, I guess. It's two weeks off. Like I said, I'll probably leave Monday. I'll take the train to Toronto, then on to Vancouver."

"It's a long trip."

"Yeah." Her face brightened. "It really is fun. I've done it every year or so since I moved here when I was eighteen. It's like being on holiday with fascinating people. A train's a special world. Normal rules don't apply."

He always traveled by air, but he'd watched old movies with Kat. *North by Northwest. Silver Streak.* Trains were sexy.

Damn. He could see it now. Kat would meet some guy, fall for him, have hot sex, end up taking him rather than Nav to the wedding.

Unless . . .

An idea—brilliant? insane?—struck him. What if he was the guy on the train?

What if he showed up out of the blue, took her by surprise? An initial shock, then days together in that special, sexy world where normal rules didn't apply. Might she see him differently?

If he analyzed his idea, he'd decide it was crazy and never do it. So, forget about being rational. He'd hustle upstairs and go online to arrange getting money transferred out of the trust fund he hadn't touched since coming to Canada.

It had been a matter of principle: proving to himself that he wasn't a spoiled rich kid and could make his own way in the world. But now, principles be damned. Train travel wasn't cheap, and this was a chance to win the woman he loved.

Unrequited love was unhealthy. He'd break the good buddy limbo, stop being so fucking pathetic, and go after her.

But first, he had to set things up with Kat so she'd be totally surprised when he showed up on the train. "Yeah, okay." He tried to sound casual. "I'll be your token good guy. I'll fly out for the wedding."

"Oooeeee!!" She flung herself into his arms, a full-body tackle that caught him off guard and almost toppled them both. "Thank you, thank you, thank you." She pressed quick little kisses all over his cheeks.

When what he longed for were soul-rocking, deep and dirty kisses, mouth to mouth, tongue to tongue. Groin to groin.

Enough. He was fed up with her treating him this way. Fed up with himself for taking it. Things between them were damned well going to change.

He grabbed her head between both hands and held her steady, her mouth inches from his.

Her lips opened and he heard a soft gasp as she caught her breath. "Nav?" Was that a quiver in her voice?

Deliberately, he pressed his lips against hers. Soft, so soft her lips were, and warm. Though it took all his willpower, he drew away before she could decide how to respond. "You're welcome," he said casually, as if the kiss had been merely a "between friends" one.

All the same, he knew it had reminded her of the attraction between them.

She would be a tiny bit unsettled.

He had, in a subtle way, served notice.

Token good guy? Screw that.

He was going to be the sexy guy on the train.

His, Unexpectedly

What a fabulously perfect June morning: a stretch of coastal California highway unfurling like silver ribbon ahead of me, the top down on my old MGB, a sun visor shielding my eyes, the ocean breeze cooling my cheeks.

Open roads meant possibilities. What was around the next curve? A sliver of white sand beach, a field of bright orange California poppies or one of grape vines, a hawk drifting high in a clear blue sky?

Or, to be practical for once, a gas station. Mellow Yellow was running on fumes.

Yeah, I'd named the butter-yellow convertible I'd bought when I was eighteen. My mom used to play the old Donovan song when my sisters and I were little, and we all sang the chorus. Little known fact about Mom: though she was now one of Canada's top legal eagles, she used to play sixties music with her kids. Given what she was like now—so f'ing serious all the time—I had trouble believing it myself.

Reality check. On the plus side, the open road. On the less plus, the end of that road, the house where I'd grown up, in Vancouver, British Columbia. I only made it back there once or twice a year. Same with my two older sisters; my family loved better at a distance. But this time we had no choice. Our baby sis was getting married.

When I arrived, it'd be same-old, same-old.

Jenna, we can't believe you're still driving that old clunker. Tell us you didn't pick up any hitchhikers along the way. That'd be my parents. Born to worry, not to mention criticize.

You certainly took your sweet time getting here. Thank heavens we weren't actually counting on you to do anything for the wedding. My two older sisters, Theresa and Kat, were know-it-alls. Not that either of them really wanted my help anyhow.

As for Merilee, I could almost hear her squeal from here. *Jenna, I knew you'd make it home for my wedding!* But there'd be relief in her voice, because she really hadn't been so sure.

Yeah, the whole gang would be at the house. Including good old Matt, Merilee's fiancé, and—surprise, surprise—a couple of additions. It seemed Tree and Kat were bringing dates to the wedding. Knowing both of them, that had to mean they were serious about these guys.

Oh man, was I dying of curiosity. Not that I wanted the same for myself. For me, single was perfect. There were too many fun, interesting, sexy men out there to settle for just one. Besides, I'd learned my lesson at seventeen. Falling in love shot my judgment all to hell. It made me stupid. And that stupidity had cost me my dearest dream.

When I caught myself stroking my barren belly, I jerked my hand back to the steering wheel and tossed my head. The past was the past. I was almost thirty now and my life was amazing. My family'd never understand me, but—I grinned smugly at the sight of a gas station ahead—the universe approved. It provided pretty much everything I needed at just about the right time.

I pulled up to a pump and got the gas flowing. Waiting, I stretched, enjoying the sun on my skin. I took off my visor and ran my fingers through hopelessly tangled curls, then hiked my patchwork tote onto my shoulder and went inside to pay.

My wallet was stuffed with bills, mostly tips from waitressing gigs in Santa Cruz, where I'd been living for the last couple of months. That was my travel money, together with what I made from selling my used surfboard.

A quick trip to the ladies' room, a fresh application of sunscreen, a refill of my stainless steel water bottle from the tap, and I was ready to hit the road again. Unfortunately, when I turned the key in the ignition, Mellow Yellow didn't share my mood. Not a thing happened.

"Please, please," I pleaded, trying again. "Come on, don't do this to me." A woman filling up at the next pump sent me a sympathetic smile.

"The joys of owning an old car," I said, climbing out again and glancing around.

The older style station had an adjoining set of service bays, so I headed over. The doors were open, revealing an ancient truck in one bay and a modern SUV in the other, but I didn't see any sign of life. "Anyone around?" I called.

An overall-clad man—fiftyish, with a balding head and full mustache—emerged from an adjoining room. "Hey, there. Help you?"

I read the name tag on his pocket and smiled at him. "Hi, Neal, I'm Jenna. Sure hope you can. My car's dead at the pump."

"Okay, Jenna, let's have a look."

When we walked outside, he grinned. "Hey, a classic B. Nice."

"Yeah, sweet. When it starts."

After five minutes of cranking it over and peering under

the hood, he raised soft brown eyes to me. " 'Fraid your alternator's shot. Gonna need a new one."

I groaned. "How long and how much?"

"Have to get one from San Francisco or farther afield. Run you a couple hundred, prob'ly, unless I find a rebuilt. Then you got two, three hours labor."

Shit, shit, shit! I'd scraped up gas money for the drive home, but fixing the car would take almost all of it, and I didn't have a credit card.

"Want me to locate the part, get you the price?"

"I'd appreciate that."

"Sure. Likely take half an hour." He tipped his cap back and scratched his forehead. "Diner down the road, Marianne's, has good coffee and home cooking."

"Thanks."

I wandered in the direction he indicated. Though I didn't have money for restaurant food, I needed a place to wait. And to ponder what to do next.

Leave the car with Neal and spend my gas money on a bus trip home? Get the car fixed and hope the universe would rain money on me? Or, option three: phone home. My parents, Tree, and Kat had all volunteered to pay for plane fare, but I was independent. If I called . . . well, that expression *No questions asked* wouldn't apply. They'd want to know how I'd screwed up this time.

Organization, planning, contingency plans—all that stuff was their shtick, not mine. And vastly overrated. I loved being a free spirit.

A Volkswagen Westfalia camper passed me and turned into a parking lot. I'd reached the diner Neal had recommended, a cute building with white paint and blue shutters. A half dozen cars and a couple of trucker rigs sat in the parking lot. The camper pulled into an empty spot on the far side, under the sparse shade of a palm tree.

The driver's door opened and a man jumped out, a magazine in one hand, then headed toward the diner. Hmm, not bad at all. Loose sage-green tank top and khaki cargo shorts, longish medium brown hair, and lots of brown skin over nicely muscled arms and legs.

My gaze sharpened with interest. I'd done a lot of surfing in Santa Cruz, when I wasn't working on a peregrine falcon survey or waitressing, and had scoped out lots of excellent bods. This one, at least from the back, was right up there. He might even top Carlos, the Mexican surfer-dude I'd hooked up with until a couple of weeks ago.

I wandered past the camper. It was pretty beat-up, covered with save-the-environment stickers, and had a British Columbia license plate.

Hmm. The universe might not have rained cash, but maybe it had sent a different solution to my dilemma. Maybe it had rained me down a ride and a sexy chauffeur.

Mark Chambers closed the door of Marianne's Diner and glanced back through the paned window. The woman he'd passed as he turned into the parking lot was walking toward the building.

Sunshine backlit her so he couldn't make out her features, but saw a dazzling halo of white-gold curls, a slim silhouette, and a long, loose skirt that was so filmy the sunshine cut straight through it, outlining her long legs. All the way to the apex, where the breeze plastered the fabric against her thighs and the sweet triangle between them.

Lust rippled though him, thickening his blood, shocking him. He didn't make a habit of lusting after strangers—usually he was so caught up in work he barely noticed women—but the picture she made was strikingly erotic. And it was . . . hmm. Months since he'd had sex, now that he came to think about it.

"Good afternoon," a voice behind him said, and he swung away from the door.

Behind the restaurant counter, a middle-aged African-American woman with short, curly hair and round cheeks smiled at him. "Take a seat wherever you like."

The place, a renovated fifties-sixties diner, was maybe half full, all the patrons seated in booths or at tables. He chose a bar stool and dropped his reading material, the latest issue of the *Journal of Experimental Marine Biology and Ecology*, on the blue Formica counter. "Thanks. Could I get a coffee and a menu?"

"You bet." She poured a mug of coffee and handed it to him along with a plastic menu. "The fruit pies are great if you're in the mood for something sweet."

For him, things fell into one of two categories: those to be taken seriously and those that weren't worth paying attention to. Food fell in the latter category.

Coffee, though . . . He lifted the mug to his lips and sniffed. Mmm. Rich, robust, not acidic.

He should have asked if the beans were fair trade, but he doubted the answer would be yes, and he needed coffee. Every man was entitled to one indulgence. Though, to be strictly accurate, as he tried to be, it was more of an addiction. Even if the stuff was poorly made, as was so often the case, he'd still drink it. Now, he savored the scent a moment longer, then lifted the mug to his lips and took a sip.

Well, now. Another sip, to confirm his first impression. "This is excellent," he told the woman approvingly. If you were going to do a job, you should do it well.

Behind his back, the diner door opened and closed. It'd be the blonde. And it would be rude to swing around and look.

"Thanks," the woman behind the counter said. "You should try the fresh strawberry pie."

"Strawberry pie?" The feminine voice from behind him was light, eager, like a kid who'd been offered a present.

A moment later, she slid onto the stool beside him, and this time he did look.

She was stunning in a totally natural way. Her face was heart-shaped, fine-boned, glowing with a golden tan and a flush of sun across her cheeks and nose. A tangled mass of white gold ringlets tumbled over her shoulders, half hiding a scattering of colorful butterflies tattooed on her upper arm and shoulder.

Then he gazed at her eyes, and oh, man. They were the dazzling mixed blue-greens of the Caribbean, and he was diving in, losing himself in their depths.

Vaguely he was aware of the diner woman saying, "So you'll have the strawberry pie, miss?"

He blinked and dragged himself back before he drowned.

The blonde's delicate tongue-tip came out and flicked naturally pink lips, and again lust slammed through him. She shook her head and said wistfully, "Just a chamomile tea, thanks. So, are you Marianne?"

"That's right, hon. This is my place. One chamomile coming up."

Chamomile tea? That jarred him out of his reverie. Might as well drink lawn clippings in hot water; it'd taste as good. Alicia, his biological mother, had been big on the stuff. And why didn't the blonde order the pie she'd sounded so enthusiastic about? Was she one of those constant dieters?

She sure didn't need to be. He'd seen her legs through that filmy flower-patterned blue skirt. Above it, her faded blue tank top revealed toned shoulders and arms. Full little breasts, unconfined by a bra.

Pink-tipped nipples. Not brown. Somehow, he knew that.

Shit, what was wrong with him?

Besides a growing erection that made him glad his cargo shorts were loose and his tank untucked. He'd been in tropical places where women walked around almost naked and not had so strong a reaction. Okay, he was a man of science. He could analyze this phenomenon logically. It was a simple combination of a bodily need that had gone too long unsatisfied and a woman who was a lovely physical specimen. Perfectly understandable, even if disconcerting.

When he returned his gaze to her face, she urged, "Have the pie." Ocean-colored eyes dancing, she added, "Maybe if I'm really, really nice to you, you'll let me have a taste." Her tongue flicked out again.

Blood rushed to his groin as he imagined that pink tongue lapping his shaft. The blonde would be appalled if she had any idea what he was thinking.

Unless . . . His friend and colleague Adrienne—whom he'd known since grad school—said women found him attractive, though he never noticed it himself. The blonde couldn't be flirting, could she? No. No possible way. She could have any man she wanted, so why would she want a science geek like him?

The diner woman put a small china teapot and a mug in front of her and she said, "Thanks, Marianne."

"I'll have the pie," he choked out.

"Sure you will," Marianne said with a knowing grin. She glanced at the blonde. "Whipped cream?"

"Is there any other way?"

He imagined the blonde painting his cock in whipped cream and licking it all off, and wanted to bury his face in his hands and groan. Since he'd first seen her, he'd been . . . bewitched. Except, there was no such thing as bewitchment in scientific reality. This was very unsettling. He rather desperately fingered the scientific journal he'd brought in with him. If he buried himself in its pages, he'd be on safe ground.

"You'd rather read than talk to me?" she teased. "My feelings are hurt."

"Uh . . ." He glanced back at her.

Her impish grin revealed perfect white teeth. "If we're going to share . . ." She paused.

He held his breath. Share? What man wouldn't want to share any damned thing with this woman?

"Pie," she finished, "I figure we should introduce our-selves." She held out a slim hand with short, unpainted nails and several unusual rings. "Jenna Fallon."

"Mark Chambers." He took her hand warily. Sure enough, when she shook firmly, he felt a sexy sensation. A cross between a glow and a tingle spread up his arm. He hurriedly let go, picked up his coffee mug, and took a sip, trying to regain his equilibrium. "You live around here, Jenna?" Likely so, since she'd been on foot.

She shook her head, curls dancing, revealing a couple of simple stud earrings in each ear, then settling. "I'm from Canada. Been living in Santa Cruz, working on a peregrine falcon survey that's run out of UC Santa Cruz."

"Great," he said with relief. She was into the environment like him. A colleague, not a woman. Well, of course she was a woman, but he was okay when he dealt with them as col-leagues. He was actually okay in bed, too; sex was one of the activities that deserved to be done well, and his partners always seemed happy. It was the in-between stuff, the social part, that gave him problems.

Carefully, she poured a disgustingly weak greenish brew from the pot into her mug, sipped, and smiled. Eyes bright, she said, "It's part of a really successful conservation pro-ject. Did you know the falcons are an endangered species in California? In 1970, they only found two nesting pairs. Now, after a captive breeding program, there are over two hundred and fifty."

On firm conversational ground now, he said, "Yeah, the DDT and other pesticides almost did them in. Thank God those have been banned, and the captive breeding programs worked." He studied her. "Bet it was a challenge to track them down. They have a habit of nesting in remote areas."

When her eyes widened in surprise, he said, "I'm a marine biologist, and I've learned a fair bit about marine birds.

Oddly enough, I've been in Santa Cruz too. Working on a research project at UCSC's Long Marine Lab."

"Seriously? Isn't this wild? We never met in Santa Cruz, yet we both happen to walk into Marianne's Diner at the same moment." She grinned. "The universe is pretty amazing."

"Yes, it is." A place of science and of still-to-be understood mysteries. A place mankind seemed hell-bent on destroying. He knew people often found him rigid, but he had no patience for those who didn't give a damn about this incredible world.

Marianne refilled his coffee and put a plate in front of him. He barely glanced at it, except to note two forks, until Jenna enthused, "Now, that's a work of art."

He took another look. Flaky-looking crust, plump red strawberries suspended in glaze, a mound of whipped cream. Not bad at all.

Jenna told the other woman, "Neal at the service station sent me your way, and I'm sure glad." She picked up a fork, then gazed up at Mark with wide, expectant eyes.

How could he say no to those eyes? "Go ahead. I have a feeling I'd have trouble stopping you." He only spoke the truth, but she grinned as if he'd said something amusing.

She carved off a sizable chunk—an entire, huge berry, a portion of crust, and a hefty dollop of cream, and opened those pink lips wide to take it in. Her eyes slid shut, and she tilted her head back, humming approval as she chewed, taking forever to consume that one bite. The sounds she made and the blissful expression on her face reminded him of slow, very satisfying lovemaking.

His cock throbbed and he swallowed hard, wanting what she was having.

Finally she opened her eyes and beamed at Marianne. "Perfection." Then she frowned down at the plate and up at Mark. "Aren't you having any?"

Pie, she meant pie. "I was . . ." *Watching you get orgasmic.* "Uh, waiting for you to taste-test."

"It's delicious." She dug in her fork again. "Here."

Next thing he knew, that laden fork was in front of his lips. Startled, he opened and let her slide the hefty bite into his mouth.

"Close your eyes," she said. "Things taste better that way."

Yeah, if he kept staring at her beautiful, animated face, he wouldn't taste a thing, so he obeyed even though he felt weirdly vulnerable about shutting his eyes while she gazed so expectantly at him.

Normally, when he ate, his mind was on work not on food, but now he concentrated as he chewed. Ripe, juicy fruit, the sweetness of the glaze, a rich, buttery taste to the pastry, and unsweetened cream with a hint of vanilla. Each flavor was distinct and the way they blended together was . . . perfect.

If all food tasted this good, he'd get as addicted as he was to coffee.

He finished the bite and opened his eyes. "She's right," he told Marianne. "That's the best pie I've ever had."

"Glad you like it," the woman said, grinning as if she was enjoying a private joke, then turned to deal with new customers.

He turned to Jenna, who held her empty fork poised. "Go on," he said, "we'll share."

"Thanks." Speedily, she prepared another forkful and stuck it in her mouth.

It was as pleasurable watching her savor the food as eating it himself. All the same, he plied his own fork and matched her bite for bite as they finished the pie. When all that remained was a streak of scarlet on the plate, he said, "Not that I mind sharing, but it seems to me you were hungry enough to order a piece of your own."

"It has nothing to do with hunger," she said wryly, "and everything to do with finances."

Huh? She couldn't afford a piece of pie?

"I'll order you another piece," he said quickly. "Or a sandwich. Whatever you want."

"You're totally sweet, but I'm not starving to death. Just watching my pennies. Speaking of pennies, though . . ." She flicked her head so her pale gold curls shimmered. "Are you just out for a day's drive or are you actually heading somewhere?"

"Vancouver. The Canadian one," he added so she'd know he didn't mean the one in Washington State. He lifted his mug for another swallow of coffee.

"Yeah? As it happens, so am I."

She slanted her body to one side, raised a slim, bare arm, and cocked her thumb in classic hitchhiker body language. "Got room for one more? I'll split you on the gas."

He almost spewed coffee. "You want a ride to Vancouver? You're *hitchhiking* to Vancouver?"

She made a face. "Dude, you sound like my parents. No, I'm not *hitchhiking*. I'm asking you for a ride." A mischievous grin lit her face. "Of course if you say no, I guess I'll be forced to stick my thumb out at the side of the road. And you know, it's dangerous out there for a girl on her own. Never know what might happen. You don't want that on your conscience, do you?" Her teasing tone told him she wasn't serious.

But he was. He was always serious. And it *was* dangerous out there. Surely she wouldn't really hitchhike. "How did you get this far?"

She picked up her mug. "By car. But the alternator packed it in back at the service station, and I'm stranded."

"So, get it fixed," he started, then paused. "Oh. If your finances don't run to pie . . ."

She nodded. "Exactly."

"Put it on a charge card." He wasn't a fan of running up credit, but that had to be better than hitching or bumming a ride with a stranger like him. Not that he wasn't boringly trustworthy, but Jenna had no way of knowing it.

"No charge card," she said airily. "I don't believe in them. If I don't have the money to pay for something, I don't need it."

A good philosophy. And yet she believed in taking rides from strangers. This was one of the oddest women he'd met in a long time. Along with being the hottest and most bewitching.

"How do you know I'm not a serial killer?" he asked.

She grinned. "Serial killers don't share pie with their victims."

He frowned at her frivolity. "You just met me."

"Your camper's awfully cute." She flicked her head in the direction of the parking lot.

He had to admit the Westfalia with all its environmental stickers looked pretty innocent. All the same, "Ted Bundy wore a cast and looked like the boy next door."

She gave a long-suffering sigh. "Yeah, I'd probably have fallen victim to Ted Bundy. So, you're telling me you are a serial killer? A serial killer who reads the *Journal of Experimental Marine Biology and Ecology?*"

He snorted. "Of course not."

Her eyes twinkled. "So we're good, right?"

She was incorrigible and she'd bedazzled him. Suddenly doubting his own judgment, he asked, "How do I know *you're* not a serial killer?"

She chuckled. "Good one. Just when I was thinking you were too stuffy for words."

He was. Again, she'd misinterpreted his serious question as a joke. Or was she avoiding answering? "Are you insulting me so I won't notice you didn't answer the question."

Another chuckle. Dancing eyes. "A sense of humor, and smart too. As well as having a great bod."

Huh? Yeah, he was smart, but he didn't have a sense of humor and his body was . . . functional. And, at the moment, lustful. He glanced down, hoping his clothes camouflaged his erection. She'd been checking out his body? Or maybe she really was a criminal and this was another tactic to put him off guard.

Jenna turned to Marianne, who'd returned with the coffee pot. "Marianne, what's your opinion? Do I look like a serial killer to you?"

The older woman chuckled. "Honey, if you do that boy in, I don't think it'll be with a knife."

"Not all serial killers use knives," he pointed out. The statistical odds were against the pretty blonde being a killer, but all the same . . . "And, though most serial killers are male, there have been a few female ones." The thought crossed his mind that if he fell victim to Jenna Fallon, he well might die with a smile on his face.